MYSTERY MAN

The prosecutor tried again. "You're certain, Dr. Hunter, that it's the defendant, Elizabeth X— Elizabeth Xavier Carleton—you were with the night of the murder?"

"Yes, sir. I spoke to her, bought her a drink—a daiquiri—and we talked until midnight. Then I escorted her to a taxi."

"Have you ever seen the defendant again, Dr. Hunter? Or spoken to her?"

"No I have not. She is a beautiful, interesting woman. I was alone. She was alone. We began a conversation. I quickly realized who she was. That is all."

Elizabeth closed her eyes, recreating Christian Hunter in her mind's eye. She knew she would never forget him. Tall, slender, intense blue eyes, a face both sensitive and intelligent.

She had never seen him before in her life. Who was he? What did he want . . . ?

FALSE Pretenses

FALSE Pretenses

CATHERINE COULTER

AN ONYX BOOK

NEW AMERICAN LIBRARY

A DIVISION OF PENGUIN BOOKS USA INC.

PUBLISHER'S NOTE

This book is a work of fiction. Names, characters, places, and incidents either are the product of the author's imagination or are used fictitiously, and any resemblance to actual persons, living or dead, events, or locales is entirely coincidental.

Copyright © 1988 by Catherine Coulter

All rights reserved. For information address New American Library.

False Pretenses previously appeared in an NAL Books edition published by New American Library, a division of Penguin Books USA Inc., and published simultaneously in Canada by The New American Library of Canada Limited (now Penguin Books Canada Limited).

 ONYX TRADEMARK REG. U.S. PAT. OFF. AND FOREIGN COUNTRIES
REGISTERED TRADEMARK—MARCA REGISTRADA
HECHO EN DRESDEN, TN, USA

SIGNET, SIGNET CLASSIC, MENTOR, ONYX, PLUME, MERIDIAN and NAL BOOKS are published by New American Library, a dvision of Penguin Books USA Inc., 1633 Broadway, New York, New York 10019

First Onyx Printing, May, 1989

1 2 3 4 5 6 7 8 9

PRINTED IN THE UNITED STATES OF AMERICA

Anton C. Pogany

1

New York City
January 17, 1989

The microphone was shoved into her face.

"Do you think Dr. Hunter's testimony is going to get you off, Mrs. Carleton?"

"No comment," snapped Rod Samuels.

"Come on, Mrs. Carleton, do you think the jury will believe the shrink?"

A snicker. "Nothing like a handy witness waiting in the wings."

"The D.A. is furious, Mrs. Carleton. What do you think the verdict will be, Mr. Samuels?"

"Not guilty, of course," said Rod Samuels.

Her face showed nothing, she said nothing, merely stared straight ahead, aware of Rod's hand holding her arm firmly, pulling her toward the limousine. Timothy's silver Rolls-Royce. He'd been so proud of it, so proud. *What do you think, Elizabeth? Just feel that finish. It's something, isn't it? Even old dour Drake approves.*

"Is the D.A. right, Mr. Samuels? Did you bribe the shrink?"

"What will Elizabeth X do if she's freed?" shouted another reporter.

"Spend all her dead husband's money, that's what!"

Elizabeth X. Elizabeth Xavier Carleton. So clever, those reporters. She had been the notorious Elizabeth X for over six months. She felt Rod tighten his grip on her arm. She felt the jolt when he shoved a reporter aside. The door of the limousine was open, Drake standing beside it, his face a cold mask, his mouth an angry thin line. At what? she wondered vaguely. At the surprise witness for the defense? At the endless harassment from the media?

Rod pushed her into the limousine and quickly seated himself beside her, grabbing at the door handle.

"No comment!" he shouted at the sea of reporters as one hand searched for the window button.

The windows were electric and wouldn't work without the motor being on.

He slammed the door. There was a loud yelp. A reporter's sleeve was caught in the door. Rod cursed, opened the door, released the sleeve, then slammed it again. Elizabeth watched Drake quickly make his way around the car and open the driver's door.

A flash went off in her face, then another, and another.

She lowered her head, her pupils shrinking at the bright pricks of light.

How many times had Rod shouted "No comment"? How many times had she been blinded by flashes? Who cared anymore about her? She wondered why Rod didn't have a comment this time. *Because he believes you guilty of Timothy's murder, that's why.*

"Are you all right, Elizabeth?"

She nodded, saying nothing, not turning her head to face him.

"It's almost over," he said, and with a deep sigh leaned back against the rich gray leather seats. "Keep your head down. There are TV cameras as well. It will be over soon, Elizabeth," he repeated. "No matter what Moretti tries, he won't break Christian Hunter."

Was it over? She still vividly saw Anthony Moretti's face distorted with disbelieving rage at the defense witness. The ambitious D.A. of New York City had headed this case since the beginning, a case he had no intention of losing.

Until the surprise witness for the defense.

Until Christian Hunter, who had testified with calm, nearly insolent conciseness, had made him look like a fool.

"What is your name, sir?" asked Rod Samuels.

"Christian Hunter."

"What is your occupation, sir?"

"I am a doctor."

"Dr. Hunter, where were you the night of July 10 of last year?"

"I was walking in the Village, alone, until about eight o'clock."

"And after nine o'clock, Dr. Hunter?"

"I went into a bar on Greenwich, the Flying Moon. I stayed until midnight."

"Did you see the defendant there?"

"Yes, sir, I did. I spoke to her, bought her a drink—a daiquiri—and we talked until midnight. Then I escorted her to a taxi."

"Have you ever seen the defendant again, Dr. Hunter? Or spoken to her?"

"No, I have not."

"You are certain it is the defendant, Mrs. Elizabeth Carleton, you were with?"

"Positive."

"You are equally certain of the times?"

"Positive."

"Dr. Hunter, six months is a long time ago. How can you be so certain of the date?"

"I was thrilled to meet Mrs. Carleton," Christian Hunter said. "I have been a fan of hers for five years now. For me it was like meeting the President."

"Thank you, Dr. Hunter. Your witness, Mr. Moretti."

Anthony Moretti stared at the man in the witness box. He had thought at first to simply look at the jury, shrug, and have no questions for this obviously lying cretin. Now he knew he couldn't get away with it. Hunter looked unruffled, completely in control, almost bored. Who was this Hunter anyway? Hell, it wasn't fair that the prosecution had to disclose every goddamned thing they had and the defense could pull a stunt like this. He calmed immediately. It was a setup, pure and simple. Someone had bribed Hunter. He'd demolish him, show him for the crook he was. That bitch would go to jail, he'd escort her there himself.

Moretti walked calmly toward the witness box, paused a moment, gave Hunter a long look, and shrugged. He heard the surge of excited whispers from behind him.

"Dr. Hunter, what is your specialty?"

"I am a psychologist."

"I see. So you're not a real doctor, then? You didn't attend a medical school."

"No, I did not. I have a Ph.D. from Harvard."

He's a fake, a damned fake shrink. "I see. And just what do you treat?"

"What I treat depends on what walks through my door."

Laughter.

Moretti showed no reaction. He waited for the laughter to die. "Do you treat many liars, Dr. Hunter— pathological liars?"

"Never treated them, Mr. Moretti. One doesn't treat one's friends, after all."

More laughter.

Slippery, smart-mouthed bastard.

"Why, Dr. Hunter, psychologist, didn't you come forward at the time of Mrs. Carleton's arrest?"

"I was in Greece. I returned only one week ago. I had no idea of what had happened in my absence."

"What were you doing in Greece?"

"I was holding my sister's hand while she gave birth to a seven-pound boy, then divorced her husband."

Laughter. The open court had played in Moretti's favor during the trial, but not now.

Moretti bit his cheek. He felt the excitement radiating from Rod Samuels, the damned bastard. He felt the tension building from his staff, heard them shuffling papers behind him. He saw the jury leaning forward, intent, all twelve of them, hanging on every word.

Moretti calmly examined his fingernails. There was an ugly hangnail on his thumb. "Wouldn't you say," he asked, not looking up, "that six months is rather a long time for hand-holding and being away from your practice?"

"You don't know my sister. Nor do you know my practice."

More laughter. Judge Wattson Olney's gavel came down in three quick bangs.

"You don't read newspapers, Dr. Hunter?"

"Not while I'm overseas, no."

"One would think, wouldn't one, Dr. Hunter, that an educated man, a psychologist, would keep himself informed of world events? This particular event has appeared in papers all over the world."

Christian Hunter sat forward very slightly. "That is why I returned, Mr. Moretti. My sister happened to mention the trial, and I recognized Mrs. Carleton's photo."

"I see," said Moretti with a fairly creditable sneer. "You didn't want to be responsible for this poor innocent woman being found guilty?"

"That's right, Mr. Moretti."

Moretti stared at him. "Ah, the baby was born by then?"

"Yes, but the divorce wasn't yet final."

Moretti paused, drew himself up, cast a derisive glance toward the witness, then an I-told-you-so look toward the jury. "How much were you paid to return to New York, Dr. Hunter?"

"Objection!"

Judge Olney frowned. "You will not badger the witness, Mr. Moretti."

"But, your honor—"

"I would like to answer, your honor," said Christian Hunter.

Olney frowned at the witness. If the man had been bribed, a possibility that Olney found quite likely, he was a master of the game. Slowly he nodded. Let the man hang himself if he wanted to. Moretti would tear his gullet out.

"After my testimony, your honor, I should be delighted to review my portfolio with Mr. Moretti and let him speak to my accountants. I have no need for money. I have more than enough for my needs. I cannot be bribed."

The buzz of conversation increased. Olney pounded his gavel, impressed in spite of himself. He'd been so certain, so very certain that the pale young woman was guilty. But now . . .

It was then that Moretti realized that it was *the* Christian Hunter. Christian Westford Hunter—a psychologist, sure, but one who didn't need to do anything except belch in satisfaction after he ate the goddamned haute-cuisine meals prepared by his French chef.

Shit. He hated smug, rich bastards like Hunter. Psychologist, bull. A hobby, nothing more. Why was he saving her neck? Why?

But Moretti wasn't ready to throw in the towel, not yet, not by a long shot. If need be, he could get a postponement from Judge Olney. Hell, the judge knew the bitch was guilty. He asked in a deceptively bored voice, "Why do you think, Dr. Hunter, that Mrs. Carleton didn't state that she was with you that night?"

"I haven't the faintest idea," Hunter said, glancing briefly toward Elizabeth. "She didn't even know my name, except for my first name. Perhaps she thought no one would believe her."

"Your honor," said Moretti, "please instruct the witness to confine his answers!"

"Your question, Mr. Moretti," said Judge Olney, "didn't require a simple yes or no."

"Did you know that Mrs. Carleton didn't ever mention that she was in this bar with you? I believe that requires only a yes or a no."

"No."

"Don't you find that curious, Dr. Hunter?"

Christian Hunter merely stared at him.

"Don't you find that curious, Dr. Hunter?" Moretti smashed his fist down on the railing of the witness box.

"Very well," said Hunter. "As a psychologist, I know of many cases of trauma where the person completely blocks out what happened. It is a defense mechanism, you see."

"You're saying that Mrs. Carleton blocked out murdering her husband?"

"Objection, your honor! The district attorney is twisting the witness's words."

"Sustained."

"So, Dr. Hunter, the defendant blocked out meeting you? A case of convenient amnesia?"

"I believe it is a strong possibility. I had the impression that Mrs. Carleton was disturbed that evening. She didn't know I was a psychologist, of course, and—"

"You wanted to pick her up? Go to bed with her?"

"Objection, your honor!"

"Sustained."

"Didn't it occur to you—within the past week, of course—that she was disturbed because she was planning to murder her husband?"

Rod Samuels said nothing at all.

Christian Hunter smiled. "I fail to see how that is possible, Mr. Moretti. As I understand it, the murder was committed during the time Mrs. Carleton was with me. I do not believe that planning anything is a crime. If it were, I should say that our judicial system would collapse in no time at all."

"As a psychologist, wouldn't you say that murdering with an ice pick—excuse me, a *silver* ice pick—is more the act of a woman than of a man?"

"I don't have dealings with murderers, at least none that I know of. Your opinion on that would be more to the point than would mine."

"Do you think, Dr. Hunter, that anyone from the bar would recognize Mrs. Carleton? Back up your tale . . . story?"

Christian Hunter shrugged. It was an elegant shrug

that dismissed Moretti from the human race. "I suppose you would have to inquire," he said. "However, I tend to doubt it. The bar was dark and I fetched the drinks. We were seated in a high-backed booth."

"Very dark, Dr. Hunter?"

Hunter smiled. "It was light enough so I could see a filling in one of her molars."

Moretti was battering his head into a stone wall. Rod Samuels knew it. Elizabeth Carleton had never testified, so she couldn't be examined by Moretti. The jury knew it. The jury believed Hunter. It shone from their faces like a beacon. Rod Samuels found Elizabeth's hand beneath the table and squeezed it. It was cold as ice and limp.

He hadn't told her about Hunter.

Moretti tried again. "You are certain, Dr. Hunter, that it is the defendant, Elizabeth X—Elizabeth Xavier Carleton—you were with that night?"

"Positive."

"Why? How can you be so positive when the bar was dark? After all, lots of people have fillings in their molars."

Hunter showed no signs of embarrassment, no signs of anything at all. His thin face was impassive. When he spoke, it was clearly without guilt. "She is a beautiful, interesting woman, in dim light or in bright. I was alone. She was alone. We began a conversation. I quickly realized who she was. That is all."

"Just why do you think a beautiful, interesting, *married* woman was alone in that bar, Dr. Hunter?"

"Search me."

Damn you, you Ivy League bastard! Moretti felt his armpits grow damp. He was losing and there was nothing he could do about it. Still, he had to try.

"You didn't ask her?"

"No. We spoke about her career. I'd heard her play at Carnegie Hall every time she'd performed there. She's quite good. I have a fondness for Bach, as it happens."

"Did you know that her husband was sixty-four years old?"

"No. We only talked about music."

Elizabeth closed her eyes. The limousine slipped into the traffic on Forty-second, headed uptown. She wondered vaguely when Drake would cut over to the East Side. She wasn't in the mood for sightseeing. She saw Christian Hunter in her mind's eye. She would never forget Christian Hunter. Tall, slender, intense blue eyes, a face both sensitive and intelligent, perhaps a bit too long, a bit too thin. A professorlike man who had an English look, a tweedy look. He seemed an aesthete, a man who rarely dirtied his hands in this world. But that wasn't true. A psychologist saw a lot, perhaps too much. And he had handled Moretti well, with little apparent effort.

She had never seen him before today in court.

Who was he? What did he want?

She felt Rod's hand holding her arm again. Drake cut through the park and crossed Fifth at Eighty-fourth. She looked briefly toward the Metropolitan Museum. Hordes of people, as always.

There was little traffic as he went eastward to Madison, then turned uptown to Eighty-fifth. The neighborhood was quiet, tree-lined, old. Drake turned smoothly into the driveway. It had actually been two residences years before, but one couldn't really tell, for the bow windows on the second floor were identical, the entrance to the east blocked up and covered with shrubs. She looked up as Drake helped her out of the limousine. She loved this house, all four stories of it. It had a mansard roof, so French-looking that it always made her smile, remembering her years in Paris. And there were narrow black iron grille balconies at the second floor and at the fourth. From the outside, the house was unobtrusive, nearly severe save for the romance of the roof and balconies. It fit in well with its neighbors. No one would ever guess that one of the richest men in the world lived there.

She walked silently beside Rod into the lobby. It

was a lobby, she thought, and it was in a house, and there was a doorman. Gallagher looked up and smiled broadly at them.

"Liam," Rod Samuels said curtly.

"I heard about the witness on the radio, Mrs. Carleton," Liam blurted out. "I am relieved, ma'am."

"Thank you, Liam." Was he the only one who believed her innocent?

Rod escorted her to the ornate 1920's elevator that Timothy had installed intact from an old building he had torn down on Wall Street. It creaked and groaned as it ascended, as was proper, as Timothy had wanted. How many times had he grinned and rubbed his hands together when the thing lurched between floors? *"Makes me feel like a ten-year-old again to hear that, Elizabeth."*

"Thank you, Rod."

He started. Those were the first words she'd spoken to him since they'd left the courthouse.

"It's nearly over now, Elizabeth. You'll be acquitted. Moretti can have the week postponement—he can have a month—it won't make any difference. He won't break Christian Hunter. This time next week, we'll be celebrating."

Elizabeth flexed her fingers unconsciously in an exercise she'd done away from the piano since she was five years old.

"Will we?" she said.

The elevator slugged to a halt. Rod pulled the wrought-iron gate open, stood back, and waited for her to exit directly into the foyer.

"I'm tired," he said, rubbing the back of his neck. "I think I'll sleep for a week once Moretti has thrown in the towel."

How odd mundane things were, she thought. She'd been selfish and inconsiderate. "Please, Rod, come in for a drink. You know you're fond of Kogi's martinis."

"Yes, I think I will. This time next week, Elizabeth, it will be champagne."

She said nothing. A Japanese man, who came only to Elizabeth's chin, burst into the living room, smiling widely. He was wearing his white coat and black slacks and his prized mustache was brushed and gleaming.

"Welcome, Mrs. Elizabeth, Mr. Samuels. I am pleased."

"Thank you, Kogi. I believe Mr. Samuels would like one of your famous martinis."

"Certainly, Mrs. Elizabeth."

He deftly took her coat, gloves, and purse, then provided the same service for Rod. Kogi had been with Timothy for fifteen years, and he'd stayed on. Stayed on with his master's accused murderer. He'd never said a word to Elizabeth and she had been too much of a coward to ask him what he thought.

"Please to sit down," said Kogi.

Rod sat on the pale gold sofa. Elizabeth wandered about the living room, a marvel of modern sculptures, most of them naked women and men in bronze and marble. One large woman was posed in front of the bow windows. Several Rodins were among the collection. So much chrome and glass and silk, not to mention the twenty-foot Tabriz in pale peach and blue that covered the thick white carpet. Very expensive, all of it, and very elegant, and about as subtle and restrained as the celebration for the Statue of Liberty. Elizabeth didn't actively dislike it, she simply ignored it for the most part. Her eyes went to the seven-foot Steinway grand piano set in the far corner by another set of long windows. Timothy had bought it for her as a wedding present, three years before. On the wall beside the piano were three Picassos, from his Pink Period. Two of them were nudes, pathetic figures against their rose and terra-cotta backgrounds.

Elizabeth walked toward the piano, forgetting Rod, forgetting the awful nightmare that had begun seven months before.

She sat down, flexed her fingers, and began Bach's Italian Concerto. She loved the key of F. It was so elegant, much more so than the furnishing of this elaborate mansion. And Bach was so clean and predictable, every chord she played calling for the next and the next, in an even pattern, an even flow.

She didn't open her eyes until she reached the second movement. She couldn't play it. It was slow, haunting, sorrowful. She ached and hurt.

"Would you like something to drink, Elizabeth?"

She blinked up at Rod, who was standing beside the piano, merely looking at her. What did he think? she wondered. He always looked so cool, so in control, so impenetrable, with those dark eyes of his.

"Perhaps a glass of Chablis." She saw Kogi from the corner of her eye already holding her glass of wine, and smiled.

"I forget how beautifully you play," Rod said, sipping on his perfect martini. Of course Timothy always demanded the best. In his drinks, in his servants, in his lawyers. In his lawyers who defended his wife against a murder rap. "Won't you continue, Elizabeth?"

"The second movement makes me sad," she said, rose, and smoothed down her dark blue wool skirt.

He watched her accept the crystal goblet of white wine from Kogi. She had beautiful hands, her fingers long and slender. Strong hands, strong enough to stick a silver skewer . . . He watched her delicately sip the wine. If only Moretti knew that Elizabeth never drank anything other than wine, that she would never touch a daiquiri.

He wondered what she was thinking. He'd wondered that so many times, not just during the past months, but since he'd met her before she married Timothy. She always eluded him, always escaped to her music or to her blank silences. But she said now, very quietly, "Rod, who is Christian Hunter?"

He'd expected her to ask him that much sooner. But Elizabeth was different. He'd always despised her, not only for her differentness—for God's sake, a musician— but also for her serenity, her calmness, her ruthlessness.

She *had* been ruthless. Timothy was a goner from the first time he'd met her, from the first time he'd heard her play that haunting Chopin prelude at Carnegie Hall.

He wasn't so certain now.

He wanted to hate her. He wanted to believe her guilty. He wanted . . . He ran his free hand through his gray hair. It wasn't that she was a sex goddess, for heaven's sake, or a woman who lured men with blatant offers. She was different, cool, reserved, kept too much to herself. He wondered if she'd ever wanted to have sex. It couldn't have been that way with Timothy, sixty-four-year-old Timothy Carleton, who exuded raw power and arrogant presence. Here Rod was, only fifty-one, a young man compared to Timothy, yet she'd never even hinted that he was anything to her but a friend, a slightly distant friend.

Old, old Timothy.

And she'd married him.

He realized that she was waiting for him to reply, and for a moment he couldn't remember her question. Oh, yes, who was Christian Hunter? "Don't you know who he is?" he asked, watching her closely.

Elizabeth turned to look down at the street from the bow windows. For many moments she was silent. Even her body was completely still. How could such a serene woman be capable of cold-blooded murder? But he'd believed her guilty.

"I never saw him before today in that courtroom," Elizabeth said, not turning. "But surely you know that, Rod. Where did you find him?"

"Is that true, Elizabeth?"

He didn't want to hear the truth, he realized suddenly. He wanted to keep protecting her, as he'd done the past six months. He wanted . . .

"You must know that I've never seen Christian Hunter in my life." She turned on those words, pinning him with those intense green eyes. Gifted-artist eyes, Timothy had told him, flushed, in love with this enigmatic woman.

Rod shrugged. "He sought me out, told me his story. I put him through the blender and I knew he would be believed by the jury. He is the most credible witness I've ever seen."

She stood stiff, ramrod stiff.

"Why? He saved you, Elizabeth. I don't know . . . Yes, I do know. Without him the jury would find you guilty. Were it not for Christian Hunter, you would go to prison for life."

She knew that well enough. The jurors had regarded her throughout with distrust and the natural wariness and envy of the very rich. "Yes," she said finally. "Yes, I know. He told Moretti that he was rich. Odd how they would believe him and not me. What does he want, Rod?"

"I don't know. Your estate is vast, Elizabeth." He paused, but just for a moment. "There's more, of course. The family, as you well know, is going to fight the will. I've held them off with the trial. But now—as soon as the jury brings in the not-guilty verdict—it will start in earnest. Don't think they will change toward you because you've been exonerated."

Her hand released the delicate silk curtain. "I don't care, you know that, Rod. I've never cared. You should realize that by now."

He was silent.

She stared at him. "No, I guess you don't know, do you?" she said slowly, thoughtfully. "There is no one for me, is there?"

"Elizabeth . . ." he said, his hand clutching at his martini glass.

"No, don't." She wasn't stupid or blind. She saw his uncertainty, understood it. She drew a deep breath. "No, you don't know, do you, Rod? Now we've another battle, have we?"

"Yes," he said simply. "We do. Are you going to be up to it, Elizabeth?"

She didn't answer immediately. She was thinking: Timothy, what am I to do? Fight your family? Your brothers? Your own sons and daughter? Your mother, for God's sake?

"Where did you find Christian Hunter?"

He felt himself stiffen at her cold tone. "I told you, he came to me."

"You should have consulted me, Rod."

Yes, I could have, but you didn't make a whimper, did you? You let him tell his story and didn't make a sound. "I suppose I could have," he said aloud. He drank down the rest of the martini. "Moretti won't break him."

"No, perhaps not. But, Rod, what price will Hunter ask? What is it that he wants?"

"I don't know, Elizabeth. I truly don't know."

2

Elizabeth stared at the black letters of the *Post* head-line: "ELIZABETH X SAVED BY SURPRISE WITNESS."

Rod Samuels had been right, about everything. Moretti hadn't broken Christian Hunter. Dr. Hunter had broken him, never tiring, never mixing up his story, even after four brutal hours of pounding from the district attorney.

She looked up at Rod, saw the triumph in his dark eyes. Triumph at winning, at beating Moretti, whom he considered an uneducated fascist. Rod was rubbing his hands together. They'd escaped the media. Gallagher had very efficiently locked the lobby doors in their faces.

"The man was a marvel, wasn't he?" Rod said, accepting a flute of Veuve Clicquot from the beaming Kogi.

"Yes," said Elizabeth. "I thought Moretti would kill him, he was so furious."

Rod regarded her closely. It seemed to him that he was always looking at her for the slightest hint of what she was thinking or feeling, for her voice never gave her away. "The jury took only an hour."

"Yes," she said again.

"Moretti couldn't dig up a scrap of dirt on Hunter. Even his ridiculous IRS ploy backfired on him."

When will Hunter want to see me? Elizabeth wondered. She said aloud, "You knew he would do that, of course. You were brilliant, Rod, telling the court how you also had been audited for the past fifteen years and asking the jurors how many of them had been too. What a chance you took!"

"It wasn't a guess, Elizabeth. I knew three of them had."

She marveled silently at his mind. "Have you ever lost, Rod?"

He grinned at that. "Yes, my ex-wife took me to the cleaners."

"Were there no surprises?"

"Not a one. I'd covered everything with Hunter, I even badgered him like Moretti would. Even the bartender at that place in the Village knew Dr. Hunter, said he was a regular, that it was very likely you could have been with him that night."

"What does he want, Rod?"

"I've told you, Elizabeth, I don't know. He's said nothing about wanting anything. He's never told me that his testimony wasn't the absolute truth. On the contrary. Could it be that he was right? Could you have blocked out everything that night, including him?"

"No."

"Perhaps you felt guilty that you were with him while Timothy was being murdered? It all was a terrible shock."

"No," she said again, wearily. "I didn't block out a thing. I wish I could have."

She realized that Rod was nearly desperate to believe that she had suffered some sort of mental or emotional trauma. Was it so important to him to believe her innocent of her husband's murder?

"It's over, Elizabeth," he said. "I told you what would happen."

"Yes, you did." But was it over? She closed her eyes a moment, remembering clearly the horror she'd felt when she'd come home alone and found Timothy lying on his study floor, the leather-handled silver ice pick in his chest. A clever, useless toy—how Timothy had enjoyed interesting toys—never used except for show in its holder on the silver ice bucket, except to murder Timothy. And she'd touched it, of course, tried to pull it out of him. But it hadn't come out and she'd realized then that he was dead. But his face, his hands, were still warm. . . .

"All of it was circumstantial evidence in any case," Rod said. Moretti had hammered and hammered away in his final summation. Motive, opportunity, her fingerprints on the silver ice pick, the endless hostile testimony from all of Timothy's relatives.

"You can never be tried for Timothy's murder again, Elizabeth."

She wished she could laugh. Even cry. But there was only a vast emptiness inside her. She moved automatically to her piano. She played the Chopin prelude Timothy had loved. It was very short, only one page, and in C minor. Barry Manilow had used it as the basis for one of his popular songs. Whenever she played it now, she thought of the song's words in her mind.

She finished, laid her fingers lightly over the keys, but didn't look up. "I want to return to the concert circuit."

Rod was silent for many moments. "I don't think it would be a good idea just yet, Elizabeth. There are too many people who would be . . ."

"Unkind? Vicious? You believe all Timothy's family would come and throw things at the stage?"

"Possibly. Likely. Almost certainly."

"Timothy wasn't going to divorce me, Rod."

"As Moretti claimed? No, I know that, Elizabeth." He paused a moment, and pulled a cigarette out of his gold case. He lit it, inhaled deeply, and said in a very deliberate, lawyer's voice, "He was, however, seeing another woman. She is younger than you. Twenty-five, I believe. She's also an artist, a painter."

He watched her closely, but she showed no emotion, merely asked, "Really, Rod? Are you certain? Why didn't the district attorney bring that out?"

"I am somewhat persuasive, Elizabeth."

"You paid her off?"

"Yes, of course. He had no plans to divorce you. She had no bearing on anything." He waited. Wouldn't she even want to know the woman's name? What happened to her? Instead, she said very calmly, "It was true, you know, Rod. What Moretti claimed. Timothy was going to change his will back."

"No, he wasn't. You're wrong, Elizabeth. His sons, as you well know, were a disappointment to him. Bradley is a ruthless snake, smooth as silk on the outside, but I wouldn't trust him to park my car. As for Trent, he's a self-righteous prig who should have been a monk. Timothy's fault, of course, and Laurette's. Never let the boys . . . well, steer their own course. Did you know that Trent's one pitiful act of rebellion was joining a religious cult? Timothy put a stop to it quickly enough. All of them were fools to treat you so badly."

She smiled at that. "At least they've always been consistent, Rod."

"They won't break the will. Timothy was very careful to leave them all adequate sums, not just a single dollar as an insult. You will have the bulk of the estate, and that includes a good number of diverse companies, both national and multinational, under the ACI umbrella. Conglomerates, if you will. The power and the responsibility are enormous, Elizabeth."

She repeated what she'd said to him several times before: "I'm a musician. I know nothing about business. It's ridiculous. And I'm a woman. Even in my world, Rod, there is endless discrimination. In the business world I would be destroyed, probably very easily, knocked out with scarcely a whimper."

"Not if you're backed up by a battalion of men who know what they're doing. I've already assembled those men, Elizabeth. They will be loyal to you and protect you. Since Timothy's death, Bradley and his uncle in particular have been undermining any power you could have. Laurette has controlled the reins. It has to be stopped, and very soon."

"I can't imagine Michael Carleton having the time to stick his fingers in Timothy's many pies. He's nearly as wealthy as Timothy."

"I can say a lot of things about Michael, but he's brilliant and has endless energy, and he has the Carleton drive for . . . well, everything. Oddly enough, as you know, he's also under his mother's thumb. Laurette won't let any of them go, not until she's dead."

"Timothy always said there had to be a strong hand at the helm." She splayed her hands in front of her. "Not these hands, nor several dozen strong hands."

"You will simply have to learn, won't you? You can't break up ACI."

She frowned at his steadiness, at his certainty. "Do you still believe me guilty, Rod?"

Her question was unexpected, and his expression, for an instant unguarded, gave him away. "Elizabeth . . ."

She shook her head sadly. "I didn't kill him, Rod. It is true that I had the opportunity, but I didn't have a motive—you see, I was going to leave Timothy. I didn't tell you that before because . . . well, it had no bearing on anything, and Moretti simply never thought of that."

He continued to stare at her, his thick peppery brows drawing nearly together over his nose. "Why?" he asked finally.

"I know you don't believe I was, but it's true. I . . . well, I couldn't take it any longer. He was becoming quite odd, you know, abusive actually. But what woman would give up such wealth? What woman would just walk away from all this? That's what you're thinking, isn't it?"

He said, "Then who killed Timothy?" *Abusive? What had he done to her?*

"I don't know. I've asked myself that question a hundred times. No, more like a thousand times."

He wanted to believe her. God, he wanted to be-

BUSINESS REP

TRAVEL&L

P.O. Box 2093
Harlan, Iowa 51593-20⁣

ams

re Made Of

nter my subscription to Travel & Leisure.
ice is $30 for 12 issues. That's a savings of $6
cover price.

_____

(please print)

_____

Apt. No.

_____

State   Zip

_____

arge my American Express Account.
yment enclosed.   ☐ Bill me.
eck here and sign below if you would like us to provide
ontinuous renewal of your subscription until you advise
to cancel.

_____

ure

e allow 8-10 weeks for delivery of your first issue. Canadian
s add $8.

JK3S8

lieve her more than anything. "Did Timothy know you wanted to leave him?"

"No, I don't think so. All those hours I spent walking about that night—that's what I was thinking, planning. No one knew."

"You should have told me, dammit!"

She merely looked at him, aloof, remote from him, from everyone. "Why? You didn't tell me about Hunter." Her look also told him that she hadn't told him because he wouldn't have believed her.

"There was a reason for that. I was afraid that you would say something, do something that would jeopardize the outcome."

"This isn't at all like Perry Mason, is it, Rod?"

He was pleased at the flash of humor. It had been a long time, such a long time since he had seen her smile in genuine amusement.

Was she truly innocent? He didn't know, God help him.

"No," he said, "it's better." He accepted another glass of champagne from Kogi, the ever-present Kogi, who hadn't been with his master the night of his murder. Not at all uncommon. The servants' quarters were on the fourth floor. None of them had heard a thing, not a single creak from the elevator, nothing. And Gallagher had left his post to go to the deli for his dinner. A long-standing habit. Anyone observing him for a day or two would know about it. Rod shook his head at himself. None of it mattered any longer. She was free.

He drank down the champagne. "Monday, Elizabeth," he said. "Monday in my office, all the clan will gather. You must be there, of course."

She closed her eyes, but their hate-filled faces filled her mind's eye. "Is your office large enough, Rod? They might bring cannon, you know."

He smiled. "Not really. We'll be in the boardroom. Have Drake drive you down. If there are any media jerks hanging around, he can get rid of them. It will begin at ten o'clock in the morning."

Silence stretched between them. He wanted to tell her that he would do his damnedest to protect her, when she said, "I'm willing to give them everything."

"No!"

"But why, Rod? They're not my family, they never accepted me. They hate me. They believe I murdered Timothy."

"No grand gestures, Elizabeth. Even that wouldn't save you from the press, or the Carletons' hatred, or their continued condemnation."

He watched her do her finger exercises, an unconscious gesture that fascinated him, as it had fascinated Timothy initially. "One of them must have killed him, Rod. There are no other people who would have had a motive. And you've told me that Timothy said nothing to any of his family about changing his will in my favor."

"You could be right," he said. "But they all have excellent alibis, you know." But couldn't one of them have hired someone? He was doing it again. He wasn't Perry Mason's Paul Drake. Dammit, it was over. He had to let it go, just as Elizabeth did.

"Yes," she said, "yes, I know." She tried to smile at him, and found it almost painful. "I'll think about everything, Rod. I'll see you on Monday morning."

Rod was nearly home before he realized that she hadn't drunk any champagne.

The Abercrombie-Carleton Building, a sixteen-story prewar structure on Park Avenue at Thirty-sixth, suited Laurette Carleton just fine. She smiled each time she saw the eight huge Doric columns that reached to the third floor, and their smaller, less pretentious cousins that soared only between floors ten and eleven. So long ago, she thought, she and Timothy had pored over those plans endlessly. He'd been so very young, yet much of the creation was her eldest son's. As George, her chauffeur, assisted her out of the Carleton white Cadillac limousine, she frowned a bit as she looked upward toward the soot-stained facade. "The building needs a bit of a face-lift." George merely nodded.

"Like most of us," Laurette added under her breath. The first floor was a huge lobby with six banks of elevators along the back. The ceiling was beautifully painted and carved by Italian craftsmen who had come to America during the thirties and forties. It was more complex and more striking than the Woolworth Building, at least in Laurette's opinion. The Italian marble floors gleamed as they always did on Monday mornings. She took the private elevator to the sixteenth floor. Men and women stopped their work as she passed, to smile at her, to say good morning. She was ushered to the boardroom by one of Bradley's assistants.

She realized that she was very tired this morning as she sat at the boardroom table. She'd been tired since the jury brought in that not-guilty verdict. She had wanted Elizabeth to go to jail for the rest of her life, but that was to be denied to her. She slowly ran her veined fingers over the smooth, aged mahogany of the immense boardroom table, and listened to the growing furor from all her relatives. Not really listened, for she had heard all the arguments, all the rage for so long now that she could have spoken for each of them in his own words. Michael had the floor now, his deep voice resonant, more reasoned than the others, but not cloaking his anger from her. For a man of fifty-six he still looked remarkably fit, the result, she knew, of the daily exercise he took in his own gym. He had the look of his father, Mason Douglas Carleton—heavy-boned, broad-faced, but handsome with his pale blue eyes and strong chin. Good teeth, she thought. She closed her eyes a moment against the ever-present pain. Timothy hadn't had such good teeth, but of course, he had been sixty-four.

"The woman will be here soon," said Michael. "Make no mistake, any of you: Rod Samuels will continue to protect her, just as he bribed witnesses for her, but we must break that damned will."

Ramsey Denebar, Michael's own age and of recognized brilliance in lawyering, said nothing, merely continued to polish the thick lenses of his glasses, his thin lips only slightly pursed. Laurette knew what he was thinking, had figured out all his little habits during the past thirty years. He didn't think they had a chance of breaking the will.

Laurette wished vaguely that it were Christmas and all her children and grandchildren were gathered at her estate on Long Island, their only concern which round of parties to attend. And how much egg nog to drink before dinner.

Brad and Trent, Timothy's two sons, were arguing quietly. Catherine, her beautiful granddaughter and Timothy's only daughter, merely twenty-three, but as aggressive and devious as any of her uncles and brothers, studied her perfectly manicured fingernails. She's saving it all up, Laurette thought; she doesn't want to waste her fury on the family. Laurette's third son, William, was speaking to Ramsey about his trip to Australia, aboard his own yacht, of course. Dear William, who didn't care a farthing about the empire, only his own pleasures. Perhaps he had the right of it, at least on rare occasions, Laurette thought. She didn't care to admit that she'd given birth to a ne'er-do-well, a black sheep. She wondered why he'd bothered to come.

"I think all of you should come with me," William was saying, more loudly now. "A month away from the filth of New York, free on the open seas—"

"Shut up, Will," said Michael, frowning toward his brother. "Unlike you, we have responsibilities. That woman mustn't be allowed to walk away with the Carleton fortune."

William raised a very black eyebrow. "That woman was married to Timothy. He never thought of all this as the Carleton fortune, it was the *Timothy* fortune. And he did leave it to her."

"You think he should just be allowed to give it all away? You know very well she must have influenced him unduly."

"Yes, Uncle Michael," said Catherine, "and then she murdered him."

Ramsey spoke for the first time, but only after he'd adjusted his glasses just so on his rather broad nose. "I would suggest," he said in his cultured, mild voice, "that all of you keep your more scurrilous opinions to yourselves. It won't help. Elizabeth Carleton was found not guilty, you know. I would prefer not to handle a libel case."

Catherine leaned forward, her eyes glittering. "Then what do you suggest we do, Ramsey? Bow our heads and let her have her way?"

"We will probably cut some kind of deal," said Ramsey. "I doubt that Samuels will be unreasonable." He turned away from her and began to shuffle the papers before him on the table.

"I agree," said William Carleton, sending his older brother a baiting look. "Live and let live, I say. There's enough for everyone, even a small country thrown in." Michael never turned down such a look, and Laurette watched his face grow slowly mottled with anger. He used that tanning machine of his too much. His skin looked more leathery than William's. Only the words had changed, she thought, watching Michael's mouth gape open like a fish's, but William had baited his older brother since his first birthday.

Then Rod Samuels walked into the long room, Elizabeth at his side. The woman had a certain style, Laurette thought, watching Elizabeth take her seat on Rod's right, and it had nothing to do with her very expensive clothing, clothing that Timothy had forced upon her, she admitted grudgingly. An exquisite Hermès scarf in vivid blues broke the studied starkness of the Armani double-breasted gray wool suit she was wearing, its narrow waist set off by a wide black leather belt. Laurette studied Elizabeth's face, seeing the quiet quality, the aloofness and reserve that had drawn in Timothy. And Timothy was dead. Her heart began to pound. She wanted to kill Elizabeth. She forced herself to draw slow deep breaths.

"You are all here, I see," said Samuels. "Ramsey," he added, nodding to his colleague and occasional enemy for the past twenty years. "Laurette, you are looking well."

"Thank you," she said. Her eyes shifted to take in Elizabeth's pale composed face. "You have been acquitted, Elizabeth," she said. "Now we may get this will business finalized. I trust you will be reasonable about it."

Elizabeth looked at her mother-in-law as she spoke. Timothy had told her once that his mother hadn't changed in the past twenty years. It was probably true. At eighty-three, Laurette still had an imperious, very regal look, her white hair still thick, her white skin like smooth parchment. And she was so strong, so certain of herself. Elizabeth had always felt like a scraggly waif in her presence.

All of them, she thought, staring about the table at the battalion of Carletons, all of them were confident and self-assured, except perhaps for William, who simply didn't care.

"Well, Elizabeth?"

Laurette's voice was sharp, but Rod said smoothly, "As all of you know quite well, Timothy left the bulk of his empire to Elizabeth Xavier Carleton, his third wife. None of you have been left out. None of you have been embarrassed by the terms."

Brad Carleton, Timothy's eldest son, sat forward in his chair. "You're joking, Samuels! This . . . woman doesn't deserve a dime of the estate! Further, she knows nothing about business, much less the empire my father built. She would destroy everything. God knows that a woman—"

"Now, my boy," said William mildly, staring at his nephew, "you surely don't wish to continue with that particular train of thought." He gave his gamin smile to Elizabeth and said, "Congratulations, my dear. Your ordeal is finally over."'

Trent Carleton said sharply, "Uncle Will, none of this really concerns you, does it? After all, you aren't one of my father's real heirs. I agree with Brad. *She* mustn't be allowed to dissipate my father's fortune, his life's work."

"I doubt three hundred people could dissipate your father's fortune in a lifetime, Trent," Rod said.

"My dear boy," Will continued to Trent, "your esteemed father left me a million dollars. It would appear that I *am* an heir."

"A piddling amount that you will spend in six months," Michael said. "It hardly counts, with the hundred millions involved."

Laurette frowned a bit. They were all acting ridiculously. Each and every utterance could only anger Elizabeth and make her dig in her heels. She cleared her throat, and that simple action, used hundreds of times in the past with instant effect, brought all faces to her.

"Elizabeth," she said in her low, cultured voice, "I agree with William. Your ordeal is over. However, the question of Timothy's estate now looms with equal importance. We are his family. We care about the future of Timothy's holdings. Michael, Brad, and Trent are completely familiar with all Timothy's corporations and their operations. You are not. You know nothing about business, isn't that true?"

Elizabeth wondered if Laurette really wanted her to say something. She compromised and nodded. It was true, as she'd told Rod. She knew nothing.

"There, you see," Laurette said, giving Elizabeth one of her rare smiles, one, however, that did not reach her eyes. "I suggest that you simply leave the family, but not, of course, as you came into it. I would think that the sum of, say, ten million dollars would be satisfactory compensation for your three years."

Rod Samuels laughed. Even Ramsey Denebar looked startled at the insult. Elizabeth was on the point of telling Laurette that she could keep her ten million dollars, that she never wanted to see any of them again, but she felt Rod's hand cover hers under the table.

He knows me too well, she thought.

"Now, Laurette," Rod said, "you can't believe that we would consider such a thing. You must also realize by now that the will can't be broken. However—"

Elizabeth cut him off. It was now or never, she thought, feeling their hatred of her, flowing toward her in waves that made her want to flinch away. "I should like to say something, Rod. Laurette, your offer . . . well it isn't what I expected." She was sounding like an ineffectual idiot. "What I mean is that I wouldn't consider taking ten million dollars from Timothy's estate. In fact, I don't intend to—"

Catherine Carleton interrupted her, rising gracefully to her feet, her palms pressed against the tabletop. "You wicked, evil woman! You married my father for his wealth, lorded it over all of us for three years, then murdered him when he found out exactly what kind of trollop you are! All of us know that you bribed that man to testify for you. You aren't worthy of a dime of my father's money!"

Elizabeth didn't change expression, nor did her body make a single movement. She said finally, her voice flat, "I did not kill your father, Catherine."

"You lying slut! You even aborted my father's child because you hated him, didn't want to ruin your life—"

"That's quite enough," said Ramsey Denebar firmly. He knew what Elizabeth had been about to offer, but he'd been too surprised to say anything before Catherine's outburst. Now he wondered what she would do.

Elizabeth said again, her voice stronger this time, "I repeat, Catherine, I did not kill your father. And you are forgetting facts. I miscarried the child. You are purposely being blind, Catherine."

Rod Samuels drew a surprised breath. He felt Elizabeth draw her hand away from his, felt the tension in her body. He could think of nothing to say for the moment, and watched her rise slowly from her chair. She looked at each member of the family in turn, then said in a calm, detached voice, "I have no intention of leaving any more of Timothy's estate to any of you.

You are all rapacious and greedy and unloving. You will not break the will. I won't let you. In fact, if you try, I won't hesitate to use all Timothy's resources to fight you. And if, by some slim chance, you do manage to break the will, there will be next to nothing left. I bid you good day."

She turned and slowly walked from the boardroom, quietly closing the door behind her.

Elizabeth sagged against the door. She could hear the raging voices, but they were now apart from her. She wanted to vomit, and quickly looked toward the rest room.

"Mrs. Carleton, are you all right?"

Millicent Stacy's worried voice sounded beside her, and she forced herself to nod. She met the older woman's eyes, and saw sympathy in them. That in itself was a shock. "Yes," she said, "I'm all right now."

"Why don't you go into Mr. Carleton's office, ma'am. I'll bring you a glass of water."

Elizabeth did as she was told. She accepted the water from Mrs. Stacy, Timothy's executive secretary for twenty-two years, and the woman left her alone. She sat on the soft gray leather sofa wondering vaguely what she had done.

Rod Samuels found her sitting very quietly some thirty minutes later. She looked shell-shocked, he thought. He said, "You did marvelously, Elizabeth. I'm proud of you. Timothy would have been proud too."

"I'm a fool," Elizabeth said. "You know I was going to give them all of it." He nodded. She continued, "I was such a fool to let Catherine rile me."

"But the dam burst, didn't it? You won't go back on what you said, will you?"

She looked undecided, and he said, his voice cold, "I believe it important for you to make a will immediately, leaving your entire estate to various foundations and charities in the event of your death."

Her eyes widened in shock. "Come, Rod, that's

ridiculous! You can't believe they would want to kill me!"

He was silent for a long moment, then said softly, "You didn't kill Timothy. Someone did. If it was one of the family, what makes you think you'd be immune?"

She closed her eyes. Her world had tilted since last July 10, had become crazy, and she had become helpless. She wasn't helpless now. She looked at him, thrust her chin out, and said, "Draw up the will."

"Good. You can be certain that I shall announce to every Carleton son, daughter, grandchild, and pet, the terms."

"It's all craziness," she said, leaning her head back against the soft leather. She didn't move as she continued, a touch of humor in her voice, "Include yourself, Rod. I'm relatively certain that you won't try to do away with me."

"Don't be too certain," he said. "Didn't I tell you that my wife took me to the cleaners?"

She opened her eyes and leaned forward. "You've been an excellent friend to me. I appreciate it. And I do thank you, for my life."

He wanted to tell her that it was Christian Hunter—and none other—she should thank, but he didn't. He picked up his hand-tooled leather briefcase and opened it. He handed her a thick packet.

"What is this?"

"You're leaving, Elizabeth. Inside are tickets to Paris. You will stay there for three weeks and enjoy yourself. At the George V, of course."

"Paris," she repeated blankly.

"Yes, it's time you got yourself together. You need a rest. You leave tomorrow."

She was clutching at the tickets even as she said, her voice doubtful, "Didn't you tell me that everything was falling apart? That Michael and Timothy's sons were trying to undermine me?"

"Three weeks will make no difference. I did cut something of a deal, Elizabeth, I had to. Ramsey is no fool."

She simply looked at him, waiting in that aloof, reserved way of hers.

"Brad will continue as chief executive officer of ACI. Trent will take over the computer companies headquartered in Silicon Valley in California. But, Elizabeth, both of them will report to you. You will be their boss. Do you understand?"

"Yes," she said, "I understand."

"Good. Now, go home, my dear, and do your packing."

She looked undecided, and Rod simply waited. She was thinking about her old piano instructor, Claude Bouchet, and his motherly wife, Marthe. She was thinking of all the mansard roofs she would see. She smiled. She would like to see them again. Paris. A beautiful place to . . . To what? she wondered. To heal, she thought. She smiled. "Yes, Rod. Thank you."

He watched her leave, her shoulders squared, her stride firm. She was intelligent, very much so. But could she learn quickly enough, be committed enough? He snapped his briefcase closed and looked slowly around Timothy's huge corner office. He bet she didn't realize that she would have to be here, behind Timothy's desk.

And he wondered again, as he had throughout the past week since he had decided beyond doubt that he believed her, who had killed Timothy.

3

She smiled just a bit at the sharp memory. "Paris makes me horny, Elizabeth. Wait until you see the bathtub in our suite at the George V."

She'd lost the child shortly after she and Timothy returned from Paris that first time. She shook her head. She wouldn't think about that now. The limousine drove smoothly from Orly into Paris. It was overcast, drizzily and dull, a typical February day in Paris.

A Monsieur Malieau had met her at customs, punctiliously showed her an I.D. that had the letters ACI on it, and guided her through quickly. Elizabeth thanked him, but didn't know his relationship to Timothy. An underling, she assumed, from one of his French companies.

She hadn't asked. She didn't want to know, not just yet in any case. He led her to a limousine, then left her with a formal bow.

When the limousine smoothly turned off the Champs Elysées onto the Avenue George V, Elizabeth saw the huge hotel looming on her left, its towers and facade as gray as the afternoon. She could feel its luxury, its calm beauty, reaching out to her until she saw the mass of photographers and media people surging toward the limousine. She heard one of the men shout out, "Elizabeth X! *Elle est ici!*"

She closed her eyes, but just for a moment, then said sharply to the driver, "Go, now. Quickly! *Allez!*"

He pulled smoothly away from the entrance, the

photographers and press running behind them. How had they known? Rod wouldn't have told them. Monsieur Malieau, of course.

"Where do you wish to go, madame?" the driver, a thin, intense-looking young man asked her in perfect English.

Her mind had retreated again as it had for six months, away from herself, away from the hurt and pain.

"Madame?"

Elizabeth blinked. "Can you recommend a small hotel, perhaps on the Left Bank? Private and small?"

She saw the assessing look he gave her and realized that this young man would probably phone the press as soon as he deposited her somewhere. How many francs would someone pay him for the information?

She said nothing, merely waited. He said at last, "Avenue Bosquet, madame. There is a very private hotel there, called La Petite Mer."

The little sea, she thought, then said clearly, "Fine. You may take me there." Then she would take a taxi.

Elizabeth ended up on the Rue St. Andre des Arts in a very small hotel whose concierge, Madame LeBeau, appeared to be more interested in the dank weather than in another American tourist. She did raise a brow at the Louis Vuitton luggage, but said nothing.

"You will be alone here, madame?" she asked in heavily accented English. Her look clearly said that she wanted no men trailing after her into *this* hotel.

"Quite alone," said Elizabeth as she follow the woman into an elevator as old as or older than Timothy's. Her room on the third floor was small, clean, and its view was of chimney pots and dirty windows in the building across from her. There was a small, ancient bathroom, the kind that was charming only when it wasn't expected to work. But Elizabeth didn't care. Timothy had teased her, saying she was the only person he knew who could get jet lag from the Concorde. It was true. She was exhausted. She hung up her clothes, smiled at the narrow bed, and eased down, pulling the pale yellow chenille spread over her. She slept until ten o'clock that night.

When she emerged for a late dinner, she almost took a taxi to Les Deux Magots, then shook her head at herself. No, it was one of Timothy's favorite cafés, and she imagined there would be people there who would recognize her. She wanted anonymity. It had stopped raining, and the students from the Sorbonne filled the streets, many of them couples, laughing, kissing, eating hamburgers from the Wimpy's on the Boulevard St. Michel. She was alone. She found a small café near the Seine on the Rue de la Renaissance, and from her table she could see Notre Dame, its towers ghostly in the floodlights. Men came and went, and she tried to ignore them, or to say as little as possible. It was past midnight when she returned to her hotel to fall into her narrow bed, her mind a bit fuzzy from the wine.

The next day, Elizabeth dutifully placed a call to Rod in New York.

"You're staying where?" he asked her again, for the connection made their voices sound indistinct, almost disembodied.

She told him where and why, and he made a disgusted sound. "I suppose it had to be Malieu, and I'll see that the little bastard hears about it."

An underling, Elizabeth thought, but she didn't feel a bit sorry for him. Rod told her to enjoy herself at least three times, and Elizabeth finally hung up, a slight smile on her face.

She wandered about Paris for three days before she called Claude and Marthe. She was invited for dinner the following evening. She was ready to see them.

Claude had short, sausage fingers, and it had always amazed Elizabeth to see those utterly unartistic fingers caress the piano keys to such exquisite effect. He was near sixty now, his body as short and squat as his fingers. His eyes were as black as coal, his thick hair white. His benign appearance was changed only when he gave piano instruction to the long line of cretins, his favored name for any and every pupil, including herself, Elizabeth remembered. Marthe Bouchet was as rotund as Claude, but taller, built as solid as a football lineman, Timothy had once said. Her tongue was acerbic and she was endlessly kind.

The Bouchet home was near the Bois de Boulogne, set off the road and surrounded by thick maple trees. Elizabeth was excited, and she had dressed carefully, praying that they wouldn't bring up the trial. Her thoughts went again to Christian Hunter, as they did many times a day. What did he want? There was no answer, of course. Lights were blazing from the two-story brick house, and there were at least a dozen cars parked about the grounds. Oh, no, she thought, and considered slipping away. I could call them and plead a headache, she thought, but she wasn't fast enough. Marthe herself, dressed in a black silk tent, appeared under the lights at the front door and called to her.

Elizabeth paid the taxi driver and in the next moment found herself engulfed in Marthe's massive bosom. French endearments flooded her and she was squeezed until her ribs creaked.

"Just a little party for you," Marthe told her, patted her cheek, and drew her inside. Martha helped her out of her wool coat; then she was passed into Claude's embrace, then released to see a living room filled with people.

"You will not worry, my dear," said Claude, seeing her dismay. "None of them will disaccommodate you, I swear it. If they tried, I should break their untalented fingers or twist off their tone-deaf ears." He laughed a bit at that, and Elizabeth imagined that he was quite serious. "But musicians, my dear, their minds never stray into the real world. Now, had you butchered a Mozart sonata, that would be another matter!"

Butchered. With a silver ice pick. Elizabeth tried not to flinch, because Claude was beaming at her. She managed a smile, but it was weak and uncertain. To her surprise, she was introduced as Madame Elizabeth Xavier, the very talented pianist from America.

She saw recognition in most of their eyes, and watched their faces sharpen with speculation. Not all of the guests were French, of course. Claude prided himself on reeling in "cretin" talent from all over the world. The last person Marthe directed her to was an American, and Elizabeth knew he was American before he even opened his mouth. He had the look of a successful American businessman, his air of confidence palpable.

She felt herself pulling away, wanting desperately to leave, but Marthe had a killing hold on her arm.

"This, my dear Elizabeth, is Rowen Chalmers, a banker from Boston. A man of the real world."

Elizabeth waited for recognition, a sneering disgust, that avid look that she hadn't managed to handle with a show of indifference, but he merely smiled at her and took her hand.

"A pleasure," he said, his voice deep. "I have heard you play, of course. A great pleasure."

"Yes," Elizabeth said, still wary. "Thank you. What are you doing here, Mr. Chalmers? Are you also a pianist?"

She realized that he was attractive, but no more than that until he smiled at her abrupt question. He had even teeth and a dimple in his left cheek. "My only talent is in admiration. Would you like a glass of champagne?"

She nodded. And waited. Marthe gave her another beaming smile and left her to her countryman.

He handed her a glass of champagne and deftly moved her a bit to the side. "Please call me Rowe," he said.

But she didn't want to call him anything. She wanted to leave.

"That is a lovely dress. Did you get it here in Paris?"

"No, Givenchy exports to New York, you know." The beige cashmere was conservative, high-necked, long-skirted. It also reeked of elegance, and Timothy, having recognized elegance always, insisted she buy it.

She sipped at her champagne, her eyes on the tiny bubbles floating upward in the glass.

His deep voice cut into her thoughts. "I suppose that Marthe and Claude didn't inform you of their little party in your honor."

"No," she said.

"It is a pity, of course, but you can't hide forever, you know."

"Excuse me, Mr. Chalmers," she said. She'd taken two steps when she felt his hand close over her arm.

"Forgive me, Mrs. Carleton. I meant no insult. I knew Timothy and I know also that you didn't kill him. Now, may we begin again?"

But Elizabeth felt a spurt of meanness flow through her at his too-smooth handling. "Just why do you think I didn't kill him?" she asked. "Wasn't he terribly rich and rather old? The perfect target for a greedy young wife?"

He took no offense. "You have been dreadfully hurt. I'm sorry for it, but I think it must be faced, then we can forget about it." He saw no encouragement on her pale face, and continued, his voice deeper, "I have already forgotten. Now, will you be playing for us this evening? Some Scarlatti, perhaps?"

She played three Scarlatti pieces after the buffet supper, and the applause warmed her. Rowen Chalmers stood near the grand piano, his eyes never leaving her face. She wondered who he was, and how he knew Claude, much less Timothy. Her arms were tired when she finished, and she gave a crooked smile to Claude, waiting for his inevitable criticism. He didn't disappoint her, and she found it more warming than the applause. It was like stepping back in time, back five years, before Timothy.

"You played the trill in the third measure like one of my cretins," Claude said. "Your technique isn't bad, but you are sadly out of practice, my dear Elizabeth. You will come and Claude will make the fingers limber again, eh?"

Rowen Chalmers said near her ear, "Actually, I

thought you ruined the seventh measure on the second page. Too much a show of technical gymnastics, too little finesse."

She laughed. "You and Claude need to compare notes."

"Actually, it was so moving I wanted to cry."

That drew her up. She said very quietly, "Thank you, Mr. Chalmers." She saw Marthe waving her arms in typical French fashion to one of her guests. "A pleasure meeting you, Mr. Chalmers," she said, and left him standing next to the old stone fireplace, a thoughtful expression on his face.

Claude was calling for a taxi when Rowen Chalmers said from behind Elizabeth, "I'm staying near your hotel. I have a rented Peugeot. It runs quite well. I would be delighted to drive you back."

Claude paused in his dialing, his dark eyes on Elizabeth's face. He was being kind, she knew, but she didn't want to have anything to do with anyone, particularly an American. An American who had known Timothy. She stood, uncertain, and watched Claude gently set the receiver back into its cradle.

"You go with your friend, eh, Elizabeth? Marthe and I, we see you again, perhaps, before you go back home."

Elizabeth felt indecisive, a condition she hated, a quality in herself that had only grown worse over the past months. She felt confident only when she was playing.

"I promise to treat you just like Claude does," said Rowen Chalmers. "I shall insult your technique, criticize your trills endlessly, even call you a cretin if you like."

"Very well," Elizabeth said. She felt churlish suddenly. The man was merely being polite.

"If you wish to borrow some of Claude's music, I can wave it in front of your nose and tell you that you're not worthy of polishing piano keys."

Her smile came easily now. "Thank you," she said. The Peugeot rode smoothly. Elizabeth leaned her head back against the leather seat and closed her eyes. "How do you come to know Marthe and Claude?" she asked, not turning to face him.

"I'm what you would call an emissary for patrons of Claude's. They couldn't make it over and asked me to come and see to things, with a sizable check in my hand, of course."

"Who are they? Perhaps I know them."

"They wish to be anonymous. I, on the other hand, love to hand over their money and take all the credit for their good deed. Are you a patron?"

She smiled. "Yes, I am. For three years now."

"I am also here in Paris alone, for another two or so weeks. I'm divorced. I haven't any children. I don't rape women, abuse animals, or belch after a good meal. I am entirely harmless. Would you spend the day with me tomorrow? I'd like to roller-skate through the Louvre. A slower pace would take at least three days."

Elizabeth turned her head slightly to look at him. His profile was toward her, his face in shadow. He was handsome, she supposed objectively. Probably in his mid-thirties. His hair was a light brown, thick, well cut and styled, his brown eyes intelligent. She'd already looked at his hands, a habit of long standing. Large hands, well-shaped long fingers, the nails clipped short and buffed, just like hers. Why not? she thought. It would be nice just to be with another person, to talk about nonsense, anything but the past.

"All right," she said finally. He turned his head at that moment and gave her a relieved smile.

"Thank you. I was sure you would say no. I was beginning to think that I had lost my touch."

She stiffened just a bit, but his smile was warm, with no hint of smugness.

"Or perhaps I had some of Marthe's spinach soufflé between my front teeth."

"No, your teeth are fine," she said. "Where does one rent roller skates?"

*   *   *

Elizabeth awoke with a smile, with no sense of the heaviness that had become a part of her during the past months. She hummed as she coaxed the faucet to give her some rusty hot water. She dressed in Lagerfeld black wool slacks and matching turtleneck sweater. She fashioned her hair in a chignon and topped it with a black hat, then slipped on the long bright red Lagerfeld cashmere coat and black gloves. She felt jaunty. She felt young and carefree. It was an odd feeling.

Actually, Rowen Chalmers was staying at the Bristol Hotel, and it was there he took her to breakfast. He was wearing gray wool slacks, a white shirt, and a matching gray cashmere sport coat. He looked very fit and very American. He was tall, she realized, taller than she'd thought. He seemed to sense her renewed wariness and made no push to speak of anything in particular over breakfast except the gray and overcast day.

They took a taxi to the Louvre, and Elizabeth felt her uncertainty, her shyness in the presence of a man who was not Timothy, fading as they mapped out their strategy. She wanted to see *La Gioconda*, he, *Winged Victory*. And the impressionists, of course.

"There are so few women," Elizabeth said absently as they wandered through the vast rooms.

"Berthe Morisot and Mary Cassatt," he said when they reached the impressionists. "Actually, I've been trying to buy a Cassatt, but I doubt I'll succeed—unless I have it stolen, of course."

She blinked at him, certain he was joking, but he looked perfectly serious. "If you stole it, then people like me wouldn't be able to see it," she said finally.

"People like you, Elizabeth, could also have it stolen."

Timothy's money, she thought. So much of it. She simply shook her head.

"I'd like to visit Napoleon's tomb," she said. And they did. It seemed natural to have dinner that evening, and Rowe, as if sensing her dislike of any place where she might be recognized, suggested a small restaurant near Montmartre.

Elizabeth loved oysters and did justice to a full dozen. "I grew up in the Midwest," she said, licking her fingers. "Oysters were considered somehow sinful. Claude introduced me to them when I came here to study with him. Now when I see an oyster, greed clouds my eyes."

Rowe looked up from his veal. "I grew up in Boston," he said, "and every time I see a pot of Texas chili, both greed and tears cloud my eyes."

"Do you still live in Boston?"

"About half the time. My parents are there, of course, doing their best to keep the developers out of Back Bay. I live in New York the other half of the time. I have an apartment there."

"I see," said Elizabeth. She spoke brightly of the Tuileries.

He left her at her hotel after setting an outing for the next day. His kiss was cool and undemanding. She liked him. He made her forget.

They went on a dinner cruise the following evening on the Seine. The night was clear, the temperature in the upper forties, the stars brilliant.

There weren't many tourists, not in early February, but of those there, she recognized several honeymooners. While they stood at the railing, Rowen took her gloved hand.

"I know about your father, of course. I regret never having heard him play."

"He was of the old school," Elizabeth said, carefully keeping her voice neutral. "And immensely talented. He was quite taken aback when I wasn't the boy he expected. But he accustomed himself to my sex by the time I was three years old. And my life's work was decided."

"When did he die?"

"He and my mother were both killed seven years ago, in a car accident caused by a drunk driver."

"You have no brothers or sisters?"

She shook her head, a slight smile touching her lips.

They talked about her years at Juilliard, her years of study with Claude, but Rowen always stopping short of her marriage to Timothy.

He, she learned, was also an only child, and came from old Boston money. "I run the family business—banking, as a matter of fact—and according to my mother, it keeps me out of trouble. A gorgon, my mother. A look from her would send the oysters scurrying off their half-shells."

They shared a bottle of Aloxe-Corton at a café next door to Elizabeth's hotel. "You're very nice," she said after a comfortable pause.

He arched an eyebrow. "I wish you wouldn't sound so surprised," he said, and toasted her.

"And undemanding," she added, studying the checked tablecloth.

He laughed at that. "Oh, I would very much like to take you to bed, Elizabeth, but some things are more important."

She cocked her head at him, saying nothing. She was shocked at his easy mention of sex, but she didn't want him to know it. She was, after all, twenty-eight years old. She had been married . . . and there had been the other experience as well. She shivered a bit, firmly repressing the memory.

"Like trust," he continued, his voice more serious. "Shared interests, friendship."

"An odd thing for a man to say, isn't it?"

"No. At least I don't think so. What will you do, Elizabeth, when you return home?"

"I'm not yet completely certain. My . . . lawyer doesn't believe I should go back on the concert circuit yet." She stopped, her eyes glazing a bit.

"He's probably right. But the public is fickle. Perhaps in a year or so. You owe it to that same fickle public. Your talent is something to be shared, not hidden away."

"Thank you for saying that," she said.

"Not at all. Perhaps you're considering staying here? To study?"

"No. There is Timothy's empire to consider now."

"Surely that's his family's concern. What has it to do with you?" He saw her face tighten, her eyes grow dim, and said quickly, "I'm sorry. I don't mean to pry or upset you."

"Thank you," she said again, and he accepted her silence on the subject with a slight nod.

They drove along the Loire the next day, then stopped to visit Fontainebleau. That evening he took her to the Moulin Rouge.

That night she returned with him to the Bristol for a brandy. She knew what she was doing. When they reached his suite, he turned from the closed door to face her. "You don't have to sleep with me, Elizabeth."

She felt ridiculously shy, her confidence as a desirable woman very close to zero.

"I think you're a very beautiful woman. I want to make love with you, but I won't pressure you."

"I know," she said, her voice faint and faraway.

He came no closer, watched her fiddle with the bracelet on her left wrist. It wasn't an expensive bracelet, he saw, rather an antique she probably had bought at a flea market before she met Timothy. She said suddenly, "I haven't slept with anyone since Timothy . . . since long before he died."

He pictured her in bed with that old man and flinched. He said calmly, "Musicians are odd ducks, aren't they? Alone with their pianos or violins or whatever. No real time for relationships. Perhaps it's time you joined the common herd, Elizabeth. It's got things going for it, I think."

Why not? she thought. She was in Paris. Rowe was a kind man, a man whose company she enjoyed immensely. He made her laugh, made her forget. He seemed to understand. And she had lived in a sheltered, regimented environment most of her life. The three years with Timothy had made her even more isolated. Yes, she thought, she was a grown woman and she had a right to do whatever she wished. And she was free. She wondered what it would be like to feel again.

"Perhaps you're right," she said, and tried to smile confidently at him. It was a pitiful effort, but he ignored it, saying, "Are you wearing one of those sexy teddy things?"

"Yes," she said, "yes, I am. It's . . . well, it's kind of lavender."

"With lace?"

"Yes, with lace."

"I should very much like to see it," he said, and walked toward her.

4

"Practice makes perfect," he said, amusement in his deep voice. He nibbled her earlobe. "You've heard that all your life, haven't you?"

"Yes," Elizabeth said, "I have, but not in this particular context." She forced her eyes open, wondering if all men wanted to talk after sex. Timothy had always wanted to, had always seemed pleased when he felt he'd performed up to par. She had never been quite sure what par was for him. She was so sleepy. Her body felt drained, and muscles she hadn't been aware she had were aching. It was then that she realized he was surprised at her words, his pupils larger in the dim light, showing that surprise. She heard herself say in a false, indifferent voice, "It seems you believed the district attorney's oft-repeated tale that I was sleeping with every man in New York."

He smiled, relieved at her show of humor. "Well, I suppose, looking at you, knowing you, I can't imagine men keeping their hands off you." He stroked his hand down her side, bringing it to rest on her hip.

"You suppose too, Rowe, that I can't keep my hands off men? What a stupid thing to say. I just had sex with you, didn't I?" She suddenly wanted to cry. It wasn't just sex. It was . . . She closed her eyes again. It was being close, so very close to another person, and caring.

"I've hurt you with my big mouth, haven't I?"

She said nothing.

"Elizabeth, forgive me. You're very special. I suppose I simply thought that a woman of your age would know a bit more than the basics."

"I told you I hadn't slept with anyone since Timothy." She hadn't *slept* with anyone before Timothy either. She clamped down on that other memory. She had to forget it. Sooner or later she would.

She felt him shrug. "Yes, you did, and I'm a damned fool." He moved away from her, onto his back, his arms cradling his head. "You've rather thrown me, Elizabeth," he said after a moment, staring up at the ceiling. "I've never met a woman like you. I suppose I wanted you to fit into some sort of pattern that I can easily understand. But you don't. Fit into any pattern, I mean. It's rather alarming for a man of my age to get it between the eyes."

She smiled at that, feeling the tension ease. "You're forgiven," she said, and snuggled next to him.

"I don't suppose you're up for more practice?"

She wasn't, but his wistful, little-boy tone made her want to soothe him. "All right," she said, and she was surprised at the shudder that went through his body at her words.

They drank Tattinger and nibbled on Brie. And they practiced. Rowe seemed to be insatiable and Elizabeth was willing enough. She savored the closeness, the feeling that he cared about her, cared about what she thought and what she felt. She told him late one night in their small hotel room in Rheims, "You have a beautiful body. I really never realized . . ."

He said in a matter-of-fact voice, "Timothy was sixty-four. I don't imagine that any of us look particularly marvelous at that age. He was a lucky man, Elizabeth. I hope he realized it."

"Perhaps at first he was pleased with me. Rod Samuels, my lawyer, told me that he was having an affair with a younger woman, an artist, a few months before his death."

He stiffened, his arms tightening about her ribs until she squeaked.

She made light of it. It was, after all, rather pathetic. Poor Timothy, who didn't want to be mortal, who didn't want to believe he was sixty-four. "She was twenty-five, not my advanced twenty-eight. New and exciting, I suppose. And I would imagine that she was very talented. Timothy was drawn to talent, evidently not just of the musical variety."

Rowe said after a moment, "I would have thought that the D.A. would have had saliva dripping down his chin at such a find."

"Mr. Moretti didn't know about her," Elizabeth said.

"Thank God for good lawyers."

"Well, it's over. I probably shouldn't have even mentioned it. Poor Timothy."

"No, poor Elizabeth. But now you're free." And he began kissing her.

Elizabeth didn't realize how happy she was until it was time for them to fly back to New York. They were eating dinner in Rowe's suite at the Bristol. She didn't like the caviar, but didn't say so. *It's beluga, Elizabeth! Eat up, and forget you're from wherever you grew up.*

"You're very quiet, darling," he said, reaching over to clasp her hand.

"Yes," she said. "I don't want to go back."

"I hope I'm a big part of that."

"You are, Rowe."

"This isn't just a fling, Elizabeth, not for me in any case."

"But when we get back, you'll be very busy. Your business responsibilities, the banks in Boston—"

"I spend equal amounts of time in Boston and New York. I have good people working for me. When I'm in New York, I don't have to worry that my vice-presidents are stealing from the coffers."

"Or when you're in Paris?"

"Exactly. My father was a workaholic. I try hard

not to be." He took another bite of caviar and Elizabeth could see the black fish roe on his tongue. "I'll be flying to New York with you. I have a condominium on Park near Sixty-seventh, as I told you. I think you'll like it."

"Yes," she said, "I probably will."

"There are good things waiting for you—your music, preparing for concerts again."

She felt him studying her closely, and was warmed by his concern. "No, not yet. My lawyer is right. I'd risk dreadful publicity if I went back now. I'll wait."

"And practice for a year? Perhaps with Claude?"

She shook her head. "Unfortunately, I've made a commitment. I'm going to do my best to take over Timothy's many business interests."

"You can't mean it!"

She cocked her head at him, a faint smile on her lips. "I'm afraid I do. Not that I want to, Rowe. I told Rod I was a musician, that I know nothing about business."

"Then why? Why not give the family their due? Not to mention Timothy's sons."

"I almost did," she said quietly.

"What happened?"

She felt herself tensing at the memory of that dreadful meeting in Timothy's boardroom. "Do you know Laurette Carleton?"

"I've never met the matriarch, but I've certainly heard of her. She must be old as the hills by now."

"Perhaps, but she's as sharp as she ever was, which is occasionally terrifying. Truly, I'd intended to renounce all of it . . . until Catherine."

"What did she do?"

He saw that she didn't want to go into it, and quickly added, "Some more champagne, Elizabeth? Forget all of it, if you wish."

"No," she said, giving him a quick smile. "You're very kind, Rowe. Do you know Catherine?"

"I met her once, yes. She's the prototype spoiled little rich bitch."

Elizabeth considered that, and nodded. "Probably true, but she does have great reason to hate me, which she does, quite verbally, at least at that last meeting. She made me so angry that I would have taken over the space program had that been an option."

"That bad, huh?"

"It was dreadful," she said quietly.

"So cut Catherine out and leave all the business to Trent and Brad."

"It sounds like you know the Carletons as well as I do."

"The Carletons and the Chalmerses go back a long way. Old money, I guess you'd say. Newport in the summers, at least in the bygone days. Now it's the Aegean and St. Moritz. Brad and I went to Harvard together, as a matter of fact. I had a couple of years on him, but since he was a Carleton . . ." He shrugged.

Elizabeth played with a bread stick. She said finally, "I don't really understand, Rowe. You've been very nice to me, when someone from your background would usually consider me an upstart, a greedy nonentity."

"I should have added that I consider most of the Carletons utter bastards."

She heard the ring of truth in his voice and relaxed.

"I don't care if you screw them royally."

"There's nothing royal about any of it."

"I'll help you, Elizabeth, if you're set on this course."

It was an immense offer, one that Rowe had to know would consume a great deal of his time, if he were serious.

"Thank you," she said. "I'll think about it. If I'm not to run the businesses into the ground, I'll need all the help I can get."

"And men you can trust."

"Yes," she said. She grinned. "Do you know that I have no idea what the modern businesswoman wears to work?"

"Christian Dior suits, undoubtedly. Or de la Renta."

"You're sounding like Timothy. I was trying on a

non-designer dress once and I thought he would have a fit on the spot."

"You haven't learned to be a snob yet, Elizabeth. Your jewelry, for example, isn't from Cartier or Tiffany's."

She stared down a moment at her bare third finger. The huge diamond ring was in the Carleton vault.

"Let's go to bed, Elizabeth."

She lay in bed, a sheet pulled over her, watching Rowe pull on a condom. He'd taken responsibility without even asking her. She appreciated it, for she'd wondered, in those few moments after he'd asked her to sleep with him what she was going to do.

"I've been off the pill for about a year now," she said.

"Stay off them if you want to," he said, and walked to the bed.

"My dentist wears gloves now, and she tells her women patients she's getting them used to the feel of condoms in their mouth."

"What's this lady's address?"

Elizabeth faced Rod Samuels across his special table at the Quilted Giraffe. A quiet table, but one where one could be seen. He'd just waved the waiter away, his eyes wandering about the restaurant, noting who of importance was there.

He brought his attention back to her, his voice gentle as he said, "You look marvelous, my dear. And a true CEO in that outfit."

"It's a Karan, Rod, expensive enough for Timothy to approve of, and actually quite comfortable." She fingered the white sleeve. "This, I was told, is cavalry twill."

"Here's to the army." He raised his glass of Perrier in salute.

"Now, what's going on here?"

"Very well, Elizabeth. After lunch, you and I will meet the management team that I've assembled. Brad knows nothing about it yet. I want everything in motion before he discovers he no longer holds the reins. That way . . ." He shrugged.

"Yes," Elizabeth said. "I understand what you mean."

He raised his glass of Perrier again. "To the new CEO of ACI."

Elizabeth grinned. "I'll never get used to all these crazy acronyms."

"Get used to CEO, my dear, because that's what you are now." He clicked his glass to hers. "Another thing, Elizabeth, even though Laurette and Michael are on the board of directors, you've nothing to worry about. All the others are in your pocket, so to speak. You'll get no guff."

She fiddled a moment with the tiny shrimp on her plate. "Have the Carletons calmed down yet?"

"It seems so to me, but as you know, none of us are on the best of terms now. I do hope, though, that I get to see the look on Brad Carleton's face when he's confronted with the battalion of dynamos I've assembled. Their salaries, benefits, and profit sharings are immense, Elizabeth, but it will be worth it, not just to you, but to all the areas of responsibility under their aegis. Now, my dear, we have a few more minutes before you assume your new role. Tell me about Paris."

Elizabeth found that she didn't want to say anything about Rowe Chalmers, not yet. It was all too new, too fragile. She would see Rowe this evening. She settled by saying she found Claude the same as ever and Paris as interesting as it was before.

"Fascinating, actually," she admitted finally, and Rod wondered at the small smile that reached her eyes, making them luminous. A man, he thought. She met a man and had a holiday fling. He wanted to tell her: Bully for you, Elizabeth. But he said nothing. Instead, after he handed the waiter his credit card, he asked in a lowered voice, "Anything from our Christian Hunter yet?"

"I was out of the country. There were no messages from him, if that's what you mean."

"You will tell me, Elizabeth, if he contacts you?"

"Probably."

"Are you ready?"

She nodded and rose. As she slung the strap of her purse over her shoulder, she saw Catherine Carleton at a far table, across from a man she'd never seen. They stared at each other, and to her shock, Catherine smiled and gave her a small wave.

Elizabeth felt a frisson of fear. Don't be a fool, she told herself. She can't hurt you, not now, not ever again.

Still, Rod wondered why she walked so stiffly from the restaurant.

"That's the dragon lady?" Chad Walters asked lazily, following Elizabeth Carleton with his eyes as she walked gracefully between the tables.

"Yes," said Catherine. "That's the gold-digging little slut who trapped my father and murdered him."

"I'd acquit her," he said. "That lady's got class. Quite a musician, I hear."

"Not from me, you didn't!"

"No more sour grapes, Cathy. Finish that salad and let's go fuck."

Catherine's eyes glittered. "Fine, you bastard, just as long as you realize who you're fucking."

"Honey, the way you scream, I always know. You did trim those fingernails of yours, I trust."

"Screw you, Walters. And you can forget that whore stepmother of mine. She's frigid as the ice in your drink."

"A frigid whore," Chad said in that slow voice of his. "An interesting concept."

Catherine sighed. "Odd how I never curse except when I'm around you. Come on, let's get out of this place. If one of my sainted grandmother's friends sees me with you, she might try to do me out of my monthly allotment of hard cash. And you wouldn't like that, now, would you?"

"No," Chad said without apparent loss of aplomb,

"I certainly wouldn't, but then again, you get the million from your father's will soon, don't you?"

Catherine wished more than anything at that moment that she could be free of him. But she couldn't, not yet. "Yes," she said, "very soon."

Elizabeth loved the Windows on the World restaurant high atop the World Trade Center. The night was clear, with nearly a full moon and little smog to mask the stars. And she was with Rowe. She felt the tension of the long afternoon begin to fade. He ordered her a glass of Chablis and a lime and soda for himself. He smiled at her and she began to talk. About Benjamin Hallimer, an ace moneyman, as Rod had introduced him, about Edgar Derby, who was a power in computer systems and communication, of Coy Siverston, a strategist who could work on six different problems or deals at once, so Rod had told her, and Oran Wicks, a detail man. And, of course, Adrian Marsh, a young wunderkind from Harvard who would be both her right and left hand. She paused when their meal arrived, and felt herself tense up again.

"You must tell me if I'm boring you, Rowe. I'm such a novice at all this, but the gentlemen were most patient with me."

"I'm not at all bored, sweetheart. Tell me all about it. After all, what is a lover good for if he's not also a confidant?"

Lover. It sat oddly in her mind. She was being silly, for she did sleep with him. A lover. Her first lover.

"What are you thinking, Elizabeth?"

She flushed just a bit, and shook her head, concentrating on the beef Wellington.

Rowe said, "So you'll take care of old Brad with this power team?"

"Yes, so Rod assures me. Brad knows nothing about any of it. It's to be a surprise. In fact, there'll be an unexpected audit of Brad's business expenses for the past six months next week. Rod is convinced, as are the rest of the Noble Six, as I call them, that Brad is doing his best to 'screw the slut.' That's why everything's cloaked in such secrecy."

Rowe reached his hand across the table and began toying with her fingers. "I wish you and your Noble Six luck, Elizabeth. It sounds like you'll have old Brad just where you want him—without his sharp teeth."

"I'd prefer to live and let live, but no one trusts Brad. Nor do they trust Michael Carleton, Timothy's younger brother. He's the one who truly frightens me. He's so desperately controlled and driven."

"Is there anything I can do, Elizabeth?"

She clasped his hand. "Just be here for me, and if you have advice, please, I'm all ears."

"And beautiful hands as well. I had a new Baldwin delivered today. Will you play for me when we get home?"

Home, she thought. Another concept that sat oddly in her mind, but then again, it was difficult for her to think of Timothy's home as hers. Rowe's condominium occupied the entire tenth floor and it was filled with eighteenth-century French and English antiques. She was almost afraid to touch anything. She was still, deep down, a bourgeoise from the Midwest.

What would happen? What did she want to happen?

It was nearly midnight when she began to play. The action on the new Baldwin grand was stiff, so she broke it in with Gershwin, then moved to Chopin. She was wearing one of Rowe's shirts, a white oxford with a button-down collar. Very conservative. She wasn't wearing anything else.

He led her back to the bedroom. She was on the point of sleep when he said against her ear, "My darling, have you mentioned our relationship to Rod Samuels?"

She shook her head against his shoulder. "No, it's too private. It's not part of my . . . well, reality with him."

"Good," he said. "I don't want to share you with anyone. You're mine, Elizabeth, all mine."

She thought she heard him whisper that he loved

her, and she fell asleep filled with a sense of safety and belonging.

Christian Hunter sat behind his Victorian mahogany desk in his library, a gold pen held between his fingers, a blank sheet of stationery before him. Rowen Chalmers. Something had to be done about him. He stared down at the blank paper, then wadded it up and tossed it into the wastebasket. It hit dead center and he smiled. He'd played basketball in college. He hadn't lost his touch. He must remember to move the wastebasket a bit farther away, perhaps against the wainscoting so he could bank some of his shots.

He pushed the button on his private line, then dialed a number he knew very well.

A gravelly voice answered.

"Hunter here. Talk to me."

The man talked, at great length. When he stopped, Christian said nothing for several moments. He propped his feet up on his desk. "Excellent," he said finally. "Continue. I'll call you on Tuesday."

He gently set the phone back into its ornate cradle and leaned back in his chair, his hands clasped behind his head. When he heard the soft knock at his study door, he frowned, but only for an instant.

"Christian?"

"Just a moment, Susan," he called back.

She was waiting for him in the bedroom, wearing only the very expensive peach silk negligee he'd bought for her. She was blond—dyed, of course, but that didn't bother him overly—and she was wearing the tinted green contacts he'd ordered for her.

She was beautiful, he thought, watching her for a moment. But her breasts were too big. He walked to the stereo and put on a compact disk. The Amsterdam Baroque Orchestra filled the silence with the Third Brandenburg Concerto.

He felt himself growing hard and began to kiss Susan.

"Can't we ever listen to something neat? Like the Beatles, Christian?" she said, squirming against him.

"No, we can't. You're only twenty-one, Susan. The Beatles were before your time."

"The Boss then," she said, giving him a grin. She felt his fingers press against her. "How about the Tunnel of Love?" His fingers moved. She climaxed in the allegro third movement.

5

🍀

Jonathan Harley felt the headache grow, pounding at his left temple, a steady building of pain that made him close his eyes and sit perfectly still. He never had headaches and it disconcerted him. He thought of calling to Mrs. Maxwell to bring him aspirin, thought of it until he heard his wife's voice, shrill, demanding, calling to him.

Another scene, another screaming match with no winner, not that there ever could be a winner, of course. So much change, he thought, change that brought a wife whom he no longer knew or understood. He had, he realized, stopped caring about Rose three years before, when he'd found out about the Italian gigolo she'd met on a cruise ship. And slept with. And admitted sleeping with to him.

"Jonathan!"

His eyes felt red and unfocused. He heard his own voice, blank with the growing pain. "In here, Rose." A pause, then, "Please bring some aspirin."

She didn't. "What's the matter?" she asked, coming into his study, her new evening gown swirling about her ankles. The diamonds glittering at her throat made his eyes hurt.

"I have a terrible headache," he said.

She laughed. "A woman's excuse, darling. But I didn't come to see if you wanted to go to bed. You aren't dressed. The Banbridges are expecting us in thirty minutes."

"I'm not going," he said. "I told you last week and last night that I wasn't going. There will be at least fifty guests. I won't be missed. Have a good time, Rose."

She hated him in that moment, truly hated him. He spoke to her as if she were some sort of boring lackey; he didn't give a damn about her. She said, her voice sharp, "My parents will be there. In case you've forgotten who they are, Jonathan, they are the Pillsons. The Andrew Pillsons. They will expect to see you."

"Give them my best."

"Bastard!"

"Please, Rose, my head is coming off. If you want to fight, it will have to wait."

"Everything and everyone waits for *you*, don't they? You, the famous Jonathan Harley, oh yes, famous *now*. If it hadn't been for my father—"

"Rose, you don't want to be late."

"You are a monster, a selfish, hateful monster. I suppose you'll leave soon enough after I do. Your headache will disappear like magic, and your little tart will drool over every word you say. Who are you screwing now, darling?"

"I'm not screwing anyone, Rose." *Particularly not you, not my wife. And I don't want to, ever again.*

"Of course I wouldn't expect an honest answer. You will come with me, Jonathan. You must come. You will not humiliate me, not again."

"I wasn't aware that I had ever humiliated you."

"So calm, so very controlled, aren't you? You've turned into a robot, no feelings—"

"I thought I was a monster," he said, and wished he'd kept his mouth shut. He just wanted to be alone now, with some aspirin, in an empty, silent room.

". . . you don't care about anyone, do you? Nothing except your rotten business, and all your cheap women, of course."

"I care about Harley Electronics, certainly. If I didn't, you wouldn't be wearing diamonds, Rose. You wouldn't have a maid, a housekeeper, a cook, and a chauffeur. There are no cheap women." He actually felt his lips curve into a smile. "If I screwed around as much as you think I do, there wouldn't be any business left. I'd be dead from exhaustion."

She felt anger soar through her. It was impossible to score a point on him, he was too articulate, too detached, too manipulative. "So you admit there are some women?"

"Only one, three years ago, as you well know. My paltry sort of revenge—unworthy, I know."

"Will you always throw Pietro up to me?" Her voice caught on a sob, and he waited, praying she wouldn't go into hysterics. "He wanted me, believed I was beautiful and special."

"Rose, I will throw up, but not Pietro. Please, go to your party. Have a good time."

She stood very still, and stared at a portrait of their cottage in Nantucket behind him on the wall. The colors were soft, the scene stark. Odd how the artist had caught the different lights. Next to the painting was a photograph of the two of them standing on the beach, the cottage in the background. It had been taken some three years before. Jonathan was wearing faded jeans and a plain white shirt, the sleeves rolled up to his elbows, sneakers on his feet. She was in shorts and a halter, barefoot, her long blond hair blowing in her face. Both were smiling brightly. So long ago. He still looked the same, she thought, gazing toward him now behind his desk. Black, black hair, olive complexion, and eyes as dark as an moonless night, a bit of nonsense she'd told him once, years before. They'd been a striking couple, Jonathan as tall and as lean now as he'd always been, a runner and an athlete who took care of himself, and she, petite, blond, and very fair-complexioned. She felt suddenly vastly older than that smiling young woman in the photograph. She felt wrinkled inside, and useless.

She said slowly, looking straight at him, "If you don't come, Jonathan, I will leave you."

"That is the idea. Don't drive yourself, particularly if you intend to drink."

But he knew what she meant, and she knew that he knew. They stared at each other, so far apart now after eight years of marriage. They were strangers, but even the détente was no longer present. They were enemies and strangers. *A stranger in a strange land? A stranger from a strange land?* He couldn't remember. She said nothing more, merely turned on her heel and left the study, banging the door behind her.

He didn't wince, he made no movement at all. He supposed he should get a divorce. He supposed he knew it had to happen, he'd just avoided thinking about it, even in their worst fights. He'd spent more hours working during the past three years than ever before in his career. It was a coward's way, he knew. He was a coward, a coward with an appalling headache. He pulled himself to his feet to go find some aspirin.

It was close to ten o'clock that evening before he felt human enough to return to his study and do some work. Anything to keep himself from thinking about Rose and her threat. Once, she'd been Rosie, his Rosie, soft and sweet. Long ago. He thought of the company, *his* electronics company that he'd built. Sure, he'd had help from Rose's father in the beginning, but it was his, all his. He was thirty-five. Thirteen years of his life were in that company. Divorce would rend not just his life but also the company. He had control, clear control, but a settlement would prevent his plans for further expansion, perhaps even draw him perilously close to only a fifty-percent ownership. It was an appalling thought, particularly since one of his good friends, Peter Anchor, told him the rumors he'd heard through a friend of his in New York. Carleton Industries was sniffing around. ACI—Abercrombie-Carleton Industries. That ridiculously diversified conglomerate wanted an established, very profitable high-tech electronics company to go along with their shoe companies, their steel factories, their foreign hotels, their textile companies, their publishing house, God only knew what else.

He felt paralyzed. Who the hell was running that sprawling octopus? There'd been nothing out of the board of directors, not a sound. He remembered that the young wife had been acquitted of Timothy Carleton's murder. The stock fluctuated alarmingly and *The Wall Street Journal* speculated endlessly, but everyone was keeping quiet. Not that it mattered; the family owned enough shares to put the power where it pleased, the board only an assembly of old men who nodded their agreement.

It's just a rumor, nothing more. You've been in on enough of those tactics to know it could be just that—a rumor.

Carleton's sons? Were they in charge? Or Timothy Carleton's brother, Michael? No, more than likely it would be Timothy's own children. What was the older one's name—Brad, yes, Brad Carleton, a spoiled unethical bastard if ever there was one. And dangerous, very dangerous.

Jonathan forced himself to calm down. He pulled out a yellow notepad from his top desk drawer and methodically began to write down questions. He'd get the answers he needed by the end of the week. His handwriting was crisp, his lines straight.

Man really in charge?
Weaknesses?

Jonathan paused. He could write down a hundred more questions that needed answers, but first he had to know who was now running things. It always boiled down to one man and how skilled that one man was in maneuvering; his tactics, his strategy, his resources. But when he began to write his list again, it was issues that would face him in a divorce action. He felt his headache returning with a vengeance. He felt even sicker when he realized that there was no child-support question on his list. His three-month-old son, Alex, had died in his crib. One morning he was dead, no illness, nothing. Nothing to understand. Sudden infant death syndrome they called it. Acceptance was beyond him for a very long time. Rose—then Rosie—hadn't wanted any more kids, and at the time he couldn't blame her for that. But now, after five years . . . it was too late.

He wouldn't lose control of his company. He couldn't. He'd do anything to anyone before he'd let that happen.

Anything.

Brad Carleton sat behind his father's desk and sipped at his coffee in its delicate Wedgwood cup. No one had said a word when he'd moved. And he intended to stay. That bitch wouldn't get him out, not a chance.

When his personal secretary, Nan Bridges, rang to tell him two gentlemen were here to see him, he told her to have them wait. Slowly, very slowly, he straightened the papers on *his* desk, put his feet up, and buzzed Nan.

He smiled at the two gentlemen who entered his office, and waited a good minute before he rose.

"Mr. Carleton," the taller of the two said. He didn't extend his hand. "I'm Coy Siverston and this is Adrian Marsh. We are here, sir, at the behest of the CEO of ACI, Elizabeth Carleton. We request your controller's assistance in an immediate audit of your personal business expenses."

Brad nodded to the men and said, "I see. Anything else, gentlemen?"

Coy cleared his throat, and Brad saw the big gold tooth near the front of his mouth. "The Carleton Textile Company, the Brammer-Carleton Lumber Company, and the Morrissey-Carleton Food Company."

"In short, the three companies over which I exercised autonomous control before the death of my father."

"That is correct."

"I assume you have contacted my company presidents?"

"Yes, we have. This morning."

Brad merely smiled at them. "Have at it," he said, and waved a dismissing hand.

Coy gave him a startled look, and felt the same surprise from Adrian. From what they'd heard, Brad Carleton should be screaming and cursing them at this point, not smiling.

"Very well," said Coy, and they went out.

Their teams were into the three different company books within the hour.

On Thursday evening, three days later, Rod Samuels called Elizabeth.

"Well, it's over," he said.

"And?" Elizabeth asked.

"Tip-top shape. The books, that is. It appears old Brad has only lost some money, but no hanky-panky. I would have sworn—"

"You should be pleased, Rod. A son stealing from his father isn't something one can readily accept."

There was silence on Rod's end and Elizabeth shifted the telephone to her other ear.

"But I *knew*, Elizabeth, I knew he was on the take. Coy told me that Brad was so calm and mellow that it was like he was a Californian with nothing more to concern him than how high the waves were. And Brad isn't like that. He's the most uncontrolled, the most emotional of the Carletons when he's crossed. There's something wrong. I can smell it."

"It appears you smelled wrong, Rod. Perhaps Brad isn't what you thought. Perhaps—"

"Bullshit."

She said nothing for a moment. "What do you wish to do now?"

"Find out who spilled the beans to that little snake."

"Even if someone did, what difference does it make? It seems to me that we should forge ahead now, and not try to pin someone, a someone who probably isn't very important anyway. Loyalties are funny things, Rod. Incidentally, I've read the three business books you gave me, studied them until my eyes were red. I feel like the stupidest person alive. It's like a different language, and even though I understand the words, they don't have the same meaning. Like 'return on investment,' 'earnings-price ratio,' 'cash flow.' It's amazing. I'd never even heard of the SEC. All the rules and regulations."

He smiled into the phone. "You needn't worry about it. You don't have to understand everything, Elizabeth, not for a good while yet. I've arranged a formal PR release to the press, a meeting with the board, a meeting with all company presidents. You will be calm, charming. Timothy's—or rather your—speech writers are preparing drafts of what you're to say to all these disparate groups. I myself will be present at the meeting between you and your headquarters executives."

This is insanity, Elizabeth thought. But she'd come too far now to say no, even though she knew she should. She said instead, "I don't understand how you've kept everything secret, Rod."

"The Carletons haven't wanted it to get out that they no longer control ACI. You see, Elizabeth, they're waiting for you to throw in the towel."

Was that a strategy or a tactic? she wondered.

"Have you studied the organizational charts?"

"Yes, for what that's worth," she said, thankful that he couldn't see her grimace.

"Good. Just try to learn which name goes with which function, all right? And don't worry, Elizabeth."

"Will Brad be there?"

"Certainly. As will Michael. As for William Carleton, he's now in Australia, and couldn't be bothered. Laurette will be there, of course."

She swallowed.

"Elizabeth? The press will go bananas on this. Prepare yourself. It will all blow over within a month. Turn down all requests for interviews. Be firm—you don't know how persuasive *Fortune* reporters can be. All right?"

What could she say? The words "No comment" were second nature to her. "When is the first meeting?"

"I'll send your new executive assistant to you this afternoon and he'll review everything with you."

"That's Adrian Marsh, right?"

"Yes. Harvard Business School. He started out in investment banking, then came on board with ACI five years ago. He's married, two children, and smart as the dickens. As I told you, a wunderkind. His impressions of people are appallingly to the point and accurate, and he knows all the operations." He paused a moment, then said, "If you don't get along with him, just let me know."

"Don't worry. I'll be a saint."

"Another thing, Elizabeth. Adrian's loyal to his bones. We'll weed out the traitors in time."

Traitors, she thought blankly. She felt like a foreign country.

"Oh yes, I also told Adrian if he succeeds in this assignment, he's got the corporate vice-presidency for strategic planning."

Adrian Marsh, Elizabeth thought that afternoon when he arrived at her home, looked more like a bodyguard than an executive assistant. He was heavy, not fat, just so muscled that he looked bulky. He was olive-complexioned, his eyes dark, and his jaw square. And he spoke slowly, in a gentle, very deep voice with a Southern accent. He was kind, at least he was to her.

"I report only to you, Mrs. Carleton," he said after shaking her hand and seating himself. "You can trust me. I realize that might be difficult for you after all the garbage you've gone through. I do know every operation very well. And I know the men. If, however, you feel uncomfortable with any of my advice, you are to say so. I know I don't look like an Adrian. Most of my friends call me Adman. I will answer to almost anything. Now, if you don't mind, I would like a glass of water."

He lumbered off to the kitchen in his slow, measured walk, leaving Elizabeth seated on the sofa, surrounded by papers and a sea of reports, to smile after him.

At the end of a two-hour meeting, she was surprised to find herself not at all alarmed. She felt excited, more confident. She realized sometime later that it was Adrian's doing. At no time was he at all condescending or patronizing. He had oversimplified explanations, and she appreciated it, for he had said with his slow smile that showed a crooked front tooth, "A lot of this stuff is garbage, Mrs. Carleton, prepared by paper pushers to prove that they produce something. What's important, of course, is the paper pushers themselves. Tomorrow I understand you'll be coming in to the office. Mine is next to yours. We'll be spending our time on their profiles. If you know how a man thinks, Mrs. Carleton, and you study some samples of his work, you can make excellent judgments and decisions."

She got him to admit that he preferred Gatorade to water, the only two things he ever drank. "A longstanding habit from college football," he'd told her. She watched his massive throat contract as he downed the entire glass in one long drink.

"There's just one other thing, Mrs. Carleton," he said at the door. "Your office."

She looked at him rather blankly. "I don't wish to change a thing," she said, thinking he wanted to know if she planned to redecorate.

"Actually, you will," he said. "You see, Brad Carleton has moved in."

She felt a twist of nausea in her stomach. "Why?"

The man's got balls, and he knows you haven't. "I suppose it doesn't matter why. It's just that you, ma'am, you in person, will have to tell him to move his carcass out."

Elizabeth felt her heartbeat quicken. Fear—the fear of unpleasantness, the fear of confrontation, the fear of failing and looking like a fool.

"I'll be right with you, Mrs. Carleton. You will simply be firm and he'll be out by ten o'clock in the morning."

Adrian shook her hand and she felt his strength.

There was someone for her, she thought. She slept soundly that night, even though she hadn't seen Rowe. He was in Boston and wouldn't be in New York until the weekend.

"What do you want?"

"Good morning, Bradley," Elizabeth said, her voice calm, controlled, a slight smile on her face. She knew he hated *Bradley*. Timothy had always called his son that when he was displeased. Adrian stood beside her, a solid rock in a dark blue three-piece suit.

"I repeat, what do you want, ma'am, or should I say 'widowed ex-stepmother'?"

Elizabeth felt a ripple of anger, but there wasn't an ounce of tension coming from Adrian. In fact, he looked a bit amused, not at all intimidated by Brad Carleton. She realized that Adrian wouldn't let her fold. She swallowed and said, "This is now my office, Bradley. Please remove yourself to your former office immediately."

"No."

She shrank back, Adrian felt it. He said slowly, his Virginian drawl very pronounced, "I suggest you do as Mrs. Carleton says, Mr. Carleton. Otherwise I will be obliged to call Carleton's security guards to assist you."

Brad looked at the man, looked at him closely. He knew Adrian Marsh, of course, knew the man was brilliant. He was called the Adman. But he didn't look at all brilliant, he looked like a dumb jock. Still . . .

Brad forced himself to smile. Slowly he turned and spit on Timothy's desktop. He looked at Elizabeth, full in the face, picked up his briefcase, and walked out, saying not another word.

Elizabeth was shaking.

"Sit down a moment, ma'am," Adrian said. He cupped her elbow in his beefy hand and led her to the sofa. "You did just fine. Just fine indeed."

"Did he fire Millicent Stacy, Timothy's secretary?"

"Yes, he did."

"Could I have her back, Adrian?"

"Certainly. She will need her two assistants as well. Doubtless she'll be here after lunch, no later."

She still looked pale, and he fetched her a glass of water. How, he wondered, could this pathetic female handle anything? She knew nothing, nor was she equipped to deal with the vast complexities of ACI. But she had the oddest effect on him. He wanted to protect her, teach her, even though when he'd accepted the position, he'd wanted to howl. But he wasn't stupid. With any ability at all, he would be the power behind the throne. He wouldn't hurt her. No, indeed.

He felt like her father. He was three years older.

"Here," he said. "Have a drink and just gather yourself together a bit. We've lots to do today."

Elizabeth nearly burst into tears when Millicent Stacy came into her office, gave her a gentle look, and told her with a motherly pat not to worry about a thing.

6

Elizabeth felt the tension ease as Rowe's strong, supple hands kneaded her back.

"Better, sweetheart?" He lifted her hair and kissed the nape of her neck.

She sighed and turned over. "Much better. Thank you, Rowe. I've missed you."

"And I you," he said, and kissed her mouth.

It took him a very long time, but he brought her to orgasm before he took care of himself.

She smiled up at him, completely relaxed now, and strangely enough, alert. "You are a very nice man, Rowe Chalmers."

"I know," he said. "You just lie still, Elizabeth. I'm getting the champagne."

They sat in his four-poster eighteenth-century French bed, claimed to have belonged to one of Marie Antoinette's ladies-in-waiting. Elizabeth had only laughed when Rowe told her, but he was serious, the bed had a pedigree. He settled a tray in front of them and poured her a glass of champagne, Perrier Jouet, his favorite, then offered her a cracker and cheese.

She was wearing the royal-blue silk top to his pajamas and he was wearing the bottoms.

"Tell me about your week," he said, and promptly fed her a cracker. "I read all the articles about the final takeover by the late Timothy Carleton's widow, and the rubber-stamping by the board, with the exception of the two senior Carletons, of course. At least everything is out in the open now, and all the nastiness will die down, you'll see."

"That's what the Adman says to me, almost hourly."

He arched an eyebrow, and she laughed. "The Adman is Adrian Marsh, my right hand." She told him about the confrontation with Brad Carleton, and he merely laughed.

"But he actually *spit* on his father's desk!"

"What did you expect? For him to fold his tent and stroll off into the sunset?"

"No, but I was so scared. A piano never faces you down, not like people do, particularly people who hate your guts."

"This Adrian Marsh—do you trust him?"

"Completely. He looks like a football player, talks like a Southern evangelist, has an excellent mind, and is kind."

"Tell me about the board meeting with dear Laurette Carleton."

Elizabeth drank her champagne first, her expression thoughtful. "It was odd, really. I was flanked by Adrian, Rod, Oran, Coy, Edgar, and Ben. Did I ever tell you about Coy Siverston?"

He shook his head, but he knew all about Coy Siverston. A formidable opponent, a formidable ally, a man who rubbed elbows with international bankers and politicians. He was a management and organizational genius.

Rowe said nothing as Elizabeth told him what he already knew. "Unfortunately, he's with me on a short-term basis, so Rod told me. He'll get everything in tip-top shape, then take himself off. According to Rod, he loves nothing more than a challenge. I guess he took one look at me and beheld the challenge of the century." She grinned. "He has this huge gold tooth that blinds you when he smiles."

"Don't let anything blind you, Elizabeth," Rowe said. "Tell me about Laurette."

"She was regal, her usual self, but she wasn't at all nasty. She treated me like an insect, of course, but that was about it. And the papers were right, it was a rubber stamp. At least there were no allegations from Laurette about me murdering her son."

"Both she and Michael Carleton knew they couldn't stop anything. Better to bow gracefully to the inevitable, I guess she thought."

"Rod is certain she's up to something," Elizabeth said, frowning a bit. "You know, I feel sorry for her, at least I did today. It's been all very tragic for her, you know."

"Stop, Elizabeth, if it distresses you. As for the old lady, she isn't used to losing. Don't let yourself feel sorry for her. Rod might be right. She may be up to something. I wonder what it could be. You've muzzled Brad."

She shook her head. "Aren't you getting bored with all my war stories?"

"Not a chance—at least not until I can get it up again. Then I'll create my own war stories, with me the ravager and pillager."

"And me the fair maiden being dragged away from her musical instrument by the marauder?"

"Yes, to mine—my instrument, that is."

She told him about all her meetings, in great detail, and he listened, bless him, he did listen. "Of course, Adrian and my other noble guys don't want us to discuss any strategy with those who have loyalty to the other Carletons."

"What strategy is this?"

"Goodness, where to start? Well, I learned today the difference between a merger and an acquisition and how it's done. This SEC group and all their regulations make my head spin. My team want to acquire Bell-Haverson. The company's not at all well-managed, they tell me, and they're first on the list, on *their* list, I should say. They told me that they've already started buying up stock, and something about how you have to register your intentions with the SEC after procuring four-point-something in stock. And other marvelous terms like a 'white knight'—that's where the

company doesn't want the takeover and looks for someone else to buy and—"

"Yes, I know about white knights and gray knights,
and so forth."

She grinned at him. "I keep forgetting that you
know all these things that are the greatest mystery to
me."

"Do your Noble Six believe Bell-Haverson will try
for a white knight?"

"No, they're—we're—planning on a friendly takeover, with lots of goodies for the executives at Bell-
Haverson. Evidently we need to round out things with
a high-tech electronics company, and this one is it."

"Yes," Rowe said thoughtfully. "It makes a great
deal of sense. Bell-Haverson is a major government
defense contractor. Yes, it is quite a sensible move at
this point. Get ACI's foot in yet another door."

"You think it's a good idea, then?"

He smiled at the uncertainty in her voice. He kissed
her. "Yes, I think it's a good idea. And now, sweetheart, I think it's time for me to be the ravaging
marauder again."

When Elizabeth thought about it, she knew that her
growing confidence, her ability not to shrink when
approached by the media, was because of Rod, Adrian,
and Rowe.

She was happy for the first time in so long that she
couldn't even remember. Perhaps with Timothy during that first year? Maybe. It was all growing so hazy
now. She had begun to think of her group as the
Nobel Seven, for Rowe, perhaps more than the others, had taken over, and she felt safe and protected.
With the excellent advice she was given every hour of
the day, she found herself back at her piano, practicing and practicing.

She was a figurehead and she didn't mind in the
least. She put off meeting with presidents and general
managers of the other ACI companies. She didn't

want to leave New York. She didn't want to leave Rowe.

On April 12 ACI stated its intentions with the SEC for a friendly takeover of Bell-Haverson. It was something called a tender offer, a term that made Elizabeth laugh and shake her head in bewilderment.

It floated through Elizabeth's head, making barely a ripple in her contentment.

Until Adrian marched into her office on the fourteenth, his muscular neck mottled red with anger.

"Read this," he said, and pointed at a marked column of *The Wall Street Journal*.

Elizabeth read the article. "I . . . I don't understand, Adrian. You told me that Bell-Haverson was a friendly deal."

"It was. At least that's what we understood."

"But they found a white knight?"

"Yes," he said, nearly spitting out the word. "It's damned impossible, really. It's insane. It's as if they . . . well, we can forget it, blast it!"

"We won't get the company?"

"Haven't you been listening to me, Elizabeth?" He raked his fingers through his dark hair. "Forgive me. No, we won't get the company. It's really not worth breaking our butts over it. It's all over before it's even had a chance to begin. You want to know who bailed them out?"

Elizabeth looked back down at the article. "It says something about MAI. Who are they?"

Adrian felt another wave of exasperation flow over him. Then he stilled his impatience. She'd lived with only her music for so long. How could he expect her to know? But she should know. He said very slowly, "Your brother-in-law, Michael Carleton, is chairman of MAI. That stands for Michael Abercrombie, Elizabeth."

"Laurette's maiden name," Elizabeth said dully. "Did Brad do this?"

"He could have spilled the beans to his uncle, I suppose, but he didn't know about it, Elizabeth, couldn't have known about it. The level of secrecy has been high."

"One of the Noble Six, then. Or one of our lawyers or investment bankers."

"Could be," he admitted, and eased himself into a chair that groaned under his weight. "Damnation, this is a kicker! Maybe even one of the secretaries, though Millicent has been the only one involved and her mouth is tight as a clam. It's just that none of us expected it. All possibilities are discussed thoroughly—you know that. But this came out of the blue."

"What will we do now?"

"Lick our wounds, try to shore up any leaks, then go to the second high-tech electronics firm on the list."

"Who's that?"

"A man by the name of Jonathan Harley owns it. He's good, very good, and has views for expansion himself. Our problem will be a stock buy-up, enough to take over. I understand he's in the middle of a divorce and his wife will take him, and that includes Harley stock. She already owns about ten percent and will get even more in the settlement."

"How soon?"

"A while yet. The divorce is just getting started, according to our sources. We'll just have to wait awhile. When we move, it'll be fast."

"This one will be hostile?"

"That's for sure. And, Elizabeth, not a word to anyone. Not even to Kogi or Gallagher or Drake."

Adrian saw that she looked upset, and rather help-less, a look he hadn't seen in several weeks. He soft-ened just a bit. "Look, why don't you just forget the entire business for now. It will be several months yet. Just put it out of your mind, and don't worry."

Because Elizabeth wanted to forget all of it, she did put it out of her mind. She went on a baroque kick, immersing herself in Bach, back in the eighteenth century, when things were simple and there were no such things as white knights or black knights or any other color.

She had her music and Rowe Chalmers, and signed her name when Adrian placed papers in front of her. Her hours in the beautiful corner office decreased.

She was content.

She thought about marriage and a home and children.

She asked Rowe on Saturday evening, "When will I meet your parents?"

He paused a moment, and she saw the flicker of something she read as appalling in his eyes. Before he could answer her, she said, forcing a small tight smile, "It's all right, Rowe. It's too soon, I was foolish to forget. To your parents, I'm that scarlet woman, or whatever. After all, I was acquitted, found not guilty, but the murderer wasn't unveiled like he always is on *Perry Mason*." She'd begun watching *Perry Mason* reruns every day at noon. It was like a daily catharsis when the real murderer spilled his or her guts in the final two minutes of the show.

Not real life at all.

"Just a while longer, my darling," he told her.

But his parents had to know about them, she thought. They'd been photographed several times and written up in clever articles that made her want to yell with the unfairness of it all. To protect him, she'd asked each of her Noble Six to escort her now and again. And the papers made it seem like she was the Merry Widow.

And there was nothing, absolutely nothing from Christian Hunter. Instead of making her feel relieved, deep inside she knew fear. She could forget him for hours at a time, but when she remembered, the fear blossomed and she was swamped with anxiety. She wanted to call him, but she was too afraid.

Life went on as it inevitably did, but unpleasantness didn't touch her. Until one Friday night.

Adrian and his wife, Elaine, invited her out to dinner, and because Rowe was out of town, she accepted. Elaine was a small, vivacious woman who ordered her

huge husband around like a puppy. Elizabeth liked
her and did her best to make the woman feel at ease
with her. They went to Chanterelle, a small restaurant
in Soho with *nouvelle* French cuisine. Elizabeth ate
oysters with white truffles, and conversation centered
on the Marshs' home life and their two children.

Then Elizabeth spotted Catherine. She was with the
same man as before, many months before when Elizabeth had been with Rod Samuels at the Quilted Giraffe. They appeared to be arguing.

"Elizabeth, what's wrong?"

She pulled herself back to Adrian's concerned voice.
She found she was hunching down in her chair, raising
her wineglass so it hid her profile. She shook her head
and tried to smile.

"Is someone here you don't like?" *"Afraid of" is
more like it*, Adrian thought, growing more concerned.
Such a small restaurant, off the beaten path. Still
Elizabeth only shook her head again, and asked Elaine
a domestic question.

Adrian looked about and spotted Catherine Carleton. He knew about her, of course. Beautiful, young,
spoiled. Even though they'd just barely finished their
entrée, Adrian said pleasantly, "Why don't we get out
of here now. There's this special place I want to take
you gorgeous women to, for a brandy."

He knows, Elizabeth thought, and gave him a grateful smile. She grabbed her purse and started to rise.
The waiter saw her motion and rushed to the table to
assist her.

Catherine was drunk. And furious. Chad Walters
was a bastard, and demanding more money from her.
Or he wouldn't provide her with the cocaine she wanted
so desperately. It was top-grade. She had no other
contacts. Then she saw the waiter from the corner of
her eye, and then Elizabeth. She saw red.

She felt a wave of dizziness as she jumped to her
feet and shook her head. "You god-awful lying bitch,"
she said. She thought she'd whispered it, but she heard

Chad say sharply, "Shut up, Cathy, and sit down! God, everyone is staring!"

But she didn't. She was out of control and couldn't seem to stop herself. She'd said it aloud and she wasn't about to stop now. She strode to Elizabeth's table. She saw Elizabeth's face, utterly devoid of color, and knew that she'd heard what she'd said.

"I mean it," she said, her voice shrill. "You bribed that man, and you got away with murder! You did it, I know you did. You killed my father!"

The restaurant was deadly silent. It was like a tableau, Elizabeth thought vaguely. Everyone had struck an attitude.

"Catherine," she said very clearly, "you're not well. Go home."

"What, dear stepmother? Leave you in peace? Are you sleeping with him too?" She sent a mocking glance at Adrian. "Perhaps a little ménage à trois?" Then she was trembling, knowing she'd gone too far, but the rage, the anger, propelled her. "I know, I know you did it. I'll see you—" She got no further.

Adrian leapt from his chair, grabbed Catherine, one huge hand covering her mouth, and dragged her through the restaurant and out the door. Chad Walters tossed Elizabeth a mock salute, which she didn't see, and strolled through the restaurant after Adrian.

"No, Elizabeth, don't say anything. Let's get out of here."

Elizabeth felt Elaine's hand on her arm and followed her out like a witless child. She heard the building sea of conversation in their wake. It would never stop, never. She wanted to die. Once they were outside, she looked blankly upon a scene that would have made for an excellent Hollywood set.

Adrian was shaking Catherine like a dog. Chad Walters merely stood by watching, a mocking smile on his lips. And a group of people was gathering to watch.

The police would come quickly, Elizabeth thought, and the ever-lurking paparazzi, and the media. Oh, God!

She heard herself in a loud, shrill voice: "Come along, Adrian. Now, quickly. Let her go."

Adrian released Catherine and felt her long nails score down his cheek. "You damned bitch," he said, turned on his heel, and walked quickly to Elizabeth and Elaine.

"Please take me home," Elizabeth said, surprised that this sorry excuse for a voice was hers.

"Yes, I think we can get out of here now," Adrian said. He was holding both women very close. "You all right, Elizabeth?"

"Yes. Elaine," she began, turning to Adrian's white-faced wife, "I'm so sorry. Please . . ."

Elaine didn't say anything. Nothing like this had ever happened in her life. For God's sake, she'd grown up in Fort Worth, Texas, her father was a math professor at TCU. Her only publicity was Girl of the Month in high school, and she hadn't even made that during the school year, but during August. She felt strangely disembodied. She heard Adrian talking, heard Elizabeth. She raised her head, looked directly into Elizabeth's eyes, and said, "I don't want to ever see you again."

"Elaine, it wasn't Elizabeth's fault!"

She shook off her husband's hand and marched down the street.

Elizabeth sagged against the brick wall behind her. She saw that Adrian didn't know what to do. Which one of them to leave?

She started laughing. "Let's go, Adrian. Find me a taxi, then see to Elaine."

She laughed until Adrian assisted her into a taxi and gave the driver her address.

"Hey, lady, you all right?"

The driver was a middle-aged man with a beer belly and a Bronx accent.

"Yes," she said. "I'm just ducky."

She didn't leave the house for three days.

The appalling scene made all the papers, of course, but Elizabeth didn't see them. Kogi told Gallagher to keep out all newspapers and all reporters. Kogi turned on the answering machine, reviewed all the messages himself, and passed only those from people he trusted.

Rowe returned from San Francisco the following Tuesday and immediately went to Elizabeth's house. Gallagher looked at him like he was the savior of the world.

Rowe thought Elizabeth looked like hell. Like she'd been through hell, and wished she hadn't come out.

He held her, saying nothing. She didn't cry. She didn't say anything. Rowe dismissed Kogi and Mrs. Jeffers, the maid, and took Elizabeth to bed. He didn't make love to her, merely held her, stroking her back. God, she felt as though she'd lost twenty pounds. Thin and white and nearly boneless. Her pain was palpable.

Finally he said, "All right, Elizabeth, that's enough. It's Catherine we're talking about, Catherine, who is twisted and sick, not you. You've got to pull yourself together now. I'm certain you've ignored all the business, including your Noble Six. You're needed, sweetheart. Now, you're going to put your face on and we're going out. To Elizabeth, New Jersey, if you like. But we're going out."

"I want to go to Hoboken," she said, and it was there they went, to a small Italian restaurant that was surprisingly good. They called it their Hoboken Find.

Elizabeth received an apology from Elaine Marsh, delivered by an embarrassed Adrian.

"Tell Elaine to forget it," Elizabeth said, patting his massive shoulder. "I don't blame her, not a bit. It was just as awful for her, I know." She drew a deep breath and forced a smile. "Now, what's going on?"

Jonathan Harley knew he was going to lose controlling interest. And he hadn't enough money to buy back the stocks to make the difference. He was broke in terms of ready cash. His plans for expansion were down the tubes. Rose had walked out, and the Pillsons had risen against him, all their power focused on him, one man who only wanted to be left alone.

He'd lost weight, and his secretary, Midge, Sweet-

Talkin' Midge, as he sarcastically called her, said to him, "You look like a railroad track, like you could lie down and have Amtrak run over you. What do you weigh, anyway?"

He didn't know.

"I'd say one-seventy, and you at least six feet, two inches. Idiot. Here, eat!" And she plied him with cartons of Chinese food. Then she spoke to his cook, Mrs. Mallson, and enough food for a battalion appeared on his table every evening.

He went to Boston to visit his cousin and family. He had sense enough to realize that he was in bad shape, and not knowing what else to do, found himself three different willing women and made love to all of them on successive nights until he was insensate.

But then he'd wake up in the morning and wonder where the hell he was and who the woman was who was lying beside him.

One woman, he thought her name was Nancy, said to him when she saw him come out of the bathroom naked, "You're a handsome man, Jonathan. You're a very nice man and an excellent lover. But you're destroying yourself. It's not a pleasant sight. Go home and get your shit together."

He did, surprisingly enough.

Midge cheered when he invited her out to lunch at the Bookery.

"Is this my belated Christmas present, boss?"

"No," he said. He raised his wineglass. "A toast, Midge. To Nancy."

Midge rolled her eyes. "You're the sweet-talking one, boss, not me. Who's this Nancy? What's her last name?"

Jonathan merely smiled and shook his head. "Search me," he said, and drank deeply. He rubbed his hands together. "Did you bring your notebook, Midge?"

"For goodness' sake, we're supposed to be having lunch!"

"Lots to do. Okay, eat your calamari, even though it makes me sick to watch you."

"Do you know *my* last name, boss?"

7

Christian Hunter didn't say a word; he was too surprised.

"Who did you say, Mrs. Hightower?" he managed at last. His knuckles were white on the receiver.

"A Mrs. Carleton, Doctor."

He looked at his Italian loafers. There was a smudge on the toe of one of them. He rubbed the toe behind his other leg.

"Dr. Hunter? Would you like me to have her call back? Leave a message?"

"No, I'll take the call. When and who is my next patient?"

"It's Mr. Pencini, at two o'clock."

"All right. Put on Mrs. Carleton."

Mrs. Hightower's voice was her usual flat monotone. She hadn't made the connection between the Mrs. Carleton on the phone and *the* Mrs. Carleton, Elizabeth X. In fact, she'd never shown a bit of interest in his sudden appearance in a murder trial except to say as she handed him a pile of letters to sign, "I suppose you know what you're doing," and that was it.

Christian wondered if he were losing his mind, thinking about staid, bored Victoria Hightower at this particular moment. He cleared his throat. "Hello, this is Dr. Hunter."

Elizabeth discovered that she didn't quite know what to say. She gripped the phone in a stranglehold.

"Dr. Christian Hunter?"

"Yes, Mrs. Carleton," he said, and he felt himself go warm at the sound of her voice. It was soft, frightened, uncertain.

"I simply couldn't wait any longer," she said. "I've been going crazy, if you want to know the truth. I need to know."

It was too soon, he knew. A couple more weeks, then he'd be ready. He said, his voice gentle and reassuring, his patented shrink's voice, "Mrs. Carleton, I'm leaving for Vienna tomorrow night. When I return, we can meet. Not in public. That wouldn't be wise."

"I see," said Elizabeth. "At my house then, Dr. Hunter."

"Say two weeks from Friday?"

"Yes . . . yes, that would be fine. *I must know!*"

"I realize that, Mrs. Carleton. I will see you at seven in the evening. Good-bye."

Just like that, Elizabeth thought, staring at the buzzing receiver in her hand. Two weeks. At least there'd be an end to it. And she would know. He would tell her. She'd know if he were saint or sinner, God or the devil. Very slowly she replaced the receiver in its cradle. Then she frowned. Would he never have gotten in touch with her? Was she forcing something she shouldn't touch? Over seven months had passed. Seven months of complete silence. She knew it had been the accidental meeting with Moretti, the New York district attorney, that had forced her to do this.

She hadn't really imagined that a sneer could be other than a pat noun or verb in a book. But Moretti's sneer hadn't been at all pat. It had been filled with fury and contempt. She'd been alone, in front of Bloomingdale's, of all places.

"So," he said, stopping beside her as she stared into a window filled with lacy lingerie. "If it isn't the murderess, free and in our midst."

She froze, turned, and looked directly into his sneering face.

He waved a hand toward a lace bra and panties. "To seduce yet another lover, Mrs. Carleton? You need this kind of help, don't you? Men eventually get frightened of you?'"

"No, Mr. Moretti," she said, "no to all of it. My husband's murderer is still free. You never wanted to find him or her. You just wanted me. I was so handy, and your political ambitions were so pressing."

The cords in his neck stood out, she saw, with rage, but his voice was venomously soft. "I wish Samuels had put you on the stand. I would have broken you in five minutes. Everyone would have seen what you are. You're a miserable human being, *Mrs*. Carleton. But you're rich, very rich, aren't you? You can buy, steal, bribe anyone and anything."

"You, Mr. Moretti, are a blind fool." And she'd marched away, her shoulders squared, her head high. But she was full of misery inside. Nothing but naked misery.

She knew then that she had to call Christian Hunter. She had to.

"Something wrong, Mrs. Carleton?"

She forced herself to turn away from the phone and smile at Kogi. "No, nothing." *I'll know in two weeks. Two weeks.*

"Mr. Rowe come to dinner tonight?"

"Yes, Kogi, he is. Will you make sushi? He is very fond of it."

Her life was a successive march of light and shadows. Automatically she went toward the light, to her piano. She played Scarlatti, Rowe's favorite composer, for three hours. No one disturbed her.

She received the letter the following day.

Just a few lines, very neatly typed, no signature.

And she felt as if someone had slammed her in the stomach.

Mrs. Carleton:
    On Thursday night drive to Laurette Carleton's estate on Long Island. Eight-thirty should be the

right time. Do not announce yourself. Walk around to the library. You will learn how MAI knew to buy Bell-Haverson, among other things. If you are wise you will tell no one. No one.

That was all. She stared at it, even shook the single sheet of paper. The betrayer. But she already knew who the betrayer had been. Avery Ramson, a man who was high enough up, an assistant to Coy Siverston. He'd killed himself, and left a suicide note stating he was dying of cancer. That was it.

She wadded the paper and threw it against the wall, then closed her eyes, not wanting to see anything, but the images raced before her, threatening, insane images. I can't go on like this. She grabbed the phone to call Adrian. His secretary, one of Millicent Stacy's assistants, came on the line at the second ring.

"Janice? This is Mrs. Carleton. Is Mr. Marsh there?"

"I'm sorry, Mrs. Carleton . . . no, here he is now. Just a moment, please."

"Elizabeth? What's up?"

Adrian's voice, so solid, like him, and trustworthy and loyal. *Tell no one.*

"Elizabeth? Are you there?"

"Mr. Adman," she said. "How . . . how are you?"

There was a surprised pause. "I'm okay. What's up?"

"I . . . Nothing, really, Adrian. I was just thinking about Avery Ramson."

"Why?"

"It's just a shame, that's all. You know that big ad campaign for MacKenzie-Carleton Foods?"

"I know it well. We lost well over a million dollars on it."

"That was after Avery's death."

"Yes, I know. But secrecy with campaigns like that . . . well, the fact is that it was in essence stolen. It happens, Elizabeth. Really. Let it go."

Did it really just happen, like that? Forget it?

"Elizabeth, what's wrong?"

She forced a smile, realized he couldn't see it, and laughed at herself. That laugh eased him.

"I was just thinking, Adrian, about a lot of things, that's all. I know you must be very busy—"

"Never too busy for the boss."

"Yes, well, give my love to Elaine."

"You're very kind, Elizabeth," he said, and she knew he was thinking of that awful evening and the scene with Catherine.

When she rang off, she wandered around the house, then donned dark glasses and a coat. She spent three hours walking, just walking. *You're walking just like you were the evening Timothy was killed.*

She wanted to call Rowe. She needed him more than ever, but he was in Boston and wouldn't return until Friday. She would show him the letter then. *But what about Thursday night?*

Rowe called her late that evening.

"A fund-raiser, sweetheart. Hope you weren't asleep."

She had been, but of course denied it. "No, I was thinking about you. I miss you, Rowe."

"No more than I do you, Elizabeth. You sound down. Anything wrong?"

She wanted to tell him, pour it all out, let him handle it. But it was her problem to resolve, all hers. It wasn't fair to bring Rowe into it. He'd be furious. He'd probably hire a task force to go to Laurette's estate.

"No, nothing's wrong. I have tickets for a benefit for the New York Philharmonic Friday night."

"Sounds good to me, if it doesn't go on too long. I want your body, lady."

She tried to laugh. "I'll be waiting, Rowe."

"With bells on?"

"With anything you wish."

"You sure nothing's wrong, sweetheart?"

"No, nothing. Friday night, Rowe."

She took two sleeping pills at two o'clock.

*   *   *

It was cloudy, the air heavy with coming rain. She'd rented a car, a small dark blue Mustang. She hoped it wouldn't rain. She didn't know where the windshield wipers were. Luckily she'd located the headlights.

Traffic was light on the expressway. Laurette's estate was in Southampton. She reviewed the security in her mind. As far as she could remember, there was only a burglar alarm, and she wouldn't trip that. No, she was only going to listen at the glass doors at the library. No dogs, no guards, no electric fences. She felt like a thief, a criminal, and could imagine the gloating look on Moretti's face if she were discovered lurking about the Carleton estate.

Who sent that letter? Why?

It seemed her life was a series of questions, questions with no answers, except she would find one answer tonight.

She felt cold, but her armpits were damp.

She was even dressed like a thief, all in black, down to her low-heeled boots, up to her hair that was braided and tucked under a black ski cap.

She should have asked Adrian to come with her.

She should have begged Rowe to come home.

The Carleton estate was just ahead. The house where Timothy had been born and raised. It was off Cowslip Road, fifteen acres, grounds groomed religiously, trees lining the perimeter. Elizabeth pulled the Mustang off the road, next to the six-foot stone fence. She stopped short, and laughed softly. A musician climbing over a stupid wall.

Even her gloves were black. She was over the wall in a matter of moments. She saw the lights ahead. The vast library, the scene of every family conclave, was on the east side of the house. She didn't need her small flashlight.

What am I doing here? Have I lost my mind?

She kept walking, slightly bent over—like a thief.

What if I'm caught?

She wouldn't think about that, but she could see the

headlines: "CARLETON WIDOW ARRESTED FOR TRESPASS-ING: D.A. SALIVATES."

Oh, God, what was she doing? What was she supposed to overhear?

Another betrayer? Adrian? Rod? Oh, please, no.

She skirted the wide circular drive. There were four cars in front. Quite a family gathering.

Elizabeth was breathing hard, not from exertion, but from fear, when she eased next to the library windows. Laurette loved fresh air, every month of the year. Several of the windows were three inches open. Did the person who wrote that letter know that?

She peered into a window. It was Laurette, Elizabeth knew, who had refurbished the Carleton library many years before, using the library from the Duke of Marlborough's Blenheim as her model. It was an overly long room, three walls covered with bookshelves, all of them filled, the wooden floor covered with a dozen small Tabriz carpets, and its effect, at least to Elizabeth, was oppressive and melancholy.

Laurette was seated like Queen Victoria in a high-backed chair away from the fireplace. Behind her, displayed proudly, was her collection of Fabregé clocks. Timothy had given her the exquisite dark blue one for her birthday two years before. On her left Michael Carleton stood, quite at ease, a smile on his lips. He looked thinner, she thought, but still fit, his face so tanned he looked as though he'd sailed to Australia with his brother, William. And there was Catherine, seated on a love seat, laughing, wearing crimson silk lounging pajamas. Brad was leaning against the mantel, his hands stuffed in his pants pockets, his shoulders hunched. She saw Laurette's butler come into view.

He spoke quietly to Laurette. Elizabeth couldn't make out his words.

Why was she here? To hear the Carletons' plans to ruin her?

She froze, and her heart began to pound, slow, sharp beats that made her nauseated.

Rowe Chalmers walked into the library with that cocky walk of his that she loved to watch.

"You're late, darling," Catherine said, waving a hand. "Not that I'm not delighted to see Elizabeth's own personal stud, of course."

"Shut up, Catherine," Michael said.

Rowe nodded toward Laurette, but made no move to sit down.

Brad pushed away from the mantelpiece. "What news have you for us, Chalmers?"

Laurette's voice rang out, sharp, clear, in command. "We will have a bit of civilization before we proceed. What would you like to drink, Mr. Chalmers? Scotch? Bourbon?"

"Nothing, Mrs. Carleton," Rowe said. He sounded so normal, as if he were talking to Kogi or to her.

"Very well. Now I suppose we can get down to business. My grandson asked you what news you have."

"None," said Rowe.

"Come now, darling," Catherine said, sitting up on the edge of the love seat. "Surely all your after-sex talk isn't about Elizabeth's beautiful toes."

"I have told you that Elizabeth has withdrawn more and more from the active business."

"She still must know things," Laurette said. "Strategy that Brad isn't let in on."

"I told you about the sales campaign. That struck a significant blow," said Rowe.

Michael said softly, "Such a pity that old Avery snuffed himself. The perfect scapegoat."

"You should know," Rowe said, his voice low. "You pushed him hard enough."

"Come now, Mr. Chalmers," Laurette said in her most imperious voice. "It was you who requested this meeting, not us. What is it you have to tell us?"

Rowe looked at each of them in turn. He wanted to kill them, all of them, very slowly. He said, "I have fulfilled my end of the bargain. I want out. Mr. Carleton"—he pointed a finger at Michael—"he promised me that it would end."

Michael looked amused. "Really, my dear boy, it wasn't my fault that your father squandered the family money through his miserable management and gambling. You need money to bail out your precious bank. And this is the only well in town."

Rowe looked directly at Laurette. "Why do you want to hurt your son's corporations? Why do you want to destroy what he built?"

Laurette said very softly, "Revenge, Mr. Chalmers. I want Elizabeth Xavier Carleton to know that she can't murder my son and get off scot-free."

"I do believe," Catherine drawled, "that our dear stud is having attacks of conscience. Is dear Elizabeth that good a lay?"

"Don't be crude, Catherine," Laurette said, frowning slightly. Catherine hadn't used to be so unladylike, but during the past six months or so . . . She would think about it later, these changes in Catherine. "Mr. Chalmers will continue to feed us information until we are satisfied. You will have another million dollars deposited in your personal account as soon as we know the next high-tech electronics company scheduled for buy-out."

"For God's sake, Elizabeth doesn't know!"

"Ask her," said Michael.

"She'll tell you anything, won't she, Rowe?" Catherine crossed her legs. "You worked fast enough in Paris. You've got her just where you want her. Panting."

"She didn't kill your son, Mrs. Carleton."

Laurette studied his face, and hers didn't soften. "Is my granddaughter right, Mr. Chalmers? Are you falling, as they say, for that woman?"

Rowe didn't answer.

"She murdered him, all right," said Laurette. "I have no doubts, not a one. Perhaps you'd best watch your back."

"You know the terms, Chalmers," Michael said sharply. "Don't try to back out on us. Don't try to marry Elizabeth Carleton. You know what will happen if you try."

"We need more information, Mr. Chalmers," Laurette said quietly. "The security network that man Adrian Marsh has set up is very nearly impenetrable."

"We couldn't even set him up with the best-looking hooker in New York," said Michael, honest surprise in his voice. "Have any of you *seen* his wife?"

"I did," said Catherine. "I thought both she and Elizabeth would expire in the restaurant."

"I will speak to you later about that, Catherine," said Laurette, frowning at her granddaughter. "I detest ill-bred scenes."

Catherine gave an elegant shrug.

"When do I get out of this?" Rowe asked.

"According to my information, which is entirely correct, of course," said Michael, "you are still in need of about five million more. You've got a ways to go yet, Chalmers. Now, I believe you will be with Elizabeth this entire weekend, right?"

Rowe nodded.

"Then I suggest that you get cracking. You have a good deal of experience with women. Elizabeth can't be all that different. Hell, talk her into being more involved with business. And, Chalmers, do find out about the next takeover, won't you?"

Rowe stared at each of them in turn. Five million dollars, and everything would be safe. He would be saved, and his father wouldn't be disgraced. "I hear that steel shipments have been stolen, lost, and otherwise detained."

"Small beans," said Michael. "All that does is give the managers ulcers."

"And cut into direct profits," said Rowe.

"You are dithering, Mr. Chalmers," said Laurette suddenly. "What is the matter? The truth, if you please."

"Elizabeth loves me. I can't continue stringing her along without marriage. She wants marriage and a family, I know it. She wants a commitment from me."

"So did my son, Mr. Chalmers, so did my son, and look where he ended up."

"Lie," said Brad. "You're a marvel at that, Chalmers."

Rowe turned on his heel and strode toward the door. He heard Michael call after him, "Just remember the five million. I'll call you on Tuesday evening. Be home, Rowe, and have some information for me. Worthwhile information, or I promise you, you will regret it."

It had begun to rain, a steady, cold downpour. Elizabeth didn't move, not until she heard a car, Rowe's car, screech down the driveway.

8

"Good evening, Mr. Chalmers."

"Hello, Kogi. How are you?"

"Just fine, thank you, sir," Kogi said as he took Rowe's black umbrella. "Mrs. Carleton be out in a moment. A drink, Mr. Rowe?"

"One of your martinis, Kogi." Left alone for a moment, Rowe walked to the long set of floor-to-ceiling windows and peered out into the heavy rain. He didn't want to go out again, particularly in this god-awful weather, but Elizabeth loved the symphony.

"Good evening, Rowe."

He spun around, a wide smile on his lips. "Elizabeth," he said, and strode toward her.

God, she looked beautiful, in a long white satin gown with narrow straps over her shoulders. She was wearing an emerald pendant around her neck that reached the cleavage between her breasts. He felt his breathing quicken, and reached for her.

Elizabeth stepped back, to stand on the other side of her piano. "How was Boston?"

"Muggy and hot, as usual, about the same as here, except you've got the rain."

"When did you get in?"

"An hour ago. I went to my place first to change."

"Yes," she said. "You look very nice in a dinner jacket, Rowe. Very nice indeed."

"You know, sweetheart, we don't have to go out

this evening. I would just as soon not share you, not as gorgeous as you look."

She smiled at him. "Thank you. No, I really don't want to go out tonight either."

"It has been a long week," he said, giving her his special smile. "Too long away from you."

"Kogi has prepared us one of his special dinners. I trust you're hungry?"

"You can count on that, lady. Now, about food . . ." He broke off and gave her his best comical leer.

"Ah, here's your martini and my white wine. Thank you, Kogi. Mr. Rowe and I will dine in, say, thirty minutes?"

"Yes, certainly, Mrs. Carleton," Kogi said, and took himself back to his kitchen.

"To us, Elizabeth," Rowe said, and clicked his glass toward hers.

"Yes, to you and to me."

Elizabeth sipped at her wine, watching him. She gave him a sweet, wistful smile and said, "When will I meet your family, Rowe?"

"Not as soon as I'd like," he said. "My parents can't abide the humid weather and are leaving tomorrow for Bermuda."

"I see. How long will they be gone?"

He shrugged. "A couple of months, I suppose. They have a house in Hamilton, you know."

"No, I didn't know, but it makes no difference, does it?"

"No," he said slowly, "I suppose not. What have you been doing, Elizabeth?"

"This week? Ah, I decided to give my music a bit of a rest. I spent most of today with Adrian and my other nobles." She sighed. "I do miss Avery. Poor man."

"Are you certain you wish to embroil yourself in all that nonsense again?"

"Rod and Adrian have convinced me to. And, of course, we need to replace Avery. We reviewed applications this afternoon."

"I see. Wanna give me the job?" He skirted the

piano as he spoke, and drew her into his arms. "Then I could be with you every day and you could chase me around my desk."

He kissed her. Then he grew still. He leaned back and looked down into her face. "What's wrong, Elizabeth?"

She rested her fingertips against his jaw. "Nothing, it's just that . . ."

"Just what?"

"Well, I started my period today, Rowe."

He gave her a moan that turned into a grin. "I keep telling you that that doesn't have to be a problem, my little Puritan."

He kissed her again. "You're not feeling too hot?"

"No, not really. Forgive me, Rowe."

He groaned again and stepped away. "I guess all my appetites will have to be saved for Kogi's dinner."

"That's the idea," Elizabeth said.

Kogi served them a Caesar salad followed by a pork roast with potatoes au gratin and green peas.

"I think I'll try to steal Kogi from you, Elizabeth. Delicious, as usual."

"Yes, and he's made strawberry tarts for dessert."

"I don't know how you stay so thin."

"He only serves this kind of food when I have company. I usually rate only a broiled chicken breast and a little rice. And I walk a lot, you know."

"When you're not practicing."

"Or now, when I'll be involved in top-level business talks."

He forked down a bite of potato. "Who are you considering to take Avery's spot?"

"There is one man we're particularly interested in. His name is James Houston, and oddly enough, he does now live in Houston, Texas. He's brilliant in marketing, and with enough inducement, I just bet we can get him here to New York."

"Never heard of him," Rowe said. "Who is he with now?"

"He's ready to leave the top marketing position

with Brammerson Oil. Even though oil prices aren't as depressed as they were, he's still reviewing his options, as the business folk say."

"Sounds pretty smart to me," said Rowe. He sat back in his chair and patted his flat stomach. "Call me stuffed. I just wish I could work off the calories in bed, Elizabeth."

He took her hand in his and gently squeezed her fingers. "Are these talented hands insured?"

"Yes, by Lloyds, as a matter of fact. Timothy insisted, three years ago. It seems rather silly to me, but he acted like he was giving me a special present."

Kogi served them espresso, and with a nod from Elizabeth, cleared the table and left them alone. Elizabeth took her coffee with her to the living room and sat down in a chair, not on the sofa.

"Will you feel well enough to give me my own private concert tonight?"

She nodded.

Rowe set down his coffee cup and put his feet up on the glass coffee table. "You're awfully quiet tonight. You haven't run into any obnoxious press, have you?"

"As a matter of fact, I did. Not the press, though. The district attorney, Anthony Moretti. In front of Bloomingdale's."

Rowe sat forward, his entire body tensing with anger. "What did the bastard say to you?"

"Nothing more than he's said at great length in the past. That I was a murderess and rich and thus could buy off anyone I pleased. That I was a slut and my lovers should watch their backs in case I tired of them and wanted them out of the way."

"You could sue him, you know."

"The media would go bananas with glee if I did." Her eyes glittered. "I'd probably beat out any political scandals in the newspaper. Perhaps you, as my lover, should take heed, Rowe."

"Stop it, Elizabeth!"

"You're right, I'll cease this moment." She jumped to her feet and walked swiftly to the piano. Unexpectedly, she played jazz, and very well. He'd never heard her improvise before.

Later, when he held her in his arms in bed, she in a long flannel nightgown, she told him about their proposed target high-tech electronics firm.

"I can't do it."

"What did you say, Elizabeth?"

Elizabeth started, realizing she'd spoken aloud. "Oh, nothing, Adrian. Just thinking with my mouth open. Tell me about the Cordie stock."

"Weirdest thing about that," he mused, leaning back in his chair. "The stock's gone haywire with the rumors of a takeover."

"Any speculation on who's doing the taking over?"

"Sure. It's the Laufferson Group."

She said very softly, "What is the relationship between the Laufferson top people and Michael Carleton?"

His chair came forward with a sharp thud. "Why, Elizabeth? What aren't you telling me? How did you know about this?"

"Just answer my question, Adrian."

"None that I know of," he said. "Now, why don't you tell me—"

She raised her hand and her voice was cold. "No, Adrian. There's a tie-in, I'm sure of it. Please put someone or several someones on it and get back to me this afternoon."

He nodded; he had no choice in the matter. She was acting differently, very differently. She tended to be reserved, aloof, but now there was something else about her, something more . . . determined. She was keeping something from him, most definitely. But what could she possibly know about Cordie? He knew that she wouldn't speak frankly with him, at least at the present time. She'd made that clear enough. He said, "I'll call you as soon as I know something."

"This afternoon, Adman," she said.

She gave him a semblance of a smile and headed toward the door of his office. She turned and said,

"Incidentally, you know that man who left Brammerson Oil? Mr. Houston?"

"Sure, what about him?"

"Find out who just hired him."

He stared at her, but she was gone. James Houston. He'd turned out to be a real flake, upon very close scrutiny by one of their top investigators, a man who had little imagination beyond selling barrels of oil. And he used his staff mercilessly, stealing their ideas, giving them no credit.

At three o'clock that afternoon Adrian and Rod Samuels were admitted to the Carleton home by Liam Gallagher.

Elizabeth was dressed in a leotard, doing exercises to a Jane Fonda tape. She smiled as they entered, and wiped the sweat off her forehead. "In force, I see," she said as she turned off the VCR. She shook their hands. "Hello, Rod. I gather you have the information I requested, Adrian. You could have phoned, you know."

"No, I couldn't," Adrian said slowly.

"Elizabeth, what the hell is going on here?"

"Do sit down, Rod, Adrian." She sat on the floor, crossing her legs in lotus fashion. "Talk, please."

Adrian shot a look toward Rod, drew a deep breath, and said, "You wanted to know if there was any connection between the Laufferson Group and Michael Carleton. There is. The chairman of the board of Laufferson is a personal friend of Michael's. As a matter of fact, Michael bailed him out of a financial bind some five years ago. He owes Michael, big."

"And Laufferson is going to buy Cordie," Elizabeth said.

"So it would appear," said Rod. "How did you know, Elizabeth?"

"Next answer, please, Adrian," she said, and Rod frowned. She looked like a shapely kid sitting there on the floor in her pink leotard, her blond hair pulled back in a ratty ponytail. But her voice was sharp, hard, as were her eyes.

"Very well. James Houston was hired just yesterday by a textile company based in Atlanta. They offered him the sky."

"Can I assume that this textile company is some sort of division of MAI?"

"Yes, it is."

Elizabeth smiled. It wasn't a pleasant smile.

Rod sat forward on the sofa. "Please, Elizabeth, you know something."

Elizabeth uncurled her legs and rose, slinging the towel about her neck. "Well, there it is. Now, gentlemen, I would like to make a recommendation. We've been having all sorts of shipping problems with Millsom Steel. The manager there is pulling out his hair and we're losing money and credibility with clients. Hire some private detectives, Adrian. I believe they'll quickly discover that these problems have nothing to do with incompetence or Murphy's Law or gremlins. The Carletons are paying people to wreak havoc. Find out who those men are, Adrian, and take care of them."

"It sounds to me as if you have a tap on Michael Carleton's phone." Adrian meant it as a joke, albeit a weak one, but Elizabeth appeared to give it serious thought.

"You could say that I do. Incidentally, let's do put a tap on Brad's office phone. Oh, and, Adrian, do have a weekly check to see that our phones aren't bugged." She smiled a real smile this time, adding, "I enjoy watching MacGyver on TV. I learned on that show all about bugging and debugging. It is done, isn't it?"

"We do a check monthly, Elizabeth," Adrian said.

"Now do it weekly. And I hope you can trust the guys doing the checking?"

"I . . . I suppose so."

"Please be certain, Adrian." She gave them both a bright smile. "I guess that will be all. I'll be in the office tomorrow morning bright and early."

"Why?" Rod asked, standing.

"It's time I took my responsibilities more seriously, don't you think? I have so much to learn."

* * *

No more rumors. Not a one. Jonathan Harley smiled as he jogged past Betsy Ross's house. He was safe. Harley Electronics was safe.

The divorce would soon be final, and ah, there was the rub. He had to get his hands on enough money to buy out Rose's stock. He quickened his pace. Who to get the money from?

Would Rose sell the stock, or hang on to it and hassle him endlessly? She was already seeing another man, a wealthy physician, a man old enough to be her father. Perhaps she did see him as a father. Andrew Pillson was a powerful figure in her life. Jonathan shrugged as he jogged. It was no longer his concern. Next week he would be free. Finally.

He'd found himself several times during the past months driving home from the office, only to realize that it was no longer his home, but Rose's. He hadn't moved out yet. Rose was in Italy with her wealthy physician. He wondered if he shouldn't get on the ball and find himself a condo. He didn't know when she would be home, but if she arrived and he was there, it would give her the greatest pleasure to boot him out. He passed another jogger, a young woman, who gave him a marvelous smile, nodding as she went by him.

He was indeed free. Never before in his thirty-five years had he even considered recreational sex. Now he had several very lovely young women to thank for his education. Tonight he would see Cynthia MacBain, no socialite, but a jazzercise teacher at a local health club. It was a good thing, he thought, that he'd kept himself in shape. If he were older and flabby, he'd probably have intense performance anxiety. That or an early heart attack. She had probably consulted on different positions for the karma sutra.

Jonathan slowed to a walk, rather like a racehorse, he thought to himself, cooling down. He felt full of energy, full of renewed life. He couldn't wait to get to the office and hassle Midge.

"Well, boss," Midge said brightly as he strolled

through the glass doors, "you've got lots of calls already."

"Business or social?"

She grinned at him. "You devil, you. A bit of both. Put them in order, and I'll pour you some coffee."

Life, he thought, as he picked up his phone to speak to his production manager, was improving at a fine rate.

And he knew where he'd get the money he needed. No problem at all.

"I don't understand it," Michael Carleton said, a deep frown furrowing his forehead. "I just don't understand it."

Laurette carefully laid down her soup spoon and nodded to Lydia, the maid, to leave the dining room.

"What is the problem?" she asked.

"The men I hired to . . . well, see to the problems at Millsom Steel. They're gone, disappeared. Not a word, nothing."

"When did you discover this?"

"Yesterday afternoon. I had a meeting scheduled with my contact."

"He didn't see you, then?"

"No, not a word, as I said."

"I shouldn't worry about it just yet, my dear," she said, and picked up her soup spoon again. It was fresh turtle soup, her favorite, and she didn't want it to get cold.

Michael hated turtle soup. He watched his mother eat, and fiddled with a bread stick. "It's not just that," he said at last.

"Oh?" Laurette's soup spoon paused midway between her bowl and her mouth.

"That man James Houston. According to my vice-president of marketing, the man's not nearly as sharp as he originally appeared to be. I can't believe that the men at ACI wouldn't know that. Yet, they were going to hire him."

"It's early days yet, I think. He must have something. The men running ACI aren't fools, you know."

"Yes, I do know," said Michael. He felt the now familiar burning pain in his belly. Damned ulcer! He forced a smile. "At least the Cordie buy-out is proceeding nicely. That has to strike a big blow."

"Elizabeth's strategic planning group must be furious," said Laurette placidly. She lifted the small bell beside her left hand and rang it. Lydia appeared swiftly and silently to serve the next course.

Michael liked lamb chops, particularly the way his mother's chef prepared them, with rosemary and just a nip of garlic.

Laurette watched him eat, saying nothing for several minutes. Then, "I spoke at length with Catherine. I have no control over her any longer, Michael. Now that she's gotten hold of her father's money, she's gone wild."

"I know. It's that Chad Walters who's responsible. I hate to tell you this, Mother, but he's a dealer, from what I hear, and Catherine is probably hooked on cocaine."

Laurette said very slowly and very precisely, "I suggest you get rid of Mr. Walters. I will take care of Catherine."

Michael didn't understand the shiver that ran through his body at her words. She was nearly eight-four years old. And yet . . . and yet . . .

"Yes, Mother," he said. "I think the best approach would be—"

"I don't wish to hear the details, Michael. Just get rid of him. There will be no more scandals in this family."

"Yes, Mother."

"Bradley is thinking of marriage."

That was a surprise. "Who?" Michael asked blankly.

"A girl I approve of," said Laurette. "Her name is Jennifer Henkle, and her father is Senator Charles Henkle of Alabama."

"But, for God's sake, why?"

Laurette frowned at him.

Michael stalled. How to tell his mother that the rumor was that her eldest grandson preferred men to women? Sometimes he wished he were a shepherd living in the Pyrenees with the Basques. Surely he wouldn't have an ulcer there.

"In any case," Laurette continued after a moment, "this weekend, Jennifer will be here to meet all the family. I think you will also approve of her. She's very quiet, pretty, and from good, solid stock."

"She's not a musician, huh?"

"You are not at all amusing, Michael."

"No," he said on a sigh, "I suppose not."

"Timothy was always very strong, you know."

Yes, Michael knew. He'd hated his brother for it, many times. He remembered the times Timothy had called him a soddy little wimp. Well, Timothy was gone now.

Laurette continued, her voice a bit dreamy, "I used to be furious with him when he would disagree with me on something. He'd just give me that special smile of his and tell me to take up knitting. Yes, he was a strong man, a strong son."

"Now you have me, Mother," Michael said.

Laurette gently patted his cheek. "Yes, I do, don't I? We are doing well, Michael. Very well."

When he kissed her parchment cheek upon leaving that evening, he felt the bond between them, not as strong as the one she'd had with Timothy, but it didn't matter. He felt her fragility, and was frightened, until she said quite clearly, "Do see to Chad Walters, my dear."

9

Christian Hunter looked at Liam Gallagher, saw the recognition in the doorman's eyes, and nodded. "She's expecting me. At seven."

"Yes, sir, Dr. Hunter," Liam said, "I know, sir." He quickly buzzed upstairs.

"Dr. Hunter is here, Kogi. Yes, that's right."

Christian fingered the gold leaf in the ancient elevator, grabbing the railing when the cage lurched between floors. Affectation is still affectation, he thought, no matter its guise. He grinned at that and tried to admire the damned elevator.

He was greeted by a Japanese houseman who couldn't have weighed more than one hundred pounds even in lead-soled shoes. His age was impossible to tell. Thirty? Fifty? Like the doorman, there was recognition in Kogi's eyes, and something else it took him a moment to identify. It was wariness, Christian realized, concern that he, Christian, would hurt Mrs. Carleton. He found himself shaking his head in response to that look.

Kogi took Christian's coat and his leather gloves, but said only, "Dr. Hunter. Good evening, sir."

Christian nodded, then looked up and went still. He couldn't believe that he was finally seeing her, was finally in the same room with her. Alone, or very nearly.

"Good evening, Mrs. Carleton," he said. He walked toward her, and took her hand. He didn't shake her hand, as she expected, he kissed her wrist. He breathed in the scent of her before releasing her hand. Elizabeth looked at his bent head, felt his cool fingers still holding her hand. She gently pulled away.

"How was Vienna?"

Vienna? "Oh, it was most charming, as usual," he said.

"Were you there for pleasure or for a medical convention?"

"Both, actually."

"You would like something to drink, Dr. Hunter?"

"Please, call me Christian, and yes, I'd like a glass of white wine. I'm quite easy to please, just so long as it is white and very dry."

She smiled a bit at that. "Me too. White and dry, that is."

Elizabeth nodded to Kogi and gestured to the sofa.

"You have a lovely home, Mrs. Carleton."

"Thank you," she said quietly. "It was my husband's, you know."

The phone rang loudly.

Elizabeth stared toward the phone, praying that it wasn't Rowe. She'd put him off this evening, telling him that she had a business appointment. She heard Kogi pick it up, murmur something, and that was that.

"You were expecting a call, perhaps?"

"Oh, no, not at all. Please, do sit down, Dr. Hun . . . Christian. And call me Elizabeth." She looked at him squarely and added, "Since you saved my life, I would think that last names are a bit ridiculous."

"I would agree," he said as he seated himself.

"When I first saw you in the courtroom, I thought you were English."

"An affectation," he said, smiling at her, "that I didn't outgrow. My mother was the youngest daughter of an English baron, a country gentleman. I was raised to believe that English tweed announced a man of refined and expensive taste and that a properly trimmed mustache announced an intellect of great depth. Smoking my pipe, of course, announces that I, like many

Americans, am hooked on tobacco. You don't mind, do you?"

"Not at all. My father smoked a pipe. I love the smell."

She watched him go through the pipe ritual. He did it gracefully, easily, from long habit. The sweet smell floated through the air.

"Ah, our wine. Thank you, Kogi."

"To your new life, Elizabeth."

"Yes, thanks to you."

She sipped her wine, wondering what to say to him. What to do? What to expect?

"It's been a very long time," she said at last.

"Yes, quite a long time," he agreed. "I see the press has at last forgotten about you."

"For the most part. A relief, I assure you."

"I did see you once, a couple of months ago, at Lincoln Center, with Rowen Chalmers. An impressive man." He watched her closely. Her face paled, then grew cold and set.

"Perhaps," she said, "one could say that about him."

"I know his family, of course. His father is something of a fool, I believe, but his mother excels in good works and the like."

She said nothing.

Kogi announced dinner and she had the oddest sense of déjà vu, when he seated her at the table, of that evening with Rowe. Tonight Kogi had made his shrimp Provençale, so delicate and light it melted in your mouth.

"You're a psychologist."

"Yes. It is something of a hobby with me. The district attorney was correct in that."

"Have you many patients?"

"Perhaps a dozen, that's all. Since I have no need to worry about the more mundane aspects of survival, I can select the patients who interest me most."

"I see."

"For example, I have a middle-aged businessman, quite a successful businessman actually, who one day, for no apparent reason, took off all his clothes and marched into a meeting with his boss, who happened to be a woman. He tried to rape her."

The bite of wild rice remained suspended on her fork. "Wh-what happened?"

He grinned, showing a deep dimple in his left cheek. "Actually, the woman was bigger than he was. She cuffed him, kicked him to the floor, and he had a heart attack. He's been in therapy with me for about three months now. He has no memory of the incident."

The rice fell off her fork. "You made that up!"

He laughed and shook his head. "No, I swear it's true. I did, however, have a special set of suspenders made for him. They clip together in the back and cannot be unclipped in the front. Thus if he ever feels the urge again to disrobe, by the time he succeeds in getting his pants freed of the suspenders, the urge should be long gone."

"And his lady boss?"

"She's also in therapy, I understand, for guilt. She did nearly kill the poor man. She's not my patient, however. I thought that would be something like a conflict of interest."

"Would you like some more of Kogi's bread?"

"Why not?"

He had beautiful, graceful hands, she thought, watching him spread butter on the slice of warm bread. If he weren't so graceful, his movements would seem studied. He had an artist's hands, long, narrow fingers.

"Do you play an instrument?" she asked.

"I did try when I was younger. The violin and the piano. Unfortunately, I have about as much talent as that salt shaker there. I'm one of your great unwashed admirers, actually."

"So you said in court."

"That much, at least, was true."

He sounded like he was agreeing that the weather was awful, nothing more, nothing less.

"Tell me about more of your patients."

He did. Even as she listened wide-eyed, she suspected that he was embroidering quite freely on the truth.

". . . you see, the daughter continued to claim, quite loudly in fact, that she'd been sexually abused by her stepfather. Most interesting, for the stepfather was impotent and had been for a number of years. It turned out that the daughter was trying to protect her mother from spiteful gossip. It was being said at their country club that the husband/stepfather couldn't get it up, and the mother/wife was most embarrassed by the gossip. By accusing the stepfather of sexual abuse, the daughter was trying to prove that the stepfather/husband could indeed perform in bed."

"Whatever did you do this time?"

"We managed to work it all out eventually. I found a surgeon who could correct the impotence problem, and now that little girl is likely being chased about in truth by her stepfather."

Christian listened to her laughter, felt the sweetness of it flow through him, warming him. Slowly he set down his coffee cup. "I suppose, Elizabeth, that you have heard enough of my professional tales."

"I don't know," she said, looking at him straightly. "Avoidance is sometimes a necessity for one's soul, and sanity, I suppose."

"True, but you do wish to know, don't you?"

"Yes, I do."

"It's very simple, really. I know you didn't kill your husband."

It was said with such candor, such simplicity, that for a moment she could only stare at him.

"How could you be so certain?"

He lit his pipe, taking his time. "I have heard every concert you've ever given. You create, you interpret, you birth beauty and emotion. You have lived your life from within, if you will. I don't believe that individual people ever touched you, touched that deep inside part of you enough to engender anything like a hatred that could lead to murder. You couldn't kill anything, it would be meaningless to you, something that couldn't even exist in your worst nightmares. In fact, I'll bet you can't bring yourself to kill a spider."

He paused a moment, sucked in on his pipe, but she remained silent.

"You see," he continued gently, "you don't even understand the concept of taking another life. It is as alien to you as it would be to me to strip off my clothes and try to rape a woman associate."

Elizabeth studied her coffee cup. "You make me sound like some sort of unfeeling being who has sacrificed humanity for art, that it's something in my genes that has made me odd, different."

"Different, certainly. The attainment of perfection in any endeavor requires immense inner focus and drive. Some aspects of a normal person's development couldn't appear in you. There was no room for them. I'd even be willing to wager that as a teenager you went through none of the awful throes young girls experience with the opposite sex."

She smiled at that. "Actually, the tendency was there. However, my father was much stronger than hormones. I suppose that he convinced me that a healthy dose of contempt was the only appropriate response to boys."

"Is that why you married Timothy Carleton? To replace a strong father?" He watched her withdraw, and said quickly, "Forgive me. I don't mean to pry. I suppose it's those shrink genes in me that demand to know things about people, to understand things. Nosy genes, I guess you'd call them if you were being kind. Occasionally obnoxious genes."

"That's all right. Perhaps you have a point. I really have never dissected my motives about Timothy. If I had, perhaps I would never have married him in the first place. I wasn't all that young when I married him, so I can't use the excuse that I was too immature, too young to realize what I was doing." *Lying, Elizabeth, and to a shrink!* She lowered her eyes, hoping he couldn't see the lie in them. Never would she tell anyone why she'd married Timothy.

"Ah, but you were. Years don't mean a thing, you know."

"Dr. Hun . . . Christian, am I going to have to pay you a fee for this analysis?"

"Forgive me again, Elizabeth." He was quiet, refilling his pipe, going through what her father had always called the calming ritual.

"Do you use that as a way to gather your thoughts?"

"What? Oh, the pipe. Probably, yes, quite probably."

"You still don't know that I didn't kill my husband. You spoke words only, marvelously logical words, but still only words. No one can guess what drives another person to do things, even violent things. If you will remember from the trial, I did have the opportunity, my fingerprints were on the weapon, and I supposedly had an excellent motive."

"The motive being money?"

"That and of course freedom from a distasteful marriage to an old man."

"You could never be so stupid."

"Stupid? As in leaving my fingerprints on that ridiculous silver ice pick? For not having something of an alibi during the time he was being killed?"

"What were you doing that evening? Where were you?"

"Actually, I was in Central Park, inviting the muggers to have a go at me, which none of them did, fortunately or unfortunately, depending on how you look at it."

"I had understood that you were to be at a special fund-raiser that evening."

Elizabeth cocked her head at that. "Yes, how did you know?"

"It all came out, as I recall."

"There was so much—I suppose I've forgotten just how much. Well, I didn't go, as it turned out. It was a pity. Think of how many people could have given me an alibi. Of course, then the D.A. would have claimed that I'd hired someone to kill Timothy."

"You're still very bitter."

"Wouldn't you be?"

"Yes, but unlike you, my first priority would be to get even. For instance, I'd back a troll if he were running against Moretti. I think I'd also try to stuff a sock in Catherine Carleton's big mouth. That young woman is a menace, though more to herself than to anyone else." He paused a moment. "I read about your confrontation with her at that restaurant."

"It wasn't particularly pleasant. Catherine is a sad case."

"She doesn't seem to pick her men carefully, I hear."

"How in heaven's name do you know so much, Christian?"

He said slowly, "You didn't read about Chad Walters?"

"Who's that?"

"A real stud to the ladies, in vulgar terms, especially rich ladies, and a dealer. He's dead, supposedly killed by one of his connections. A thoroughly nasty business."

"Was he the man with Catherine that evening at the restaurant?"

"Yes, he was."

"And he's dead."

"Yes. No great loss to society."

Elizabeth felt a chill run from her neck to her toes. "It seems most propitious—his death, I mean."

"His line of work was particularly risky."

"And Catherine had an alibi?"

"Certainly. She was, as I heard, vacationing briefly in Nassau when it happened."

Both of them were silent a moment, each with very different thoughts. Christian said finally, "Would you play for me, Elizabeth?"

"I will, certainly, if you tell me why you did it."

"I did tell you."

"No, you gave me a string of very unlikely character tags. Why, Christian? I'm entitled to know."

"I've lost all my money and intend to blackmail you for the next fifty years."

She tried to smile, but couldn't quite manage it. "Well, that at least I could understand." She waited, but he said no more.

She rose and walked to her piano, but didn't sit down on the bench. She ran her fingers over the shiny ebony very slowly, with great concentration.

"Elizabeth," he said from behind her. "Haven't you ever trusted someone—completely, irrevocably? Believed in someone, despite everything to the contrary?"

"Yes, I did, but the *contrary* part was rather overwhelming. I was a fool, a mushbrain—well, you certainly aren't interested in that." Oh, yes, she'd believed in Rowe, trusted him implicitly. She shuddered, pain rippling through her, making her stomach knot. *I'd get even.*

Well, that's what she was doing. She forced her shoulders back and sat down. She played the Pathétique Sonata, filling the room with Beethoven's fury and pain and grandeur.

She was midway through the second movement when her fingers would no longer obey her. It wasn't that the pages were sad or depressing or hit her between the eyes, it was just . . . She replayed the same measure, then very softly lowered her head and began to sob.

Christian stayed where he was. The second movement always touched him, but he didn't believe that the heavy, tragic sounds that melt a stone had moved her to tears. He said nothing, merely waited.

"Would you like a Kleenex?"

She gave a small laugh. "No, thank you. I don't wear mascara so I don't have to worry about black streaks on my cheeks."

"Go to the third movement."

"Yes, I will. Had I done that in front of an audience, they would have thrown tomatoes, then carted me off."

He watched her exert control over herself, and admired her immensely in that moment. She played the third movement with verve and panache. But without emotion. When she finished, she was breathing hard. She said, smiling toward him, "When I was ten years old, and would practice that sonata, my father would yell at me, telling me that he would rename it the Pathetic Sonata. He'd spent the past six months trying to make me understand the concept of pathos. I never really got it, but 'pathetic' I understood very well. It took me years to play the sonata through without blundering."

"Now, I think no one would question your understanding. Thank you, Elizabeth. That was magnificent. You've given me great pleasure. Now, it's late. May I see you Monday evening? Andre Galreau is playing Mozart at Lincoln Center. I should very much like to share it with you."

"Yes," she said slowly, rising. "I should like that. Galreau is a fine artist."

Adrian switched on the tape player, and Elizabeth and Rod listened to Brad speaking to his uncle, Michael Carleton.

"It makes no sense!" Brad said.

"I know. It appears that James Houston is a loss. A mistake. It's a pity that we simply didn't allow dear Elizabeth to hire him."

"Well, I shouldn't be using the office phone, it's not smart. I just wanted to fill you in."

"We'll speak more fully on Thursday night. Your grandmother's house. Same time, Brad."

"All right."

"One other thing, Brad. This girl you're supposed to marry."

Brad's voice, mocking, a bit bitter: "She's a senator's daughter and, according to Grandmother, has quite the appearance of a good breeder. Unfortunately I met her at a political dinner in Washington and began squiring her about."

"I hope you know what you're doing."

"Oh, I know, Uncle, I know."

Silence. The sound of the line being disconnected.

There was a long silence. Rod said, a small, very cruel smile playing about his mouth, "I wonder what that's all about. Uncle Michael worried about Bradley marrying a senator's daughter? Seems like what Laurette would want."

"I'll find out," Elizabeth said.

"How?" asked Adrian, sitting forward, folding his beefy hands.

"Trust me," she said. "I have ways."

"There's still a leak, obviously, but it has to be lower down."

"Yes," said Adrian. "That business about James Houston. In this instance, the leak backfired."

"I trust Brad isn't taping our conversations?"

"No, not anymore, Elizabeth. Talk about dog eat dog, or in this case, bug eat bug."

She hated it, the acting, the lying, the sheer misery of pretending. Faking an orgasm was perhaps the most difficult. She did, then waited for Rowe to climax. She forced herself to hold him close, forced herself to kiss his shoulder.

Christian was wrong, she thought. I could kill another human being. I could, but then I'd have to do myself in.

"Elizabeth, what's wrong?"

Smile, pretend. "Nothing, Rowe. I just have a lot on my mind, that's all." She felt him pull away from her, and her entire body relaxed, finally freed of its betrayer.

He said nothing.

"What do you think about Brad Carleton and his romance with this senator's daughter?" she finally asked.

"I could care less."

"No, seriously, Rowe, I heard this rumor that Brad really didn't want to get together with the lady, indeed that Michael Carleton is quite concerned about it."

"I wouldn't know," Rowe said. He lay on his back, lightly scratching his belly.

"Come now, you were telling me how old money

sticks together, how one's dirty laundry is always washed in private."

"You want a rumor? Another one that isn't very nice? Well, old Brad is reputed to be queer. I haven't the faintest idea if that's true or not, but there it is."

It fit, Elizabeth thought. Oh, yes, it fit. But what to do with a tidbit like that?

"How's the banking business, Rowe?"

He turned on his side to face her. "There, alive, well, and all that. I'm thinking of hanging a lot of it up, as a matter of fact."

You mean you'd take the Carleton millions you've earned and skip the country?

"Then again, I'm just spouting off." He sighed. "Forgive me. I'm just tired, that's all. How's your business coming along?"

"Funny you should ask. Actually, there's a pretty important bit of news that came to my ears just today. I need to give Adrian my decision on it very soon. It's about an Army defense contract on a new jet fighter, the G108. I think it's a good idea to go for it, and most of my associates agree. And it seems that we've got the inside track, what with important contacts and all that. Without the new contract, I'm afraid we'd have to make some pretty substantial cutbacks in the military division of Cragon-Matthews. What do you think?"

"That's a tough one. Why don't I ask around and get back to you?"

"Friends in equally high places, huh?"

"Not really. Just some men who are bright as hell and love to give their opinions, usually unsolicited."

"All right. I'd appreciate it, Rowe. Can you let me know their collective opinion by . . . Friday afternoon?"

10

The article was there two days later, on the front page of *The Wall Street Journal*, and rumors were flying. The Army was steadfastly denying everything, but still people talked and speculated. After all, there were *reliable sources* involved.

Adrian looked grim. "You knew about this, Elizabeth, don't try to deny it. God, it sounds like a new car about to roll out of Japan. The G108? Where the devil did that come from?"

"I think that's a nice name for a new jet fighter," she said. "Don't forget that you did mention something about a new Army contract to me and the situation with our military division at Cragon-Matthews."

Adrian sipped on his very hot, very strong black coffee. "Yes, but from the inside information we'd gotten, the best thing to do was pass. You knew that, and you also knew that it was a new land-based missile. Now this." He pointed a finger to the article.

Elizabeth said, "Most odd, isn't it? Why are you so exercised about it, Adrian?"

He had no chance to reply, for Coy Siverston was announced and came in. He was smiling, something of a malicious smile, and Elizabeth could see his big shiny gold tooth. He was carrying *The Wall Street Journal*.

He said to Adrian, "I got a kick out of this. Oh, hello, Elizabeth," he added as something of an afterthought. "This is Michael Carleton's doing. I scent his style, as will many other people. He does look like a complete ass, doesn't he? His credibility will go down the tubes, at least for a while, until it blows over." He paused a moment, frowning over his glasses. "I also have this inescapable feeling that he was set up."

"Do sit down, Coy," Elizabeth said.

"Yeah," said Adrian, "that's what I think. I also think Elizabeth set him up, but she won't tell me how she did it."

"Trade secret, gentlemen."

Coy stared at her. He thought her a charming young woman, a young woman very much over her head. No, Adrian had to be wrong. Elizabeth Carleton was a figurehead, nothing more. He slowly removed his glasses and slipped them into his vest pocket, his mind working with its usual speed and methodology. He'd always thought of himself as the Sherlock Holmes of big business. He said at last, "There are no trade secrets, Elizabeth. Now, do tell us what you know about all this, if anything."

Under Adrian's fascinated gaze, her eyes grew very cold, hard, her lips tightened. My God, he thought, what is going on here? He nearly jumped when she said, "I have no intention of telling you anything, Coy. Now, if you will excuse me, gentlemen . . ."

She left the office, leaving Adrian and Coy to stare at each other. Adrian said slowly, thoughtfully, "She's changed. It's scary as hell."

"Nonsense," said Coy, who, if he didn't understand something, dismissed it without further thought as being inconsequential. "She's being coy, eh? She doesn't know a thing. How could she? She's a musician, for heaven's sake."

"As I recall, Coy, you were wrong about something last June 14. Maybe this is your error for this year. She's changing, Coy, changing and learning at an alarming rate. But what's worse is that she's become secretive. Oh, why do I bother with explaining things to you?"

"Because, dear boy, I am your senior by a number

of years that I don't choose to disclose, and you owe me proper deference and respect."

"Bull," said Adrian. "Are you going hunting this weekend with Bruno?"

"No, poor old fellow's at the vet's. He's got a urinary problem, damn and blast."

"Before you take off, Coy, there's something else. Something else Elizabeth told me. Make of it what you will. Brad Carleton is evidently thinking of marrying a senator's daughter. The rumor is that Brad is also gay."

"Probably bisexual. Pretty common nowadays," said Coy unemotionally. "It doesn't appeal to me, but . . ." He shrugged.

"Yeah, if you could screw your dog, Bruno, you'd probably consider that equally as common!"

"Getting pretty big for your boots, aren't you, Adman?"

"Still a size twelve."

Coy grinned. "I'm shoving off now, my boy. While you sit on your behind trying to come up with new fairy tales, I work." Coy paused at the doorway and said with absolute conviction, "You're wrong about Elizabeth. There's no way she could have had anything to do with this military nonsense."

"Blind idiot," Adrian said under his breath as Coy left the office.

Elizabeth sat on the bench in Central Park, unaware of the brilliant display of multicolored leaves around her. It was early September, but the East Coast was having a freak cold spell. She was wearing gloves and in her right hand she was clutching a rumpled newspaper page. She watched several children playing tag, screaming out, laughing, arguing. Just like adults, she thought, except that they don't play for keeps.

Slowly she smoothed out the page again and stared down at it. It was a grainy photo with a caption beneath from a small Boston rag called the *Tattler*. It had been sent to her anonymously, just as that first note she'd gotten. She still had no idea who it was, her unknown champion—at least she assumed it was someone on the bandwagon for her. That someone must know that she was still seeing Rowe after that night at Laurette Carleton's mansion. And that someone wanted her to stop. That realization was a bit chilling, and she looked around her briefly, perhaps expecting to see that someone lurking somewhere, watching her.

She looked down again. Despite the flaws in the photo, Rowen Chalmers looked handsome, debonair, beautifully dressed in a black dinner jacket, as did the young woman pressed close to him. "ROWEN CHALMERS ESCORTS AMANDA MONTGOMERY TO DEMOCRATIC FUND-RAISER." His hand was cupping her elbow and she was looking up at him. The look on Rowe's face was anger, toward the photographer, she supposed, and protectiveness for his companion. She simply looked at the photo, her expression unchanging. Finally she folded it into a small square and dropped it into her shoulder bag. Her thought at that moment was: Rowen must be very stupid or very sure of himself to squire another woman about, even in Boston.

Rowe was in New York. She would see him this evening. Oh, yes, she would see him all right.

She'd used him long enough.

She'd gotten even.

Now it was time to save herself.

Elizabeth dismissed Kogi after dinner that evening. Rowe smiled at that, a smug male smile, Elizabeth thought, watching him through her lashes. He thinks I can't wait to jump into bed with him.

She gave him an enticing smile.

But Rowe was in no hurry. "How about a brandy, Elizabeth?"

"Okay," she said.

She watched him pour the brandy from the Waterford decanter into two snifters.

"You're beautiful," he said, and raised his glass to hers. "God, I'm tired."

He sat down on the sofa and patted the spot next to him. "Come talk to me, sweetheart. How are you doing with your jock executive assistant?"

My God, are they after Adrian?

"He's a bit peeved with me at the moment," she said, which was certainly the truth. She eased down beside him and felt his arm come around her shoulders, pulling her against him.

"Impossible or the man's an idiot."

"Ah, well, you see, I approved a contract that he disapproved of. It made perfect sense to me, but Adrian was spouting about this and that, and loopholes and tax problems and various assorted other headaches."

"What kind of deal was it?"

Elizabeth smiled into her goblet of brandy, swishing it about a little. "Would you believe a contract on Brad Carleton?"

He grinned at her. "That fellow giving you more trouble?"

"Nothing that I can't handle."

"My money's on you, Elizabeth." He downed the rest of his brandy, leaned his head back, and closed his eyes. Elizabeth said nothing, merely waited. Without changing position or opening his eyes, he asked, his voice sleepy, "Do you want or need my advice, Elizabeth?"

"Probably, but later, all right?"

He cocked an eye open. "Sounds good to me." He uncoiled his tall body and came to his feet. He stretched out his hand toward her. "Shall we, my darling?"

She let him draw her to her feet. She felt his hands stroke down her back, cupping about her buttocks and bringing her up against his body. She felt his breathing quicken as he kissed her. She kissed him back with all the expertise he'd taught her.

"You go ahead, Rowe. I'll be with you in just a moment."

She kissed him again, very deeply, letting her hands glide down his chest, lightly teasing his belly. She slipped her fingertips under the waistband of his pants.

He was breathing hard when she slowly stepped back. She stood quietly, the seductive smile still firmly in place.

"Don't take too long," he said, and kissed her chin.

"No, I won't."

Five minutes later, she heard him call out, "Elizabeth! I'm waiting and my body's all yours."

Indeed it is, she thought.

He'd kept only the bedside light on and the rest of the large room was in shadows. Elizabeth paused in the middle of the room, her eyes adjusting to the dimness. Rowe was lying naked atop the bedcover, his hands behind his head. He was certainly ready, she thought dispassionately, glancing over his body.

She sat down beside him. When he started to bring his arms forward, she stopped him. "No, Rowe, not just yet."

"I'd like to take off those clothes of yours, darling."

"Not yet," she repeated.

"Initiate, then. I'll love it," he said, and she saw that his eyes were heavy with desire.

"Oh, I fully intend to, Rowe." Slowly she brought out her left hand from the folds of her wool skirt. She was holding a silver ice pick, and before he could understand, could react, the point of the ice pick was against his throat.

"Wh-what?"

"You've become a stammerer, Rowe?"

"Elizabeth, what are you doing? What . . . this is a stupid joke! Come on now, stop it."

She pressed the sharp tip forward, just a bit, not enough to break the skin. She merely stared down at him. She saw him go from amusement to uncertainty.

His body was rigid, all physical desire dead as ashes, his eyes on her face.

"It's very sharp, isn't it?" she said quietly. "Please don't move. My hand isn't all that steady. Yes, it's very sharp. Don't you recall that I was on trial for murdering Timothy with a very fancy silver ice pick? Not this particular one, of course, I think the D.A.

still has that one, but thanks to Christian Hunter, it's not in his trophy case. I had Kogi buy a new one. Of course he had to buy the complete ice bucket with it, but the cost was worth it. I wanted it to be exactly the same. It's particularly sharp, isn't it?"

He looked desperate now, but he didn't move and his voice was light, very soothing. "You don't know what you're doing, Elizabeth. Come now, sweetheart—"

"Another one of your phony endearments, and I'll try for your jugular."

He stared at her, swallowing convulsively. "My God, why?"

"Don't you recall that the D.A. firmly believed that Timothy was going to divorce me? And I found out later, as you know, that my husband had, in fact, betrayed me with another woman. Probably plural, but it doesn't matter."

He knew then, and his Adam's apple bobbed. "You saw that ridiculous photo, didn't you?"

"Actually, I did, but it didn't matter, Rowe. Not one whit."

God help him, she was jealous, despite her words to the contrary. He must reassure her, make her believe him. "Amanda means nothing to me, Elizabeth. I was her escort, that's all. There's nothing at all between us."

The ice pick pressed inward, and his eyes went black with fear.

"You think I'm upset because I saw you with another woman, don't you?"

"Elizabeth, you know there's no one else! I wouldn't lie to you. There's no reason for me to."

"Please don't move, Rowe. My hand really does feel kind of sweaty. Actually, I want to thank you. You have taught me many things, so many things."

"What do you mean?" He'd stall her, he thought frantically, she hadn't half his strength. When she relaxed a bit, he could get the ice pick away from her. God Almighty, what was wrong with her? This was insane!

"With the ice pick against your throat, are you still inclined to believe that I didn't murder Timothy?"

"Of course you didn't!"

"You would stake your life on it?"

"Elizabeth—"

"No, it's time for you to listen to me, Rowe. I did indeed see the photo of you with Amanda Montgomery, as I told you. I also said that it didn't bother me. It's true, I wouldn't lie to you. You see, Rowe, I know that you betrayed me. And that betrayal was the one that hurt, really hurt. But how can one disbelieve what one sees, what one actually hears?"

"What are you talking about?"

"I do remember, though, how you told Laurette Carleton that I didn't kill Timothy, how you did defend me to that old witch. Are you still so very certain of that?" The ice pick lightly pricked his throat.

"Don't!"

"Sorry, my hand slipped. You'd best lie very still, Rowe. Now, about your certainty of my innocence."

"Of course you didn't kill Timothy, you couldn't!"

"You did sound very certain of that when you told Laurette."

"I . . . I don't know what you're talking about."

"Such exquisite timing, and all the planning. Dear Elizabeth all by herself in Paris, the most romantic city in the world. Dear Elizabeth, so very vulnerable, so very alone and hurting, so fragile. I must say that you and the Carletons worked very quickly. In you, they found the perfect man for the job. It is true, Rowe, by the time we returned to New York, I was fancying myself in love with you. No, don't say anything! You'll have your chance, but not yet.

"What you will say when you do talk . . . well, we'll see. I have come to the inescapable conclusion that women who are infatuated—or all *eat up*, as a Southern friend says—are mushbrains. All their critical faculties are suspended. Since I was never in love with Timothy, in the romantic sense, I hadn't before experienced that particular aberration. But you were so very smooth, everything you did and said was so very perfect. You were my lover and my confidant. Your word, I believe. You wanted to help me, you were so noble, so kind, and so very busy with your own business. As I said, I was a mushbrain. I was thinking about children, a station wagon, a home in Connecticut. Perhaps even a shaggy dog to sit by my piano. I was thinking about finally belonging, being loved for myself." She paused a moment, her throat clogging.

"Damn you, I want to cry! Not over you, ou can be sure about that, but for that poor pitiful fool I was. I was at Laurette's estate that Thursday night some weeks ago, standing right outside the open library windows. I saw and heard everything, Rowe. Everything."

"Then you know they were blackmailing me." The truth, he thought, watching her face. As much of the truth as he could manage.

"Yes, they were. I had no idea you were a gambler, Rowe."

"It was my father, Elizabeth. He nearly wrecked the banks. I had to do something! Surely they said something about that?"

"By my reckoning, since I discovered your little scheme, you should have gotten another three million from the Carletons."

"Only two and a half."

"I'm sorry that there won't be more coming, Rowe. I suspect you'll just have to latch on to an heiress. Does Amanda have money?"

"Yes."

"Actually, I'd hoped that it had cost Laurette and Michael more by now. After all, the value of your information appeared, on the surface at least, to be of good quality."

He was silent, understanding now. "You fed me false information to pass along to them."

"Yes, I did. I had intended to have a screaming match with you immediately, but, well, let us say that I wanted to have the awesome experience of using you. James Houston, for example. It wasn't much, but it did set things a bit cockeyed. My masterpiece, though, was the Cordie takeover. And of course, I did put a stop to all Michael's shenanigans with our steel company. Other things, of course. I'm sure you'll be able to trace everything that happened since that memorable evening."

"I didn't want to hurt you, Elizabeth. Please, you must believe me. I care—"

The ice pick pressed deeper. "Don't say those words, Rowe." Her voice was shaking. She'd thought she had such control over herself. She stopped, forcing herself to take deep, steadying breaths.

"You know, Rowe, if I did kill Timothy, for his supposed desire to divorce me, then it would seem that I have much greater motive to dispatch you to hell." She saw the sweat on his forehead. He was truly afraid now. Of her. What a novel experience to have someone actually afraid of her.

"No, Elizabeth, you've got to understand why I did it."

"I know why you did it, Rowe. You still need two million dollars, don't you? Well, I'm sorry about that, but it appears that you'll just have to propose very quickly to Amanda. There is just one more thing, Rowe. If you say a word to the Carletons—and I will know if you do—I will ruin you. Your precious banks will cease to exist. I won't force you out, I'll destroy you and your precious family with you. Do you understand me?"

"Yes," he said. "I understand."

She saw the fear leave his eyes, but she no longer cared. "You know, Rowe, you're the one who should be tried for murder. You killed Elizabeth Xavier Carleton. She no longer exists. She wasn't all that bad, just a lonely, very insecure woman who'd just gone through the most awful experience a person could have. What you did to her! She was clay in your hands, so malleable, so very trusting. I do wonder if it's true that most women will do whatever a man wants, if, of course, they believe they're in love with him. It's amazing, truly amazing. Another thing, Rowe, you will never, never try to cross me in the future. Make up whatever story you like to feed to Laurette and Michael, I really could care less how you extricate yourself from their net. Just always remember that my net is larger and more deadly. Now, you look quite foolish lying there sweating like a pig."

She moved off the bed very quickly and strode toward the bedroom door. She whirled about, wondering if he were enraged, if he would come after her. But he was sitting on the edge of the bed, staring at her, not moving.

"I want you out of my house in ten minutes," she said, and closed the bedroom door behind her.

She was on the point of having the piano removed. She wanted no reminders of that other Elizabeth. But there was Christian, and he delighted in hearing her play, and he had saved her life.

Kogi faithfully dusted the piano, though the lid was closed most of the time.

She didn't bother with any Armani suits. She went to Bergdorf's and bought six suits off the rack. They were all severely tailored, expensive, but not, of course, designer. She liked the look. The new Elizabeth Carleton.

She told Adrian two days later, on a Wednesday morning, without preamble, "I know you know I've been learning things about business. However, now I fully intend to take over. You can either help me to the fullest extent of your power, or I will find someone else. I won't tell you why I've made this decision. Suffice it to say that the decision is made and is irrevocable. There is a power now, and it is Elizabeth Carleton, not Timothy Carleton or any power-hungry minions: I'd like to meet with the rest of our group. There's a project that I wish to begin immediately. You will please inform our team that my first priority is to get rid of Brad Carleton. I want a meeting in my office at three o'clock this afternoon, and I want suggestions on how to accomplish this goal. Do you have any questions, Adrian?"

He stared at her. She said nothing more, just looked at him patiently. Suddenly he smiled. "I have a couple of excellent books for you to read, Elizabeth. Why don't you look them over while I inform the others of the meeting and the agenda."

"Thank you, Adman," she said. "Get me the books."

"That's just the beginning, Elizabeth."

"I know."

Elizabeth looked around the table at the five men. They were still in shock, she thought, and suppressed a grim smile. She'd seated herself at the head of the table, the power seat, and said, "Since Timothy's death, each of you has come to exercise tremendous power in your specific area. You've done quite well. Each of you is used to dealing with change, indeed, you're masters at initiating changes that benefit both you and ACI. Now it is I who am doing the initiating. I'm taking over and I wanted you to hear it from me. If any of you have a problem with working for me, you may leave now."

Coy Siverston said slowly, "Adrian said you wanted to learn enough to step in."

"Yes."

"I should like to know why, Elizabeth. I don't think it's too much to ask. For example, are you displeased with our running of things?"

"I have already said that each of you has done well. Now, as to why, that is none of your business. I'm quite serious, don't think I'm being a frivolous woman. I will no longer be a figurehead. You will work for me, not around me or over me. Is that clear to everyone?"

Silence.

"I see," Elizabeth said. "I suggest we take a poll. Let's begin with you, Adrian."

"I want to head up the strategic planning of ACI. Of course I'm behind you."

"Coy."

"You have no experience, Elizabeth, you are a musician, a woman."

"All true. Your point?"

"It will be difficult, not only for you but for all of us. I'll agree if you agree to listen to us, really listen to us."

"I agree. I'm not stupid."

"Very well," said Coy.

The three other men each agreed, as she'd known they would. Edgar Derby, her very overweight computer genius, was sweating as if he'd soon be out of a job. Had the Carletons gotten to him? She shook her head, remaining silent. No, she didn't think so.

"Now," she said. "Let's move on to my priority project. Adrian, do you have suggestions on how to get Brad Carleton out?"

Before he could reply, Rod Samuels came into the office. "Sorry I'm late, Elizabeth. Gentlemen."

"Sit down, Rod. We've actually just begun. From now on, this project will be known as OBC. Oust Brad Carleton. You see, I'm already learning how letters stand for things. Rod is here because he's our expert on the legal end of things. Now, Adrian, please continue."

". . . his books checked out clean as a whistle, as you know."

"Yes, I know. The reason they did was that there was a leak. That leak no longer exists. I can assure all of you of that."

"How can you be so certain, Elizabeth?" Rod asked. "Who was the leak?"

"I am certain and I won't tell you who the leak was. I will assure you that it was not poor Avery. Coy, let's have another surprise audit of Brad's books." She watched Coy write something in his ubiquitous notebook.

"Edgar, what do you think?"

Edgar Derby had little to say. He popped down one

of his high-blood-pressure pills. Benjamin Hallimer scratched his bald head and mumbled inanities. He desperately wanted to get off by himself and do some thinking. It was his way. Oran Wicks looked interested, but uncertain, faced with this new Elizabeth.

Elizabeth turned finally to Rod Samuels. "Rod?"

"Forget the legalities, forget the deals made with the estate. Go for his balls."

"My sentiments exactly," said Elizabeth. At the blank looks around the table, she explained, "Brad is reputed to be gay. He is also thinking of marrying a senator's daughter. Now, does this give you any ideas?"

Adrian said very softly, "A private detective, photos perhaps, leverage."

"This is hardball," said Coy.

"The very hardest," agreed Elizabeth. "Let's get under way without delay. Now, let's go to the next item. I want to know, I mean *really* know, all our major companies and their top management. I've given myself six months. Adrian will make up an agenda. I'll spend three days studying each company, then we'll pay the management an on-site surprise visit." She paused a moment, then looked around the table at each man in turn. "If," she said very quietly, "anything discussed among us goes outside this room or if any of the management turn out not to be surprised by my visit, I will fire every one of you. No exceptions."

Adrian and Rod remained after the other men had filed out, each with his assignment.

"There's one other thing," Elizabeth said. "Adrian, remember that awful scene with Catherine Carleton that evening at the restaurant?"

"Too well," he said on a grimace.

"Do you remember the man she was with?"

"Vaguely. Why?"

"His name is . . . was, Chad Walters. He was murdered. He was a drug dealer and the police have in essence closed the book. Gang-related and all that. I've given it a lot of thought. I don't think it was."

"I don't quite understand," Rod said, looking at her closely.

"I think one of the Carletons, Laurette probably, had him killed. You see, Catherine was on the verge of making a pretty nasty scandal. Walters probably had her hooked on coke. I want to hire another private detective to check into it for us. Can you handle that, Rod?"

"My God, Elizabeth! The Carletons are a lot of unpleasant things, but murderers?"

"You forget that someone killed Timothy," she said very quietly. "I didn't. Who else comes to mind?"

"For God's sake, not one of his family!"

"Perhaps you're right. I don't know. But if they were responsible for Walters' death, that information would give us more leverage, more power." She paused a moment, her hand now a fist. "I've got to know."

Two days later, on the second page of the New York *Post*, it was reported that the police had arrested a small-time cocaine supplier, Juan Ramirez, for the murder of Chad Walters. The man's motive was that Walters was trying to take over his operation in Atlantic City. The evidence cited seemed conclusive.

"Damn," Elizabeth said. "I really thought that you'd stop at nothing, Laurette." She paused a moment, then continued aloud to her empty bedroom, "Laurette, you and Michael are either the luckiest people alive, or you're smarter than I thought."

Probably the latter, she thought.

11

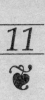

"I'm proud of you, Elizabeth. You are in control of your life. To you, my dear."

Elizabeth smiled at Christian Hunter and clicked her wineglass to his. "Thank you, Christian. It's been a wild three months. I have no problem at all sleeping now. The minute my head hits the pillow, I'm out like the proverbial light."

Christian glanced at the newspaper on the coffee table. "The Boston *Globe*?"

"Yes," she said, and picked it up. "It contains the engagement announcement of Mr. Rowen Chalmers and Miss Amanda Montgomery. His second marriage and her third. I was wondering if I should send a gift or perhaps a letter of condolence to Miss Montgomery. Although," she continued, looking away from him, "she should have enough experience now to know when she's being duped."

Christian heard only the mocking amusement in her voice, and relaxed. "You were well rid of him," he said.

She kicked off her shoes and put her feet up on the table and leaned her head back against the sofa cushion. "You know something, Christian?"

"Not yet, but I'm patient."

She laughed a little. "I'm at last feeling worthy to be a member of the human race. I'm still scared that I'm going to do something or say something very stupid, but I get less scared every day."

"Just make sure you don't lose your humanity along the way, Elizabeth."

"As in ceasing to trust people?" Her voice was light, but his sensitive ears picked up her cold determination.

"As in there are people that can and should be trusted. As in me, Elizabeth."

"I do trust you, Christian. After all, you saved my life. Why would you want to destroy it?" He said nothing to that, and she continued after a moment, "I've simply learned to keep business and personal matters completely separate. It keeps things simpler."

She didn't see the pained look on his face. He began to fill his pipe.

"I'm proud of you," she said after a moment, her voice teasing. "You aren't playing shrink with me."

"The last thing you need is a shrink, my dear. However . . ."

"Yes?"

He was sucking ferociously on his pipe. "You need to spend more time with me."

"If I'm not mistaken, Christian, we are together at least twice a week." She sighed, turning her head to face him. "Have I told you lately how much I appreciate you? You don't care if I'm rich or poor. You just care about me. A friend like you must be unique."

A friend. Nothing more, at least not yet.

"Play for me, Elizabeth."

She wiggled her toes. "Just so long as you don't expect me to put my shoes back on."

He wanted Chopin, and that's what she played. For him. She never played for herself anymore. When she looked up finally, she saw that his eyes were closed. "Are you asleep, Christian?"

He didn't move a muscle. "No. More, if you please."

Because she hadn't practiced in a long time, she was aware of a slight burning in her forearms. No more Chopin etudes. She skipped to her favorite theme song from James Bond, "Nobody Does It Better."

"Is that supposed to tell me something?" he asked lazily when she finished.

"You got it. Now it's late and I have an eight-o'clock meeting tomorrow morning. Friday night, Christian?"

"Yes," he said, rising. "I've got a new place to take you. The star is a black jazz pianist, and he improvises so well he should be recorded while he's doing it."

She watched him shrug into his tweed jacket. He was becoming so dear to her. Solid, that was Christian. And he never pushed her. She raised her face for his parting kiss.

It was light, barely brushing her lips. "Good night, Elizabeth."

Christian took the elevator downstairs, bade good night to Gallagher, knowing that after his departure Gallagher would lock up the building tighter than a tick. He took a cab to Susan's apartment on Fiftieth near Madison. She was waiting for him, just as he knew she would be, just as she was supposed to be.

He was hard, trembling with desire. "Now," he said.

Why don't you get her to do this? But Susan didn't say it aloud. She led him into her bedroom and unzipped his pants. He never took long, not after spending the evening with *her*.

Then he lay on the bed on his back, saying nothing.

Susan had long ago learned to keep her thoughts to herself and her mouth closed. She brought him a glass of brandy.

What, she wondered, did this Elizabeth Carleton have that she didn't have? Money, that was all. But money couldn't matter to Christian. He was so rich, she bet he didn't even remember where all his assets were. No, there was something else that woman had, a very big something.

Finally she said, her voice tentative, "I'm taking piano lessons."

That got his attention. He reached for his pipe.

"What do you think, Christian?"

"I think you should do as you please, Susan. It's late. Thank you. I'll see you on . . . Friday—late, I'm afraid."

"Yes, Christian. All right."

She watched him dress and shove his pipe into his coat pocket, and wanted to cry.

Senator Charles Henkle took the sealed envelope handed to him by his housekeeper with an impatient nod. He was late for a meeting, but the letter was unusual. It had been hand-delivered, and "PERSONAL AND CONFIDENTIAL" was written in big block letters at the bottom. Perhaps, he thought, ever cynical, it was another contribution from an unknown person or persons, who would more than likely let his identity be known soon enough if he, Charles, accepted the contribution. He wandered to his desk and sat down. He picked up his antique letter opener and carefully slit open the envelope.

It contained a half-dozen eight-by-ten photos. Nothing more. He picked one up and turned it over, and froze. It was in glittering color. Brad Carleton was naked on his hands and knees. Another man, younger, was pumping into him, the look on his face sheer ecstasy.

Slowly, one at a time, Charles Henkle looked at each of the photos. They were excellent photography, he thought vaguely. So much detail, so many close-ups. The one that made him truly ill was of Brad kissing his partner, his tongue deep in the man's mouth, his hand on his cock.

He carefully put the photos back in the envelope and locked it in a drawer. He walked from his study to the bathroom and vomited. His first thought after he'd rinsed out his mouth was: Has Jenny slept with him? My God, what if he has AIDS? Then he wanted to kill Brad Carleton. It was a simple, clean desire.

He left his home in Georgetown, not wanting to see either his wife or his daughter. He thought about showing the photos to Jenny, then dismissed the idea.

He returned home at midnight, went into his study, firmly closing the door behind him. He reached for the phone. All right, you little bastard, he thought, let's see if you're home, and if you are, you damned son of a bitch, another man better not answer the phone.

He was gritting his teeth on the third ring.

"Hello? Brad Carleton here."

He got a grip on himself. "This is Charles Henkle," he said. "I want to see you, Brad. I want you to fly to Washington tomorrow. I'll meet you at La Fourchette at precisely noon."

"But . . . what's the matter, sir? Jenny's all right, isn't she?" Brad ran his hand through his hair, trying to get his wits together. He'd been deeply asleep, and it was late, very late. He heard his soon-to-be-father-in-law's deep breathing on the other end of the line. What the hell was going on? He said again, more sharply, "Sir, is Jenny all right?"

"Yes. Just be here, Brad."

Jonathan Harley walked out of the First People's Bank of Philadelphia at precisely ten o'clock in the morning. He was wearing a smile that made people he passed start, then smile back at him involuntarily.

"Ten million dollars," he said aloud. "Out of the woods. I'm safe." The loan had a thirty-day call-in after three months. It was plenty of time, and the interest rate wasn't all that exorbitant. Too, those were only paper terms. He knew his banker well, and if he needed it, he could get as long an extension as he wanted. He'd buy up another hunk of Rose's stock— through a go-between, since she'd probably spit in his face if she knew he was the buyer. Then he'd expand as he'd wanted to do.

"Went well, I see," said Midge, reacting to the beautiful smile on her boss's face.

"You got it," Jonathan said.

"Congratulations."

He nodded, and strode into his office like a man who knew he was now in control.

"You deserve it," Midge said under her breath. "You're rid of that bitch of a wife and now you've got enough money to make a real go of it." She grinned down at her word processor. If she were ten years younger and not in love with her husband, well, just maybe . . .

Ten minutes later, Jonathan walked from his office. His face was utterly white. Midge jumped to her feet. "What happened?"

He silently handed her a letter, one she hadn't opened because it had been marked "PERSONAL AND CONFIDENTIAL."

The envelope had no return address on it. It was blank save for Jonathan's name and address. Her hand was shaking as she smoothed out the single page. She finished reading it, then looked up at her boss's face. It was no longer white. He was flushed with anger, and his jaw was working.

"The bastards, the damned bastards," he said, more to himself than to her. "I won't let them get away with it."

Actually, Midge wanted to tell him, it wasn't bastards at all, it was a woman, one very big, very powerful woman. Elizabeth Xavier Carleton. And she wanted Jonathan's company.

Charles Henkle ordered a Perrier. He never drank during the day, but he sure wanted something stiff right now. His eyes remained trained on the door of La Fourchette. Young men in business suits streamed in, young government men for the most part. This restaurant wasn't popular with his cronies and he'd picked it for just that reason.

He saw Brad step toward the hostess exactly two minutes past noon. Punctual bastard.

He didn't rise. Brad's face was a study of concern. "Sir," he said, and stuck out his hand.

Charles said, "Sit down, Brad."

Brad pulled back his hand and sat down, his eyes carefully studying the older man's face. Charles looked older, more tired, and Brad could see strain in his eyes. Why all the secrecy and this command performance?

"You're well, sir?" he asked, with proper deference.

"No, I'm not," said Charles. "Nor am I the least bit hungry. I simply asked you here because I didn't fancy meeting in some park. I suggest that you order a drink, Brad."

Brad ordered a Scotch. What was wrong? Why was Charles babbling about meeting in a park?

Charles waited until Brad drank a long swallow from his Scotch glass. Then he said very calmly the words he'd rehearsed so he wouldn't physically assault the young man: "You aren't going to marry Jenny. Indeed, you'll break it off with her. I would suggest that you claim you've met another woman, you can't help yourself, you don't want to hurt her, all that nonsense. I'm certain you can carry it off once you give it enough thought."

Brad very carefully set down his glass. His mind was racing. "What is this all about? You know I love Jenny. You know there isn't another girl."

"No, I don't imagine there is," said Charles, his voice laced with irony.

Brad frowned and a small thrill of fear began to travel through him. He said nothing for a moment, his brain frantically sorting through possibilities. He stared at Henkle's thick wavy white hair and clear blue eyes, imagining cynically that his constituency believed him the epitome of a statesman, an honest and honorable man. In God's name, what was the old man's problem?

"Lunch, gentlemen?"

Charles shook his head and waved the waiter away.

"As I said, Brad, you'll break it off with Jenny. I'll give you three days to come up with the best story. No longer."

This ridiculous old man telling him what to do, just because he was a bigwig in the government? Brad could buy and sell him three times over! "No, I won't," Brad said. "As I said, I love your daughter, and she, I might add, loves me."

"I know she loves you, more's the pity. Her heart will mend, however. Don't make me get dirty, Brad."

"What the hell are you talking about?"

"Very well." Charles opened his briefcase and extracted one photograph. He handed it to Brad facedown.

He watched the young man's face go slack with shock.

He watched his mouth work, but nothing came out. Charles leaned forward over the table and said very softly, "Now, you dirty little bastard, you will do just as I said."

Brad reacted without thinking. He shredded the photograph.

"I have five others, each quite detailed," said Charles.

"How did you get these?"

He sounded defeated, and scared, scared as hell. Charles felt no pity for him, not an ounce. "I got them, that's all I need to tell you. Just one thing— have you slept with my daughter?"

Brad wanted to shout at the old man that he'd screwed Jenny a good hundred times, but he wasn't stupid. If he said he'd slept with her, there was no telling what Henkle would do. "No," he said. "I haven't slept with Jenny."

"You'd better be telling me the truth, Carleton. I'll ask Jenny, you may be sure of that, and she always tells me the truth."

Brad gulped. "Very well. We did sleep together, but just two or three times. I always used a condom, I swear it!"

Charles wanted to kill him. "You lying little slime. You deserve to die." He lowered his voice to almost a whisper. "If you don't do exactly what I tell you to do, I'll see that everyone in the entire world sees these photos. Do you understand me?"

"Yes, I understand."

"Good."

"If I do as you say, will you give me the photographs?"

"Worried, aren't you? Yes, I'll give them to you." Charles laughed. "You see, you filthy scum, someone sent the photos to me, anonymously. So someone else knows, knows all about you. You'd best cover your flank. You've nothing to fear from me if you break off with my daughter. Now, I'm leaving. You sicken me."

Charles tossed a twenty on the table. He handed Brad the envelope of photos. "You might want these," he said, "for inspiration. Just remember that I have another set."

Brad didn't know what to say. He felt a certain amount of relief, despite his fear. He was aware of the contempt flowing from the senator. What did he know about anything? He swallowed down angry words, and watched Charles walk from the restaurant.

Brad looked at his grandmother, so proud, so queenly-looking, as was her wont. *Queenly*. He would have laughed at the thought had he been able. Odd how he never thought of her as old, not really. Objectively, she was ancient, a relic. She should be his little white-haired grandmother, a bit dotty and all that. God, what a joke. He was beginning to believe that she'd live forever, and control all of them until they died off. He glanced toward his Uncle Michael, who was seated near Laurette, his expression one of mild curiosity.

"Now I suppose you will tell your uncle and me what this is all about?" Laurette asked in her calm, well-bred voice.

Brad closed the library doors very firmly. "I'm not going to marry Jenny Henkle," he said.

Laurette merely arched an eyebrow at her grandson. "May I ask why?"

Brad pictured Jenny's face in his mind for a moment, seeing her bewilderment, her shock, then the tears that streamed down her face. Pitiful little female. He realized that he'd cared more for her at that instant than he ever had before. And she loved him, really loved him, at least she thought she did.

He said, "Jenny broke it off."

Michael merely stared at him. "Bull," he said. "The girl would kill for you."

"Why?" asked Laurette, her voice sounding mildly interested, no more.

"She decided that we wouldn't suit."

Brad knew the moment his Uncle Michael realized the truth. Not all of it, not the nastiness, but enough of it. He sucked in his breath and his face went pale. "It's just as well," he said. "Yes, it's just as well."

"Both of you are being ridiculous," said Laurette. "I want this marriage. You will go through with it, Bradley. If you have already spoken to Jenny, you will call her back . . . no, you will go see her, on your hands and knees, if necessary."

"That's impossible, Grandmother," Brad said, sending an agonized look toward his uncle.

Michael shrugged. "She knows," he said.

"I know," Laurette said in a crisp voice, "that you have this unfortunate . . . propensity for men, Bradley. Is that what Michael is talking about?"

"Yes, it is. Her father knows and he threatened me with exposure if I didn't break it off immediately."

Laurette closed her eyes a moment. She felt the familiar pain in her kidneys, at least she thought it was her kidneys. It could be anything. It wasn't fair. There was so much to do . . . so much. At times like this, she wanted to just get up and leave the room, leave everything to Michael. But Michael wasn't Timothy. He would flounder like a raft in a storm. "I will speak to Senator Henkle," she said.

"No, Grandmother, you can't!"

"I assure you that I can."

"He . . . he has photos." There, he'd said it. It was out in the open.

"Show them to me," Laurette said.

Michael jumped to his feet. "No, Mother, please, no!"

"Don't be a fool, Michael. I assure you that I've seen everything there is to see in my eighty-four years. The photos, if you please, Bradley."

Silently Brad handed her the envelope. He watched her pull out the photos, one at a time. There wasn't a sound in the room. Michael had dropped his head into his hands. Brad felt frozen to the spot, his eyes on his grandmother's face. He felt shame, so much shame that he wanted to choke on it. She showed no expression.

She still said nothing as she replaced the photos in the envelope. "Does Henkle have copies?"

"He told me that he did. He told me he would give them to me once I'd broken off with Jenny."

"I believe him," she said. She continued thoughtfully, "Now, of course, the important thing is, where did he get the photos?"

"I don't know. He said they were sent to him anonymously."

"Elizabeth," she whispered.

Michael started. "Come now, Mother, really! Not Elizabeth!"

"Both of you are fools. Just because she's a woman, just because she has no business experience, you discount her. You know as well as I do that she found out about Rowe Chalmers and, shall we say, neutralized him. She's growing stronger by the minute. Come, Michael, you know that she has taken over ACI. Now this."

She looked at the envelope for a moment, then placed it in a drawer of her desk. She locked the drawer.

"First things first," Laurette said, willing the pain to subside. She despised painkillers. They numbed and slowed her mind. "Henkle," she said. "Our dear Senator Henkle."

"It's over," said Michael.

"I'm beginning to think that Catherine, despite all her wildness, has more guts than you do, Michael, and you, Bradley. Now, you will indeed break off with the fellow in those photographs. No, don't argue with me, Bradley! Break it off. Then you will arrange to see Jenny again."

"But why, Grandmother? You know as well as I do that Senator Henkle would act."

"Photographs," she said very gently, "don't have to be the doing of only one person. No, indeed." Timothy had taught her that many years before. She couldn't remember the details now, but it had worked. Timothy had laughed and rubbed his hands together, and she had learned that ruthlessness was the key to the game.

Brad stared at her, at first not understanding. When he did, he wanted to puke. "I can't," he said.

"You will do as you're told," said Laurette, out of patience with him now. "You will call Jenny and convince her that breaking off with her was a mistake. To convince her of your love, you will take her to a motel that we select in advance. You will make love to her very thoroughly. I trust you will be able to manage that with aplomb. Then we will pay a visit to Senator Henkle. With photos of our own."

A week went by. There was nothing about a breaking of the engagement of Bradley Carleton and Jennifer Henkle.

"I don't understand," Elizabeth said.

Rod sat back in his huge leather chair, his expression thoughtful. "I don't either, yet."

They did, that afternoon. Elizabeth withdrew photos from an unmarked envelope. They were of Bradley and Jennifer Henkle, naked, in various positions. Some of them were on a bed, some on the floor. The close-up details were devastating. That poor girl, Elizabeth thought, hating herself in that moment for starting the whole thing. Jennifer Henkle was innocent, and now this.

There was a note enclosed that said only, "If you publish the photos of Bradley Carleton, these will also be published. They will ruin Senator Henkle and his entire family."

"Hardball, Elizabeth," Rod said softly.

"That's one to Laurette, isn't it?"

"Unless you want the Henkles on your conscience."

Elizabeth rose from her chair and unconsciously smoothed down her wool skirt. "No, you know I wouldn't go that far."

"I wonder what the senator will do," Adrian said aloud.

The wedding date of Bradley Carleton and Jennifer Henkle was announced the following day. Just one month after Rowe Chalmers would be married.

Elizabeth's OBC project died on the spot. "But only until we can come up with something else," she said. "He'll make a mistake, a big one. Then we'll strike."

That evening, Christian wondered what was wrong with her. She was withdrawn, silent. He began kissing her, the first time drawing her tightly against him. She did nothing, didn't react one way or the other.

"I've got to do something, Christian," she said at last when he released her.

Christian sighed inwardly. "Something I can help you with, Elizabeth?"

She wanted to say yes, to pour it all out, but she didn't. Rowe had taught her well, too well. "Forgive me," she said, trying to soften her words. "It's something quite foolish, really, Christian. Nothing that should concern you. I'm sorry to be such a bummer." She gave him a big smile and hugged him. "You're so important to me," she whispered against his shoulder.

"Yes," he said, kissing her hair. "I want to be." He wondered if she were thinking of Rowen Chalmers, and bit his lower lip in rage. But he couldn't ask her.

12

❦

"I want to know what *you* want, Catherine. You're twenty-four years old. You graduated from Harvard. I want you to tell me what you want to do with your life."

Her granddaughter looked thin, the flesh of her face drawn too tightly over the bones. There were dark shadows beneath her expressive eyes, attesting that she wasn't sleeping well. Laurette wondered if perhaps Catherine were still ill. Ill, she thought with a wince at her ridiculous euphemism. Catherine had spent nearly two weeks in a private sanatorium in Vermont, and supposedly had no more addiction to cocaine. But she was still irritable, still nervous, her body flinching at any unexpected sound.

Laurette said softly when Catherine didn't answer her, "I want you to be happy, my dear. But you must be strong now. You must search for your direction."

Catherine laughed, but it wasn't a healthy sound. "My direction," she mused aloud, staring away from her grandmother. "I don't know. I really don't know."

"I remember how well you did in mathematics, my dear. You were the top of your class, remember?"

It seemed a century ago to Catherine. "Yes," she said, "I remember."

"I even remember when you wanted to become a wildcatter," Laurette said, giving Catherine her special smile. "You were five years old and you'd just gotten a kitten. You heard your father talking about oil drilling and announced that that was what you wanted to do if you could find more cats like Marvin."

Catherine grinned at that. "Goodness, Grandmother, I hadn't thought about that in years! I remember you laughing and kissing me."

There hadn't been much laughter or kissing of late, Laurette thought. Life had become so complicated. She said gently, coming back to the present. "You did so well in your first three years at Harvard."

"Yes, until . . ."

"Until you decided to be a flighty, useless rich girl."

Catherine sucked in her breath, her eyes flying to her grandmother's face. "That's cruel."

"Perhaps, but it's the truth. You're no longer five years old, Catherine. You're a grown woman. It's time you acted like one. It's time you did something with yourself. A life without goals is a sorry excuse for existence. Do you remember your Great-Aunt Marion? She had face-lifts every couple of years, bought clothes until she had to have more closets built to hold them. But she had no goals, Catherine. She wasn't ever a happy woman."

"I don't suppose so," Catherine said. "I remember Father saying she was crazy."

"No, she was a woman who elected to live her life through other people. Through her husband and perhaps through me, her older sister. All those ghastly rules about women and what they should and shouldn't do. She never got beyond those strictures, never saw herself as free to be what she wished." Laurette paused. She must be getting old, all these memories, all of them set in concrete now. There was the present and Catherine and she had to help her. She said abruptly, "Now, my dear, Chad Walters is dead, as is your unfortunate drug habit. It is time to face up to things."

Catherine didn't reply. That pain, that never-ending elusive pain, continued to gnaw at her. She hadn't loved Chad, but his death had come as such an awful shock. She was tempted to laugh about her drug addiction. But she felt too awful. She needed to buy more coke, *had* to. She said finally, "Look at Jenny Henkle, a woman of the eighties. She went to a good school, if I remember correctly. She won't do anything except have babies and buy clothes and order servants about. Once she's a Carleton, that is. She's just like Great-Aunt Marion, isn't she?"

"Not really. She has no particular talent or desire to be something beyond what is offered. Do you consider yourself like Jennifer?"

"No, Jenny's so sweet and innocent."

Laurette pictured those photos of Brad and Jenny in her mind, and winced just a bit. At least Brad had promised no more men.

Catherine rose to her feet, unable to sit still any longer. She loved her grandmother, occasionally feared her, as did every other member of the family. But Laurette couldn't help her with this. God, she needed some coke. She couldn't seem to think about anything else. Her *direction*, for God's sake!

"I'm really very tired, Grandmother. I think I'll go on up to bed now."

Laurette wanted to shake her, wanted to tell her that all of a sudden she'd wake up and be eighty-four years old and wonder what had become of all those years. She drew on her patience. "Very well, my dear. You do need your sleep. We'll talk again tomorrow."

An hour later, Catherine had slipped out of her grandmother's house and was on her way to New York City. Her nose was running again. Thank God her grandmother hadn't noticed. She reached for a Kleenex.

Her hands were gripping the wheel when she finally entered the city. Where to go? Where to buy cocaine? Chad had always provided all she needed, all very high quality. But Chad was dead.

She forced down the tears. Dammit, she hadn't loved him. He was a criminal, after all, and she had paid all the bills. She had to have some coke.

Catherine drove down Broadway very slowly, her eyes on the streets. She cut over at Thirteenth Street to Fifth and continued down to Washington Square. She drove more slowly now, alert to the people on the streets. She was drawing attention, her bright red Porsche the focus of the milling men who lounged in the doorways and on the corners. She saw a tall black man with a well-dressed white man speaking in the recessed doorway of a darkened building. She saw something change hands. Her heart speeded up. She slowed the car. The white man nodded, turned, and walked quickly away. She sniffed and jerked the wheel. The black man looked up, and she could feel him studying her, her car. She started to roll down the window; then she saw his eyes. They were cold, terrifying. He waved at her and started toward the car. It was then she saw another man in the shadows. He lifted his arm and she saw a gun.

"Oh, God," she whispered. He was close now, and she felt frozen.

His hands reached out for the door handle. Catherine gave a small cry and slammed in the clutch and down on the gas. The Porsche jerked and coughed. She heard a shout from the man, and forced herself to ease more carefully on the clutch.

She looked back, seeing him standing in the street. He gave her an obscene gesture, and shouted something she thankfully couldn't understand. She couldn't see the other man, the one with the gun.

Catherine was trembling. She grabbed a Kleenex and wiped her nose. It was red. Her blood. She was crying and the blood was mixing with her tears. A pale red drop fell to the white of her cashmere sweater.

She finally pulled the Porsche over on a deserted street. She was somewhere on the East Side, in a residential district. She didn't know how she'd gotten here. She leaned her head against the steering wheel and sobbed.

The knock against the window glass nearly made her stop breathing. She jerked about, a scream rising in her throat, to see a cop standing beside the Porsche, looking at her with some concern.

She wanted suddenly to laugh. Should she tell him she was trying to buy cocaine but a man had terrified her? Should she tell him about the other man, the one with the gun? Should she tell him that she couldn't bear herself any longer and she wanted to die?

"Miss? Are you all right?"

Catherine got a hold of herself and tried to swallow her tears. The cop was young, his face fresh. One of New York's finest, and not too long on the beat, she thought. She rolled down the window. "I'm fine, thank you. I just felt dizzy for a moment."

Dizzy, hell, he wanted to tell her, but he didn't, of course. "I suggest you go home. It's late, and you don't want the crazies to be all over you."

At least his lecture was short and to the point, Catherine thought. She said yes, and thank you, and watched him walk back to his squad car. He waited. Catherine sighed, started the Porsche, and drove sedately down the street. Yes, she thought, I'm going home. But not back to Long Island. She'd almost reached her apartment when she realized that her grandmother would be worried. She didn't want her to know that she'd taken this insane drive into New York. She turned the Porsche around.

As she drove back to Long Island, she played over her grandmother's words. What did she want to do with her life? Catherine shuddered. She didn't want her nose to bleed and run until it rotted off. She didn't want to be driven ever again as she had been tonight. *I nearly went to the streets.* But the high, the feeling of absolute superiority . . .

She thought of her father, the famous and infamous Timothy Carleton. He'd loved her, shown her attention until Elizabeth came along and seduced him. Then he'd had no time for her, Catherine. No, no, she didn't want to think of that pain.

Her grandmother was right about another thing. She needed a goal, no more wandering about, doing absolutely nothing. Her last thought was of Elizabeth and her certainty that she had murdered her father. And then she knew what she would do.

Laurette heard the muffled sound of a car and knew it was Catherine's. She slept so little now, each spurt of sleep a blessing when it came. But awake, she heard every sound, every noise, and her mind had to identify its source. What to do about Catherine? She would speak to her again soon.

Laurette rose from her bed and walked to the long windows. Slowly she pulled back the drapery and stared out over the moonlit grounds. Oddly enough, she thought of Christian Hunter. How she'd wanted to destroy him for what he'd done. She'd tried to get at the man, but his assets were too diversified, his holdings too solid. His reputation was impeccable. For the first time, she allowed herself to wonder if he had told the truth at the trial.

She turned slowly from the windows, and heard the drapery fall softly back into place. The man had to have lied. There was simply no one else who could have killed Timothy. No one except Elizabeth.

Timothy.

Laurette sighed, and walked to the wall thermostat and turned it up. She was always so cold these days. Even her very bones felt cold. She felt the heat gush out at her legs through the vent, seep through her old, infinitely comfortable robe. It felt so good. She had lied to Catherine, unfortunately. Timothy had no use at all for women except for sex. Had he lived, he would have continued to treat his young daughter as a bit of useless fluff, a beautiful bauble with no particular value save in marriage. And she would have probably done nothing about it, nothing at all.

He'd told her once, laughing and hugging her after she'd given him a very perceptive bit of analysis on a business deal, "Hell, if you weren't my mother, I'd have married you in a flash. No other woman can touch you."

Look at what he'd done to Elizabeth. She'd been nothing more than a beautiful bauble, tremendously talented, of course, but that had only been the draw for Timothy. And she'd been ruthless enough to twist him about, to make him change his will. Then she'd killed him.

The blessed heat was warming her blood now, and she was becoming drowsy. She walked back to her bed and slowly lay down, pulling the thick covers over her. But her mind kept wandering back, back to a particularly vicious scene she'd witnessed, but never spoken of.

Timothy, strong, ruthless, mean sometimes. Particularly toward his first wife, Eileen. Gentle, weak Eileen. Of such good family, but of no character at all. No spine. He hadn't struck Eileen until after she'd given him two sons. When the doctors had told him that there could be no more children, he'd turned on his gentle, weak wife.

"What good are you, you stupid cow?"

Eileen, cowering, wincing, trying to escape his vicious words, and Laurette, standing just outside the door, a dozen red roses in her hands, ready to be placed in the vase in the corridor.

"God, I detest you," Timothy had shouted. "I'd kill you, you idiot bitch, if I could get away with it!"

No, Laurette thought, closing her eyes, I won't remember, I won't think about it. But the images came on, and the awful words.

"Please, Timmy, I—"

"Timmy! God, you nauseating cunt! You're hurting my sons with your mealymouthed stupidity."

The sound of a hand striking flesh. The awful whimper.

"I want you out, Eileen. I never want to hear your whining voice again. I never want to have to see that face of yours again!"

"But, Timm . . . Timothy, I—"

The striking hand, the scream.

I've got to stop this, Laurette thought. Dear God,

I've got to stop him! But she didn't move, for he yelled at that moment, "And one more word out of your stupid mouth about my mother and I'll flay you, do you understand? You're not fit to be in the same house with her."

Pride flowed through her, making her move away down the corridor now, the roses forgotten. Her son, her defender. He was right. Eileen was a useless, stupid woman. She would let Timothy take care of her.

And he had. Eileen had moved to Spain. She'd seen her sons, Brad and Trent, twice a year after that. She'd died five years later. No one had known what she'd died of.

Laurette shuddered now. Timothy had mentioned her death over dinner one evening, between the soup and the main course.

Then Charlotte had come along and he'd married her. And she'd given birth to Catherine. At least Charlotte was still alive, living, the last Laurette knew, in London. She'd heard from Charlotte but once, a telegram received just after Timothy's death. It had read simply: "SUCH A PITY. STOP." Laurette had clearly pictured the look of malicious glee on Charlotte's face.

Then Elizabeth. And she'd murdered Timothy.

Elizabeth was tired, so tired that all she wanted to do was fall in bed and sleep for a week. Flanked by Adrian and Coy, she'd paid unannounced visits to three of their largest American-based companies. A textile company in Atlanta, a lumber company in Seattle, and the headquarters of a grocery-store chain in Cleveland.

In her protected, isolated environment on Park Avenue, she'd never really understood the scope of her power. Now she did. The men they visited had recognized it, but hadn't known how to handle her. They gave her endless attention, but serious questions, she soon realized, were directed to Adrian or to Coy. At one meeting with the president of the Copperton grocery stores, she'd giggled involuntarily at what she came later to call the good-ole-boys ritual. It had sounded ridiculous at first. Unfortunately, she thought, it soon came to sound very normal.

She realized other things very quickly. There were very few women in positions of responsibility and power. She'd met a woman in Atlanta who was vastly talented and who hadn't a prayer of becoming anything more than the sales manager. Elizabeth smiled. She would take care of Melissa Graves. She couldn't wait to send the president packing, the condescending fool.

Suddenly she no longer felt tired. She walked purposefully into her study. Yes, she thought, gazing about, it was hers now. All traces of Timothy were long gone. She'd had the entire room redecorated, made it utterly feminine, knowing deep down with each change she approved that Timothy would have hated it, scorned it and her, calling her a useless idiot.

She sat behind the beautiful Louis XVI desk and picked up the phone. She dialed the special number, waited a moment, then began dictating.

When she'd finished, she sat back in her chair and grew thoughtful. Melissa Graves would realize her hard work and her dreams. *All because of me, a woman with power*.

She thought of the stream of women she'd seen at the three companies, secretaries mostly, fetching coffee for the men, looking pretty, watching her as if she were some sort of alien. A woman they couldn't possibly understand. And she'd thought that the women's movement had accomplished something, that women could do anything they had the talent to do. It was the eighties, after all, the end of the eighties.

She'd realized it wasn't a question of male versus female. It was a matter of power, and very few of the women had any.

She did.

She fell asleep, her mind filled with plans.

The following Wednesday morning at precisely ten o'clock, she was sitting at the circular conference table in her office, Coy and Adrian facing her. She'd made her announcement some fifteen minutes into the meeting.

"Come, Elizabeth, surely, you can't mean to . . ."

Elizabeth merely looked at Coy patiently, wanting now to hear his opinions. "Yes?" she prodded.

"Look, Elizabeth, this woman, what's her name? Graves? She doesn't know what to do, she hasn't the ability to see beyond the next meal for her husband, for God's sake!"

"But isn't she the sales manager?" Elizabeth inquired, her voice mild.

"Yes, but what with appearances, Pierson couldn't leave her where she belonged."

"And where was that?"

"A sales rep! Sure, she did just fine. From the looks of it, she's doing passably well as sales manager, but to promote her to vice-president of sales! It's ludicrous!"

Elizabeth smiled at him. What poor Coy didn't know! She'd flown Melissa Graves to New York and met with her privately. What an earful she'd gotten after the woman had finally realized she could trust her. "I agree, Coy."

"Good. Now, we can go on to other matters. This situation at the Paris headquarters—"

"Actually," Elizabeth interrupted him smoothly, "I do agree that a vice-presidency for Melissa Graves isn't at all appropriate. Adrian, please check into Pierson's contract. I want him out by the end of the month. Melissa Graves will take his place."

Coy stared at her. His mouth worked, but nothing came out.

Elizabeth said very gently, "Coy, the woman is so talented it's frightening. She's been kept down because of that good-ole-boy network that's so alive and well, particularly in the South."

"You can't do that!"

Elizabeth merely smiled at him, then said very pleasantly, "I beg your pardon, Coy, but I can do just as I please. Don't you understand that yet?"

He didn't, obviously, and he shot an agonized look toward Adrian.

Adrian, wisely, just shrugged.

"Why don't you study her personnel file, Coy. I think you'll be quite surprised when you do, if, that is, you're willing to look at it objectively. And study Pierson's performance for the past year. I believe it was you who said the man was about as innovative as a cabbage. You said that to Adrian, but I overheard you say it. Then come back and give me your opinion."

Coy rose a bit unsteadily. He couldn't meet her eyes; he was too stunned, or perhaps he was too angry.

"I'll read the personnel files," he said, turned on his heel, and stalked toward the office door.

"Do also study the productivity records, Coy."

Adrian whistled, then waited silently until Coy was out of the office.

"Coy's older, Elizabeth. He's been, shall we say, insulated from everyday workings and progress. He's unused to dealing with women in business."

"Except for secretaries who bring him his coffee?"

"Don't be so rough on him. You've thrown him."

"I should hate to lose him, Adrian."

"I don't think it will come to that. And now, Elizabeth, would you like to go over the organization charts for the three companies we visited? See what level the women are at?"

"Yes, I would."

Jonathan Harley stared hard at his lawyer and longtime friend, Josh Simpson. "They want a meeting," he said.

"No harm in hearing what they have to say," Josh said.

"It's not really a *they*," Jonathan said, bitterness filling his voice. "It's a damned woman! Elizabeth Carleton. The one who murdered her husband!"

"I recall she was acquitted, nearly a year ago, in fact."

Jonathan snorted.

"That means not guilty, Jonathan, decided by twelve men and women. Jury trial and all that."

"I don't care if she killed ten men. I just don't want her killing what's mine."

"You could lose everything," Josh said gently. "Have you any idea of the wealth and power of ACI?"

"Yes. This woman, this Carleton broad, what is her role, exactly? I've heard rumors that she's well-ensconced."

"Did you read the article about a woman down in one of their Atlanta companies who will be promoted to the presidency? It seems that Elizabeth Carleton kicked out the man who was running things and put the woman in his place. She has plans for the women in the other ACI companies as well, from the scuttlebutt I've heard."

"The place will fold in six months," said Jonathan.

"Jonathan, you're only thirty-five years old. For heaven's sake, my boy, you grew up during the women's movement. You went to Yale with women! You were a freshman the first year women graduated, right? You shouldn't be spouting neolithic attitudes, for God's sake."

Jonathan set down his coffee cup. He felt so angry he wanted to hurl the cup against the wall. "I know," he said finally. "I don't really mean it. What I don't know is why they're coming after me."

"I can answer that easily enough. You're a success. They want to buy you out and keep you on as president. If that is your wish. You'll make so much money from the sale—if you decide to sell, that is—you could even go to California and start another electronics company."

"No."

Josh thumped his pencil up and down on the desk. "All right, then. I would recommend that at this initial meeting, you keep your anger to yourself. You know as well as I do that a poker face is more important in business than it is at five-card stud. The pot's much bigger."

"Do you think that woman will come?"

"Could be. You'd best play it very cool, Jonathan."

Jonathan cursed.

"Best moderate your language, old son."

13

Catherine Carleton pushed the buzzer. Her hands were sweaty.

On the second buzz, the door opened and an older woman, dressed in severe black, looked out at her.

"Yes, miss?"

"I'd like to see Mr. Chalmers."

"He's working out in that gym of his," said Mrs. O'Brien. "He never sees anybody when he's working out."

"It's very important," said Catherine, her chin up, her tone patrician. "I don't care to wait." It worked. Mrs. O'Brien quickly stepped back.

"Just tell me where he is and I'll announce myself."

Mrs. O'Brien pointed down a long corridor off the living room.

Catherine heard him grunting as he counted. She peered into the small gym, as well-fitted-out as her Uncle Michael's. Rowe Chalmers was flat on his back, on a bench, lifting weights. He was wearing nothing but a pair of blue gym shorts, and Catherine realized that he was very well-built.

"Mr. Chalmers," she said in a clear voice once he had reached the count of fifty.

Rowe sat up slowly, his eyes fixed on Catherine. He reached for a towel and wiped the perspiration from his face. He continued looking at her as he wiped off his chest. What did she want? He'd taken all he was going to take from the Carletons.

"Well?" His voice was cold.

Catherine stood her ground. "I wanted to speak to you, Mr. Chalmers."

" 'Mr. Chalmers' is it? How polite you are! No more 'stud' or any of your other complimentary names?"

"That's correct," Catherine said calmly.

"Talk, then. I can't very well throw out a Carleton, now, can I? At least for five minutes, and that's all you've got, lady."

She stood in the doorway of his gym, feeling wary, even frightened. But I have to know, she kept telling herself over and over. "May I sit down?"

"Sure." He waved toward a hard-backed chair some ten feet away from him.

Catherine walked to the chair and sat down, legs together, her hands folded over her purse on her lap.

"Well?"

She blurted out, "I understand you're getting married in a couple of weeks."

Rowe arched a dark eyebrow. "So, you can even read. Amazing. Maybe you didn't buy your way through Harvard after all."

She felt a flush of anger course over her cheeks. "I understand she's something of an heiress."

Rowe laughed. "If you're here representing your family's interests, Miss Carleton, I suggest that you leave right now. If you want to threaten to blackmail me with my fiancée, well, go ahead. I can't stop you. But Amanda knows all about my relationship with Elizabeth Carleton. Not the reasons for it, but certainly that I was sleeping with her."

"No," Catherine said. "I'm not here representing my family. In fact, I really didn't come to talk about your getting married. It just came out. Forgive me for being clumsy."

"What game is this?" Rowe rose, slung the towel over his shoulders, and walked toward Catherine.

"No game."

"Then what the hell do you want?"

"You don't have to be so rude!"

"Rude? To you, a blood-sucking Carleton? Why, bless my boots, I've offended a *lady*."

Catherine sucked in her breath, and with it, the scent of him, his sweat. "I'm here to talk about Elizabeth."

"You must know that I haven't seen Elizabeth in some time."

"Yes, I know."

"You were also at the family conclave when I told them it was all over between us."

"Do you know yet how she found out about you and your activities with us?"

"No, I don't. And frankly, I don't care, not anymore. In fact, I'm glad she found out. My life wasn't particularly pleasant during that time."

"You were making love to her, weren't you? Wasn't that pleasant?"

"Ah, now some cattiness from you." He shrugged. "You were making me wonder there for a while, with your Little Miss Sweetness and Humility act. Now you're back to being a selfish little bitch."

"Stop it!" Catherine jumped up from her chair. "You jerk, you got over three million dollars from us!"

"Yeah, and it wasn't enough."

"And that's why you're marrying this heiress!"

"Right again. Now, are you through?"

Catherine shook her head. She'd failed, she hadn't handled him right, not at all. He hated her and all her family, and she supposed she couldn't blame him. "Please," she said, putting her hand on his arm. "Elizabeth."

Rowe looked down at the white hand and its beautifully sculptured fingernails. "I have nothing to say about Elizabeth."

"Only one question, please."

He just looked at her.

"I remember once when you were at my grandmother's house, you said you believed Elizabeth was innocent. You believed that she hadn't killed my father. I must know, Mr. Chalmers—Rowe—did you truly believe what you said? Do you truly believe she didn't kill my father?"

He continued to look at her, no expression on his face. She saw a rivulet of sweat streak down his left cheek.

"I've got to know!"

Rowe said very quietly, "Yes, that's what I told you. That's what I truly believed."

"But now?" Catherine held her breath.

"Now," he said slowly, "now I don't know. I truly don't know."

"Why?"

He laughed, and strode away from her. He pointed to the door of the gym. "That, Miss Carleton, is none of your business. You're leaving now. Your five minutes are up."

"Yes," Catherine said. "I'm leaving. Thank you."

Rowe stared after her, not moving. Without meaning to, he lightly rubbed his fingers over his throat.

"A new patient, Dr. Hunter. A Miss Sarah Elliott. She wouldn't tell me why she wanted to see you."

"She's here?"

"Yes, Doctor."

Christian frowned at the intercom. "All right, I'll speak to her. Send her in, Mrs. Hightower."

But just for a moment, he decided. He didn't want any more patients. He was frankly growing bored with their problems. The door opened and Mrs. Hightower ushered in a slender young woman of medium height. She wore tinted glasses and her hair was short, black, and curly.

He rose. "Miss Elliott?"

"Yes." Her voice was soft and helpless.

"Please sit down."

Catherine sat down in the comfortable brown leather chair across from his desk. She searched his face for signs for recognition, but there weren't any. The black wig was obviously a good idea. He looked quite professional and his expression held just the right blend of detachment and concern.

"What may I do for you, Miss Elliott?"

"I used cocaine for some months and am having difficulty breaking away."

Christian said, his voice very cold, "I don't deal, Miss Elliott."

"No," she said quickly, leaning forward in the chair, "I know. I'm here for help. I haven't used coke for some time now, but I still have something of . . . well, I guess I'd call it a psychological addiction. Can you help me?"

Her clothes were rich, her accent declaring old money and lots of it. She was quite pretty, but too thin, the result of the coke, no doubt. Christian was perceptive about people, and rarely wrong. She was telling the truth about the cocaine. Rich little girl hooked on coke. He wondered how to get her out of his office.

"Look, Miss Elliott. I have more patients now than I can handle. However, I can send you to one of my colleagues, a very thorough and conscientious man. I think—" He broke off suddenly, staring at her face. It had crumpled, and tears were streaming down her cheeks.

"Miss Elliott, I . . . Here." He gave her his handkerchief.

She removed her glasses and he saw that her mascara was running. It was somehow endearing, and pathetic. No, he told himself firmly, you don't need this. Send her to Matthews.

Catherine blotted at her eyes, and saw the black on his handkerchief. She said, "I'm sorry. I can have it washed and will bring it back to you."

"It's no problem, I assure you. Keep it."

"It has your initials on it."

"Yes."

"Please don't make me leave, Dr. Hunter. I was told that you were the very best person in New York. Please, I need help."

Catherine nearly choked on the plea. Pleading with the man who had gotten Elizabeth off. Merciful heavens, she hated him!

Christian sat back in his chair, his fingers playing with a pencil. He watched her sniff just as a child would. She was younger than he'd originally thought. In her early twenties, he guessed.

"Your nose is bleeding," he said. For an instant she looked utterly stricken; then he watched her dab his handkerchief at her nose. "It will stop in a couple of months." At least it should, he thought. He had no idea of the magnitude of her addiction.

"I've ruined your handkerchief."

"It doesn't matter. Look, Miss Elliott, I really don't know what I could do for you. Truly, you already know the symptoms of quitting coke. Are you still having trouble sleeping?"

She nodded, and he saw the circles beneath her eyes.

"I wouldn't prescribe anything to help you sleep, you know. It's something you've got to do on your own. Basically, you've just got to hang in, and no more snorting. There are, of course, outpatient clinics for drug abuse."

"I know, it's just that I . . ."

"Yes?"

"My boyfriend was mur . . . arrested some weeks ago for dealing. I just don't know what to do." She kept her head down. She'd nearly blown it. Surely Dr. Christian Hunter had read about Chad.

My God, he thought, eyeing the pitiful young woman. He said matter-of-factly, "He was supplying you with the coke, I take it."

She nodded.

Christian sighed. "Very well, Miss Elliott. I agree that you need someone to talk to." He looked down at his appointment book. "Can you come in, say, tomorrow at ten o'clock?"

"Yes," Catherine said. "I can come." She rose at

the same time he did. They shook hands. "Thank you, Dr. Hunter."

He watched her walk from his office. A brief frown marred his features. Her walk was somehow familiar to him. But no, that wasn't possible. He'd never seen her in his life. And now he'd taken her on. He didn't think she would need much, just someone to listen. His role would be that of a priest, but he wouldn't have her kneeling in a church for hours as penance. He'd just charge her an immense fee for his time.

His intercom buzzed, and he picked up the phone. His heart began beating faster. It was Elizabeth on the line.

"I just wanted to tell you that I would be a bit late this evening, Christian."

"More long hours?"

He heard her sigh. "Yes, most of the time I love it, except when it interferes with other things I like equally well."

Like, not love. Well, he had to give her time. Her experience with Rowe Chalmers, coming so close on the heels of the trial had made her especially vulnerable and wary at the same time. But she had changed; he wasn't at all blind to it. She tried to keep the new and sometimes terrifying hardness from him, but it came through.

"Shall I pick you up at nine o'clock, then?"

"That would be just fine. Thank you, Christian, for being so understanding."

"My pleasure, Elizabeth." He hung up the phone. He should call Susan and tell her he would be late. He prayed that she wouldn't play "When You Wish Upon a Star" for him again. It was in the key of F, just one flat, and she never could remember it.

Elizabeth flew with Adrian and Coy to Philadelphia early on a Friday morning. Her private jet was met by a black limousine. She said nothing on their thirty-minute drive to Jonathan Harley's offices in downtown Philadelphia. She was reviewing in her mind what she knew of the man. He was recently divorced. It had been a very acrimonious divorce. He'd grown up poor, attended Yale on an athletic scholarship, married a very wealthy Philadelphia socialite, the daughter of Andrew Pillson, and made his millions in the subsequent years. He was smart, ruthless, cunning, and in his mid-thirties. She'd seen a photo of him. He looked hard as nails. Perhaps it was because he was so dark. His hair was as black as her onyx ring. Looking at that photo, she'd felt some pity for his wife.

Elizabeth couldn't wait to meet him.

Midge looked up at the trio coming into the executive offices. She was angry and nervous and her eyes went immediately to the woman flanked by the two men. Elizabeth Carleton. The woman who had so much money she couldn't begin to throw it away, the woman who wanted to destroy Jonathan and all he'd built.

She forced herself to say politely, "Yes?"

Elizabeth said, "I'm Elizabeth Carleton, here to see Mr. Harley."

Midge forced herself to rise from her chair. "If you'll be seated for a moment." She quietly opened the door to Jonathan's office and slipped in, closing the door behind her.

"She did come," Midge said. "She's got two men with her."

He looked so tired, she thought, waiting patiently for him to say something.

Jonathan rose from his chair, automatically straightening his tie. He managed to give Midge a crooked smile. "Please don't spit on her Gucci shoes. You might as well send them in."

She was beautiful, he admitted, but otherwise she appeared just as he had believed she would. Cold, hard, dressed severely in a light gray wool suit, the jacket buttoned over a pale blue silk blouse. She looked very self-possessed. Hard to believe that she'd been a musician such a short time ago. He couldn't imagine her seated at a piano, belting out Mozart.

"Mr. Harley," Elizabeth said, nodding her head only slightly before accepting his outstretched hand.

"Mrs. Carleton," he said, releasing her expensively gloved hand very quickly.

"This is Adrian Marsh and Coy Siverston."

The men greeted each other, if not warmly, at least civilly.

Jonathan waved toward the circular conference table. "Please sit down. Midge, could we have some coffee?"

"Sure thing," Midge said.

Elizabeth's eyes followed Midge, unconsciously assessing her. Her eyes were intelligent. She was also very pretty, and obviously loyal to Jonathan Harley. She finally turned her attention to Jonathan Harley. He and Coy were discussing golf, and she waited patiently for the man talk that seemed to begin every meeting to run its course. But no, they had to have a couple of minutes to discuss the wretched season the Steelers had endured, and their chances for next season.

Midge came back in carrying a beautiful silver tray with fine china cups and a silver coffeepot.

Am I supposed to pour, Elizabeth wondered, while the men continue with their important sports talk? But Midge did that job, quietly and quickly. Elizabeth saw the woman look a bit furtively toward her boss, and wondered if they were lovers. The woman's eyes held concern and worry. Elizabeth realized she was applying a male standard, and felt ashamed. Perhaps Adrian looked at her that way—with concern and worry.

Elizabeth took a sip of her coffee, then rattled her cup just a bit back onto its saucer. She said, her voice cool, very contained, "Gentlemen, shall we begin?"

Jonathan had been aware of her every expression as he put in his mandatory two cents about football. He realized with a spurt of anger that she was amused at their talk, as if they were little boys eager to impress each other. Hell, how else to keep the room from being utterly silent while each person was casing the others? He'd sometimes thought that God had created sports just for this purpose.

He sat back in his chair, automatically assuming his most powerful pose, his legs stretched out in front of him, crossed at the ankles, his arms crossing his chest. "Begin with what, precisely, ma'am?"

Elizabeth knew he hadn't wanted to have anything to do with ACI, but his arrogance made her tense. "You agreed to meet with me, with us, Mr. Harley. Do you normally conduct meetings when you don't know the objective?"

"I would imagine, ma'am, that our objectives are diametrically opposed."

"Actually, Mr. Harley," Coy said quickly, wondering at Elizabeth's unwarranted attack, "we're pleased that you agreed to see us. We've been very impressed with your handling of Harley Electronics—"

Jonathan interrupted him smoothly. "My *handling*, Siverston? You make it sound like I'm some bright president put in charge by a board of directors. This is my company and my handling of my company is impressive because it's mine."

"Not entirely, Mr. Harley," Elizabeth said.

"Ah, yes, I know that Rose sold you some stock. But not enough, ma'am. Not enough."

Adrian entered the fray, sitting forward, his face intense. "Mr. Harley, as you know, ACI is a tremendously profitable company—"

"Don't you mean conglomerate? Innumerable holding companies? So many swallowed companies—merged or just plain acquired—that you don't even know the extent of them?"

"I assure you, Mr. Harley," Elizabeth said, her voice like ice, "that we know and manage and provide support and capital to each and every one of our companies. ACI isn't a monster swallowing up the world. Under our ageis, your company will not only expand, you will realize more profits than you could possibly imagine."

"No way, lady," he said before he could stop himself.

"Also," Elizabeth continued, ignoring him, "you must realize that we would like to buy your company outright."

"No way, lady," he said again, this time because he wanted to. He saw her lips purse, and it pleased him.

"Of course, if you didn't wish to give up your company outright, I'm certain we could work out a very advantageous contract with you. As Mr. Marsh said, we're impressed with your—"

"No way, lady," he said, interrupting her. He liked the refrain. It was making her mad as hell. People said things when they were angry, made mistakes.

"Don't you wish to know what our offer is?"

"No."

"Mr. Harley," Coy said, "if you don't wish to sell outright, perhaps we can convince you that a . . . ah, coming-together with ACI really is in your best interests. Please allow me to enumerate the advantages."

Coy pulled a bound notebook from his briefcase and proceeded to enumerate, very completely, very thoroughly. Jonathan Harley appeared to listen to him carefully, but his face was an expressionless mask, his body perfectly still.

Elizabeth watched his eyes for some clue to his thoughts. She saw nothing. He was rude, she thought, rude and crude and hard as nails. And he disliked her personally. She wasn't stupid, and it wasn't just because he didn't want to sell to ACI. It was probably because he hadn't ever had to deal with a woman before and he believed it beneath him. *Or because he believes you are a murderess.*

Or a combination of the two.

She shook her head and tried to pay attention to Coy.

Her eyes kept straying back to Jonathan Harley. The man appeared to be carved in stone, she thought. He was large—she hadn't realized how large a man he was until he'd shaken her hand and she'd had to crane her neck upward to his face. She imagined that intimidation was one of his favorite tactics. She had met several high-powered executives who used their size to their advantage. Except they had treated her like a delicate little doll, their subtle condescension making her grit her teeth. Of course, she had been *their* boss.

She didn't know if she preferred outright rudeness to condescension.

Coy wound to a halt. Still Jonathan Harley said not a word. Adrian immediately filled the gap, only to be interrupted by Harley. "I should like some more coffee, I think. All that talk has made me thirsty. Ma'am?"

Elizabeth stared at him and at his outstretched coffee cup. The silver tray wasn't within easy reach, and he expected her to serve him! She drew on the control she'd learned over the past months. "Adrian," she said politely, "Coy, would you two please leave us alone for a moment?"

Adrian shot her a concerned frown, but Coy merely nodded. Both men left the office.

Elizabeth waited until they'd closed the office door behind them. "I'm not a servant, Mr. Harley," she said.

He said very deliberately, "You're a woman, aren't you?" He watched her eyes narrow with anger. He'd scored a big point, but he wasn't pleased with his approach. Still, he guessed it was the way to treat her, to keep her off balance.

"I suggest, Mr. Harley, that if you wish more coffee, you buzz for your own private servant."

"Midge isn't a servant, private or otherwise."

She'd shaken him just a bit, she thought. His voice was clipped, cold, but his expression was still impassive.

"No, perhaps she isn't. She is probably too bright to do more than she has to with her boss."

"Look, lady—"

"My name is Elizabeth Carleton."

"Yes, I know. Elizabeth X."

She flinched, hearing the awful label the media had

pinned on her. He saw it and she saw that he saw it. He sat back in his chair again, fully in control of the situation. She wanted to scream at him, but knew she couldn't. She managed to say calmly, "Do you normally resort to sexism when confronted with women, Mr. Harley?"

"I don't deal with women," he said, and there was disdain in his voice.

"I see. They have no place in the business world?"

"You got it, lady . . . Mrs. Carleton. As I understand it, you didn't know how to balance a checkbook before your husband's untimely death." If he'd been in her shoes, he'd have killed anyone for that remark. He waited, seeing what she'd do, what she'd say.

"He was murdered, Mr. Harley. You needn't be sarcastic. I find your behavior quite inappropriate."

"Tough shit. You're playing in the big league now. Get used to it."

Elizabeth said very softly, "Mr. Harley, you haven't any idea of what the big league is. Your company is nothing more than a goldfish, and the tank you're swimming about in doesn't compare favorably to the ocean, which is ACI."

"Your simile sucks," Jonathan said.

"And your language is fit for the streets!"

"I'm certain you heard much worse during your trial."

She jerked back, and he saw the wasteland of pain in her eyes. For the first time, she was human, and it bothered him. He couldn't weaken, wouldn't weaken. She was the barracuda in her damned ocean. He said with deliberate cruelty, "I also understand that you have been seeing a great deal of Dr. Christian Hunter—after a suitable amount of time since the trial had elapsed, of course."

"You know nothing about anything, Mr. Harley."

He disliked the quivering in her voice, but he was swift to move in on the kill. He'd found a major weakness and he had to take full advantage of it. "Of course," he continued, his voice bland, "no one can figure out just how you managed to bribe the good millionaire doctor. Did you promise to be his lover? It would appear to be the case now. I trust you're excellent in bed, ma'am, for he took an awful risk in saving your hide."

Elizabeth closed her eyes a moment. Why was she so surprised at his tactics? It was the big league, hardball, only this was the first time that it wasn't *her* big league and her rules. Damn him! He was nothing!

She heard him continue, his voice taunting now and very soft, "Of course you had to wait a goodly amount of time, didn't you?" He sat forward. "As I recall, you hopped into bed with Rowen Chalmers immediately. Marriage to an old man for three years must have left you pretty horny. Unable to wait it out, Mrs. Carleton?"

I mustn't let him continue. I mustn't let him do this to me!

"Mr. Harley," she said, pleased at the smoothness of her voice, "I am here to conduct business with you, not to listen to your stupid, senseless insults. Now, I am prepared to pay you two hundred million for your company."

"No way, lady."

"Your refrain is becoming as boring as your insults, Mr. Harley."

"You're right," he said, smiling, a cruel, cold smile. "Nor is my refrain at all accurate. Let me try again: No way, bitch."

Elizabeth rose slowly from her chair, leaned forward, pressing her palms against the tabletop. "I will ruin you, Mr. Harley. I will take your company and I will personally see you in the gutter."

He didn't move, and his smile widened. "Ah, you plan to murder me as well, ma'am?"

She couldn't help herself. She picked up her cup of coffee and flung it at him. Unfortunately, she thought blankly as she watched the coffee splash onto his neck and the front of his suit, it wasn't hot enough.

He calmly picked up a napkin and began to mop himself off. "This is one reason I don't deal with women," he said, not bothering to look at her. "So emotional, so little control."

"You would drive all control from the devil himself!"

"You've dealt with the devil," he said, looking at her now, "so I guess you would know. What, ma'am, you can't find anything else to throw at me? Good, now, may I escort you out of *my* office?"

Oddly enough, in that moment Elizabeth realized what she'd done and how he'd outflanked her. She even smiled at him, and was pleased to see him start in surprise. She said very softly, "No, Mr. Harley, you needn't show me out. I know the way. I fancy that when I have your office refurnished, I'll leave the coffee stains in the carpet. They look almost as satisfying on the carpet as they do on your shirt."

She picked up her purse and walked to the door. She turned at the door. "I'll see you ruined, Mr. Harley. As you so accurately pointed out, this is the big league. Good day. Perhaps it will be your last."

"I doubt that," he called after her. "Two can play the same game, though I doubt it'll be much sport with a woman."

14

Elizabeth said nothing, merely nodded to Adrian and Coy. They left the office in silence.

Adrian cleared his throat to speak once they were in the limousine.

"We'll go home," Elizabeth said, forestalling him, her voice clipped.

"Yes," said Coy. "I suppose we should."

An hour later Elizabeth watched Philadelphia fade away below them.

"Elizabeth."

Unfastening her seat belt, she turned to face Adrian.

"Would you like to tell us what happened?"

"Mr. Harley plays hardball, that's all. He plays with great panache and cruelty."

"Oh," said Coy.

"You shouldn't have sent us out," said Adrian.

"I have the feeling it wouldn't have mattered to Mr. Harley one way or the other. Now, gentlemen, how do we get hold of his company and ruin him in the bargain?"

Adrian said, "He owns, as you know, Elizabeth, fifty-one percent of the stock. He has a completely free hand with his board. No matter how much we buy, we can't change that. We can force a seat on his board, hassle him somewhat, but that's about it."

Elizabeth fell into deep thought. She said finally, just as they were nearing New York, "I want a thorough analysis on all Mr. Harley's financial dealings.

As both of you have taught me, we need leverage. Find it for me."

"Elizabeth," Coy said, leaning forward, "why can't we just forget him and his damned company? There are others, perhaps not as profitable, not as stable, but who cares? We can bring in our own management team and solve any problems. Harley's little. He doesn't matter."

A goldfish. "No," she said, "I want Harley's company. No other."

Coy and Adrian exchanged glances.

Catherine didn't see the proverbial couch in Dr. Christian Hunter's plush office. She sat down in the brown leather chair that faced his desk.

"Miss Elliott," he said. "How are you feeling this morning?" He was leaning slightly forward, all his professional attention focused on her. He wasn't at all stupid. But then again, she would tell him the truth; there was no reason not to.

"Awful," she said.

"You had difficulty sleeping last night?"

She nodded.

"Tell me about the man who was arrested, the man you were close to."

Well, most of the truth. "His name's not important. He's a pretty small-time drug dealer, as I understand it. Actually, he was using me. I was paying his way and he provided me with first-class coke."

Christian noticed that her nose was running. She sniffed often.

"How do you feel about that? About being used by him?"

Catherine paused, feeling hurt and confusion wash over her. "I didn't mind, not at first."

"Do you have a photo of this man?"

"Why, yes, I do." Catherine rummaged through her wallet and extracted a small photo of Chad. His picture had never been in the papers. Thank God she wasn't in the picture. She handed it to Dr. Hunter.

A stud, Christian thought, silently studying the photo. An arrogant, free-meal-ticket stud. "Did your family know about him, Miss Elliott?"

"No, I don't think so. I'm not really sure."

She was lying; Christian knew it. But he gave no indication. It would take time for her to trust him. He still wasn't certain that he wanted to give her that time. He handed her the photo, but she shook her head. He arched an eyebrow in question, and she looked at the wastebasket. Christian slowly shredded the photo and tossed the pieces away.

"A good start. Now, let's talk about your family, Miss Elliott. Tell me about your father."

"He's dead."

"I see. How long ago did he die?"

"A long time ago."

Lying again. "And your mother?"

"She's living in London. At least the last time I heard, she was."

"You aren't close to your mother?"

"No. My father divorced her and paid her off. She left me."

"The family money is all on your father's side?"

"Yes."

"Were you hooked on cocaine before you met your boyfriend?"

"No."

"Why him? You are a lovely young woman, Miss Elliott. Why, understanding this man as you obviously do, did you allow yourself to become involved with him?"

A good question, Catherine thought. Too good. She thought about it honestly. "I was bored and I wanted my fa . . . I wanted to experience new things."

She tried not to show her chagrin at her near-slip. Dr. Hunter appeared not to have noticed. He left the subject of the boyfriend and asked questions about her childhood. Those weren't difficult, and she wasn't aware that Christian Hunter was busily storing away the subtle information she was unaware of providing him.

He seemed to have no particular direction in mind, and the fifty minutes passed quickly, too quickly for Catherine. She realized as she stood and shook his hand that she wanted to see him again, soon. She was appalled at herself. After all, this was the man who had gotten Elizabeth off. This was the man who, for whatever reason, had saved her father's murderess.

"Next Tuesday, Miss Elliott?"

"Yes, yes, that's fine," Catherine said. Tuesday, she thought. Then she would begin to ask him questions, learn about him. She'd catch him out; she knew she could do it.

Christian watched her walk from his office, and again he frowned. Something so familiar about her walk, her carriage. He prided himself on his memory, on his ability to perceive details that escaped others.

The fifty minutes had been interesting, once he'd realized he was following her through a maze of lies. He pulled his notebook toward him and began to write.

Laurette studied her granddaughter. She seemed less jumpy, less gaunt. There was a new purpose about her, but Laurette knew it wasn't a healthy purpose.

She said without preamble, "Why are you seeing Dr. Christian Hunter?"

Catherine's jaw dropped. "H-how do you know about that?"

"I've been worried about you, my dear, and—"

"Ha! You're afraid I'll try to buy coke, aren't you? My God, you've had me followed!"

Laurette was unruffled. "That's right. It's for your own good. Now, tell me why you're seeing Christian Hunter, and in a black wig."

Catherine's chin went up. "I need professional help and he's one of the best in the city."

"You're a terrible liar, my dear. Leave it, Catherine. Keep away from the man. He's not stupid. He will reveal nothing to you. Surely you must realize that?"

Catherine rose from her chair and walked to the fireplace. There were only glowing embers now and she felt the mild warmth flush her face. It was thirty degrees outside, the sky full of snow. She leaned down and added more logs.

"Catherine?"

She rose, dusted off her hands, then turned slowly to face her grandmother. "I'll find out the truth from him, Grandmother. He may not be stupid, but then again, neither am I."

"Of course you know that he is now seeing Elizabeth?"

"I do read the society page."

"That is the answer, of course. He's in love with her, and that's the reason he lied for her in court."

"Then he's a fool," Catherine said, her voice shrill.

"Hush, my dear. Ah, here are Jennifer and Brad. Come in. We'll have tea now."

Jennifer felt shy and tongue-tied around the Carleton matriarch, as her father called Mrs. Carleton. Nonetheless, she walked forward and planted a kiss on the old lady's parchment cheek.

"You're looking lovely, Jennifer. My grandson still amuses you?"

"Oh, yes," Jenny blurted out. She looked at Brad, flushing.

"Hello, brother," Catherine said.

"Catherine."

"How's your father, Jenny?" Catherine asked to fill the silence.

Brad's eyes flew to his grandmother's face, but her expression of benign affection never wavered.

"He's fine, just fine. Very busy, of course."

"Senator Henkle is a . . . very intelligent man," said Laurette.

If Jenny noticed the oddness of Mrs. Carleton's remark, she didn't show it. Indeed, she was too eager to please this awesome old lady. She slipped her hand into Brad's and sighed with relief when he squeezed her fingers.

"Jenny and I are off to the Nelsons'," Brad said with ill-disguised boredom. "A party, of course."

"If you'd rather not go, Brad . . ." Jenny said, her voice tentative, and Catherine wanted to snort in disgust. Jennifer Henkle was a damned wimp! Brad was already walking all over her.

"No, we must go, Jenny."

"Whatever you wish, Brad," she said, her glowing eyes resting on his face.

Lord, it was nauseating, Catherine thought. Brad and Jenny left soon and she was once again alone with her grandmother.

"The girl will be a fine addition to the family," Laurette said complacently.

"She's a weak-willed bore!"

Laurette briefly thought of those photographs of Jenny and Brad in bed, then unconsciously shook her head to clear away the images.

"She suits Brad just fine. Now, my dear, back to you. I want you to stop seeing Christian Hunter."

"Will you continue to have me followed if I do?"

"Yes," Laurette said, "yes, I will."

Catherine looked at her for a long moment, then shook her head. "I hope you're not paying your detectives too much, Grandmother. I will keep seeing Christian Hunter."

"You're a fool, Catherine. What will happen, do you think, when he discovers who you really are? And he will, my dear. Indeed, he will."

Catherine shrugged. "If he does find out, what does it matter? All he can do is kick me out of his office."

"Perhaps I should call him myself. Tell him about his patient. I imagine that would put an end to it."

Catherine's jaw tightened in anger. Before she could say anything, Laurette sighed. "My dear, you're so very stubborn. You get that from me, I suppose."

Catherine recognized the olive branch and said, "Very well, Grandmother, I'll think about it, I promise."

*   *   *

"Well, Elizabeth, here's your leverage."

She'd just walked into Adrian's office, and she stopped cold. "So soon, Adrian?"

"It wasn't at all difficult, so I can't take much credit. Harley borrowed ten million dollars not long ago. It's a three-month loan with a thirty-day call-in, but there's every reason to assume that he can get as many extensions as he wants or needs."

She felt a rush of triumph. "That's excellent!"

"He's using the money to buy up more stock, bringing him near to sixty percent, and of course, for his expansion plans."

"Get the loan, Adrian."

"Ah, there's the rub. His banker is a longtime personal friend."

"I'm learning," Elizabeth said slowly, "that money tends to neutralize friendship. What would we have to offer to get hold of it?"

"I don't know. Ben Hallimer is the one who knows everything about banks. I'll have to discuss it with him."

"You do that, Adrian," she said, and gave him a dazzling smile.

In fact, it was Christian Hunter who told her how to go about it, that evening when they were sitting in a small bar near Lincoln Center. She'd asked him merely a hypothetical question.

But Christian wasn't fooled. At least she'd begun to really trust him, he thought. That was an excellent sign, given what Rowe Chalmers had done to her.

". . . So you see, Elizabeth, all you have to do is hook up with the chairman of the board at the Philadelphia bank. You did say Philadelphia, didn't you? It's very probable that he is one of the close-knit business group. Probably on the ACI board, if he's big enough. There's always tremendous crossover, of course. He can have the board agree to sell the loan, at a reasonable profit, of course. It's not done often, usually because it doesn't come up. But the purpose of banks is not to help people, Elizabeth. Their purpose is like anybody else's—to make money."

Elizabeth was so excited she couldn't sleep. She remembered every cruel thing Jonathan Harley had said to her. Everything. Now he would learn that she was indeed a barracuda.

"I know, Elizabeth," Christian said into the phone the following morning, "that the question you asked me was purely hypothetical. However, if this Philadelphia bank just happens to be the First People's Bank, the chairman of the board is Rory Cox, a mean old curmudgeon whose son just happened to marry my first cousin. It also just so happens," he continued smoothly, "that I'm on his board of directors."

She couldn't believe it. She expelled a deep sigh of triumph. "Christian, thank you. I don't—"

"Would you like me to do any more, Elizabeth?"

She thought furiously, memories of Rowe making her cold and wary. But Christian was different. If anyone was using anyone else, it was she using him. No, that was ridiculous. If he were like Rowe, he could bring down the whole deal. "I need to think about it, Christian."

"All right," he said easily. "Just let me know. In the meantime, I'll see what else I can find out about the bank."

"Thank you, Christian. I really appreciate it—you're a very dear friend."

Friend. He winced a bit at that bland word, not at all how he wanted her to think about him. Time, he thought again; it would simply take time. He was a patient man, he always had been, but it was becoming more and more difficult.

On Tuesday morning Jonathan Harley faced his friend in his sterile office at the First People's Bank.

"What's cooking, Del? Why all the urgency?"

Delbert wouldn't meet his eyes. "It's about your loan, Jonathan."

"What about it? I've another month or so to go on

it before we renegotiate. Probably I'll want another six months."

Delbert Frazier felt like shit. He didn't know whose feathers Jonathan had ruffled, but they were undoubtedly very powerful feathers, and there was nothing he could do about it. He couldn't think of a way to soften the blow, so he said, "The bank sold your loan."

Jonathan grew very still. "You don't mean it," he said, staring vaguely at the marble paperweight on Del's desk.

"I'm afraid I do mean it. The terms are the same, of course, but as for any renegotiations . . ." He shrugged. He could have easily added, "But I wouldn't count on it, good buddy."

"Who?" Jonathan asked, but he knew. God, he knew. It had been less than a week. Big-league, hell! He suddenly pictured the coffee stain on his carpet. He wanted to kill Elizabeth Carleton.

"It's kind of weird, really," Del said, frowning slightly. "There was lots of pressure, but in the end, an Elizabeth Carleton personally bought the loan. Look, Jonathan, I would have warned you, but I didn't know, not until this morning, when old man Cox called me himself."

"I know," said Jonathan. He forced a smile at his old friend. "I know."

"If there's anything I can do, Jonathan . . ."

His mind felt like a vast wasteland with nothing at all in it.

"There are other banks, you know. It's possible that you could fix up another loan and pay this one off to this Carleton woman when it comes due."

"Yes, it's possible." But she could find out who and buy that one too. He had to think of something!

"What are you going to do?"

Jonathan rose from the soft, cracked leather chair. "I'm going to New York," he said.

Jonathan left the bank, returned home, and changed into his running clothes. He ran until he was too exhausted to move. He made it to his office at one in the afternoon.

"You want me to *what*?"

Midge's horrified voice made him smile. He repeated, "Call Elizabeth Carleton. Make me an appointment with her as soon as possible."

Millicent Stacy poked her head into Elizabeth's office. "A quick question, Elizabeth. Would you like to see a Jonathan Harley of Philadelphia tomorrow?"

Elizabeth didn't realize how much she'd been waiting for him to get in touch with her. Well, he'd only just found out. He wasn't a man to mull about for hours and hours. "No, Mrs. Stacy. Not tomorrow. I will see him on Friday, here at . . . let's say ten o'clock."

Let the cruel jerk sweat, she thought, and broke her pencil neatly into two pieces. She'd force him to mull.

"Not until Friday, boss," Midge said.

Jonathan didn't say a word for many moments. Finally, "I suppose I'd do the same thing to her. It's all right, Midge. Please make reservations for me."

"So," Elizabeth said to Christian, curling her legs beneath her on the sofa and turning to face him, "tell me about any new patients you have. Anything horrifying? Anything truly marvelous?"

"Not really. I've got a new patient—a young woman who was hooked on drugs—but she's not all that interesting. She's a liar, but that aspect just keeps me on my toes. It also made me make another appointment with her."

"Why does she lie to you? That seems like a waste of money to me. Why lie to your shrink?"

"You've got me. She'll come clean soon, though, I think. Most patients do. Now, my dear, do tell me what happened with that Philadelphia bank business of yours."

Elizabeth was silent for a moment, and Christian saw her expression change subtly, her eyes narrow a bit, her lips thin. He didn't like it, but didn't know what he could do about it.

"Everything is going just as I want it to," she said finally, and smiled.

"When, I wonder, will you be ready for a well-deserved vacation?"

"Ah, a good question. Actually, I'm having so much . . . well, not fun precisely, but I'm learning so much, and the power, Christian, the power of it all!" She unconsciously touched her hand to his arm in her excitement. "I promoted another woman, a real find, in a shoe company of all places. In the Midwest, Cleveland to be exact. She's loaded with talent and drive. If she does well there, I'm thinking of bringing her to New York."

"What do all your gentlemen think about your own private women's movement?"

"They just sigh now, no more arguments, no more fighting. But local management . . . well, the good ole boys hate it, as you can imagine."

"And you love to rub their noses in it."

She looked up at him, her expression sharp. "You're being a shrink, Christian."

"Sorry, my dear." His eyes fell a moment to her breasts, cleanly outlined against the softness of her dress. He wanted her so much it hurt.

"Rowe Chalmers is getting married in less than two weeks," Elizabeth said.

"Yes, I read about it," he said easily, but he was watching her closely. "It promises to be quite a shindig."

Elizabeth was wondering what the Carletons thought about it. She wondered if Laurette or Michael still had anything on Rowe. It would be their style to blow the whistle at the last moment. He deserved anything he got, she thought. She'd been tempted to send his very rich fiancée a letter, but didn't, of course.

Catherine Carleton didn't intend to blow the whistle, not precisely. But she was on a plane to Boston Friday morning. She had to see Rowe Chalmers.

15

Jonathan was exhausted, both physically and mentally. He'd been working out like a crazy man, then thinking just as hard. He stared out of the taxi window as the cabbie weaved in and out of haphazard traffic down Park Avenue. It was a damp, drizzily day, cold as hell, and it reflected his mood, unfortunately.

He had to do it just right. There was no more room for error. He admitted to himself, finally, that he'd made a gross mistake treating Elizabeth Carleton as he had. He'd hit her weaknesses sure enough, but in the process, he'd earned her revenge. Now he had to find just the right approach, the middle ground. Somehow.

He paid the cabdriver and got out. He found himself staring up at the impressive Abercrombie-Carleton Building and counting all those columns. He made his way through the lobby to the executive elevator, which went straight to the top floor.

The elevator doors opened directly onto an immense reception hall decorated with a melange of antiques and furnishings so modern that it should have looked bizarre. But it didn't. It looked rich, so rich that for a moment he felt tremendous doubt. He felt like the goldfish who just got dropped into the ocean.

A smiling young woman took his name, checked it against a list, then directed him down a plush corridor. He came finally into a large office at the end of the hall. An older woman, whose wooden name plate read "Millicent Stacy," rose to greet him.

"Mr. Harley?"

Her voice was smooth and kind. So, he thought, Elizabeth Carleton hadn't told her about him, the insulting male chauvinist pig from Philadelphia.

"Yes. I'm here to see Mrs. Carleton."

Millicent knew who he was, of course. She recognized the dazed look in his eyes—she'd seen it many times before when a man from one of the ACI companies paid his first visit here. Intimidation, pure and simple. The seat of power. The seat of unbelievable power.

"Please sit down a moment, Mr. Harley. I'll tell Mrs. Carleton you're here."

He sat down on what he thought was an antique French chair, praying that it would hold his weight. It did. He didn't know there were steel braces ensuring that no one could wreck the valuable chair. He picked up an annual report of ACI from beside him. No, he thought after thumbing through a few very glossy, well-designed pages, I won't look at it.

I've got to do it right this time.

Millicent reappeared after a moment. She gave him her motherly smile. "Won't you please go in, Mr. Harley? I'll bring you coffee and Danish. Will that be all right?"

He nodded, his mind racing ahead. He drew a deep breath, squared his shoulders, and walked into Elizabeth Carleton's office. It took him but a moment to realize that three of his offices could fit into this one. It was like an immaculate throne room. God, the sheer cost! His shoes made no sound as he strode across the carpeting so thick he was an inch shorter.

"Mr. Harley."

He met Elizabeth Carleton's eyes, and nodded. She looked more severe, more formal even than she had in Philadelphia, in an unrelieved blue wool suit. Her blond hair was drawn back from her fine-boned face into a tight chignon. Especially for him? She wanted to erase any thought he might have that she was a woman? He wanted to tell her that despite her man-tailored suit, she looked very much a woman, but too thin.

"Hello, Mrs. Carleton," he said. She motioned him to an oversize leather chair and seated herself at the table opposite him.

"Was your flight pleasant, Mr. Harley?"

No golf or football talk, he thought, and smiled just a bit. "Quite pleasant, Mrs. Carleton."

"Unfortunately, our winter weather is in perfect form today."

"It's the same in Philadelphia."

"Ah, here's our coffee."

"Black, please," Jonathan said to Millicent Stacy. He shook his head at the offer of a Danish.

Millicent gave him a very understanding look, and he wished he'd taken three Danishes.

He sipped the rich black coffee. It was delicious. Did ACI also own a Jamaican coffee plantation?

"You're here because I now own your loan, isn't that right, Mr. Harley?"

Fine, he thought, let her gloat, let her think she was winning, that she had won.

"Yes, of course," he said.

"I believe you have seven weeks left, Mr. Harley. Then, of course, I will expect repayment. No extensions."

"I didn't expect that there would be."

"Then why did you come?"

He didn't answer immediately, but just continued sipping on his coffee. Elizabeth found, oddly, that she wasn't enjoying herself as much as she'd thought she would. Jonathan Harley looked exhausted. She saw a few gray hairs at his temples that she hadn't noticed at their first meeting. He was dressed beautifully, though, in a three-piece charcoal-gray suit, Savile Row, she recognized. His silk tie had a conservative print, setting it off nicely against a shirt of pristine white. She waited patiently for him to begin pleading with her, begging. Surely she would enjoy that!

"I came to tell you that I will sell you my company

at the time my loan comes due, if, of course, I'm unable to repay the loan."

"Ah." He'd succumbed, completely. No wallowing in front of her.

"I agree that it's a wise course for you to take, Mr. Harley. However, I should like the sale to go through immediately."

No way, lady!

"I don't think so, Mrs. Carleton," he said easily. "I'm not ready to throw in the towel just yet. I assume you can understand that?"

"Yes, I can. However, it is quite clear, from looking over your financial obligations, that you won't have the money when I call in the loan. Your expansion plans are draining you. Your market hasn't expanded to the degree that you wish—"

"It will."

"—and you're on the verge of having some union problems."

"True. You're remarkably well-informed, ma'am." He looked around him. If he could sell the furnishings in her damned office, he would probably be well on his way to clearing away his financial problems.

"Of course." She wanted to keep her control, keep herself utterly calm and professional . . . well, perhaps rub it in just a little bit. He'd been way out of line, cruel, incredibly mean.

"So," he said, looking directly into her eyes, "where do we stand now?"

"I don't think you're standing at all, Mr. Harley," she said, allowing just a bit of malice to creep into her voice.

He felt his collar tighten, really felt it choking him. He supposed, objectively, that he'd earned it. He watched her pick up a gold pen and gracefully fiddle with it. He watched her mouth as she continued, "Actually, Mr. Harley, I'm tempted to come down quite a bit on the offer I originally made you. Made you in good faith, if you will recall."

"I wasn't terribly polite to you. It was wrong of me."

How odd that it didn't sound at all like an apology. His words sounded rehearsed.

"No, it wasn't right of you. May I ask the reason for your behavior, Mr. Harley? Why you attacked me personally, with such . . . contempt?"

"I don't want to sell my company, not to anybody. It's mine, always has been. I would have been equally rude to God himself."

"I see."

"Perhaps you do."

"I didn't kill my husband, Mr. Harley." The instant the words were out of her mouth, Elizabeth started, aghast at herself. She hadn't meant to say anything of the kind to this man. She felt as though she'd just received a tremendous physical blow, only this time she'd inflicted it herself.

"The jury agreed with you," he said, shrugging. But he was looking at her closely, realizing that her words had slipped out, and wondering why. Again, briefly, she was a human being, real, too real, and he felt uncomfortable. He had to put her back in her ocean and let her assume her barracuda guise once more.

Well, Elizabeth thought, she'd begun it, she should finish it. "No, actually the jury believed Dr. Christian Hunter. And he's not my lover."

Again, she'd startled him. Why was she saying these things? He had no idea how to respond, except to apologize, which he did reluctantly. "Perhaps he's not. I shouldn't have attacked you in that way." He forced a smile. "Actually, ma'am, I'm usually not the brutal chauvinist I appeared. As I said, I would have in all likelihood been cruel to God himself."

Stop it, Elizabeth! For God's sake, finish him off! She knew a real apology when she heard it, but she ignored it. Her voice was controlled, utterly calm again. "Now, Mr. Harley, back to business. You're refusing to sell to me immediately?"

"Yes, I am."

"My offer will go down each week that you delay."

He shrugged. "That's your decision, ma'am."

"There's another thing, Mr. Harley, that you must understand completely. I now have a bit of knowledge of companies that don't wish to be bought. They try to find a white knight, I believe it's called. Another buyer—"

"I understand the terminology, Mrs. Carleton."

"Yes," she said. "Well, what I will offer you is this: if you sign a legal agreement that if you cannot repay the loan you will sell your company to me—and no one else—in return, I will leave the original offer intact."

"And if I refuse?"

"I assure you, Mr. Harley, that I will know every move you make. If you try to find some other company with which you can merge, for example, I'll find out about it and I'll destroy you."

"That's very plain talking," he said, his voice still calm, controlled. He could break her so easily, at least physically. That thought shook him a bit. Physical dominance was abhorrent to him, yet this damned woman made him want to choke her with his bare hands. He looked at the high-neck cream blouse she was wearing and wanted to laugh at himself. He wondered briefly why she wasn't wearing any jewelry. Surely she owned enough to buy stock in Fort Knox.

"I mean it, Mr. Harley."

"Mrs. Carleton," he said quietly, his eyes fastened on her face, "I can assure you that I won't sell my company to anyone."

"Else. Anyone else, Mr. Harley."

"As you wish." Again he shrugged.

"You will have no choice!"

He merely smiled at her. Elizabeth wanted to strike him. She realized her hands were fists, that he saw they were fists, and quickly splayed her fingers. "Then you refuse to sign the agreement?"

"Why don't you give me a copy of the agreement and I'll look it over."

Elizabeth said very softly, "You won't be able to repay the loan, Mr. Harley. Come now, you must be reasonable about it."

Jonathan rose smoothly, gracefully. He stared down at her for a long time. "Would you like to have lunch? You could celebrate your victory. It's just a bit premature, but I won't mind."

She stared back, her eyes wide, completely nonplussed.

"You'll have to recommend the restaurant, though. I don't know any in this area."

"You're out of your mind if you think you can change my mind!"

"No, I don't think you'd change your mind if your life depended on it."

"Then why?"

"I'll be hungry in another hour or so. I don't want to fly back home just yet. Besides, my flight isn't until three o'clock. Just think, Mrs. Carleton, I'm giving you some free time, some of my free time, and you can gloat to your heart's content."

"I think you're crazy," Elizabeth said. Nonetheless, she rose and walked to the phone. "Millicent, please make reservations for two in my name at the Cantina."

"Mexican food?"

"I love it. Perhaps I can get you to change your mind about signing the agreement if I pump you with their Cadillac margaritas."

"What the devil is that?"

"A margarita with a shot of Grand Marnier. It's a killer."

Elizabeth shook her head at herself. They were talking like friends, she thought blankly. She immediately straightened, resuming her aloofness. "My assistant, Mrs. Stacy, will give you the directions to the restaurant, Mr. Harley. I will meet you there at—"

"I think I'd like to see your headquarters if it's all right with you, Mrs. Carleton."

Again she felt nonplussed. She frowned at him. "Very well. Why don't you return to my office at noon. Meanwhile, I'll have one of my people come up to show you around."

"Thank you."

So far, so good, Jonathan thought. He shook the woman's hand, and took himself off. He had a difficult time restraining his smile when he came face-to-face with Millicent Stacy, whose face was a study in confusion. So he had truly caught the Carleton woman off guard. Score one small point for him.

As he dutifully followed a young man about the various ACI departments, he paid attention to not a word, his thoughts on his upcoming lunch. Should he treat her like a woman? Compliment her?

The Cantina was decorated in Art Deco, surprisingly enough. Elizabeth loved it. She was safe here.

José immediately rushed forward, assisting her from her raincoat. "So pleased you are here, Mrs. Carleton."

"This is an out-of-towner, José. Make your Cadillac margaritas extra . . . macho for him."

"I shall, Mrs. Carleton. This way, please. I have your special table ready for you, of course."

Of course, Jonathan thought. Hell, he wondered if she owned the place. Her special table was set back from the others, private, away from prying eyes.

Elizabeth ordered a Perrier, and Jonathan felt honor-bound to order the Cadillac margarita. A test of his manhood. He wanted to laugh at himself for being so easily caught in his own conceit.

"A toast, Mrs. Carleton," he said once the drinks were placed in front of them. He saw her hesitate, and added, "Come, to your victory. To devastate and otherwise wipe out the nasty man from Philadelphia."

"I suppose that's close enough," she said, and lightly clinked her glass against his.

His first taste of the margarita was enough to tell him that it should be his only drink for the entire day. It packed a powerful wallop. If only she would go to the women's room, he could dump it in the plant behind him. Rose always excused herself when they arrived at a restaurant, to repair herself, she said.

When Elizabeth Carleton made no move to do anything, he said, his voice light, "You worked very quickly, Mrs. Carleton."

"Yes, I did. You made me very angry, Mr. Harley. I decided only yesterday that I wouldn't ruin you."

"So I'm a lucky man, huh?"

"I should say you could begin to count your blessings. That had, of course, been my initial plan."

"To ruin me?"

"To destroy you, actually. But I realized that you have done well with your company. You've worked very diligently to bring it to the fore of one high-tech industry. One must admire that sort of commitment and accomplishment. I would only destroy you now if I had no other option."

"Then I must be certain that you've plenty of options."

"And you must be certain that you control your mouth. I won't take any more abuse from you, or anyone else for that matter. You see, I no longer have to subject myself to that kind of thing."

"I think I'll be able to manage my mouth as well as my other parts," he said, and took another very small drink of the margarita.

Sexual banter? she wondered, frowning just a bit. Well, if it was, it was her own fault for coming out to lunch with him. It was probably a very stupid move, but he'd taken her aback. And he was right, she did want to gloat, just a bit. Well, perhaps more than a bit.

"I wonder just what it would take to make you go back to hurling insults at me?"

"Is that your style?"

"Lawyer tactics, Mr. Harley? Answering a question with another question?"

"Something you don't know, Mrs. Carleton? My law degree is from Harvard."

"You don't have a law degree, Mr. Harley."

He grinned at her. "I suppose you even know where my birthmark is?"

Elizabeth didn't like this at all. He was good, very good. "No," she said coolly, "but I do know all about your marriage and divorce."

"Ah, so you're diving below the belt now."

"A very nasty business. I would guess that if your father-in-law, or rather your ex-father-in-law, had some control at the First People's Bank, you would have been tossed out on your ear."

"Actually you're wrong there. Andrew Pillson remains a friend."

He had to be lying, she thought. Pillson, according to her reports, was ready to skin his ex-son-in-law.

He saw the disbelief on her face, and added, "He knows his daughter quite well. He also knows when to put the proper face on things."

"So it was all her fault? Naturally, I should have guessed. The shallow, spoiled woman?"

"You're trying to make me toss my margarita in your face, aren't you?"

"Just testing, Mr. Harley, just testing. You see, I learn from every encounter I have with business*men*."

Again that flash of humanity that made him vastly uncomfortable. "You're young," he said abruptly.

"Not terribly. I'm twenty-nine now."

"I venture to say that there are very few chief executives in Fortune Five Hundred companies who are your age."

"Unless they inherit."

"Yes," he said, "unless it's handed to them free of charge."

"It wasn't free of charge, Mr. Harley."

He said before he could stop himself, "Three years isn't much to pay for what you've gotten in return."

"I was wondering," she said slowly, perfectly in control, "how long you would be able to control your . . . rage."

"Do I look enraged? Ah, here's our waiter. What do you suggest, Mrs. Carleton?"

Surprisingly, Jonathan, not a Mexican-food lover,

found the burritos delicious. He said, smiling, that he wished he could order a dozen macho burritos.

"You're feeling that insecure?" she said.

"No, I was thinking rather of displaying them, with signs of course, kind of like a peacock strutting his plumage."

She wanted to smile, at the very least, and nearly choked on her Perrier.

Now, as she picked at her taco salad, she wondered again why she'd come with him. She certainly hadn't managed to put him in his place very well. He was slippery, a master of his trade.

He said after a moment, "Why do you feel you must have my company, Mrs. Carleton?"

"You weren't my first choice," she said, "but there were problems. Yes, I suppose you could call them problems brought about by my naiveté. Then I heard about you, or rather my management team brought you to my attention. I like not only your location but also the solid strength of your operations."

"If I hadn't . . . insulted you, just refused you, may I ask what you would have done?"

"Bought the loan."

"And if I hadn't borrowed the money?"

She shrugged. "I would have found another way, I suppose. Power, Mr. Harley, as I'm certain you know quite well firsthand, can be wielded in many different arenas."

"And I'm just unfortunate enough not to have as much power as you to wield."

"That's right."

"So no one in his right mind dares cross you?"

"Are you admitting that you're crazy, Mr. Harley? That you acted like a cretin?"

"Touché," he said. "May I ask you why you decided not to go back to the concert stage? Or do you still plan to in the future?"

He saw her go very still, her fork poised just above her plate. Ah, a nerve, he thought.

"I'm as yet undecided." She carefully laid the fork

beside her plate. "You're pushing again, Mr. Harley. You're not stupid, I'll give you that. You know very well why I couldn't go back, why I can't go back for a long time."

Suddenly, without warning, a flash went off, and the whirring noise of a camera.

Jonathan whipped about in his chair, saw a man grinning at him. "What the hell!" he shouted, rising.

"No," Elizabeth said, reaching out her hand to touch his arm. "No, don't. There's no need to involve yourself. No need at all."

He eased back into his chair, frowning at her.

Elizabeth called out, "José."

He was there in an instant. He leaned closer to her, listening. Then he disappeared very quickly.

"What was that all about?"

"The man will leave with his camera, but unfortunately, he will have a regrettable accident with that particular roll of film."

Jonathan simply stared at her.

"You see," Elizabeth said, wanting to laugh at his expression, "José and I have an agreement. He promised me protection, complete protection, from prying eyes, and I . . . well, I reciprocate, naturally."

"Will José's goons also break the guy's legs? Or are they your goons?"

"Don't turn soft on me now, Mr. Harley. You're ruining my image of you."

"Lady, you're tough as nails, aren't you?"

"Careful, Mr. Harley. You're slipping."

"Yes, I suppose I am," he said slowly, getting a grip on himself.

"Consider yourself in a poker game, Mr. Harley. Your major problem is that no one will deal you any cards. Well, deuces, perhaps."

I will get you for that, lady. Oh, yes, you've gone too far, much too far.

"So even a three of hearts will beat me?"

"That's correct. You see, I knew you were somewhat bright."

"You gloat very well, Mrs. Carleton."

"I'm learning."

"I've never heard you play the piano," he said, and she blinked at him in surprise at his abrupt change of topic.

"You aren't into classical music?"

"Yes, but I've just never bought you. Your late husband bought a recording company for you, didn't he?"

"No, he didn't. However, he did own one, but it's country-and-western, primarily. I believe the company is in Nashville. I haven't had the chance yet to visit with the local management. They're not a very large concern, and of course everything is a matter of priorities."

"I should imagine that it would take you at least a year to work with and meet the management of all your companies."

"Yes, at least a year," she agreed, smiling just a bit at the mixture of condemnation and bitterness in his voice.

"I don't suppose I could get you on antitrust?"

"Nope, not a chance. But I'm certain you've already explored all avenues open to you, haven't you, Mr. Harley?"

"Wouldn't you?"

She nodded. "Of course. You just must realize that I have several people whose primary job it is to do strategic planning. Their experience is awesome. There is nothing—I repeat, nothing—you could devise that they haven't thought of first."

He looked as if he would disagree vehemently, but then he shrugged, looking mildly bored.

"You must have been just a bit upset to learn that you couldn't just simply acquire my company."

"Yes, just a bit. It meant confronting you personally. I didn't like that meeting, Mr. Harley."

"I would say that if you didn't hate me before that memorable meeting, you certainly must now."

"Close enough. As I told you, I did calm down, but I didn't change my mind."

Jonathan said nothing to that. The lunch hadn't gone as he'd planned it, but then, he really hadn't had a specific plan. He'd just assumed that with a woman, he had a chance. For someone who was a musician before she became a business tycoon, she was tough, very tough. He wondered absently if she had murdered Timothy Carleton.

"I was wrong about something," she said after a moment.

"No!"

"No need for sarcasm. Your secretary. Midge, I believe her name is?"

"That's right," he said, and she saw that he'd stiffened just a bit.

"She's much too smart to sleep with you, Mr. Harley. I'm looking for very bright women. Do you believe she'd be interested in a more rewarding position? After we complete our business, of course."

"Her loyalty is to me. However, feel free to ask her."

"That's what impressed me initially. Her loyalty. Now, Mr. Harley, shall we go? I assume you have a plane to catch?"

"Isn't there a check to pay?"

"Consider, Mr. Harley, that the barracuda is feeding the goldfish . . . at least today."

16

Elizabeth sat alone in her office an hour later, replaying the luncheon with Jonathan Harley in her mind. In Adrian's words, he did indeed seem a slippery bastard. At one moment she'd believed he was apologizing for his behavior in Philadelphia, but the next, she'd wanted to put her fist in his mouth. He was unaccountable and she knew she must be careful. He was a formidable adversary. She remembered his parting words as he'd helped her into a taxi.

"Why didn't you want that photographer to take that picture? There wasn't anything to it, after all."

She gave him a cool, mocking smile. "Mr. Harley, surely you don't want to be known as Elizabeth Carleton's latest?"

"Latest what, Mrs. Carleton? Lover or victim?" And he'd given her a mock salute and stepped back.

Very slippery.

But she had him—oh, yes, she had him.

He wouldn't go to the Carletons for a bail-out. Not him. She wondered if he would indeed sign the agreement and send it back to her. He'd better, she thought.

"Oh, I'm sure he will," Adrian said some minutes later. "I hope you didn't let him get to you again?"

"No. He isn't all that stupid, Adrian."

"I still don't believe you took him to lunch!"

"You wanna know something, sailor? Neither do I."

"I assume, then, that you reached a sort of détente?"

"In the loosest sense of the word, actually, not even close to a yes. However, he'll fall into line. He has no choice. If he tries for another loan, even from an out-of-state bank, we'll know it and take appropriate action."

"You mean you want him tailed?"

"Certainly. Starting today, the minute he steps off the plane in Philadelphia. You know something else? I refuse to feel guilty about this. As you've told me and as I'm continually telling myself, this is business, pure and simple business."

"Yes, it is." Adrian left her office, made the phone call, and returned. "You ready for the board meeting?"

"Three o'clock already?"

"Does that mean time flew while you were having fun?"

"Stuff it, Adman Marsh."

Outside in Millicent Stacy's office, Elizabeth saw Adrian gather up the envelopes that contained the exorbitant fees each board member received each month, after every meeting.

She wondered if they would do anything at all if she were in truth destroying ACI. Probably not. They rubber-stamped everything. Of course, with all the Carleton leaks, they weren't told everything. She found herself thinking of Laurette Carleton, and wondering at a hatred so profound that she would try to undermine all her son had built to get back at her, Elizabeth. "And you've got the wrong person, Laurette," she said quietly.

Elizabeth's eyes fell upon the society page in the paper on Millicent's desk. She stared down at a photo of Rowe and his fiancée, Amanda Montgomery.

She frowned just a bit. But there was no pain now, no anger at his betrayal. In fact, she realized, she no longer wished him ill. Despite all his lies, his web of deception, he'd taught her so much. "Good luck, Rowe," she whispered, then straightened her shoulders and marched out of Millicent's office, Adrian behind her.

She wondered briefly if Rowe were pleased with this marriage. She rather hoped, in her less beneficient moods, that Amanda was a bitch.

Rowe Chalmers realized he liked work. "And that," he said to himself and to his office, "is a good thing, because the rest of my life isn't going to hold much more."

Well, perhaps children, but he wasn't certain about that. Amanda had, to this point, successfully skirted the subject.

"You're a lucky bastard," he continued to himself. "She's good in bed and she's loaded. I won't get any more gray hairs trying to save this sinking ship."

There was a knock on his door before it opened to admit his secretary, Doris Cummings. She was young, pretty, and efficient enough. She was also discreet. And kind.

"What is it, Doris?"

"There's a lady here to see you, Mr. Chalmers."

Rowe groaned inwardly. Amanda loved to pay surprise visits. Did she think he was off playing polo or something? Off having illicit sex in the afternoon with one of her friends?

"It's a Miss Catherine Carleton."

He stared at her, his jaw dropping.

"Hello, Rowe," Catherine said from behind Doris.

He rose slowly to his feet. "Miss Carleton." He nodded to Doris and she left the office, closing the door behind her.

He strode across his office, stopping six inches from Catherine.

"What the hell do you want?"

"Forgive me for disturbing you," she said, holding her ground. "I came on in because . . . well, I was afraid you'd refuse to see me."

"You're damned right I'd refuse!"

"I wanted to talk to you."

"That's what you said the last time. As I recall, it

wasn't particularly memorable. A waste of time for both of us.''

''I've been seeing Dr. Christian Hunter.''

Rowe stared at her. ''Seeing him? As in going to bed with him, you mean?''

''I suppose I deserve that. No, as a patient.''

A patient! What was she up to now? He frowned at her. ''What does that have to do with me?''

''You said you weren't certain anymore that Elizabeth hadn't murdered my father. If you're right in doubting her—and I know you are—I want to know why Christian Hunter lied for her. Then I want to nail him.''

He found himself responding to the plea in her voice. ''Look, Miss Carleton—Catherine—there's nothing to say. I already told you that.''

''No one else could have done it, don't you see? Only Elizabeth.''

Rowe turned away from her and walked to the long windows behind his desk. He looked over at Copley Square. He heard her move up behind him. ''Why don't you leave,'' he said.

''I can't. Not until you . . . tell me things.''

''You are very young, Catherine. Drop it. Leave it be. Move to California. The farther away you get from your precious family, the better it would be for you.'' He'd turned back to her as he spoke, and was again shaken at the pleading look on her face. He said abruptly, ''Your nose is bleeding.''

He pointed to a small box of Kleenex on his desktop. Catherine dabbed at her nose, saying nothing. He stood watching her. He'd thought of her only as a spoiled brat with a nasty mouth for so long that he had difficulty seeing her as anything else. He hated vulnerability in women, and his experience with Elizabeth, using her as he had, made him uncomfortable with himself.

''Dammit, here!''

He took the Kleenex from her and wiped the blood from her nose and near her upper lip.

"Good morning, darling. What's this?"

Rowe looked up to see Amanda standing in the open doorway, a chagrined Doris behind her.

"Hello, Amanda," he said. He finished wiping Catherine's nose and dropped the Kleenex into the wastebasket.

Catherine turned slowly, sniffing, to look at Amanda.

"What brings you here so early?" Rowe asked.

"It's not that early, Rowe. I came to take you shopping, then to lunch. Who is this?"

"She's Catherine Carleton," he said.

"Elizabeth X's stepdaughter?"

"Yes."

"How very interesting."

Catherine looked from one to the other, and felt a surge of pity for Rowe Chalmers. Then she felt a deep recognition and made a small sound. No, she was thinking, I can't be like her. Oh, God, no. But she recognized the tilt of the head, the absolute arrogance, the immediate cold assessment of another who just might be poaching on her preserve.

"Shall we go, Rowe?" Amanda moved aside to let Catherine pass.

"No, I'm quite busy right now, Amanda. You should have called me."

"Yes, you certainly do look busy, don't you, darling?"

"Miss Carleton is leaving. Now."

Catherine didn't look at him again. She would come back. She nodded toward Amanda and left the office.

She heard Amanda say just before the office door closed behind her, "Really, Rowe, must you screw teenyboppers right here in your office? Isn't that secretary enough for you? Or were you wondering what the stepdaughter was like after the stepmother?"

Catherine shivered. She didn't hear Rowe's answer. She supposed she should be happy that he was marrying that woman. She'd make his life miserable. She was already well on her way.

Catherine said to Doris, "Will Mr. Chalmers be here this afternoon?"

Doris, whose face was flushed with anger at what she'd heard Amanda say, suddenly smiled at her. "If he goes out with her now, he'll be here late."

"Do you think he will?"

"Probably."

Yeah, Catherine thought, he probably will—he needs her money. "I'll be back then," she said, "but please don't tell him. I want it to be a surprise."

"You got it." Doris watched the young woman leave. She must be as rich as Amanda Montgomery, she thought.

Rowe left with Amanda ten minutes later and didn't return to his office until after two in the afternoon. Doris shot him a look of sympathy, but he didn't notice.

Midge looked up, her breath held, as Jonathan strode into the office. "Well?"

"Just fine, Midge," he said. He handed her a folded envelope. "Mail this for me, special delivery."

"What is it?"

"It's a signed agreement to Elizabeth Carleton that I'll sell to her if I can't repay the loan at the stated time."

"You didn't!"

He just grinned at her. "Believe me, it doesn't matter. It's called distracting the lions while the Christians escape through the back door. Go ahead and read it, I know you're dying to. And, Midge," he said over his shoulder, "I do have a tail, thanks to the dragon lady—you know, as in private detective. Wanna know something else? This is fun." He rubbed his hands together as he disappeared into his office.

He came back out not ten minutes later.

"You still got that agreement?"

"Yeah, but a messenger is on his way to pick it up."

"Cancel the messenger. I think I'll hold on to it for a couple of days. Then I'll go back to New York and deliver it in person. And, Midge, you got my reservations to Zurich?"

*   *   *

It *was* fun, Jonathan thought, grinning into his rearview mirror at the discreet Chevrolet three cars behind him—never more, never less. He pulled into his driveway, saw the Chevrolet pull over down the road, and smiled again.

Binky Vaughan was bored, but then again, he was used to being bored. Harley hadn't left his house for three hours. He straightened a bit when a black sedan pulled into the driveway and a man got out. He watched him enter the house.

The man left an hour later.

Jonathan Harley didn't reappear. Binky's relief appeared at precisely eleven o'clock that night. "Nothing," Binky said to Gus, and left. "Hell, the guy's divorced. You'd think he'd at least go out with women or something."

Binky was back again at seven the following morning. After a fifteen-minute wait he saw Jonathan Harley emerge from the house and get into his car. He followed him to his office.

Jonathan blinked awake when the flight attendant came over the loudspeaker. "Fasten your seat belts, please. We'll be landing in Zurich in approximately fifteen minutes."

Catherine walked through the silent outer office and quietly opened Rowe Chalmers' door. He didn't hear her and for a moment she stood looking at him. His attention was on a bound sheaf of papers in front of him. He sighed once as he turned a page and continued his reading.

"Rowe," she said very quietly.

He wasn't surprised, not at all. "Hello," he said, not looking up for a moment. "What do you want? Again?"

"The same. Again."

He tossed his pen on top of the pages and sat back

in his chair. "And I'll say it again, Miss Carleton—
Catherine—let it go." He saw the stubborn set of her
jaw, and added, "I can't believe your esteemed Uncle
Michael or your grandmother is pleased about your
activities."

"No, but I really don't care."

She walked past him to the windows and gazed
down at the wealth of city lights below. "This view is
beautiful," she said. "I love all the Christmas decora-
tions and lights."

"Yes," he said, "yes, it is. What is it going to take
to be rid of you?"

She turned slowly. "I understand why you must hate
my family, and me."

"Most perceptive of you."

Her chin went up. "However, if you hadn't been a
moron and a weakling, you wouldn't have been ripe to
do what they bribed you to do."

"True. I should have kicked my father out years
ago. I can just picture him folding up his tent and
taking off."

"And now you're having to marry that awful woman
to fill up the till."

"True again."

"Have you an agreement with her?"

"That's none of your damned business." He rose
and she saw his anger, and the lines of weariness on
his face.

"You're working hard."

"Yes, there's so much to be done, to be mended."

"You don't have to marry her." Why had she said
that? Catherine stared at him, her eyes wide on his
face.

"She's the best catch in town," he said, amusement
in his voice. "I bet she's got as much money as you do,
little girl."

She blurted out, "Were you in love with Elizabeth?"

Rowe lit a cigarette, inhaled once, and ground it
out.

"You don't smoke," said Catherine.

"Amanda must have left them here."

"Rowe, I—"

"Please leave, Catherine. I have nothing to say to you."

"Can I buy you a drink somewhere?"

"Aren't you afraid I'll come on to you?"

"I'd be shocked if you did. Perhaps you're afraid I'll come on to you."

"That would be something, wouldn't it?" He looked at her. "Look, I don't want to go out with you, for whatever reason."

She shook her head at him, swiping the back of her hand automatically against her nose.

"It's bleeding again," he said. "Are you ill?"

"No, not anymore."

He watched her wipe her nose.

"Coke," he said. "I trust you're off it now."

"Yes, I am."

"Good. You're too young to destroy yourself."

"You sound like you care."

He pointed toward the office door. "Good-bye, Catherine."

"I'll see you in a couple of days, Rowe."

"You might as well give it up, Catherine. I mean it. Oh, shit, I can't tell you a thing . . . All right, Thursday night, at Barney's."

"Thank you, Rowe."

He watched her leave his office and ran his hand through his hair. Why had he done that?

Millicent Stacy stared at the phone for a moment, a thoughtful look on her face. She rose and went into Elizabeth's office.

"Yes? Something exciting, Milly?"

"Maybe. That was Mr. Harley's secretary on the phone. He wants to see you tomorrow morning. He wants to hand-deliver the agreement to you."

"Interesting," Elizabeth said. She wondered why. He certainly hadn't done anything in the meantime to change the situation. The men following him had reported that he'd gone about his business at the same time every day. Nothing at all out of the ordinary. Nothing at all. Perhaps this time he wanted to plead, to beg.

Her eyes glittered.

"I'll be delighted to see Mr. Harley. I think I'll even take him to lunch."

"What are you smiling about, Elizabeth?" Adrian asked, coming into her office. "You look like the cat who got the canary."

Elizabeth grinned at him. "Jonathan Harley wants to see me tomorrow, agreement in hand."

"Signed, I presume?"

"I hope he does it in front of me. With my pen."

"Do you want any reinforcements present?"

"Nope. Why spoil my fun? Now, what do you have for me?"

"Organization charts, with names and accompanying responsibilities, for the six companies located in the Northeast."

"Number of women in managerial positions?"

Adrian shook his head. "Only twelve in all. And only one from the middle rungs."

"Do you have their personnel folders, including all their performance evaluations?"

"You got 'em." He plunked down twelve folders on her desk.

Adrian thought briefly about his wife's reaction to Elizabeth's own private women's movement. She'd been horrified. He'd reminded Elaine that she grew up during the women's movement, and she was even more horrified. Her place, every woman's place, she told him, her face mottled red with anger at Elizabeth, was to support her husband. As for himself, he'd found that the more vociferous Elaine had become, the more he was supporting Elizabeth's position. It was odd, he thought now, staring briefly down at the twelve personnel folders; he'd never really thought about the women in the companies. He wasn't at all certain whether he was for or against them.

"After I've gone through these, Adrian," Elizabeth said, "we'll set up meetings with all the management staff of the companies I select, here in New York. Then we'll see."

"I assume the women will also be present?"

"Yes, I imagine most of them will. I want to see how they perform, how they deal with their male bosses, and how the men in turn treat them."

"Have you ever considered setting up a castration center in Albany?"

"No," she said, "and don't be sarcastic. It's an idea—I'll consider it. Just think of it. Our managers don't only retire, they get their performance permanently eliminated."

That evening over dinner, Elizabeth, who'd reviewed all twelve folders in great detail, was telling Christian, "There are seven of them who deserve a lot more than they've got."

She'd begun talking to him at last about work. He was more pleased than he could say. He was building her trust in him.

"Will you meet with the women individually following the meetings?"

"I sure intend to." She toyed a moment with her glass of white wine. "It's odd, I know it. I was never a part of any movement, women's or otherwise. I was always just . . . alone. Me and my trusty piano."

"And now you're using power in a positive way."

"I'm glad you understand, Christian." She gave him a glowing smile and he was so instantly horny that he wanted to fling her on the floor of the restaurant. Instead he said, "You've even made me aware. I was at a board meeting with the Westward Corporation—you know, appliances and all that—and I even brought it up. The other good ole boys looked at me like I had a crack in my brain."

"What happened?"

"I made a luncheon appointment with the CEO. Since I can buy and sell him, I think he'll be receptive to my concern."

"I think you're wonderful, Dr. Hunter." And she meant it. She recognized at times, particularly at night when she was trying to get to sleep, that he'd helped her keep some balance in her life. She said suddenly, "Let's go back to my place, and I'll play for you. Whatever you want."

"Is Kogi still keeping the piano dusted?"

"Yes, he never gives up."

"Nor will I, Elizabeth."

She went still for a moment, not wanting to examine what he'd meant by those words. He was her friend. She wanted nothing more. She couldn't handle the other, at least not now.

"It's all right, Elizabeth."

She managed a smile. "You know me too well, Christian."

"I'm trying. Are you ready? I want my savage breast soothed."

"Mr. Harley is here, Elizabeth," Millicent said.

It was all she could do not to rub her hands together. "Send the gentleman in, Milly."

"Good morning, Mrs. Carleton. How lovely you look today."

"I left all my conceited bones at home this morning, Mr. Harley, but it's a refreshing approach on your part."

"Ah, you see that innocuous comment as pandering?"

"Correct. Now, what can I do for you? I understand you've brought me the signed agreement."

"Not quite, but almost. Before I do sign it, I would like to try some new negotiations with you."

"Forget it."

"I said 'try,' Mrs. Carleton. Surely you can't blame me for that, can you?"

He didn't seem at all like a man on the brink of surrender. She frowned at him. The men following him said he hadn't done anything out of the ordinary at all—no more consultations with any banks. Of course, there could have been phone calls to out-of-state banks . . . She'd have that followed up immediately.

She said, "I trust you haven't tried any banks outside Pennsylvania."

"As in Utah?"

"Exactly."

"No, I wouldn't dream of going to Utah or any other state. I figured you'd find out about it if I did, and stop it."

"Quick as a flash, Mr. Harley."

"Of course, any bank I approached for a loan would have to know about the note you're now holding."

"Mr. Harley, what do you want?"

He smiled at her. "Just making conversation, Mrs. Carleton."

"I'm a busy woman—"

"Yes, I know. I understand you've offered lunch. Shall we discuss my ideas over lunch?"

"As you wish." She reached for her purse. "At least the weather is smiling on you today, Mr. Harley."

"Don't you think it's about time you called me Jonathan?"

"No."

"Well, that's clear enough." He offered her his arm, which she ignored.

"Milly, I'll be back at one o'clock."

"Yes, certainly, Elizabeth."

"Do you think we should stop meeting like this?" Jonathan asked when they entered the Cantina.

"I eat most of my lunches here," she said. "Because of José's surveillance, of course."

"I can't get over a Mexican restaurant with Art Deco decor. Only in New York."

Once they were seated, Jonathan said, "Are you having my phones bugged?"

She looked at him sharply. Had he known he was being followed? "No," she said mildly, "but I suppose I should consider it."

"I don't suppose you'd believe me if I told you you could certainly trust me."

"No, not on your life."

Jonathan merely smiled at her, pulled an envelope from his breast pocket, and laid it on the table. "Here's the agreement."

Elizabeth opened her purse and pulled out her pen. "And here's the pen."

"Symbolic for you?"

She said nothing.

"Down with the nasty, pushy man? Rub his nose in it? Kick him metaphorically in his private parts?"

"You're reading all my thoughts quite accurately."

"Before I sign, can we take a moment to talk things over?"

"Hello, José," Elizabeth said. "Are you ready to order, Mr. Harley?"

They both ordered Perriers and lunch.

"Now, Mr. Harley, what could you possibly have to say?"

Jonathan sat back in his chair, his arms folded over his chest. He looked completely at his ease. Completely in control. "First of all," he said, "would you consider marrying me?"

17

Elizabeth's eyes widened in surprise, but that was all. She sat back in her chair, trying to copy his body language.

"How very flattering of you, Mr. Harley," she said finally. "Do I take it that if I marry you, you would expect some sort of dowry?"

"No," he said, grinning at her. "You wouldn't have to give me a dowry. Not precisely, anyway."

"Ah, the 'not-precisely' catch."

He grinned at her, and tossed a tortilla chip into his mouth. He said, still smiling, "All you have to do is promise to keep your fingers out of my various pies. I'm not a greedy man."

"Not a greedy man, huh? And just what are you, I wonder, Mr. Harley?"

"Horny, for one thing."

"Surely you have enough funds left to relieve that particular problem."

"I have a thing for blonds."

Elizabeth said sharply, "I think that's quite enough, Mr. Harley—"

"I should have said *natural* blonds."

"Here is your burrito. You did order the *macho*, didn't you?

"Yes, indeed," he said. She watched him busy himself with his lunch, unperturbed.

"Should I take your silence for a yes?" he asked, looking at up her.

"Mr. Harley, aren't you afraid I'd do away with you in your sleep?"

Her voice was light, mocking, but once again he felt the pain in her and tried to draw back from it. "But you would have all the money, dear lady. There would be no need. You could simply boot me out the door when you tired of me."

She felt a spurt of relief. He was once again being slippery, but that was now a known quantity. Of course, she had asked for it. Never, she thought, should she forget what he truly believed about her.

She took a bite of her lunch, ignoring him.

"How is Dr. Hunter?"

"This is interesting, Mr. Harley," she said, carefully setting down her fork. "Would you care to tell me why you're purposely trying to make me want to ruin you?"

"Am I doing that? Men, I suppose, can behave stupidly—and at the most inappropriate times. Since, of course, I'm completely at your mercy, I should be kissing your toes, shouldn't I?"

"I wouldn't mind at all seeing you beg."

"All right." He picked up the pen, her pen, and signed the agreement with a flourish. "There, Mrs. Carleton. You've won. My company goes into your maw on the day my loan is due—if I can't pay it, of course."

"You forgot to mention that what you get out of it is the original offer from me. ACI stock or cash, whichever you wish."

"And a seat on the ACI board?"

"No, not possible. Console yourself with the thought of all that money."

"How could I forget your generosity? I've tried to find a likely metaphor. I like to think of what you're doing as just like someone coming up to a father who has only one child—a child he's very proud of and loves very much—and offering to buy the child, and when the father refuses, threatening ruin to the father and stealing the child anyway."

"You seem to have a flair for the melodramatic, Mr. Harley. So you basically came here to New York to plead with me, biblically, to let your children go?"

"Just one child, Mrs. Carleton," he said softly, deadly serious. Suddenly his expression changed, becoming boyish, roguish. "No, I came here to ask you to marry me. I couldn't very well do that over the phone. Besides, I needed to see you, needed to be certain that you were as beautiful as I'd remembered."

"You're weird, Mr. Harley," Elizabeth said. "Close to certifiable, even."

"You'd get along great with my ex-wife. Why don't you have dinner with me this evening? Perhaps we could go to the theater—maybe *Phantom of the Opera*?"

"Or *Elephant Man*."

"*Cats*?"

She started laughing, she couldn't help it. Jonathan stared at her a moment, then joined in.

"You don't laugh too often, do you?" he said after a moment.

"Enough," she said. She stretched out her hand for the agreement.

Jonathan merely smiled. "I'll give it to you if you come out with me tonight."

Elizabeth eyed him, wishing she could read his thoughts, understand his motives. Did he think to charm her into changing her mind about his company? That had to be where he was coming from. Well, two could play at that game. Why not rub his nose in it? Why not let him try all his little male tricks? It should be very amusing.

"All right," she said. "It sounds so delightful, how could I refuse?" She returned to her lunch, aware that he was now silent, obviously surprised, staring at her across the table. At least he hadn't believed he was irresistible to her. She wanted to laugh, to look at him and laugh, but she didn't.

She sipped her Perrier. "I don't eat at well-known restaurants, Mr. Harley, for obvious reasons. Why don't I meet you at seven o'clock this evening at the Pirouette?"

Jonathan didn't quite know what to make of how things had fallen out. What was she up to?

Then he decided what he would do. He smiled at her and said, "If we have dinner at seven, we'll have plenty of time for a club. How about it?"

"As you wish. Just not one of the famous ones— again, for obvious reasons."

He nodded. "Do I get to pay for this lunch?"

Elizabeth merely shook her head and rose from her seat. "This evening, then, Mr. Harley."

He watched her walk between the tables toward the front of the restaurant and wondered if she'd stand him up.

Elizabeth considered it at least a dozen times. The man hated her. He had to. But, she admitted grudgingly to herself that evening as she was dressing, no matter how intractable he was, he made her feel alive. Even when her blood pumped with rage at something he'd said, she felt alert, involved. She shook her head at her mirrored reflection. No, she was in no danger of becoming a mushbrain over this man. No man, ever again.

Drake dropped her off a half-block from the Pirouette, precisely at seven o'clock. To her unadmitted relief, she saw Jonathan Harley standing just inside the small restaurant door, talking to the doorman about the Mets. For the first time, she looked at him, really looked at him, and admitted objectively that he was a handsome man. He was a bit broader than Rowe, bigger-boned, his skin swarthy, his hair black. Beneath that suave, well-dressed exterior was a man of dubious motives. She wouldn't allow herself to forget that.

Thank God Rowe had taught her that a man with both looks and money was a deadly combination. And intelligence, she added to herself. And ruthlessness and cunning, and a vicious tongue, just like a snake.

"Hello," Jonathan said, looking up. "You didn't

stand me up. I was hoping you wouldn't. It took me a hell of a long time to find this place."

"It's called the telephone book, Mr. Harley."

"Tell that to the cabbie. No tacos here, I see."

"No, but the shrimp here is exquisite."

"Do you mind my saying that you look exquisite?"

"Just because I'm not wearing one of my uniforms?"

He looked her over. She didn't move, simply waited for him to finish his male inspection. "No," was all he said.

Here, Jonathan noted, just as at her Mexican restaurant, the maître d' knew her, and was completely low-key. The restaurant was small, the lighting dim, and as they followed him to their table, no one paid them any attention. No one recognized her. Of course, she wasn't dressed at all flamboyantly, but the pale blue silk dress would have caught his eye. He wondered again if this was a good idea. When they were seated behind a bank of palms, he found that most topics of conversation were off limits unless he wanted her to throw her soup in his face.

He chose business, and managed to ask the right questions to ease the silence between them.

"I have worked very hard, but there's so much to learn," Elizabeth said honestly over her endive salad. "I hadn't the foggiest idea what a merger really was, for example, and the relationship between the acquired company and ACI. But I have good people to help me. Very good people."

"I imagine that the responsibility for all those companies and their employees is enormous."

His tone was sympathetic, interested.

"One thing I've learned is that your responsibilities and mine are the same. It's just the scope that's different. Like you, I have people who are responsible bottom-line for the operations under their aegis. Again, only the scope is larger, as are their respective staffs. Coordination on the top levels can be a bit dicey as well. Incidentally, I understand you acquired two smaller electronics companies in the past couple of years."

"Yes," he said. "But of course they wanted to be bought. There was no arm-twisting."

The garlic shrimp arrived. To Jonathan's eye, the serving wasn't enough to fill up a bird. He'd never cared for *nouvelle* French restaurants for that reason—beautiful presentation and very little substance.

He watched the waiter pour the chardonnay. He watched her down one glass and begin another. What would happen if he got her drunk? he wondered. It was an engaging thought.

"If you don't mind, Mrs. Carleton, I'd like to ask you why. Why me?"

"I've told you this before, and I told you the truth. You're successful, you're profitable, and if you weren't so stubborn, we could have merged, with you remaining in power."

"That will teach me to be hardworking and reasonably bright, won't it? The American Dream, backfired."

"I have a question for you, Mr. Harley. When you have meetings that aren't going to be pleasant, at least from your perspective, do you always attack personally?"

"No."

"I believe I asked you that before," Elizabeth said, frowning a bit as she drank more of the delicious chardonnay.

"You don't have any children, Mrs. Carleton?"

It was, should have been, a perfectly innocuous question, but Elizabeth felt herself tense, remembering the pain, the blood, so much blood, all over the place. "No," she said.

"Do you want children?"

She got hold of herself. There was no reason to make him feel like a louse. He couldn't know about the miscarriage, or all the other unpleasantness. "I suppose that many women do," she said. "Yes, I guess so. I've turned twenty-nine. The biological clock is beginning to tick isn't it?"

"I have one woman manager who had her first child when she was forty."

"You have an actual, real woman in a capacity of power?"

"Uncalled-for, ma'am."

"Probably not, given what I know of you and your opinion of women. However, as you wish." She finished off her second glass of wine. For a moment she looked at the empty wineglass, her expression vague.

"You have no children," she said.

"No, I don't. I did for a total of three months."

That got her attention. "What happened?"

"Crib death. No rhyme, no reason, no one's fault. The child is well and happy one day, and the next, he's just . . . gone."

"Oh. I'm sorry." Deep waters, very deep. The father and his one beloved child. Had he placed his company in the void? Stop it, Elizabeth! For heaven's sake, the man is gifted at verbal assaults.

"It must have been very difficult for you and your wife."

For a moment he merely stared at her. Then he shrugged and refilled her glass. He nodded toward a waiter and asked for another bottle. He found himself looking briefly at her breasts. Don't be an ass, he told himself. She'd make love with Koch before she'd allow you to touch her. And of course he didn't want to touch her, except maybe to strangle her.

"As I said, no one's fault."

"Do you want children?"

Jonathan said thoughtfully, "I suppose every man wants a son to carry on after him." He watched her stiffen, and knew he'd uttered that stupidity on purpose. All he'd ever wanted was a healthy child.

That hurt. "My father did. As it turned out, he had to make do."

"Is that why you're turning your attention to the aid and succor of professional women? To right the wrongs of centuries?"

"I like to think of it as a redressing of the balance of power. Women have gotten the short end of the stick for far too long, I think."

"Women have always exercised unbelievable power, Mrs. Carleton. For example, had you and your husband's roles and ages been reversed, it would have been impossible for him to marry you, a very rich older woman. Only a young, beautiful woman can gain what she wants so quickly and with so little effort."

She was beginning to feel the least bit light-headed, and frowned at the newly filled glass of wine in front of her.

"You're exhibiting disgusting prejudices again, Mr. Harley. And here I was beginning to believe what you'd said."

"Actually I was thinking of the gates of heaven and all that," he said, clicking his wineglass to hers.

"I don't understand," she said, cocking her head to one side.

"Sex, ma'am."

She still didn't understand, but she didn't want to push for an explanation. She said, "I suppose it's true that men can no longer go out and rape any woman it pleases them to."

"No, it's damned difficult now. Ah, for the good old days."

He sat forward suddenly, his face intense. He wanted to say: What can I do to make you go find another victim? But he didn't.

"It's difficult to converse with you. Most topics are off limits."

"Tell me about your college days at Yale."

He did. "My coup in my senior year was winning the Yale chess championship. The final play-off was held between two of the colleges, the chessboard drawn on the common, the chess pieces, classmates. My opponent and I were seated in a tower above the common with a bullhorn. Each chess piece was most dramatic when he or she got knocked off. You know, clutching one's breast, flailing one's arms and weaving about, and finally falling dead, arms and legs spread."

She laughed. "And they were in costume?"

"Outrageous costumes. Medieval. My first year at

Yale was only the fourth year that women had been there. Since I didn't know any different, I thought it was great. My costumed chess queen had a victory march when the opposing king resigned. I might also add that she ignored her king."

"It sounds like fun."

"Yeah, it was. I remember, though, how some of the professors were bitching around about the dilution of academic excellence when the first women had come on board in sixty-nine."

"Until the women started carrying off the prizes?"

"That only made it worse for a while. You're talking about some real old fogies here, Mrs. Carleton."

At ten o'clock, after polishing off a second bottle of wine, Elizabeth was feeling no pain. She was giggling at his story about how one of his roommates finally lost his virginity through the intense planning of his friends. "Complete to a bottle of wine hanging out the suite window. Bless Susie. She didn't need any wine at all, but poor Brick did. His real name was Nathan, but his nickname was Brick. We named that memorable occasion 'The Night Brick Got Laid.' "

It should have raised her hackles, but it didn't.

"What happened to Susie?"

"She's a big-time lawyer in San Francisco, the last I heard. As for Brick, he's the mayor of a small town in Georgia. Funny how things turn out, isn't it?"

She told him about her first recital at age seven. "I'll never forget my father standing at attention at the back of the hall. He was more nervous than I was. I went through my Mozart like a good little trooper, only to have my masterpiece, a Chopin etude, go right out of my head. I thought my father would expire on the spot. He didn't forgive me for six months. To this day, whenever I try that particular etude, I blank out."

He laughed, but it wasn't funny. He had the urge to go choke her damned father. I'm drunk, he thought. She must be too—she's turning human.

Elizabeth asked abruptly, "Why did you want to have dinner with me, Mr. Harley? Come on, the real reason."

Jonathan said truthfully, "I was thinking of the ulti-
mate revenge of taking you to bed, of using you as a
man sometimes uses a woman. Power, Mrs. Carleton,
and ruthlessness. To punish you, to shame you, to
dominate you, for however short a period of time.
And then walk away laughing."

Elizabeth wished she hadn't drunk all that wine.
Her mind wasn't as sharp as it needed to be. She
found that she was staring at him, going over his
words in her mind.

"I told you the truth because I knew I couldn't do
it, no matter how drunk you got, or how willing."

"The reason being, of course," she said, "that if I
did sleep with you and you did what you described, I
would destroy you."

"No, but that would doubtless be the outcome. Don't
get me wrong, Elizabeth, I would very much like to
hurt you, to make you back off and leave me and my
company the hell alone, but not with sex. Sex should
be fun in itself, not a means to an end—in this case,
some kind of twisted revenge."

"I would never go to bed with you, Mr. Harley. I've
learned, you see, that men who appear to care for me
just for myself, who appear so honest and forthright,
aren't at all, and . . ." She broke off, the pain of
Rowe's betrayal flowing through her body, making her
shudder. It's the blasted wine that's doing this to me,
she thought.

At that moment he felt tremendous desire for her,
mixed with an equal amount of compassion. Who had
hurt her so badly? Her husband? "Let me take you
home, now," he said abruptly, and rose.

"Yes," she said, "I suppose that's a good idea. We
can do a club some other time."

He left her in her private doorman's capable hands.
He didn't want to see her home, he didn't want her any
closer. Because she was going to lose, fair and square.

"Good night, Elizabeth," he said, and lightly touched
his fingertips to her cheek. "Take three aspirin before
you go to bed. It never fails."

She nodded. feeling as though an earthquake were beginning under her feet. it was the first time she'd been three sheets to the wind in over six months.

She realized just before she fell asleep that he'd been calling her Elizabeth. She couldn't remember when he'd begun that. Probably after the second bottle of wine.

"I expected you back yesterday, boss," Midge said when Jonathan strolled into his office late the following morning.

"I should have called you. Sorry, Midge. I had more business in New York." Business, hell, he thought, thoroughly irritated with himself. *I was going to seduce that woman and she did me in.* Or he'd allowed himself to be done in. He wasn't certain who had done what to whom.

"You've got a call from Zurich," Midge said, lowering her voice. "Monsieur Flaucon wants you to call back immediately."

"Good," said Jonathan, and disappeared into his office.

Fifteen minutes later, he gently set the phone down and sat back in his chair. Midge appeared in the doorway. "Your ladies have also been calling. You want their numbers?"

"Yeah," he said after a moment. "Give me Christine's." She was blond, slender, and if he closed his eyes, just maybe . . .

He cursed and Midge laughed.

Christian Hunter didn't want to see Sarah Elliott, and she was sitting in his waiting room. He didn't want to see anyone except Elizabeth. He'd been parked in his car across the street from her house last night when that man had brought her home. At least the bastard hadn't gone upstairs with her. He couldn't have stood that.

The man was just a business acquaintance, that was all. But Elizabeth had been tipsy, he knew the signs.

Christian realized he was being an idiot. He'd see Elizabeth tonight and simply ask her what she'd done the night before. He leaned forward to buzz. "Send in Miss Elliott," he said.

He forced himself to concentrate on the young woman coming into his office. Again he felt that nagging sense of familiarity with the way she moved, walked. Very odd. He must be getting old. She also looked a bit tense, with ill-suppressed excitement. Coke again?

They got through the amenities, with Christian carefully studying her as she spoke. She told him she'd been out of town, but not where. Then he sat back in his chair, fiddling with his ever-present pen, and said, "What's his name, Miss Elliott?"

Catherine stopped cold in her tracks.

"The new man in your life. Who is he? Not the criminal sort, I hope."

"How did you know?"

"It was either coke or a man. You told me you were off coke, so that didn't leave much for me to think about."

"You believed me?"

"Of course. Is there any reason why I shouldn't?"

"No," she said sharply.

"Then you won't be requiring my services any longer, will you?"

Catherine closed her eyes a moment. "He, the man, he's . . . married."

Another lie, and so poorly executed.

"I see. And he has at least four children?"

"Very well, so he's not married. He is engaged to another woman and the wedding is to come off in under two weeks!"

"Well, the truth at last."

The words poured out of her mouth, all her hatred and distrust of Dr. Hunter buried for the moment, under an avalanche of feeling she herself couldn't understand. "I don't like him, not really. I wanted to know things from him, but it isn't turning out right.

He's not an honorable man, not really, and I know it. He's dishonest, an opportunist, a louse, but . . ."

"You've slept with him?"

"No!"

"But you want to."

Sleep with the same man who was Elizabeth's lover? My stepmother? For profit? Oh, God, no! That evening she'd spent with him at Barney's in Boston, at first they'd been like two sparring partners, each wary of the other, but it had changed.

"The weather's cold," Catherine had said, sipping on another whiskey, neat.

"Bullshit," said Rowe. "Only this evening, Catherine, then never again."

She'd leaned toward him, for the noise level in Barney's was ear-splitting. "She murdered my father, Rowe. I know it."

He gazed down into his whiskey glass. "It doesn't matter, not anymore, Catherine," he said finally. God, he was so sick of the whole thing, and his despicable part in it. "Even if she did, she can't be tried again. So what do you want to prove? That Christian Hunter lied? You won't, you know. He's got more brains and is slicker than any man I've ever seen. Do you think Elizabeth will suddenly collapse under the weight of her guilt and scream to the media that she truly did murder Timothy? You're being a fool, Catherine."

He saw the tears shimmering in her eyes. Unconsciously he reached his hand out and grasped hers. "Come on, sweetheart, just let it go. You've got your whole life ahead of you. Get on with it, Catherine."

"I've got nothing," she said.

"You're the oddest girl," he said, then realized he was holding her hand and quickly released it. "You're beautiful, you're rich, and it seems to me that you're also shedding your spoiled skin."

He'd said the latter in a light, amused voice, but Catherine had responded to it. "Do you really think so?"

"Yes," he said. "I really think so."

She'd leaned ever closer to hear his words, and he

kissed her. He hadn't meant to. He drew back, but not before his tongue slid over her lower lip.

"I'm sorry, Catherine," he said, and his voice was a bit shaky. "I didn't mean to do that. Now, just listen to me another minute. I honestly don't know if Elizabeth killed your father. I swear it to you. She never made any great confessions to me. I can't help you. Let me add that I feel rotten about my part in the entire affair. I wish it could be undone, but of course it can't. It might surprise you to know, Catherine, but Elizabeth, until the end, always appeared to me to be loving, very caring, and brave. No, don't pull away from me just because you don't like what I'm saying. You must understand, Elizabeth has changed from what I've heard. She's become ruthless, hard, if you will. But it was because of what I did to her. She's not a mercenary bitch, Catherine. Your father's money was never important to her."

"Then why did she marry an old man?"

He smiled at that. "You want to know something? I don't think even Elizabeth really understands why she married Timothy, or at least she'd never talk about it. But she didn't marry him for the Carleton name or the Carleton wealth. Believe it. I think it all had to do with her relationship with her own father, a cold, dictatorial bastard, from the small things she let slip. Perhaps she wanted a father who really loved her, who wanted to take care of her—not financially, but emotionally. God, now I'm sounding like a shrink. And I could just as easily be wrong about all of it. Maybe she knows exactly why she married your father, and just refuses to talk about it. I don't know, really."

"I don't like this, Rowe."

"Probably not." The uncertainty, the weariness in her eyes got to him, and he kissed her again.

They stared at each other.

"Don't ever see Christian Hunter again."

"But who killed my father?"

"Your father probably had at least a hundred enemies, men who hated his guts. That's not counting other women."

"Women! That's ridiculous!"

"Not at all. He was human, Catherine, not some sort of divine being with no faults. There were other women when he was married to all three of his wives, Elizabeth included."

"But—"

"No more, Catherine. Now, I'm leaving. If I stay, I'll kiss you again, and I don't want that. I've been enough of a jerk in the near past. No longer."

"But she's a bitch!"

"Elizabeth—"

"No, your Amanda Montgomery."

He didn't take offense. "Look, Catherine," he said at last, "life is a series of compromises. If we decide on a certain course of action, we must be prepared to accept the consequences of any decision we make. I know what I'm doing. I know the consequences. Now, go home. Do something with your life."

He'd pulled out his money clip, tossed a twenty on the small circular table, and left.

Catherine heard Dr. Hunter say something to her, and she started, pulled from her memories.

"As I said, Miss Elliott, I no longer believe myself to be of any use to you."

Catherine sat back in her chair, carefully folding her hands, to gain time. She said at last, "I saw you in the courtroom when you testified for Elizabeth Carleton."

Every muscle tensed, every sense was alerted, but nothing appeared on his face. He was much too good, was far too experienced, to allow any surprise to show.

"I thought you looked familiar," he remarked. "What were you doing at the trial? You have a ghoulish tendency?"

"No, not at all. I thought you were very good. But I knew you were lying."

"Perhaps you're the D.A.'s daughter? Ah, a reporter? That's it, isn't it?"

Christian was watching her closely, judging her expressions, trying to place her in his mind's eye. Who was she?

18

"The jury didn't believe I lied, Miss Elliott—or whatever your name is," Christian said, his voice mild, detached.

"No, they didn't. They were fools. I've just found myself wondering why you did lie, Dr. Hunter. Since it came out that you're very rich, it couldn't have been for money. So I think it's because you're in love with Elizabeth Carleton, or maybe she found a skeleton in your past and blackmailed you."

"You've a very imaginative girl," Christian said as he rose. "I believe you know the way out."

Catherine rose, uncertain, knowing that she'd made a monumental mistake.

"You're a damned hypocritical liar! You let a guilty woman go free!"

"The door," said Christian, pointing.

"I hate you!" Without thought, Catherine pulled off the black wig and flung it at him.

Christian wasn't too surprised, not now. "How do you do, Miss Carleton." He tossed the wig back at her and she caught it.

"Please," Catherine said, placing her hands palm-down on his desktop, "please tell me why you lied for her."

Christian merely looked at her appraisingly. "So, the man you've been seeing is none other than Rowe Chalmers. You'd best steer clear of him, Miss Carleton. You may go now."

"But . . . how could you possibly know?"

"You said you wanted him to tell you things, that he wasn't honorable. Rowe Chalmers is the only man I know of who could have told you about Elizabeth Carleton, the only man to fit the bill, so to speak."

"Please, you must tell me the truth!"

"Very well, Miss Carleton. I can assure you that I didn't lie. Elizabeth Carleton did not kill your father."

She found herself being convinced in that instant. His voice was intense, sincere, so very believable. She shook herself, and said in some disgust, "I really blew it, didn't I?" She started laughing as she turned on her heel and marched out of his office.

Christian stood silently for many minutes. The damned little bitch was trying her best to hurt Elizabeth. He couldn't allow that. No, he *wouldn't* allow that.

That evening, over Kogi's sushi dinner, Christian told Elizabeth about his fake patient. "She admitted everything to me, finally. Incidentally, she's been to see Rowe Chalmers. If she gives you any more trouble, Elizabeth, I want you to promise me you'll let me know."

Elizabeth was appalled. "Oh, dear," she said, and forgot about her dinner. "Yes, of course I'll tell you. How awful for you, Christian."

He shrugged. "I can handle little tarts like her. But she's got a malicious mouth. I don't like it. I don't know whether she'll let it go now. I do know that she's taken with Chalmers, even though she denied going to bed with him. Interesting, isn't it?"

Catherine and Rowe? And Amanda Montgomery . . .

Elizabeth shuddered, unaware that Christian was watching her closely. She was wondering with a sinking feeling if Rowe had told Catherine about the ice pick she'd held to his throat, how she'd mocked him, and how frightened he'd been.

Kogi appeared at Elizabeth's shoulder, carrying a small silver tray with two cognacs.

"Delicious dinner," Christian said. "A beautiful watch. I believe I recognize it. Didn't it belong to Mr. Carleton?"

Kogi beamed, his slender fingers caressing the solid gold band. "Yes, Mrs. Carleton gave to me."

Elizabeth came out of her fog at that moment. "Kogi adored that watch. I wanted him to have a memento, and since I'd given the watch to Timothy, I felt I could give it again."

"I take off only when I shower or clean."

"I don't blame you," said Christian.

"I didn't realize you'd ever met Timothy." Elizabeth shook her head. "How strange, but I simply hadn't thought about it before."

"I met him several times, the last time quite a good while before his death. I didn't mention it. I didn't really think it was important."

When they were alone again, Christian sipped his cognac, still watching her face, and said finally, "I just happened to see you last evening, Elizabeth. Who was that fellow you were with?"

Elizabeth started. "Oh, goodness, Christian, what a coincidence. That fellow was only a business acquaintance. Actually, thinking about it now, I don't know why I did agree to have dinner with him. But he's back home now, long gone. I keep thinking about Catherine. I'd just like to forget it, Christian, all of it. Let her do her worst."

"I don't trust Rowe Chalmers."

"I just hope for Catherine's sake that he leaves her alone."

Christian said, his voice dry, "My impression is that our Catherine is the one interested, not Mr. Chalmers."

"I can assure you that Laurette Carleton would scotch anything along that line in an instant. Now, before you ask, Christian, what would you like me to play for you?"

Christian sat back on the sofa, his eyes closed, listening as the beautiful Mendelssohn flowed through him. When she was in the middle of a third piece, he opened his eyes to look at her. Her expression made him frown. Her face was cold, emotionless, as if her fingers weren't part of her, as if the music had nothing to do with her. She was like an excellent performing automaton.

He walked quietly up behind her and gently began to knead her shoulders. She was tense, her muscles knotted. He leaned down, lifted her hair, and kissed the nape of her neck. "Elizabeth," he said softly, stifling a groan. He sat beside her on the bench and pulled her against his chest.

Elizabeth was startled and her thoughts were a tangled mess. No, she wanted to tell him, oh, no, please don't do that, Christian. Please don't expect anything from me! She felt his tongue lightly touch her closed lips, prodding a bit, and she drew back, alarm and fright in her eyes.

"Elizabeth," he said again, but she laughed, a nervous sound, and wriggled away and off the piano bench.

She splayed her fingers in front of her. "Please, Christian, I can't. You must understand that . . ."

Christian sighed, getting a grip on himself. "I understand," he said, and rose from the piano bench. He was expected at Susan's in an hour's time. God, he would need her tonight. At least her repertoire had increased a bit. She'd worked up to "Nobody Does It Better." She didn't do it well, but at least it was recognizable.

Laurette Carleton felt bone-tired. She was so weary of just plain living. She turned to face Michael, who was staring into his martini glass. She thought he was drinking too much these days, but now wasn't the time to speak to him about it. Later, she would straighten him out.

"Did you find out the name of the man Elizabeth was with at Pirouette?" she asked.

"Yes. Jonathan Harley. He owns a highly successful high-tech electronics company in Philadelphia."

"Why?" Words were so difficult nowadays. Stringing them together, making them make sense. How she wished Timothy were here speaking to her, not Michael. So many times in the past they could simply look at each other and understand, words not necessary.

Michael shrugged. "I can find out. But it seems to me logical that ACI wants his company. If you'll recall, there was some mention of him months ago."

"Will he sell to her?"

"He might have to. He's got a huge loan out from a bank in Philadelphia, at least that's what I heard. Nothing verified."

"Buy his loan. If he sells, it will be to us."

"Yes, Mother."

Jonathan thought it was fun. In fact, he hadn't enjoyed himself so much in months. Here was the famous or infamous Michael Carleton, in the flesh, wanting to buy his company. Revenge, of course, against Elizabeth. The deal he was offering was unbelievable.

Once he'd run down, Jonathan said very honestly, "I'm not selling to anyone, Mr. Carleton, I can promise you that."

"But she has your loan and she will call it in. I know of your current difficulties, Mr. Harley. ACI has resources you can't even begin to imagine. They—"

"I'm not selling to anyone," Jonathan repeated firmly. "Believe it."

Michael had to be content with that, but something nagged at him. "Then why were you having dinner with Elizabeth in New York at Pirouette?"

Jonathan wasn't amazed, just a bit surprised. "Your network of informants is impressive, Mr. Carleton," he said, his voice mild. "I will say it one last time: I'm not going to sell my company. As you know, I'm the majority stockholder. I'm in control and I'll stay in control."

When Michael Carleton took his leave some five minutes later, Jonathan sat perfectly still, staring at nothing in particular. He'd made love—no, he amended—

he'd had sex with both Christine and Holly since his return from New York, and he hadn't enjoyed himself. It was all her fault, that damned woman who was probably also a murderess. He sighed, and tried to get down to work. An hour later, he left his office and jogged until he was ready to drop.

He wasn't at all surprised when Midge buzzed him late that afternoon, saying, "Mrs. Carleton is on line one, boss. Elizabeth Carleton, that is."

He grinned, and lifted the phone. "Hello, Elizabeth, how's tricks?"

Elizabeth curled her hands into fists. "That's my line, Mr. Harley. I understand you had a meeting with Michael Carleton."

"That's right."

He heard her sharp intake of breath, and added, mocking her, "It appears we were seen by one of the Carleton spies at Pirouette. I guess you're going to have to strike that restaurant off your list. Back to a diet of tacos."

"Well?" She couldn't think of anything more to say; otherwise she'd spit.

"I assured Michael Carleton that I had no intention of selling my company to anyone, you included."

He heard her almost unconscious sigh of relief, and his eyes narrowed. "It's the truth, you know, Elizabeth," he added, his voice almost gentle.

"Certainly, whatever you wish to say is fine with me. I just hope you're not lying to me, Mr. Harley."

"No, I'm not lying. How suspicious you are, Elizabeth."

"Don't call me Elizabeth, and go to hell," she said, and slammed down the receiver.

"Why are you whistling like you haven't a care in the world?" Midge asked, poking her head through the door. "The dragon lady is pretty fast, isn't she?"

"I believe it's called networking," Jonathan said blandly. And he laughed.

"Their machinations are pretty awesome," Midge said, wondering at his fit of humor.

"Yep, they are. Now, I believe I've got a meeting with Mr. Dip, or is it Mr. Drop?"

"Mr. Doone."

"Well, I intend to iron out the last of our union problems. Nip them in the bud now. I'll make him a proposition he can't refuse. Show him in when he arrives, Midge."

"You got it, Godfather."

It was only five weeks until the wedding. Jenny was humming softly as she fingered her wedding gown, a Chanel creation of silk and lace, so exquisite she was almost afraid to touch it. She'd flown with her mother to Paris the previous week for the final fittings. And now she missed Brad. Very much. She hadn't seen him for nearly two weeks.

She gently zipped up the garment bag, and nodded to her maid. "Is my father home?"

"Yes, Miss Jennifer. He's in his study."

Jenny tapped lightly on the study door, then quietly opened it. She saw her father sitting in his usual place behind his mahogany antique desk, but he wasn't wearing his glasses, nor was he on the phone, as was his usual habit when at home.

"Dad, are you all right?"

Senator Charles Henkle forced himself together. His sweet, innocent daughter. Ha! He felt a spasm of rage at the thought of those indecent photographs. A father shouldn't have to see his daughter, his only daughter, being fucked. And that's what it had been. Fucked by a faggot. He forced himself to say, as he watched her walk toward him, concern written so clearly on her open face, "I'm just fine, Jenny. Where's your mother?"

That was odd, Jenny thought, pausing. He rarely asked about her mother. Particularly during the day.

"I'm not sure," she said. "I think she had some sort of charity function, a luncheon, I believe, for Greenpeace."

"Oh," said Senator Henkle. He cleared his throat. "Is there something you want, Jenny? I'm quite busy."

"Well, I'm going up to Long Island this weekend, to the Carletons'. I wondered if you would have time to come with me. At least one dinner."

"No! I mean, I don't have time, Jenny."

"Dad, what's wrong?"

He couldn't meet her eyes. Finally, drawing a deep breath, he said, "Are you certain you wish to marry Brad Carleton?"

Jenny blinked. "Of course, Dad."

"You . . . you love him?"

"Of course."

Jenny's strong suit wasn't brains. Charles had long accepted that. She was guileless, easily led, malleable, and what the Carletons were doing to her, and to him, was disgusting. And there was nothing he could do about it.

"I thought you liked Brad."

She sounded bewildered, uncertain, like a child.

He saw the photos again in his mind's eye. No, she wasn't a child, at least her body wasn't a child's, nor the silent scream on her lips when she'd reached orgasm.

"I just want you to be happy," he said finally. He wished he had the guts to expose the whole mess, and damn the consequences, or to have Brad Carleton killed. Just like his stepmother had killed his father. And she'd gotten off. Charles shook his head. God, what was he thinking? He pictured the headline and gave a ghastly smile. "SENIOR SENATOR MURDERS GAY SON-IN-LAW."

"I'm happy," Jenny said. "I promise you." She rushed to him and hugged him tightly. "I love you, Daddy."

He wanted desperately at that moment to show her the negatives of Brad and his lover, and her with Brad. To show her the kind of people the Carletons really were. His hand fluttered for an instant over the locked desk drawer. Slowly he withdrew his hand. "Go about your business, Jenny. I've really got lots of work to do."

She left him, her happiness only momentarily dimmed.

Perhaps, she thought, he just didn't want to let her go to another man. She'd been his baby for such a long time. She liked that notion. She was important to him.

Catherine was trembling, she couldn't help it. But she couldn't believe her eyes, literally. She was standing in her grandmother's study, a sheaf of photographs in her hand. She hadn't purposely intended to snoop, but she'd seen the normally locked desk drawer slightly ajar. Her grandmother had gone upstairs for a moment, and Catherine had decided to wait for her here. And she'd seen the interesting-looking manila envelope and eased it out of the drawer.

And opened it.

Brad and another man. Copulating? Or was it sodomizing? Slowly she lifted the top photo and looked at the next one. More of the same, only from a different angle.

Oh, God. Of course she'd heard rumors, who hadn't? But she'd never believed them.

More photos. Jenny and Brad. Definitely copulating. Attached to the top of one of those photos was a phone number with a Washington, D.C., area code.

What did it mean? She heard her grandmother's voice coming from the corridor and hastily slipped the photos back into the envelope and the envelope back into the drawer. She was careful to leave the drawer slightly open. Her grandmother had eagle eyes. She never missed a thing.

Oh, Jenny. That poor little Milquetoast.

What did it mean? What should she do?

She watched her grandmother walk slowly into the study, her carriage erect, as usual, her white hair pristine, as usual. She looked so damned regal, so Victorian. And yet, the photos. Catherine shuddered again.

"Hello, my dear," Laurette said, giving Catherine her special smile. "What brings you here this morning?"

What to say? Catherine felt color creep over her cheeks.

Oh, God!

"I . . . I just wanted to tell you that I don't have nosebleeds anymore!"

"That's good," said Laurette, and Catherine felt her grandmother's searching gaze on her face. Studying her like an insect under glass.

"That was all, really. And I'm no longer seeing Dr. Christian Hunter."

"Excellent. I'm delighted you took my advice. Just one other thing, my dear. What about Rowe Chalmers?"

Catherine's eyes fell. "I won't see him again either." That was probably a lie, she knew. But all she wanted to do now was escape, and think.

"I'm pleased, Catherine. Will you be staying for lunch?"

Catherine felt frantic. She knew she hadn't the courage or the ability to withstand her grandmother's inevitable inquisition.

"No, I'm sorry, Grandmother, but I have an appointment in the city."

"What kind of appointment?"

"With a dentist! One of my fillings came out the other day."

Laurette said nothing for a moment. She was wondering what was wrong with Catherine and why she was lying to her. Well, she had too much on her mind to probe, at least for the moment. Maybe she wasn't lying after all. "All right, then, my dear. Tonight, dinner. You know Jenny is coming up for the weekend today. I think a family gathering is appropriate. A welcome for Jenny. The wedding is in five weeks, you know."

Catherine wanted to puke.

"I'll try, Grandmother," she said, and escaped.

Christian stopped short and stared into the jeweler's window at the display of expensive watches. He felt a surge of panic and took a step backward, bumping into a woman loaded down with shopping bags. She glared at him, and he apologized.

My God, he thought, how could he have been so stupid? He got a hold of himself. So he'd remarked on Timothy Carleton's watch being on Kogi's wrist. So what?

Elizabeth had said she'd given the watch to Timothy. Surely he'd worn it often, perhaps every day. And he had met Timothy in the past.

It had been a minor slip. Stupid, but not important. He resumed his walk down Fifth Avenue.

He had to find out when Elizabeth had given Timothy the watch.

But very carefully, very subtly.

He'd seen the watch only once. It had been on Timothy Carleton's wrist the night Christian had plunged the ice pick into his chest.

He remembered the glitter of the gold in the lamplight very clearly. He remembered thinking vaguely that the old man didn't deserve such a lovely watch. It had reminded him of all the immensely valuable jewels found on the mummies of ancient Egypt. It had looked ridiculous on Timothy's vein-knotted wrist.

He felt the hairs on the back of his neck bristle. He felt his palms grow sweaty.

He must be very careful. He cursed himself softly at his fear. It was ridiculous. The whole thing was nonsense. Elizabeth had probably given Timothy that watch for a wedding present.

He kept walking. His fear abated. He would very easily find out about the wretched watch, then everything would be fine again.

19

Brad Carleton stared at his sister.

"You've got to call it off, Brad," Catherine said again. "You've got to."

They were standing in the middle of Brad's room at the Carleton mansion on Long Island. Jenny and her mother were due to arrive in a couple of hours.

Brad got a hold of himself. "Listen, Cathy, you'll forget what you saw, do you understand me?"

"What were those photos doing in Grandmother's desk? Whose phone number was written on the envelope?"

"Stop it, you little fool! Let me put it this way—a deal has been cut with Jenny's father. That's all there is to it. The wedding will take place."

"Do you want to marry Jenny?" Catherine asked quietly. Her revulsion was momentarily damped by the long affection she'd had for her older brother. She'd idolized him since she was a little girl.

Brad shrugged. He looked pale and very unhappy. "There's nothing I can do to change anything now," he said.

"But it's not fair to either of you! I know Jenny has about as much personality as a doorstop, but she's still a human being, Brad, she's got to have feelings."

"As you saw on those damned photos, she's also wild in bed," he said, and grimaced at the memory.

"I saw that you were wild in bed too, in the other photos."

"Look, Cathy, just leave it alone, all right? Grandmother has spoken. It's all over but the rice-throwing."

"It was blackmail, wasn't it?" Catherine asked slowly, staring at her brother's face. "Grandmother blackmailed Senator Henkle with those photos of you and Jenny."

"Yes."

"But those photos of you with that other man? I don't understand." But of course she did.

"It was Elizabeth, dear bitchy Elizabeth, who sent those photos to Henkle, but she backed off when she saw the photos of me and Jenny."

It took several moments for that to sink in. Finally Catherine said, "Is it part of the deal that you become monogamous once you and Jenny are married?"

"Yes, it is."

"And will you be?"

"I . . . I don't know," Brad said. "God, I wish I could just leave the country!"

"Me too," said Catherine on a sigh. "Why don't we go together. How about Katmandu? Bombay?"

"Even Havana." He touched her cheek. "I'm sorry about all this," he said. "But what's done is done."

"I think you should be in California, not Trent."

"Yeah, and old Trent is so straight it would make your hair curl."

"Then bring him back here and you go there. Start a new life, one that you select. You're a grown man, an adult. It's simple, Brad."

She saw a momentary flare of hope in his eyes, then the glazed acceptance. She said very quietly, "I love you, Brad, but I can't let you do this. Not to Jenny, not to yourself."

"You try to stop it, and God knows what will happen."

Catherine gave him one long last look, saw the defeat on his face, and headed for the door. She paused, and said over her shoulder, "Another thing. Do you know, I'm not convinced anymore that Elizabeth killed our father."

Brad looked at her blankly. "Then who the hell did?"

Catherine gave a bitter laugh. "You know, I wouldn't be surprised if it wasn't Grandmother. She wasn't the one to back off, and yet Elizabeth did."

"No," he said seriously. "Our father is the only one of the family she would never harm."

"At least not intentionally?"

"She can't help the way she is. And we—all of us—keep her there, on her throne."

"Why did Elizabeth back off? You would think she'd do anything to get back at us for what we've done to her."

"Who knows? Go away, Catherine. And keep your mouth shut."

Laurette watched Brad and Jenny with great complacency that evening at the dinner table. The girl would do just fine. She would do exactly what she was told. And if Brad didn't do enough telling, she certainly would. Her eyes shifted down the table to Catherine. Something was definitely wrong there. She should probably put a man on her again to find out what she was doing.

Catherine flinched every time Jenny opened her mouth, and it was invariably something that she deferred to Brad. Jenny's mother looked as if she'd caught a whale in her fishing net, so pleased, so proud of her wimpy daughter for her windfall catch. Stupid, useless woman!

What to do? Catherine was thinking.

Elizabeth sent the photos of Brad and his lover to Senator Henkle. Then she backed off. Why?

Catherine made up her mind over the medallions of veal and creamed asparagus.

Millicent Stacy frowned as she gently eased into Elizabeth's office.

"Yes, Milly?"

She didn't quite know what to say. She stood there feeling like a fool, her hands clasped in front of her.

"A fire? One of our companies bit the bullet? Come, what's up? I can take it, I swear."

"No, Elizabeth, none of the above. Catherine Carleton is outside. She wants to see you."

Elizabeth blinked. Catherine!

"Well, I suppose I have no choice but to see her. If you hear mayhem beginning, please come back, Milly. I might be strangling the girl."

Catherine was dressed to kill, Elizabeth thought as she walked into her office in a Valentino black-and-white-checked wool ensemble. Kill. What an odd way to think of it.

"Catherine," she said, slowly rising from her chair.

"Thank you for seeing me, Elizabeth."

Good God, what was going on? Catherine sounded absolutely benign.

"What do you want?"

"I'm beginning to think you didn't kill my father."

Elizabeth arched an eyebrow. "Well, that's something. Intelligence and objectivity in a Carleton."

"I suppose I deserve that. But I wanted to talk to you about something else."

"Well?"

"The photos of Brad and that other man."

Elizabeth became very still. Finally she said, "However did you find out about that mess?"

"By accident. I also saw the photos of Brad and Jennifer Henkle. Brad told me it was all blackmail and you were the one who started it off."

"True. I was an arrogant fool and I was awfully wrong."

"But then you backed off. Why?"

Elizabeth sighed. "It's not too difficult to come to a sane conclusion, Catherine. Your grandmother told me quite clearly, not in person, of course, that if I didn't back off, she'd have the photos of your brother and Jennifer Henkle all over the media. You must know that I have nothing at all against the Henkle girl.

However, the thought of her still marrying Brad turns my stomach."

"It turns Brad's too," said Catherine.

"But he'll go through with it, won't he, Catherine?"

"Yes. It's funny, you know, but I always thought Brad was the strong one among the three of us. But he's not. He's scared. He'll do as he's told."

"And what about you, Catherine? Why are you really here?"

Elizabeth realized suddenly that the two of them were standing in the middle of her office, squared off like opponents in the boxing ring.

She waved her hand toward a sofa. "Oh, sit down, Catherine. Do."

"I want to know if you can stop it, Elizabeth."

"I? Look, Catherine, I've done my bit. It backfired, like a lot of other things I've done. Some because your family got the better of me, and most because I'm so ignorant."

"You sent those photos of Brad to Senator Henkle as revenge?"

"No, as leverage against your brother. He hasn't endeared himself to me, Catherine. None of you have, but Brad was a major thorn in my side—and still is, occasionally."

"Who killed my father, Elizabeth?"

"If I knew that, don't you think I'd do something about it? God, you're a fool, Catherine! Listen, I truly am sorry about all this, particularly about poor Jennifer Henkle, but your grandmother will have her way. You know it. I know it. Now, if there's nothing else . . ."

Catherine sighed. "No, I guess not. It was stupid of me to come here. I know there's nothing you can do, and why should you?"

"Life could be simpler, that's for sure," Elizabeth said. "Instead, things seem to multiply, blurring issues, turning enemies into noncombatants if not allies." Elizabeth dashed her fingers through her hair, loosening the chignon. "Oh, Catherine, I'll try to think of something, but I can almost guarantee you that anything I came up with wouldn't work. Why don't you confront your grandmother?"

"I wanted to but I'm afraid."

"I don't blame you, but think about it."

"I suppose you know I was seeing Christian Hunter."

"Yes."

"And Rowe Chalmers."

"Yes."

"I don't know what to do!"

"Most of the time, I don't either."

Millicent Stacy appeared in the doorway. "There's an urgent call for you, Elizabeth."

"Thank you for talking to me, Elizabeth. I know I've acted a bitch toward you—"

"Yes, but not anymore, I trust. You've surprised me more than I can say. I will try to think of something. Good-bye, Catherine, and good luck."

Elizabeth waited until Catherine had left her office. She stared thoughtfully after her, then shook her head, bemused. Nothing ever stayed the same, and if it did, it was usually the bad things, the awful things. Catherine coming around? Catherine being nice? It was almost too much to take in. She'd forced herself not to think about Jennifer Henkle. Now the senator's daughter was back with a vengeance. What could she do? She was a fool to have promised Catherine that she'd try to come up with a solution.

She walked back to her desk and picked up the phone. "Yes? Elizabeth Carleton."

"Hi, Liz. Jonathan Harley."

Liz? "Yes?" Her voice was as forbidding as she could make it.

"I think it's time, dear lady, that you and I got together again."

"I don't."

"Let me put it this way: you've got to see me. If you refuse, you'll be very upset with yourself."

"Then tell me, now."

"Nope. In person. I'll see you at your Mexican restaurant this evening. Seven okay by you?"

Elizabeth frowned at the phone. What did the wretched man want now?

"Oh, very well. But, Mr. Harley, this had better be good."

There was a slight pause; then, "You can count on it, Liz. I promise you that."

"Don't call me Liz."

"At least I'm calling you. That should count for something."

"Don't push your luck, Mr. Harley. This evening at seven."

"You got it, kiddo."

There was a click in her ear. What was he up to? What she'd said to Catherine was right: every time she tried to simplify things, those things just got messier.

Jonathan Harley was waiting for her. He wasn't wearing a suit this time. He was casually dressed in brown cords and a light brown turtleneck sweater, with a tweed sport coat. He looked like a businessman on vacation, a handsome jock businessman.

He smiled up at her when she reached the table, but didn't rise. "Hello there," he said, and waved an expansive hand to the chair opposite him.

The waiter pulled her chair back for her.

"Don't you ever get tired of this place? Haven't you found another safe house?"

She shook her head.

"You can't keep hiding forever, Elizabeth."

"What do you want?"

"You want to try for a higher-level drunk tonight?"

"I was rather hoping that your plane wouldn't make it. Dining alone has its benefits, you know."

"Come now, Elizabeth, I didn't take you to bed. I left your virtue intact. Nary a whimper out of me."

She looked tired, he thought, and preoccupied. Worried. Well, he was going to set the seal on her evening. He hoped he would feel better about it. Still, he probably would be dancing on the table, grinning in her face by the time he was through.

"Cut the garbage, Mr. Harley." She turned to the hovering waiter and ordered a Perrier.

Jonathan nodded in agreement.

"You're not trying for much of a drunk with the Perrier, Mr. Harley."

"It's still a celebration drink, Elizabeth."

"You've discovered I have a terminal illness?"

"No, your insides as well as your outsides are well-nigh perfect. In perfect condition, that is."

She said nothing.

"I've thought about you quite a bit. In fact, I thought about you when I was making love to other women. It was very disconcerting."

She just gave him a weary look, refusing to rise to the bait.

"You're a barrel of laughs this evening, aren't you?"

"No, I'm tired and hassled and I'm a complete bore. Now, what is it you want?"

He started to tell her, to see the shock on her face, but he decided to hold off. "What's happened," he asked abruptly, "since the last time I saw you?"

The Perriers arrived. Elizabeth raised her glass, only to be forestalled by Jonathan.

"A toast, Elizabeth."

"What sort of toast?"

He frowned, biting back the words. Finally he said, his voice light, mocking, "To the future."

"Innocuous enough." She touched her glass to his, then sipped from it, half-wishing that she'd ordered a margarita. At least the tequila would hit her now, and make the world fade just a bit, blur it around the edges.

"Is it possible that you've missed me? That when you've made love with other men, you've thought of me?"

"Please, Mr. Harley," she said.

"What the hell is the matter?"

He sounded angry, and she cocked her head to one side, staring at him. His eyes were narrowed, his lips a thin line.

"All right. One of the major things is the sacrifice of a young woman. And it can't be stopped. There's nothing I can do, and it stinks."

"Tell me."

"No. Even if I trusted you, you could do nothing. Indeed, how could you even care?"

"Don't you trust anybody?"

"No. People do learn, even me."

The waiter came again and they ordered dinner.

"It would seem to me," Jonathan said after the waiter had left, "that you've the power to accomplish most things."

"Yes, most things. That's true, I suppose."

"You know, Elizabeth," he said after a moment, "perhaps in the future you could trust me."

"Come now, Mr. Harley, hatred doesn't change overnight, you know." But Catherine had changed, at least she appeared to have changed. Elizabeth wondered now if everything Catherine had said and done had been an act. No, at least her upset over Brad and Jennifer wasn't an act.

"It has, but not overnight, that's true."

"Please, I'm very tired, and I'm really not up to sparring with you. Just tell me what you want."

"All right," he said, suppressing a sigh. "I will." But he couldn't, not just yet. Talk about hatred. She would want to kill him.

Dinner arrived. They were silent for some minutes.

"The weather's nice," he said.

"Yes."

"I think the Giants are going to do great again. Don't you?"

Elizabeth carefully laid down her fork. "I'm walking out of here in ten minutes, Mr. Harley."

"Well, you won't walk out empty-handed, Elizabeth."

"What will you give me? An epidemic? A virus?"

"I still have a while before my loan is due."

She just looked at him, waiting.

He laid down his fork and sat forward. "I'll meet

you and your staff and lawyers, I suppose, tomorrow morning in your office at ten o'clock."

"Why?"

"I have a check for you, of course." He forked down a big bite, grinning at her. Her expression didn't change. She just became very still.

"Little girls shouldn't play in the big league," he said, wanting now to hear her yell, curse him. "You couldn't win, Elizabeth, even with all of ACI's resources behind you."

She still said nothing.

"You could do just as you pleased with your poor husband, but not with me, Elizabeth. Incidentally, I'll have my lawyer with me tomorrow. You won't keep me waiting will you?"

Damn her, why wouldn't she say something? Spit at him, try for a groin kick?

"You know," he continued after a dead-silent moment, "you're not bad, for a woman. Maybe with, say, ten more years' practice, you could be nearly as good as I was ten years ago. But it's your hormones, Lizzie, they make you emotional. You can't think as clearly as a man. As I said, you couldn't beat me."

Still she remained silent. Didn't she want to know how he had gotten the money? Couldn't she at least flay him verbally for his baiting remarks?

Finally she said very quietly, "I suppose you're right, Mr. Harley."

She very carefully drank the rest of her Perrier. She very carefully set the empty glass back on the table. She picked up her purse from the floor beside her and rose. She looked at him, then turned away and walked out of the restaurant.

Jonathan Harley cursed.

20

Jonathan walked into Elizabeth's office the following morning, precisely at ten o'clock, flanked by his lawyer, Josh Simpson. They'd gone to Yale together and Josh had been his opponent in the chess tournament senior year. He wished he could mention that to Elizabeth when he introduced them, but of course he couldn't.

Elizabeth was seated at the circular conference table with Adrian Marsh, Coy Siverston, and Rod Samuels.

"Good morning, Elizabeth, gentlemen," Jonathan said, his eyes never leaving her face. She was pale, he could see the strain in her eyes, but she was completely composed.

"Mr. Harley," Elizabeth said, nodding toward two empty chairs.

Jonathan introduced Josh.

"Now," he said, "I don't see any need for amenities this morning. I suppose Elizabeth told you why I'm here."

Adrian shook his head. "No, Mr. Harley, she didn't. Is it about an extension to your loan?"

Jonathan looked at Elizabeth, but she said nothing. "No," he said sharply, "I'm here to pay the loan off. Mr. Marsh, if you would please have your people compute what you think the balance is, we'll do a quick comparison and Josh here will go to our bank and get you a cashier's check."

There was no sound for many moments. Jonathan felt pleasure at their stunned expressions.

Coy said finally, "Do you mind me asking how you managed it, Mr. Harley?"

"You guys didn't think of Europe. And the guy you had tailing me never got close enough to notice that the man I'd hired to go through my routine for several days wasn't me. Even though I'm a small fish in the ocean compared to ACI, I do have contacts in Europe and some power. Easy, really." He didn't add that he'd gotten quite a bit of help from his ex-father-in-law, Andrew Pillson. "Besides," he added, "I hadn't been to Europe in several years. I wanted to rest a bit, along with the business."

Elizabeth said, "I have already had the loan balance computed, Mr. Harley. You may now check it with your computations."

She pulled out several sheets of paper from her briefcase and handed them to Jonathan.

The balance was the same as his. Of course. What had he expected?

He nodded to Josh. The four of them sat in grim silence around the table after Josh had left. Jonathan said, "Will you gentlemen please take a hike for, say, ten minutes?"

Adrian's eyes flew to Elizabeth's face. She nodded.

Once alone, Jonathan said, "What's wrong with you?"

She merely shook her head.

"Dammit, woman, you're a fighter! You're letting me walk on you like a dumb rug! What the hell happened?"

Elizabeth gave him a small smile. "What would you have me do, Mr. Harley? You won, you've told me that very clearly."

"Call me names."

"All right. You've proved yourself brilliant. Obviously a leader in cunning and survival, a risk-taker. I hope you rot."

He rose to his feet and began pacing her office. "I

straightened out my union problems," he said, frowning at her.

"Yes, I know."

"But you wanted them straightened out, didn't you, for your own profit?"

"Certainly. Even we unstable, emotional women can do some things right, you know."

He stood there staring at her. Her back was to him, her head slightly bowed. He saw the nape of her neck and wanted to touch her. It occurred to him that there was no reason for him ever to see her again. "Elizabeth," he said.

"Yes?"

"Damn you, stand up and face me!"

She did. "Yes, Mr. Harley?"

"Tell me you're not sleeping with Hunter for what he did for you."

That drew her out of her numb shell. He'd won, for God's sake. Right between the eyes, he'd fired straight-on. And now he was angry at her, and she simply didn't understand him. She was his enemy, wasn't she? And now, now he was the victor. Was this another way of rubbing her nose in it? She tilted back her head.

"Why, of course I sleep with Dr. Hunter. After all, since he saved me from life imprisonment, isn't he entitled to some consideration? He's really quite good. Sometimes, though, it's difficult . . . so many of my lovers are quite talented, really. But Christian ranks right up there with the best, and—"

He grabbed her and kissed her, hard.

"You're a pathetic little liar," he said, lifting his face, shaking her shoulders.

She tried to shrug, but it was impossible, he was holding her too tightly. She merely shook her head, trying to look bored.

He kissed her again. She did not respond, merely suffered him until he stepped away from her.

"A victory celebration of a manly sort, Mr. Harley?" she asked calmly, wiping the back of her hand across her mouth. "To show the little woman what she's worth? Polish off your little triumph with a show of male dominance and force my submission? With that performance I doubt you'd even make it to the ranking scale with my other lovers."

To her utter astonishment, he raked his fingers through his hair and said, "I'm sorry. That was uncalled for. I—"

There was a knock on the office door.

Just as well, Elizabeth thought, vaguely disconcerted. "Come in," she called out.

It was Adrian and Coy.

"Gentlemen," she said, forcing a ghastly smile. "If you two will please finish things up here with Mr. Harley, talk about baseball and all that sort of thing. I have an urgent meeting."

She turned back to Jonathan and saw a smudge of her lipstick on his mouth. She wondered if Adrian and Coy would notice it.

"Mr. Harley," she said, turned on her heel, and left the office.

There was no baseball talk.

Adrian saw the lipstick and wondered what the hell was going on. Coy was thinking only of that damned cashier's check and Harley's charade.

Elizabeth sat alone at home. It was midafternoon and she could hear Kogi moving about in the kitchen. Oh, yes, she remembered that Christian was coming to dinner. Her lover. One of her many lovers. She wished she could laugh.

What to do about Jennifer Henkle? Odd how losing to Jonathan Harley wasn't foremost in her mind, at least for the moment. She wondered now how she'd managed to get Jennifer Henkle out of her mind before. Probably because she'd realized quite early that there was nothing to be done.

Then Catherine had come, stirred everything up again. Made her see, made her feel guilty, as if she'd been partially responsible, which, she supposed, she had.

How, Elizabeth wondered, could Laurette Carleton force such a marriage? Obviously to save Brad from being uncovered as a gay, probably to keep him from getting diseased, to save the family from more scandal. There'd been a change in Brad over the past months, she realized now. He'd withdrawn, become more of a cipher. No, she wouldn't feel sorry for him.

She'd just have to give it up again, dismiss it from her mind. If Senator Henkle didn't care enough about his daughter to . . . To what? Create a horrendous scandal that would ruin all their lives? No, the senator had had no choice.

Think!

Leverage. That was the operative word. It sure hadn't worked on Jonathan Harley, but . . . Surely there was something she could do. Her mind went blank. In disgust, Elizabeth rose from her chair and walked automatically toward her piano. She stopped cold and stared at it.

I won't. I can't. Who cares about Jennifer Henkle? She's nothing to me. Nothing, nobody. But she'd know her if she saw her in the street, from the photographs.

She said to the piano, "You beat me, Jonathan Harley. You made me feel a total fool. Europe, you said. Switzerland, probably. And none of us considered that. Smart, slippery bastard."

There was a buzz from Gallagher downstairs.

Kogi emerged from the kitchen, wiping his hands on his apron. Flour, everywhere. Even on his watch. For an instant Elizabeth stared at Kogi's watch as he carefully wiped it with his sleeve, a frown on her brow. Timothy's watch. Something . . . something wasn't right.

"It's Mr. Harley," Kogi said, coming over to her. "He's downstairs and wants to see you."

More gloating? No, he hadn't gloated, not the way she would have thought. He'd kissed her, angrily.

"Please ask him what he wants, Kogi."

She heard Kogi's voice but couldn't make out his words.

"He say he has a surprise for you," Kogi said.

"A time bomb?" she said aloud, then shook her head. "Oh, very well, let him come up."

She was wearing jeans and a T-shirt that said "Musicians Play at Love." She was barefoot, her hair tied back in a ratty ponytail. Who cared?

She heard Kogi greet him at the front door, heard his footsteps coming toward the living room.

She rose finally, to face him. He'd changed out of his business suit and was also wearing jeans, a sport shirt, and a corduroy jacket.

"Mr. Harley, what do you want?"

"Didn't your man tell you I had a surprise for you?"

"Yes."

Jonathan thought she looked wonderful. No makeup, no severe chignon, no sexless business suit. She looked fresh, very young, and wary. As if she were afraid. Of him?

"May I sit down?"

"I suppose you must."

"Such graciousness."

"From the loser, what would you expect? Champagne? Caviar?"

"Coffee would be just fine."

She nodded toward Kogi.

"I'm sorry I attacked you this morning."

She merely looked at him. Like I'm some sort of insect, he thought. He added, mocking, "Well, not really sorry. Just out of place, I'm just sorry that I did it there, in your office. You made me mad."

"You're a man," she said, shrugging.

His eyes fell to her breasts at her movement. She wasn't wearing a bra.

"Oh, for heaven's sake, Mr. Harley, I'm not some sort of sexpot for your review! Just get on with it or get out."

He nodded and drew a sheaf of folded papers from his breast pocket. "Come here," he said, not looking up at her as he spread the sheets of paper on the coffee table in front of him.

Intrigued, Elizabeth sat down beside him, keeping some distance between them. "What's all this?"

"Hi-tech electronic companies. I found three that are in excellent shape. Great growth potential, given ACI's management system and influx of capital. More important, they want to sell, if the offer's right. I know two others that could be acquired, but they would be unfriendly."

Elizabeth was too stunned to say anything. She picked up the neatly typed pages and looked at them. She knew of all three companies, indeed, she and her management team had discussed the pros and cons of each. But she didn't tell him that, not now. She was much too interested in his motives, whatever they were.

"Why?"

He looked at her then, his eyes serious. "I don't know," he said after a moment. Then he shrugged. "I got it all together last night." He didn't tell her that he'd had his own plans to buy before she'd blasted into his life, and had had most of the figures at his disposal long before last night.

"Well, that's honesty of a sort, I suppose," she said, her head cocked at him.

Kogi brought in the coffee at that moment and deftly served it.

"Is this the Yale way, Mr. Harley? Give the loser a bone to save face?"

"No. I usually have a ball when I win. This . . . well, this is different."

"Why?"

"You."

The small word sounded utterly sincere, and for an instant Elizabeth felt something warm and glowing deep inside her. But only for an instant. Then she felt wary and very cold.

"I'm a very wealthy woman, Mr. Har—"

"Jonathan, please."

"Yes, well, I am."

"What does that have to do with the price of conch shells? I'm not exactly on skid row myself."

"Mr. . . . Jonathan, I appreciate this gesture. It's quite a surprise, truly, but—"

He cut her off, his hand slashing through the air. "Now that we have all this damned garbage out of the way, I want to see you. No more business, no more jockeying to see who can best the other, just a man and a woman."

Elizabeth reached for her coffee cup, not to drink, but to warm her suddenly cold hands. "What if I had won, Jonathan? Would you still have wanted to see me?"

"Good question," he said, his voice rueful. "I guess not. I probably would have put a contract on you."

"What makes you think I won't do that to you?"

He laughed. "You want to know something? I think maybe you've done some pretty rotten things since you took over ACI. To survive, you would have had to. It's made you wary and I understand that, but hear me, Elizabeth, I have no reason to want to hurt you, not now in any case. I want—" He broke off, staring at her, afraid of what he would say.

Elizabeth didn't want to hear what he had to say either. She jumped to her feet and turned her back to him, hugging her arms around herself. She said, "My life is a mess right now. There are so many things, so many problems—"

"Rowe Chalmers is out of your life. As far as I could tell, he was the biggest problem."

"You don't know the half of it," she said quietly. She slowly turned to face him. "Why would you want to see me when you believe I murdered my husband?"

"I don't. Think you murdered your husband, that is. No way on God's green earth could you have done something like that."

"You sound so certain. Too bad I didn't know you then. What a character witness you'd have made. Also too bad that Mr. Moretti believed so ardently that I was a cold-blooded bitch. Still believes, for that matter."

"Moretti's an ass."

"A very angry ass."

"Is there anything else you'd like to ask me, Elizabeth? To test me out, I guess?"

She rubbed her palm against her hair, dislodging the rubber band. A strand of it stood straight up on her head. Jonathan thought it endearing. He vaguely heard the phone ring.

Elizabeth didn't know what to say, and she was saved from trying to come up with something when Kogi appeared. "Excuse, please, ma'am, but Dr. Hunter is on the phone. He wants to know what time to come for dinner."

She saw Jonathan stiffen up like a poker.

Like an angry rooster who'd just spotted another rooster in his hen yard.

"Tell Dr. Hunter that seven o'clock will be fine, Kogi," she said very calmly.

Kogi nodded and left the room.

"Well," Jonathan said, rising to his feet. "I guess that sort of answers everything, doesn't it?"

"Not really," Elizabeth said, defeated.

"Just what does that mean, lady?"

"Jonathan," she said, "please. Thank you for your victor's gesture."

"Shove it," he said, and walked away from her, not looking back. She heard the front door slam.

She raised her hand, an unconscious gesture, then slowly let it fall.

"Brad, what's wrong?"

He wanted to yell at Jenny that he couldn't get it up, it was as simple as that.

"Did I do something wrong? Are you angry with me?"

Did she always have to be such a wimp? "I'm not angry at you, Jenny," he said, and rolled over onto his back. He looked up at the motel-room ceiling. Why had he brought her here anyway? He felt her hand tentatively slide down his stomach to his groin.

"Don't," he said. He heard a small sob, and felt like he'd just kicked his puppy. He turned back onto his side, facing her, his fiancée, the woman he was supposed to marry and spend the rest of his life with.

"Look, Jenny, I'm sorry. It's just that I've got a lot of things on my mind right now. It's really got nothing to do with you, okay?"

Jennifer nodded, of course. She wondered if he wanted her to go down on him. He liked sex that way, very much, but she was afraid to do it. She felt miserable and didn't know what to do about it. She said softly, "I think I'll go shower. We should be back to your grandmother's house in an hour."

Brad grunted, relieved when she rose from the bed and went into the bathroom. He wished he had someone he could talk to. He wished he could see Evan. Evan would understand, he always did. But Evan was in Greece, probably screwing every young man he could find with the buy-off Laurette had provided.

You and Trent should change places. That was what Catherine had told him. Let old Trent come back here and be under Grandmother's veined hand. Why not? He wasn't poor, he could skip out, he could do anything he pleased.

There wasn't even the pleasurable thought of destroying Elizabeth any longer. They'd been found out and all major leaks were shut off. He ran his companies, sure, but now he was under Elizabeth's hand just as much as his grandmother's. He'd been coasting the past couple of months, existing really, nothing more.

He rose from the rumpled bed. He heard the shower shut off. He prayed Jenny wouldn't come out naked. He didn't think he could stand it.

He was going to break it off. First, Grandmother. He was smiling when Jenny, wearing a towel, emerged from the bathroom.

The ballroom in the Dickerson mansion in Back Bay glittered under the chandeliers. The guests and the myriad flower arrangements were stunning, the noise level sedate. Jewels shimmered, men and women danced to the band. Catherine shook Mrs. Dickerson's hand, murmuring, "Thank you so much for having me on such short notice. You're very kind."

"Certainly, my dear. Our pleasure. How is your grandmother?"

"She's fine."

Another couple came up behind Catherine, and Mrs. Dickerson patted Catherine's hand, saying, "Go enjoy yourself, my dear. You already know many of the guests."

Oh, yes, Catherine thought, walking slowly into the ballroom, but there's only one I want to see, must see.

She took a proffered glass of champagne from a silver tray held toward her by a Dickerson servant, and sipped it.

She saw Amanda Montgomery, the center of attention in a small group of people. Rowe wasn't with her. Then she spotted him with a group of businessmen next to a potted palm in the corner. He looked very solid, trustworthy, and Catherine knew she'd been right to come. She set down her empty glass on a tray and made her way through the crowd to him.

She lightly placed her hand on his arm. He turned in mid-sentence, surprise and something else in his expression. He just stared at her.

"Excuse me, gentlemen," she said gaily. "I have come to take Mr. Chalmers away to the dance floor."

"What a ludicrous surprise. May I ask what you're doing here?" Rowe wasn't at all amused. He realized on a gut level that she looked good, so good that he'd like to haul her out to the balcony and make love to her, but that was ridiculous, of course.

"I was invited. Can't you just say hello to me, Rowe, like you're glad to see me for once?" Catherine placed her hand in his, her other on his shoulder. "Dance," she said, pressing against him.

He began to move automatically. "Catherine, if you don't stop doing what you're doing, I'm going to have to turn my back on everybody."

"I get to you that much, Rowe?"

"Bitch, you know exactly what you're doing."

"Dance, Rowe."

He sighed. "What is it this time, Catherine?"

She tilted back her head to look at his face. "You want to know something? I don't have anybody I can talk to, that I can trust. Except you, as odd as that might sound."

"Bull."

"All right. I wanted to tell you that I spoke to Elizabeth the other day. I apologized to her, at least I tried to. I've never seen her look more surprised."

He stared at her, nonplussed. "Why did you do that? You hate her guts."

"No, not anymore. I needed to know something, but I knew she couldn't help. You want to know something else? I believe that if she could help, she would."

"I believe the world is going flat. This is the evil woman who murdered your father, remember?"

"I was wrong. I've been a fool."

He eyed her. "That makes two of us," he said. "What changed your mind?"

"You, a bit, then Christian Hunter, then Elizabeth herself put the lid on it. I guess I needed someone I could see to blame. And Elizabeth was the obvious person to have done it. Now, not knowing who did it, thinking that it could be a member of my family—" She broke off, seeing Amanda over Rowe's shoulder, staring at her. God, if a look could kill . . .

She said quietly, "If I'm no longer a bitch, does that mean you're no longer a bastard?"

"You can't change the past, Catherine."

"No, but you can change the future, and learn to live with the past." She smiled a bit. "I think Dr. Hunter said something of the sort to me. He's right, you know."

The music stopped, and they stood there unmoving, looking at each other.

"Well, what's this? Catherine Carleton? What are you doing here?"

Rowe released Catherine slowly, easily. "I see you remember Catherine, Amanda. She's here because she was invited and happened to be in Boston."

"Hello, Amanda. Lovely diamonds you're wearing."

"Thank you. Why don't you go somewhere and play, Catherine? With someone else. Rowe, our dance?"

Rowe wasn't at all surprised when, at one o'clock in the morning, he returned home and found Catherine waiting for him in her car. She joined him at the front door and smiled. "Amanda did tell me to go play, Rowe."

"It's late," he said, turning the key in the lock.

"May I come in?"

"It's not a good idea, and you know it, Catherine."

She grabbed his lapels and kissed him. He finally pulled her hands away. "You do that again, and we're going to end up in bed."

She kissed him again. "Isn't that why you came here? Alone? You knew, didn't you, that I'd be here?"

He kissed her.

"Delicious dinner, as usual," Christian said, patting his stomach and sitting back in his chair.

"Yes," Elizabeth said automatically, her thoughts still on Jonathan Harley.

"You're a million miles away tonight, sweetheart."

She flinched at the endearment. "Forgive me, Christian. Business problems, always more of them, jumping out at the oddest times to make me crazy."

"Well, I want you to drop them, all right? I have something important to ask you, Elizabeth."

Oh, no, she thought, staring at him. Please, no.

"Here's Kogi with your favorite coffee, Christian."

While Kogi poured, Elizabeth's eyes were drawn again to his watch—Timothy's watch, which Christian had said he'd seen and admired.

Something nagged at her, but she couldn't put her finger on it, something she should remember. Lord, Jonathan Harley had turned her into an idiot.

"What are you thinking now, Elizabeth?"

"I was just thinking that I had to be wrong about something. Nothing important, not really. Shall I play for you, Christian?"

"Very well."

She played until he stopped her. He said very gently, standing behind her at the piano, "Marry me, Elizabeth."

She became very still.

"I love you, Elizabeth, have loved you for the longest time. Marry me."

"I can't, Christian," she said, turning on the piano bench to face him. "I'm sorry, but I can't. You are my dearest friend, you know that. But I don't love you, not like I should to marry you."

"Is there someone else?"

"No. Oh, Christian, can't we continue as we have? You've done so much for me and—"

"Yes," he said, "I have. I lied for you. I lied for you because I loved you, even then. I have tried to protect you. If I hadn't involved myself, you might still be with Rowe Chalmers, and the Carletons would have had their revenge."

She stared at him, but she realized she wasn't surprised, not really. "You sent me that anonymous letter about their meeting, didn't you?"

"Yes, certainly. I've watched over you, Elizabeth. There's that other man, the one I saw bringing you home that night. Who is he?"

"No one of any importance at all."

"Elizabeth, I'm trained to know when someone is lying. Who is he?"

She suddenly felt afraid. Something in his eyes alarmed her. Jealousy, she thought, it had to be jealousy.

She tried to smile. "Just an acquaintance, Christian. Someone I've locked horns with in business, that's all. Now, please, be my friend. Can't we—"

He grasped her upper arms and pulled her upright. Two cavemen in one day was her last thought before he bent his head and kissed her, hard.

21

He forced his tongue into her mouth; his hands tightened about her face to hold her still.

Elizabeth began to struggle. He was hurting her.

"Hold still, Elizabeth!"

She arched her back, pressing with all her strength against his chest. She managed to pull her head back. "Christian, stop it! What's the matter with you? Stop it!"

As quickly as he'd grabbed her, he let her go. He dropped her arms and stepped back.

"Marry me," he said. His breath was coming hard.

She shook her head, feeling numb.

"You have to."

Anger shot through her. "I don't have to do anything I don't want to. Now, I think you'd better leave, Christian."

He realized at that instant how much he'd blown it. He'd scared her, then made her angry. He'd lost his head. "You won't marry anyone else, Elizabeth. You can't."

"That," she said, her eyes glittering, "is very probably true."

"This man, the other one—"

"Would you just stop it? Please, leave. Christian, I just can't take any more right now."

He looked at her, really looked at her. She'd changed. He felt it. Changed irrevocably toward him. It wasn't that he'd scared her. He'd lost her. He closed his eyes a moment. He'd gotten so close, moved so slowly and carefully, and now . . . A wife couldn't testify against her husband. The damned watch . . . would she remember? What would she do?

"I'm going," he said.

She watched him pull on his jacket, stuff his pipe, the English tobacco, into his pocket.

"Christian . . ."

He turned to face her.

"I'm sorry, truly."

He said nothing.

"You damned bitch, you betrayed me! Bitch!"

Susan moaned. He was hurting her, really hurting her. He was biting her mouth, and she tasted her own blood.

"You deserve what I give you now!"

She felt him shudder, finally, felt his body go slack. He was lying on top of her, dead sweating weight on her. She was having trouble breathing.

"You betrayed me," he said.

"Oh, no, Christian," she gasped. "I'd never betray you!"

The fury, the red haze that had gripped him, began to fall away. "Elizabeth," he said.

Then he opened his eyes, reared back onto his hands, and stared down into Susan's white face. No, no, it wasn't Susan.

"Bitch," he said again softly. He struck her, the flat of his palm against her white cheek. He felt her struggle beneath him, heard her cry out, and struck her again. He watched the red imprint of his fingers on her cheek. She made a small bleating sound and he stopped cold.

He pulled away from her and sat on the edge of the bed. Susan huddled beneath the sheet, saying nothing. He'd struck her once before, not hard, and she'd thought it was just his way of being playful. This wasn't play, this was something that was mixed up, something frightful.

Christian finally rose, and began to dress. He didn't look at Susan, just said coldly, "Your rent is paid for the next month. Then I want you out."

"I can't get out fast enough," she said, and wished she'd kept her mouth shut when he whirled around, his face tight with rage. His hands were clenched, and she was suddenly very afraid.

"None of you is worth anything," he said, flinging himself down on a chair to put his socks and shoes on. "You're all deceitful, stupid cunts."

Susan was smart enough to keep her mouth shut. She thought of all the piano lessons, her endless hours of practice. And for what? To play the part of another woman, and now Christian hated that woman, hated Elizabeth Carleton. So she'd betrayed him, had she? Smart lady. And Christian had taken it out on Susan. She heard him mutter more obscenities, and that shook her. Never before had she heard him curse, yet the ugly words were spewing from his mouth.

Finally he fell silent. Susan prayed he would just leave. He did. She spent twenty minutes in the shower and the next hour packing her things. She dragged her suitcases off the bed, then looked at the wrinkled covers, the drying patches of dampness. She shuddered, her hand unconsciously going to her cheek where he'd struck her. She walked from the bedroom, into the living room, past the piano.

She paused at the front door. The beautiful apartment looked suddenly like a prison, but now she was free.

"I want you to show Jenny the photos, Grandmother."

Laurette felt her breathing grow shallow. Then she got hold of herself. "Brad, what is all this about?" She watched him, saw him standing tall and straight, defying her. She waited. He was confused, that was all. Someone had spoken to him, made him uncertain about what was best for him.

"I will not marry Jenny. You can let me break it off, or you can show her the photos and let her do it. And there will be no more blackmail, Grandmother."

"Your wedding is next month."

"No way. It's all your brainchild, Grandmother. I want nothing more to do with it."

"You will not speak in such a way to me, Bradley! How dare you, you stupid boy!"

"I may be stupid, but I am no longer a boy, Grandmother. I'm a man. How dare you try to control my life? Catherine was right, she said—"

"Ah." Laurette sat back in her chair. So it was Catherine he'd listened to. "So you went whining to your sister."

"No, actually Catherine saw the photos, quite by accident, of course. She, at least, cares about me. She came to me."

Laurette felt a sharp pain in her left shoulder, then a numbing sensation down her arm. "Brad, I care about you, I know what's best for you. You must do what I tell you. You're not a man, not yet. Not until you marry Jenny, until you give me a great-grandchild. Then you'll be a man, then you can do—"

The pain grew suddenly sharp, unbearable, and she clutched at her breast. "Oh, God," she whispered. "No, not yet, there's so much, so much—"

"Grandmother!"

Brad watched her slump forward, her head striking the desktop.

Catherine listened to Rowe singing in the shower. She grinned. She felt good—no, she felt marvelous. Then she heard the doorbell ringing insistently downstairs.

She wondered what to do. Rowe hadn't heard a thing. She slipped out of bed and pulled on his velvet bathrobe.

"Who is it?" she called out as she skipped down the stairs.

There was a moment of silence; then, "It's Amanda Montgomery. Come, Mrs. Grady, let me in."

Who was Mrs. Grady? Rowe's housekeeper, probably. She made up her mind in that moment, squared her shoulders, and opened the door.

The two women stared at each other, Catherine with a slight smile on her mouth, Amanda so stunned she couldn't move, much less talk.

"You!"

"Hello, Amanda. Are you certain you wish to come in? As for Mrs. Grady, perhaps today is her day off."

"You damned slut! Get out of my way!"

Amanda wanted to kill. She shoved Catherine out of her way and walked into the entranceway. She looked up and saw Rowe striding onto the upper landing. He had a towel knotted at his waist, nothing else.

Rowe had the sudden image of himself walking onto the stage of a very bad comedy. Catherine was wrapped in his bathrobe, her hair tousled. And Amanda was staring at him. He realized that she didn't understand, that she was incapable of believing what was right in front of her. She was used to getting what she wanted, and in this case she'd wanted him, and had him, until now.

"Amanda," he said. He didn't move. He wasn't that big a fool.

Quick as a striking snake, Amanda turned and slapped Catherine hard, so hard that her head snapped back.

"You rich, conceited, miserable—" Catherine saw red and dived for her, feeling the exquisite silk sleeve rip between her fingers. She felt Amanda's long fingers grab at her hair, and she felt the pain in her scalp. Then they were on the floor, yelling, gasping, kicking.

"Oh, Jesus," Rowe said, and bolted down the stairs. "Stop it, both of you!"

He tried to pull Amanda off, and got a fist in his stomach. A bloody cat fight, the like of which he'd seen only at the movies.

He finally grabbed Amanda under the armpits and yanked upward. She tried to kick him, all the while screaming at Catherine.

He shook her. "Stop it!" He saw Catherine scramble to her feet, but she didn't attack, merely stood there, as if she couldn't believe what was happening herself.

"Amanda," he said again, not releasing her.

"You bastard," she said. "Let me go!"

"I'm afraid to."

She jerked her arm forward, then back, her elbow connecting with his abdomen. He let her go.

And backed up quickly.

Mascara was smeared beneath her eyes. Her blouse was ripped at the shoulder and torn out of the waistband of her slacks. Amanda looked from Rowe to Catherine. "You deserve each other," she said, and pulled off the engagement ring. She flung it across the floor, and it was the loudest sound in the room.

"I'll ruin you for this, Rowe Chalmers."

"God, I've heard that before," he said. "Look, Amanda, I'm sorry about this, but . . ."

"But what?"

"You're right. You don't deserve to be saddled with a bastard like me. Good luck, Amanda."

She slammed out.

Rowe and Catherine just looked at each other.

She said at last, "She thought I was Mrs. Grady."

"Hellfire," said Rowe, raking his fingers through his wet hair.

"Your towel is slipping."

"Catherine, you should be beaten senseless. Why did you open that door?"

"At least you're not going to have to spend your life with that horrible woman. She's not a nice person, Rowe."

"And you are? And I am?"

"We're a couple of winners, yeah, you're right."

"What now, Catherine?"

"Let's go upstairs and discuss it."

"You're damned impossible!"

"Your towel is slipping."

He laughed. He realized that he hadn't laughed in so very long. It felt good. He felt free.

* * *

Elizabeth felt the warmth of the pastrami sandwich through the paper bag. It was Kogi's night off, and she'd gotten this craving. She was salivating, just thinking about that beautiful rye bread covered with mustard. Not the spicy French sort, but good old American mustard.

She'd walked to the deli on Madison near Eighty-fourth, and now, with the wonderful smell of the sandwich filling her nostrils, and the soft evening air ruffling her hair, she began to feel human again. It was growing dark, and she automatically quickened her pace.

Things could be worse. She'd made an appointment with Laurette Carleton for tomorrow. She would try to reason with the old woman. At least she was doing something positive. She was taking action.

She started humming a song from *My Fair Lady*. She looked down the street, then began to walk across.

The whooshing sound of the car didn't penetrate her consciousness until she heard someone shout. She jerked around and saw a large dark blue sedan bearing down on her. It was accelerating, madly, right at her.

She stood frozen until a rush of adrenaline shot through her. She leapt a distance she would normally have believed impossible, then twisted, landing on her back between two cars. She felt the heat of the car envelop her as it roared by. She became aware of pain in her back. The cars were practically touching, and she'd struck against the bumper of one, then bounced off the front grille of the other.

"Lady, are you all right?"

She looked up to see an older man staring down at her. He had a beer belly, and the stomach button of his shirt was missing. He was balding.

"My pastrami sandwich got crushed," she said.

He helped her up. "You all right?"

"Yes," she said.

"That maniac! He could have killed you!"

"My sandwich," she said again, looking down at the crushed bag on the street.

He shook his head. Shock, most likely. "Let me call an ambulance, all right?"

"No . . . oh, no, I'm all right. I live just in the next block."

"I'll walk you there."

He fell in beside her, ready to catch her if she fell.

"You're missing a button," Elizabeth said.

He blinked. "Yeah, the missus, it's her way of getting back at me for being fat. She won't sew it back on until I lose ten pounds. That's her offer."

"I'm sorry."

Gallagher jumped up and ran forward. "What the hell—?"

"A guy nearly ran her down. My name's Foggerty. You'd better see to the lady here."

Foggerty left her in Gallagher's shaking hands, wondering what the hell the world was coming to. Well, it was New York, and full of crazies.

"I'm all right, Liam," Elizabeth said. "Truly."

He kept a firm grip on her hands. "Tell me what happened, Mrs. Carleton."

"A man in a big car . . . he tried to run me down, just like Mr. Foggerty said."

"I'm taking you upstairs, then I'm calling the cops."

She shook her head, but Gallagher ignored her.

He took her up in the elevator, sat her down, and went to the phone. He automatically asked for Lieutenant Draper.

Thirty minutes later, Gallagher let the lieutenant in. He hadn't seen him since . . . since that awful time when Mr. Carleton had been murdered and the lieutenant had questioned and questioned Mrs. Carleton. He realized suddenly that he probably shouldn't have called Draper. But he was here now.

"What's going on here, Gallagher? It is Gallagher, isn't it?"

Liam nodded.

Lenny Draper strode into the magnificent living room. A long time, he thought, a very long time, and she'd gotten off and was still living high off the hog. He motioned to the patrolman to stand by the door.

"It's Mrs. Carleton, Lieutenant. Some man tried to run her down."

"Her deeds finally catching up with her, huh?" Draper said.

"See here . . ." Gallagher said, his face turning red.

"Don't give yourself an ulcer. I'll speak to her, all right?"

Draper saw her sitting still as a stone, on a sofa that would have paid his salary for a year. Her face was utterly white.

"Mrs. Carleton," he said, sitting across from her. He pulled a pad out of his jacket pocket. "What happened?"

Elizabeth looked over at him. She shuddered unconsciously, remembering his endless stream of questions, his scorn, his contempt and disbelief at her answers. And finally that day when he'd read her her rights. Why had Liam called him, of all people?

"What happened?" Draper repeated, seeing the shock now.

Elizabeth moistened her lips. "Would you like some coffee, Lieutenant?"

"No. Would you like a doctor?"

She shook her head and her fingers began pleating the afghan Gallagher had put over her lap. "A man," she said finally. "I know it was a man, and he was alone. He was driving a big car, dark blue I think. I was crossing the street and he revved the engine, speeded up, on purpose, you know, and he tried to kill me, to run me down."

"How did you escape the car?"

"I jumped. Just like a broad jump in the Olympics. I landed between two cars and he kept going. He was probably afraid to stop because of . . . Foggerty."

"Foggerty?"

"An older man who had a button missing on his shirt," she said, and for the first time, she raised her eyes to his face.

She was in shock, Draper saw. His face tightened. He didn't want to feel sorry for her.

"Did you see his face?"

"No."

"License plate? Anything, Mrs. Carleton?"

"No. It was too fast. I was afraid."

"Where does this Foggerty live?"

Elizabeth just looked at him. Gallagher came forward, running his fingers through his hair. "I forgot to ask him. I know he lives close, say, a block down."

Draper got to his feet. "All right, then. I'll find this Foggerty and see what he has to say. You should see a doctor, Mrs. Carleton."

He left her still seated on the sofa pleating that useless afghan.

As they exited the town house, the patrolman asked in a low, excited voice, "It's her, isn't it, Lieutenant? The woman who killed her husband?"

"Yes, and she was acquitted," said Draper.

"God, did you see that house?"

"I saw. I've seen it many times before. Find this fellow Foggerty. Evidently he saw the whole thing."

It was close to ten o'clock that evening when Moretti walked in. Gallagher just stared at him.

"Hear you had a bit of excitement," Moretti said, and his big face split with a smile.

"I'd say it was for the police, not the D.A."

"Don't be smart with me, Gallagher. Oh, yeah, buddy, I remember your name. The *lady* upstairs in her castle?"

"The doctor came and gave her a sedative. She's probably asleep."

"Good, call up. Maybe she'll tell me things I already know if she's out of it."

"Scum," Gallagher muttered under his breath. At least Kogi was home now. He called up and watched Moretti stride toward the elevator like a predator closing in on the kill. He'd been a bloody fool to call Draper.

Elizabeth walked slowly into the living room wrapped in a long bathrobe. She saw Moretti standing there, and sucked in her breath.

"What do you want?"

"Why, I represent law and order and justice, Mrs. Carleton," he said smoothly. "Mind if I sit down?"

Elizabeth wished she could order him to leave. He ignored her in any case and eased his considerable weight into her favorite chair.

"Hear you nearly bit the bullet," he said amiably.

"Yes," Elizabeth said. "I told Lieutenant Draper all I could remember."

"Yeah, I know. Lenny called me, thought I'd be interested, which I am."

"What do you want?"

"As for Foggerty, the old coot couldn't remember anything either. A pity, isn't it, Mrs. Carleton? It appears someone is after you now."

"What do you want?" she asked again. The Valium was tugging at her, making her head feel light.

"Just wondered who wants you out of the way. Do you have enough paper to make a complete list for me?"

He grinned at her.

She was aware that Kogi had moved silently to stand protectively beside her, like a little Japanese banty rooster, she thought vaguely.

"Why don't you leave, Mr. Moretti?"

"What, no list, Mrs. Carleton? How's Draper supposed to do his job if you don't cooperate?"

He's really enjoying this, Elizabeth thought dully. She felt a flood of weakness, and merely shook her head at him. "I'm tired, Mr. Moretti. Kogi, see the gentleman out, please."

Moretti called out after her, "Watch out for yourself, Mrs. Carleton. I surely wouldn't want you to follow in your husband's footsteps, now, would I?"

She was too tired, her mind too fogged to say anything. She simply turned and walked out of the living room. She heard him laughing softly behind her.

* * *

Kogi answered the phone the following morning, his voice muted. He wondered what to do, then sighed.

Elizabeth was watching television, a game show, and she hadn't moved in the past hour.

"It's Mr. Harley," Kogi said, and handed her the phone.

"Hello," she said, her voice flat and emotionless.

"What's going on? What's the matter, Elizabeth? I called your office and got some nonsense from Mrs. Stacy about you being ill."

"No, I'm not ill, Jonathan. Just very tired. What is it you want?"

"I want you to stop acting like a whipped dog."

She smiled, just a bit. If he only knew . . . A whipped dead dog. Or bitch. She stifled a laugh.

"Did you hear about Laurette Carleton?"

"No, but I've got an appointment to see her tomorrow."

"You can forget it. She had a heart attack."

Elizabeth jerked forward on the sofa. "What?"

"She's in very serious condition. A heart attack."

"But she's . . . indestructible."

"Evidently not. Why did you want to see her?"

"A private matter, Jonathan. None of your concern."

"All right. I guess I deserved that. I want you to spend the weekend with me. I have a cabin in Maine, at a quaint place called Christmas Cove."

Elizabeth stared at the phone.

"Do you enjoy boating? Hiking? A rustic cabin? The great unwashed out-of-doors?"

"Why are you asking me, Jonathan? You left in a rage."

Jonathan grimaced. "I was a fool. I apologize. I want to see you." He wanted to touch her, hold her, make love to her. But he knew if he said those idiot words, she'd probably hang up on him.

"To see you," he said again. "Just to be with you."

Something moved inside her, but she refused to give in to it.

"I've got to go, Jonathan. Perhaps some other time."
She didn't want him to say anything more. She placed
the receiver gently into the cradle.

She stared at the phone a moment, then picked up
the remote control and snapped off the TV. Laurette,
a heart attack. Her next thought was of Catherine.
She tried her apartment. There was no answer.

She sat with a glazed look, wondering what to do.
Kogi moved quietly up to her and gently placed a
silver tray on the coffee table in front of her. "A
croissant perhaps, Mrs. Carleton?"

She smiled up at him, and nodded. She watched him
pour the coffee. Her eyes fell to the watch on his
slender wrist. Timothy's watch.

"Kogi, that watch . . ."

"Yes, Mrs. Carleton?"

She frowned at it. "Oh, I don't know. Forget it. I'm
coming down with early senility."

22

🍂

It was a private hospital, of course, near Southampton. Elizabeth was directed to the coronary intensive-care unit. Huddled in the waiting room were Michael Carleton and Catherine.

"What the blazes are you doing here?"

"Michael," Elizabeth said, nodding briefly toward him. "I came to see how she is."

"Bad," Catherine said, stepping toward Elizabeth. "Just one of us at a time. Brad is with her. Thank you for coming."

Michael snorted.

Elizabeth moved more closely to Catherine. "I tried to call you when I heard."

"I was in Boston."

"I had an appointment to see her this morning, Catherine."

"Well, we can be grateful for something. What if it had happened while you were with her? She was with Brad. He finally got the nerve to confront her about Jenny and everything else. Now he feels so guilty he can barely speak."

"I don't imagine there will be a wedding now."

"You're right about that. Jenny was sobbing her heart out on the phone when Brad called about Grandmother. I thought he was going to yell at her."

"Is he going to break it off?"

"Probably. Yes, he's got to."

"Well, well, a gathering of the infamous clan. And Mrs. Elizabeth Carleton—how interesting."

Both women jerked about to see Moretti standing there grinning from ear to ear.

"The old lady couldn't have done it, huh, Mrs. Carleton? Flat on her back."

"Please, Mr. Moretti," Elizabeth said. "Please, just leave. None of this concerns you."

"Just doing my job, Mrs. Carleton. Don't you want me to question these suspects? Doesn't it seem likely to you that one of them probably tried to kill you?"

Catherine turned pale. "What's he talking about?"

Elizabeth gritted her teeth. "Night before last, a man tried to run me down. Mr. Moretti loves it."

"The road to perdition is paved with many rich feet," said Moretti. "How 'bout you, Miss Carleton, you got an alibi for the . . . ah, the night in question?"

"Go to hell," Catherine said very calmly.

"Bitches run in the family, I see," Moretti said. He poked a finger toward the ICU doors. "The old lady going to make it?"

"The doctors think she just might," said Michael.

"Did you try to do away with Elizabeth X, Mr. Carleton?"

Michael's jaw dropped.

"No, well, perhaps young Bradley. Can't shit without his grandmama's permission, can he? None of you can."

"That's quite enough," Elizabeth said. "If you don't leave, Michael will call the governor. Harassment, Mr. Moretti. Get out of here."

"Sure thing, Mrs. Carleton. Just wanted to see the gathering of the vultures."

He tossed a wave of the hand and walked down the corridor.

"Miserable excuse for a human being," Catherine said.

"He's whistling," said Elizabeth. "What were you doing in Boston, of all places, Catherine?"

To Elizabeth's surprise, she flushed. "Let's just say

that since I'm on the road to reform, I've decided to bring someone else along with me."

Elizabeth understood. It surprised her, but she said only, "I hope you know what you're doing."

"Lord, I do too. Now, what's all this about someone trying to kill you?"

"Just as I said, someone tried to run me down in the street. And no, I don't have any idea who it was."

"This is crazy. I think we should all move to California."

"Or Peru."

Catherine laughed. "That's what I suggested to Brad."

"I'll leave now. You will keep me informed, won't you?"

"Yes, I will. Elizabeth, please be careful."

Drake drove her downtown to her office. He said over his shoulder, "Did you know that the windows are bulletproof?"

"Good heavens! No, I didn't know."

"Mr. Carleton had it done. Now I'm relieved. You're perfectly safe, Mrs. Carleton."

"Thank you, Drake. I guess I don't go out for a pastrami sandwich anymore, do I?"

"No, ma'am. At least, not without me or Gallagher."

She sighed. "Who could it have been?"

"I wouldn't be surprised if it weren't that dork of a D.A."

Elizabeth laughed. "Moretti? I doubt it."

She was reading a report on the last quarter's profits from Paris at the Le Marcon shoe factory. The translation was abominable.

Millicent Stacy poked her head in the door. "Strange, Elizabeth. There's a woman on the phone asking to speak to you. She won't give her name, but she says it's urgent."

Elizabeth started to refuse, then something stopped her. She nodded and picked up the phone.

"Yes? Elizabeth Carleton here."

"You don't know me, Mrs. Carleton, but I know all about you. I used to live with Christian Hunter. Well, actually, he paid for my place, and he'd visit me. Did you break off with him?"

"Who are you? What is this all about? Are you a reporter?"

"I don't blame you for not wanting to say anything. Look, Mrs. Carleton, he was a crazy man the other night. He was talking about betrayal and all women being bitches. I just wanted to tell you. I'm leaving New York."

"My God," Elizabeth whispered into the phone. "Whoever you are, are you all right?"

"Oh, yeah, I just wanted to tell you."

"Well, thank you. Please, be careful."

The line went dead. Elizabeth sat back in her chair, her hands behind her head. So Christian had had a mistress. So what? So what if he'd been angry after she'd refused to marry him?

Susan walked out of the phone booth and waved down a taxi. The driver gave her a wink and a shrug and kept going.

"Damn," she said, and stepped off the curb, her arm raised. She turned at the sound of loud honking, and never saw the car bearing down on her. It was a dark blue sedan and it struck her, hurling her ten feet out into oncoming traffic.

Elizabeth refused a call from Jonathan Harley. She went by herself to Lincoln Center to see *Swan Lake*, her favorite ballet. Drake was waiting for her at curbside at ten-thirty.

"I've got an invitation to meet the dancers, Drake," she told him. "Could you bring the car around to the stage entrance in about thirty minutes?"

"Sure thing, Mrs. Carleton. I'll move the car around now."

Elizabeth turned away, her steps quick because she was excited. She was nearly to the entrance when the explosion sent her sprawling to the sidewalk.

There was yelling, screaming, utter pandemonium.

She saw Timothy's limousine in flames. She saw one of the doors wrench off and hurtle into the air.

"Drake!"

She jerked to her feet and started running toward the spewing flames. Someone grabbed her arm. "It's too late, lady. God, someone blew him and the car to hell and back."

The police were there within minutes.

Elizabeth stood huddled next to the curb. She watched firemen spray the car, saw them try to free Drake's body from behind the wheel. The police were going through the crowd. Several ambulances pulled up, sirens screaming.

It was unreal, a nightmare, and she was the cause.

"Lady? You all right?"

She looked up into the young police officer's face. "No," she said very clearly. "No, I'm not all right, nothing is right now. That was my car, and my driver, Drake, is dead."

She started laughing.

Someone was shaking her, but she couldn't stop laughing. She didn't know when the laughter turned to sobs.

She was aware of someone, a woman in a white jacket, slipping a needle into her arm. She was lying flat on her back, bright lights blinding her eyes.

"It's all right," a woman said. "You're suffering from shock, and no wonder. Just a few bruises, a few cuts. Now, just breathe deeply, this will calm you down."

"I should have been in that car, you know," Elizabeth said. The woman in white just patted her arm. "I should have been in that car!"

She felt tears on her cheeks, dripping to her chin. Then she felt peaceful numbness filtering into her mind, then blessed darkness, then nothing.

"Elizabeth."

She tried to turn her head away from the insistent sound of her name. She didn't want to leave the cocoon because if she did, she would know horror.

"Elizabeth, come on, sweetheart."

Whose voice was that?

"It's me, Christian. Wake up."

Christian! But hadn't that woman who'd phoned told her he was furious? "What are you doing here?" Was that her voice? She sounded like a dead frog.

"I told them you were my fiancée," he said, and grinned. "It was the only way they'd let me in. There's a cop outside, keeping the press away from you."

"Drake is dead," she said.

"I know. But you're not. You're going to be just fine."

"Until he tries again."

"She awake yet, Hunter?"

Christian turned but didn't release Elizabeth's hand. "Lieutenant Draper," he said. "She's not really with it yet."

"What's wrong with her hands?"

"Cut on shattering glass, the doctor said."

"My hands," Elizabeth whispered, and slowly raised them. Both were bandaged. "My hands."

"Your hands will be okay, Elizabeth, I promise. You can speak to the doctor in just a little while."

"I need to ask some questions, Hunter," Lieutenant Draper said. "First of all, what are you doing here?"

"I am a close friend of Mrs. Carleton's. I was driving nearby when the car exploded. I came right here."

"Close friend, eh? Sure, fellow."

"That's right, Lieutenant. Anything else?"

"Not for the moment. I'll want to talk to you some more later. Now, Mrs. Carleton, tell me what happened."

Elizabeth opened her eyes and saw the car exploding, fragments bursting everywhere. She shuddered. "I don't know. I'd gotten an invitation to visit with the cast and told Drake to take the car around to the stage entrance. I should have been in the car."

"And when he started the car, it blew. I'd say you're very lucky, Mrs. Carleton."

"Drake wasn't."

"No, but he was just a hired hand, wasn't he? Easily replaceable."

"You're despicable," Elizabeth said.

"Moretti should be here any minute. Why don't you try out that line on him?"

"Look, Draper," Christian said, standing. "Why don't you just cut all this garbage?"

"The lady's always got a man to protect her," Draper said, open contempt in his voice and on his face. "First her husband, and now you, Dr. Hunter. Where does what's-his-face fit in—Rowe Chalmers, big businessman from Boston, right?"

Christian clenched his fists. "Look, you son of a bitch, why don't you do your damned job?"

"Oh, yeah, I will. There were a good thirty people injured in the explosion, Mrs. Carleton. It would be nice if you rich folk could keep your feuds to yourselves."

He strolled out of the room, leaving Christian staring after him. "He worked on your husband's case?"

"Yes, he did," she said, and closed her eyes.

"Why didn't you tell me about the first attempt, Elizabeth?"

She shook her head on the pillow.

"Why?"

Why was he pushing? She'd thought for a while that he'd been responsible. But that couldn't be. He was here, with her, the same as he'd been before that night he'd asked her to marry him. "I got a phone call, Christian. It was from a woman who told me that she'd lived with you. She was afraid."

Christian winced. He'd been too late. "What did this woman tell you?"

"That you had visited her after I turned down your marriage proposal. She said you'd acted crazy and that she was leaving New York."

He said calmly, withdrawing his pipe from his pocket and going through the familiar routine, "It's true, in part, I suppose. I was angry and took it out on her. By the way, I told her to leave. It wasn't her idea." He lit his pipe and drew on it. He pulled up a chair next to her bed. "Forget about Susan. She's not important. Now, since the damned police don't give a flying . . . well, since they don't care, talk to me. I want names."

She couldn't very well tell him that he'd been on the top of her list. She stared at her bandaged hands.

Christian was silent, watching her. "You know, Elizabeth, the press is going wild over this. I'll speak to the doctor about when you can be released. Then maybe we can leave New York ourselves for a while until they catch whoever was responsible."

Moretti walked in, not bothering to knock. He surveyed the scene in front of him and sneered. "Draper told me you'd finally come out into the open with your protector, Mrs. Carleton. He's now your fiancé, right?"

Christian rose from the chair very slowly, until he was eye to eye with Moretti. "You will listen to me, you son of a bitch. You find the man who's trying to kill her and you do it fast. And no more of your innuendos, you got that?"

Moretti felt no fear, just blinding hatred of this man who'd lied for her. He stepped away. "Well, it appears to me that the most probable suspect is someone who can't stand the fact that you got away with murder, Mrs. Carleton. He took his time. But now he's after you."

"I didn't kill my husband, Mr. Moretti."

"The question that's been hounding me is what you paid Dr. Hunter here to lie for you. I guess you've answered that. Boundless love, Mrs. Carleton?"

"That's enough, Moretti! Leave her alone!"

"Incidentally, the old lady's still alive. Maybe she paid someone to do it."

"No, that's not her style," said Elizabeth.

"What about Rowe Chalmers?"

"I believe that Mr. Chalmers is now on the straight and narrow, Mr. Moretti. Forget him, he's got nothing to do with this."

"Any leads on the bomb?" Christian asked.

"Yeah, a homemade job, amateur stuff, but effective as hell. The ingredients would be impossible to trace. No go there. I guess you'd best stick close to home for a while, Mrs. Carleton. The press will hound you, probably protect you from further attacks."

Christian said nothing, but he sent a look to Elizabeth.

"Yes, I'll stay at home," she said.

"Why don't you check out that businessman in Philadelphia? She was buying him out. Probably a solid motive there."

"No! No, he won, Christian. He had no motive, none at all."

"What's his name, Elizabeth?"

She stared at him. Why did he want to know about Jonathan? Jealousy? No, that was ridiculous, or maybe it wasn't. She felt a headache building over her left temple. She just shook her head.

"See you around," Moretti said, and left.

"He's whistling again," Elizabeth said.

She was released from the hospital the following morning. The press discovered her escape and Gallagher had his hands full.

Now all she had to do was get rid of Christian. She watched him pace the living room. "Please go now, Christian. I'm fine."

"Look, Elizabeth, you're far from fine. Let me stay, let me take care of you. Come away with me, to England. I have some business in London, perhaps—"

"No, Christian. Nothing's changed. You're my friend, truly, but—"

"Who is that man in Philadelphia?"

Oh, God, why wouldn't he just leave it alone? "I've told you, Christian, he's only a business acquaintance, nothing more."

"Then I'll just have to find out for myself, won't I?"

"Christian, please leave. I'm very tired and there are Drake's funeral arrangements to be made."

She was jarred by the ringing of the phone. She listened to Kogi answer, heard him ask the caller to wait a moment.

It was Jonathan, she knew it. "I'll call you, Christian. Good-bye, and thank you for being there for me."

Christian gave her one long last look, then shrugged and left.

"He gone?" Kogi asked.

"Yes. Who's on the phone?"

"Mr. Harley."

She felt a rush of pleasure and relief. "Hello?"

"Well, kiddo, you're all over the newspapers and the television news. What's going on up there?"

She laughed, a shrill, thin sound that made Jonathan flinch. "Someone is trying to make me cock up my toes before it's time."

"You're right to laugh. Sounds funny to me also. I'll be there by tonight."

"No!" Suddenly she was afraid, afraid not only for herself but also for Jonathan. "No," she repeated more calmly. "Everything is under control. I don't want you involved in this mess."

There was a momentary silence. "I'm already involved."

"Please, just stay away for now. All right?"

"We'll see," he said, and hung up the phone.

Elizabeth didn't leave the house until the morning of Drake's funeral.

The media were out in full force. They yelled questions at her, and flashbulbs went off continuously in her face. Elizabeth X was alive and well again.

She saw the afternoon paper: "ELIZABETH X TARGET."

It will never end, she thought, slumping down into her chair. Never. Moretti and Draper dogged her—not to find out who was trying to kill her, but just for the fun of it.

There were at least a dozen calls from Jonathan. She refused them all. She had to keep him safe and out of it.

Laurette Carleton was improving. To Elizabeth's surprise, she refused to make any comment at all.

"I spoke to her," Catherine said to Elizabeth that

afternoon. "I told her that if she didn't pull in her horns, she was going to lose all of us. For the first time, she believed me."

"And Brad?"

Catherine was silent a moment. "He hasn't called it off yet with Jenny. Senator Henkle has been on the phone, as you can imagine."

"Why hasn't he?"

"You know, I think Brad is scared."

"I don't blame him. And I think you're right, Catherine."

Catherine looked thoughtful. "Yes. He feels alone, I think. He's scared of the future, and what will become of him. Since Father . . . died, he's been floundering around, you know, and—"

"Since your father was murdered, Catherine," Elizabeth said, her voice harsh. "He was murdered, and I didn't do it. The person who did is probably laughing his or her head off."

Catherine rose and walked to the wide windows that looked toward Central Park. "You're right," she said, not turning to face Elizabeth. "I wish to God I knew something, but I don't. I was surprised that Dr. Hunter gave out that he was your fiancé."

"No one was more surprised than I," said Elizabeth.

"You know what the press is saying, don't you?"

"Sure, even a blind-and-deaf person could figure that out. He loved me enough to save my hide and now I'm coming out of the closet, so to speak, with our relationship."

"What are you going to do, Elizabeth?"

"If I only knew what to do, I'd be doing it. Ah, Kogi, with the coffee." She smiled at him, and was slightly amused at the wary look he shot Catherine.

She turned as he poured the coffee, and once again her eyes went to the watch. Timothy's watch.

"The band is too loose for me," Kogi said, seeing her looking at the watch. "Do you mind if I have it tightened, Mrs. Carleton?"

Elizabeth froze. "No," she whispered. "No, it's impossible."

"Yes, Mrs. Carleton? Something wrong?"

"Elizabeth, is something wrong?"

"Yes," Elizabeth said. "Something is very wrong."

She remembered now, very clearly. The morning of Timothy's murder, he had broken the band of his favorite watch. She saw him in her mind's eye, saw him reaching into the top dresser drawer and pulling out the watch she'd given him, cursing even as he'd had to put it on.

He'd never worn that watch before the day of his murder.

And Christian Hunter had said he'd admired that watch.

Oh, God.

Elizabeth shook her head and jumped to her feet. She was vaguely aware that both Catherine and Kogi were watching her, concern on their faces. No, it couldn't be. There had to be a mistake. Christian had simply remembered the wrong watch.

And someone had tried to kill her—twice.

After she'd told him she wouldn't marry him.

And then that woman—Christian's mistress—had called to warn her.

"Elizabeth, for God's sake, what is the matter?"

She felt Catherine's hand on her shoulder, shaking her. She turned blind eyes to Kogi. "Please get the district attorney on the phone. I must speak to him right away."

"Are you out of your mind?" Catherine demanded.

"Maybe. Perhaps for the first time I'm thinking straight. Call Moretti, Kogi."

23

"This better be good."

"Do sit down, Mr. Moretti."

"What's she doing here?" He poked a finger in Catherine's direction.

"She's my . . . friend."

Moretti laughed at that. "A Carleton? The only daughter of Timothy Carleton? You sure about that, lady? Maybe she's just pretending. Better yet, maybe she's the one who wants you underground."

"I know who murdered my husband. I know who's trying to kill me now."

That pulled his attention from Catherine. "Yeah? You're that much better than the police?"

"It's Dr. Christian Hunter."

Moretti stared at her, then threw back his head and belly-laughed. "Oh, that's good, Mrs. Carleton." He slapped his hands on his knees. "Really good! But please, no more wasted trips, no indeed. If you want to feed me any more bull, you can come downtown. Make an appointment first."

She couldn't believe him. "Don't you want to know how I know, Mr. Moretti?"

"That Ivy League wimp lied for you, then what? Then he became your lover. What happened? He threw you over? And this is your notion of revenge, right?"

"No. It's the watch."

Catherine could only stare at Elizabeth. How could

she be so calm? Lord, if it were her, she'd be ripping his face off, the stupid prick.

"You've had a lot of time to think of a good tale, I'll bet. All right, Mrs. Carleton, lay it on me, but be quick. I've got more important things to do."

"Why don't you stop acting like an ass?" Catherine asked, unable to keep her mouth shut.

"Look here, you little . . . Tell me, Mrs. Carleton. I'm getting bored." He sat down and pulled out a cigar.

"About two months ago, Dr. Hunter was here for dinner. He noticed the watch Kogi was wearing and said that he'd always admired it when he'd seen my husband wearing it. I had given the watch to Kogi after Mr. Carleton's death—"

"His murder, don't you mean?"

"Yes, his murder. I gave the watch to Kogi because he admired it. I didn't realize, didn't remember until just a while ago. You see, Mr. Moretti, my husband had never worn that watch before, not until the day he died. I finally remembered that he'd broken his watch band that morning. He didn't like the watch I'd given him, but he had no choice but to wear it."

Moretti examined his fingernails, and puffed cigar smoke in Elizabeth's direction.

"Dr. Hunter did ask me to marry him, and I refused. Not long after that, a man tried to run me down. Then Drake and the car."

Moretti yawned, then blew cigar smoke upward and watched it float about over his head.

"If he realized that I might remember about the watch, he would want to protect himself, wouldn't he? He would know that I knew, and that I'd talk."

"Better and better," said Moretti.

"And there was that woman who called me. She said that Dr. Hunter visited her, in fact, kept her in an apartment here in New York. She was afraid of him and wanted to warn me."

Moretti sat up. "What was this woman's name?"

"She didn't tell me." But Christian had mentioned

her name. Yes, it was . . . "Susan," she said. "I think her name was Susan."

"When exactly did she call you? What time of day?"

"I'm not really certain . . . wait, it was a Wednesday morning, I think. Yes."

"That all?"

"Kogi can show you the watch," Elizabeth said.

Moretti shook his head. "Nah, not now. I've got to go now, Mrs. Carleton. Don't stick your head out of any windows, all right?"

"You stupid buffoon!" Catherine yelled at him.

"As for you, Miss Carleton, why don't you try keeping your legs closed?"

"You dumb jerk!"

"No, Catherine," Elizabeth said. "Let him go. He doesn't care."

Moretti left whistling.

Catherine and Elizabeth stared at each other.

"What are we going to do?" Catherine said at last.

"You go home, Catherine. Everything will be all right."

"Don't be crazy, Elizabeth! For God's sake—"

"Please, Catherine. Go home, I'll call you."

After Catherine had left, Elizabeth sat still as a stone, weighing her options. Her mind was clear; she felt utterly calm. She walked purposefully into her bedroom and packed one suitcase. She wouldn't need more than one.

Kogi stared at her, and Gallagher's jaw was working madly.

"You can't! The police will—"

"Look, Liam," she interrupted him, "the police think this is all a marvelous game, kind of like the fox and the hen. And I'm the hen."

She told them both about Christian Hunter.

". . . Moretti doesn't care. He thinks I'm making it all up. And there's no proof. None. Kogi, you don't remember Mr. Carleton ever wearing that watch before, do you?"

Kogi hung his head. "I felt guilty for admiring it. I

remember when they released Mr. Carleton's things, and I wanted it."

"It's all right, Kogi."

"I'll hire some men to protect you," Liam said.

"No, it's no good. Kogi, just take very good care of that watch, it's the only solid thing we've got. Now, listen, here's what I want you both to do. . . ."

At nine-thirty that evening the sky was heavily overcast and the air was cold and damp with the coming rain. Elizabeth buzzed down to Gallagher. "Check the street now, Liam. Look really carefully. If there's no one about, call a taxi."

Three minutes later, Elizabeth, her one suitcase in hand, dressed in jeans, sneakers, a heavy knit sweater, and a ski jacket, slipped out of the house and into the waiting cab.

"Grand Central, please," she said.

She hadn't told anyone where she was going, not even Kogi or Liam Gallagher. She sat back a moment, then immediately turned and searched the street behind them. Always so many cars, primarily taxis, in New York. She searched for a dark blue sedan. Nothing.

She wanted to relax, but was tight as a wound spring when the driver stopped in front of Penn Station.

She paid him, fumbling with the money, then dashed into the station. The Amtrak for Philadelphia was leaving in twenty minutes.

She stood in the ticket line, feeling exposed, as if she were wearing a neon sign over her head.

A man bumped into her and she froze. No, not Christian.

The train was on time, thank God. In two hours she'd be safe.

It was raining hard when Elizabeth came out of the Thirty-third Street train station in Philadelphia. She waved down a taxi and gave the man Jonathan's address.

"On the Main Line, huh?"

"I suppose so," she said, not knowing what he was talking about.

"Only the rich folks out there, lady." He gave her the once-over, and she wanted to laugh. She wanted to tell him that she could buy his taxi company if she wanted to.

"Yeah," she said only, "let's go."

The rain was coming down so hard, all Elizabeth could make out behind her taxi were headlights. Her heart was pounding. What if Jonathan weren't home? What if he told her to get lost?

She closed her eyes.

"We're here, lady."

Elizabeth could make out the wide circular drive, the large white Colonial house. There were lights on and two cars were parked in the driveway.

"Wait for me," she said. "Here's a twenty," she added at his look. "Wait for me."

She didn't have an umbrella. She lifted out her suitcase, slammed the taxi door, and dashed toward the front porch. Behind her she heard the taxi pull around the drive. She whirled about to see the taxi roaring through the gates into the street. He'd left her.

She walked to the front door and rang the bell. Please, Jonathan, please . . .

She rang again. She heard footsteps and sucked in her breath.

A woman pulled the door open. A very beautiful, very well-dressed woman.

"What do you want?" Rose Harley stared at the young woman, at her clothes, at her damp hair.

"Who are you?" Elizabeth managed.

"Who am I? Look, if you're one of Jonathan's bimbos, take yourself off now. I'm surprised he didn't tell you that I live here, not him."

Elizabeth could only stare at her. Not his house! Oh, God, she'd had no idea . . . "Where does he live?"

Rose laughed. "So my dear ex-husband didn't tell

you? What's the matter, do you have the clap or something equally distasteful? Or maybe you let him get you pregnant?"

"Please, it's urgent," Elizabeth said. "Tell me his address."

"I wouldn't tell you how to find a rock to crawl under!"

Rose slammed the door in her face.

What to do? The rain was coming down in a thick sheet. She was in a residential area, the houses set back and far apart. No phones.

And no Christian Hunter.

Elizabeth drew a deep breath and walked into the rain and back to the road. "It's time for a walk," she said aloud, "nothing more, just a walk, that's all. You're not going to melt. Come on, you've been spoiled. Let's go."

Every time a car came by, Elizabeth ducked off to the side of the road, her heart in her throat.

Jonathan had been living at that address until just a short time before. She didn't understand, not that it mattered at all. She kept plodding along through the rain. She heard a car slow behind her, its headlights pinning her. Oh, God!

"Hey, you want a ride?" a male voice called out to her. "You look about ready to drop."

It wasn't Christian Hunter.

Why not? She decided she'd rather take her chances with a mad rapist than feel that awful fear.

She climbed in, apologizing.

"I need to find a phone booth."

She was shivering, and the man turned on the car heater.

"Better?"

"Yes, thank you."

"Here's a small shopping area just ahead. You want to stop there?"

"Yes, that will be just fine."

"Look, you be careful, all right?"

She managed to smile at the man. She watched him

drive back onto the road, then turned to the row of lit phone booths. None of them had a directory.

She put in a quarter and dialed 411. She asked for Jonathan Harley's phone number.

The operator asked, "Jonathan Harley on Pointer's Lane?"

"No, no. He's moved. Do you have a new listing for him?"

"Sorry, miss. It's an unlisted number. I can't give it out."

"But this is an emergency!"

"I'm sorry, miss."

Elizabeth just looked at the phone, the dial tone blaring loudly.

She called a taxi.

She huddled under the cover of the phone booth, waiting. A car slowed, a big car, a sedan, and she thought her heart would pound out of her chest. It went by, speeding up.

What was the name of Jonathan's secretary? Midge . . . What was her last name? Midge . . . Ripley? She dialed 411 again. There were two Margaret Ripleys. She was dialing the first number when the taxi pulled up. She yelled to him to wait, and finished dialing.

It was an old woman.

Elizabeth dialed the second number. A bouncy young woman's voice this time. "Hello?"

"Are you the Midge Ripley who works for Jonathan Harley?"

There was dead silence on the other end. "Who wants to know?" Midge asked.

"Elizabeth Carleton."

She heard a gasp.

"Please, Miss Ripley, this is an emergency. I've got to find Jonathan. Please help me!"

What was going on? Midge wondered. What did the dragon lady want? But Jonathan didn't think of her like that anymore. He'd beaten her, and then he'd . . .

"All right. Hang on, I'll give you his number and address."

"Thank you."

The taxi driver shouted at her.

"Just a minute!" she shouted back.

Midge was back on the line with his number and address.

"Thank you, Ms. Ripley. I—" She saw a big car from the corner of her eye. A big blue or black car. She was clearly outlined in the phone-booth lights. She dashed into the cab, flinging her suitcase to the floor, and slammed the door and blurted out the address.

"Please hurry!'"

"You're getting my cab wet, lady." .

The man was smoking a cigar, just like Moretti. For an instant she saw red. "Tough! Get going!"

"Don't get yourself in an uproar," said the driver, and pulled out of the shopping area.

He'd folded, just because she'd gotten nasty. Elizabeth's eyes were trained out the back window. The big car was directly behind, very close. It was ridiculous, she was being ridiculous. How could Christian drive down here faster than Amtrak? It couldn't be him. At least not in the same car that had run her down in New York. She was losing her grip.

Still, she said, "I'll give you a hundred dollars if you get away from that car behind us. I don't care how you do it, just do it."

"The cops after you?"

"Don't be ridiculous! Just do it!"

It wasn't Christian Hunter. It couldn't be. The cab took a sharp left turn, tires skidding in the rain, and the big car drove straight ahead.

"All right. Take me to this address now."

The cabbie shook his head and clamped down on his cigar. You got kooks all the time. Was this one paranoid? He thought of the hundred dollars and kept his opinion to himself. She probably was running from the cops. None of his business.

Twenty minutes later the cab pulled into a condominium complex. "Which number, lady?"

"Three-twenty-four."

"All right. This is it. Nice setup. You got some rich friends, lady."

Elizabeth gave him a hundred and twenty dollars.

"Good luck, lady!"

Elizabeth took the elevator to the third level. Three-twenty-four was on the end, a huge corner condo with a view of downtown. There were no lights. She hit the buzzer and waited. Nothing. He wasn't here.

"I'm a fool," she said aloud. She'd tried to call him during the day, but nothing. Of course, she'd dialed his ex-wife's house. She'd even phoned his office, on a Saturday, just in case, but no answer. Just an answering machine. What if he'd gone to Maine?

She was protected from the rain, at least. She eased down, pulling her suitcase close, and pressed her back against the door. To wait.

What if Christian Hunter knows this address?

No, he didn't even know Jonathan's name.

Oh, please, God.

It was cold. She wrapped her arms around herself, but it didn't help. The ski jacket was wet, and soon she felt the cold seep through.

Jonathan was tired and worried. He pulled his umbrella open as he eased out of his car. He'd try to call her again, just as he'd tried on and off all evening. Now it was so bloody late. Kogi wouldn't tell him a thing, even after he'd identified himself.

Where was she? What if she were hurt, dead? No, that wasn't possible. Kogi would have told him. Hell, it would have been all over the news.

He'd had no choice but to go to the business dinner, and he knew he'd acted like a complete moron. And then that bloody fool Dex Grant had wanted to find a couple of hookers. He'd set Dex up, then left.

He walked the stairs to the third level, as he always did. It was dark.

Jonathan came to an abrupt halt. Pressed against his front door was what looked like a kid, wet clear through, asleep. It took him another good look to realize who it was.

He dropped to his knees, his hand on her shoulder. "Elizabeth?" He shook her shoulder.

Elizabeth was dreaming she was on a ski slope, alone. A man was shouting at her, and she twisted on her skis to see Christian Hunter behind her. He was holding a looped rope in his hands. He turned into Rowe Chalmers. He had a rifle and was aiming it at her even as he skied wildly toward her. It was like a bad James Bond film. She realized that even in her dream, and then she saw the cliff in front of her, and she couldn't stop. . . . She screamed as her skis flew over the cliff.

"Elizabeth! It's all right. Wake up!"

"Jonathan?" She blinked away the nightmare and stared up at his shadowed face.

"Yep. What are you doing here, kiddo?"

"I went to your house," she said, struggling to stand up. He helped her.

"That must have been an experience. Was Rose there?"

"Oh, yes, she was. She thought I was one of your bimbos."

They heard the phone ringing from inside.

"Come on, let's get you out of those wet clothes. Shit, it's cold."

He unlocked the door and stepped back to let her go first.

He turned on the light switch and walked quickly to the hall phone. "Midge? . . . Yeah, she's here, waiting for me. . . . No, I don't know what's happened yet. . . . Just keep it under your hat, okay? . . . No, I'm fine. . . . No, my plans are still on. Thanks, Midge, for giving her my address."

Jonathan turned back to see Elizabeth standing on the terra-cotta-tile vestibule, a growing puddle at her feet.

She looked like a waif, a very cold waif. He wanted to pull her into his arms and kiss her silly. He wanted to tell her she was safe now. Instead he said, "Come along, Elizabeth. I don't care if you get the carpeting wet. You need a hot bath."

She was vaguely aware of her surroundings—the high beamed living-room ceiling to her left, the antiques, the warm earth tones. She followed him silently down a corridor and into a large bedroom. More antiques, and a buffed hardwood floor with expensive small Persian rugs covering it. Timothy would have known what kind, where they were made, and if their pedigree warranted attention.

"Come along."

He sounded impatient with her, and she wondered if after he'd gotten her dried out—or off—he'd tell her to leave. Probably. She really wouldn't blame him if he never wanted to see her again.

She stopped in the doorway of a large bathroom. Jonathan was sitting on the side of a tub, filling it with water. Hot water.

"I think I've died and am about to go to heaven," she said, eyeing the steam rising from the tub.

"I don't have any woman-type bubble-bath things," he said, rising. "You look like a drowned rat."

"I know. Thank you."

"Do you need any help?"

"No."

"All right. Take your time in the bath and I'll put your suitcase in the bedroom."

He fetched her bag, a Louis Vuitton, thankfully waterproof. He opened it and pulled out all her clothes and left them on the bed. He went to his living room and poured himself a stiff drink. Then he lit the wood in the fireplace.

It was nearly two o'clock in the morning.

Elizabeth emerged wearing his thick velour robe some thirty minutes later. Her hair was wrapped turban style in a towel. He searched her face, and was satisfied that she was all right.

"Brandy?"

"Yes, thank you." It was ridiculous, she knew it

deep down, but she was shy, nervous, and very embarrassed. What had possessed her to come to Philadelphia? More important, what had possessed her to involve him? What if Christian . . . ?

"Here, Elizabeth. Drink down."

She did. The brandy sent dizzying warmth to her stomach.

She handed him back the brandy snifter.

"It just occurred to me that I've been a big fool," she said, not quite meeting his eyes. "I'll leave in the morning—that is, if you don't mind me staying the rest of the night."

"Shut up."

His voice was harsh, cold, and her head jerked up.

"I'm sorry, I should have realized that—"

"Just be quiet, Elizabeth. Come over to the fire and warm up."

It felt good for the moment to have someone taking care of her, telling her what to do. But she would leave in the morning, she wouldn't involve him. She must have been out of her mind to come here.

Jonathan watched her face a moment, then said, "Now, we'll iron out all the details later. Right now, I want you to tell me why you're here. Why you came to me."

"I finally realized that Christian Hunter killed my husband and he's trying to kill me."

Jonathan stared at her. "Well, I did ask for it, didn't I? Come here and let me warm you up."

She moved closer on the sofa and felt his arm come around her shoulders. He pulled her slowly toward him until her head rested on his shoulder. "Much better," he said. "Now, everything."

She told him about Kogi's watch, about Moretti, about the woman who had called her. She even told him about Catherine and Rowe Chalmers and Laurette Carleton, even about that awful night Drake had been blown up in the limousine. The fire was embers by the time she'd finished. Jonathan hadn't said a word.

"I was coming to New York in the morning to fetch you," he said.

"Why?"

"Got me, Lizzie. I'm a masochist, I guess."

"No, Jonathan, I'll leave in the morning. I never should have come here, involved you. It's just that I . . ."

"Was afraid? Scared out of your wits?"

She nodded her head against his shoulder. "The D.A. and Lieutenant Draper both think it's a grand joke. Retribution for the murderess." She shuddered then. "The press is having a field day, as you can imagine. I don't think anyone followed me. I was very careful."

"Then what are you worried about? Tomorrow you and I are going to check out of the world for a while. We're going to my cabin in Maine. Maybe the cops will take care of Hunter for us."

"Moretti is probably giving him a medal."

"Do you trust me, Elizabeth? Really trust me?"

He watched the play of expressions on her face. Suddenly she smiled. "Yes, I do. Maybe for the first time ever, I do really trust you."

"Who could be more trustworthy than an enemy turned . . . well, turned friend?"

His arm tightened momentarily around her shoulders. He rose abruptly. "You sleep in the guestroom. It's all made up. We'll leave in the morning."

"Where in Maine are we going?"

"It's called Christmas Cove."

"I knew it was some sort of holiday—I just couldn't remember. Are you certain, Jonathan?"

"Yes, very certain."

24

"We can drive straight through, or stop for the night. It's up to you, Elizabeth."

"I want to go on," she said.

"And never stop?" He turned slightly to face her.

"Yes, forever, if I could."

"Don't be afraid. There's no need now."

"I've been afraid for so long, I wouldn't know how to stop."

"Ever since your husband's murder?"

He felt her jerk at his words, but he kept his eyes trained on the highway. They were near New Haven, Connecticut. It was a cold, clear day. Traffic was moderately heavy, since it was a weekend.

"I'll never forget what it was like to be taken as a criminal to the police station. This woman pressed each of my fingers onto this inked pad. Then she handed me a Kleenex. The ink didn't come off."

"You didn't have to stay in jail, did you?"

"No, Rod Samuels got me out on a quarter of a million dollars' bail."

"I remember your husband's murder and your subsequent arrest. The press went haywire. I remember thinking that the rich bitch just couldn't get enough. I thought you were guilty."

"Everyone did. I made such good copy. *Elizabeth X.* Even Rod believed me guilty, until Christian Hunter came along. He was so convincing, so very calm. Moretti probably hated him as much as he hates me. In fact,

I know from firsthand experience that he still hates him."

"Tell me about Christian Hunter."

"You're not going to believe this, but I'd never seen him in my life until that day in the courtroom."

The car swerved. "You're putting me on."

"No. Rod didn't tell me about him, I guess because he was afraid I'd spill the beans somehow. And then Christian didn't contact me. For a good six months I was terrified that he would, and terrified when he didn't. You see, I didn't know what he wanted. I ended up calling him. He still put me off. Evidently he was holding off until he could get rid of Rowe Chalmers. Which he did. Rowe was betraying me, selling information I gave him to the Carletons. The world must be crazy—I think Catherine is in love with him."

They stopped in Hartford.

She told him about meeting Rowe in Paris at Claude's home, and she told him about the anonymous note she'd eventually gotten. And that final evening with Rowe, and the ice pick. By six o'clock in the evening, she was nearly hoarse from talking.

Jonathan said at last, "You want to know something, Lizzie? You're damned lucky I came along."

She started laughing—she couldn't help it.

He reached out his right hand and patted her thigh. "Keep laughing, it sounds good."

"When will we get to this Christmas Cove place?"

"Around midnight. You want to stop?"

"No. What are you doing with a cabin in Maine?"

"I descend from home-grown folk—Down Easters, they call us—ship captains, most of them. There were a couple of fishermen, though. Stop looking out the back window, Elizabeth. He's nowhere near us, all right?"

"I didn't think you'd noticed," she said.

"I think I've noticed everything about you from the moment we met in my office. Of course, I was ready and willing to strangle you that day."

"You did, with words."

He grinned over at her. "At least you couldn't forget n.. co ld you? It must have been fate. If I hadn't climbed your frame up one side and down the other, you might have left me and my poor company alone."

"Climbed my frame?"

"I've also got relatives in Texas. It means chewing someone out until they're in a heap on the floor."

They didn't stop in Portland. "Not far at all now," Jonathan said. "Under two hours."

"I wish I could see something. I've never been to Maine before."

"This stretch is so wild and beautiful it makes my throat tighten each time I come. No high elevations, just zillions of pine and fir trees, rocks and boulders, and the ocean, of course. The tourists haven't really discovered Damariscotta or Christmas Cove yet. They spend most of their time and money over in Newcastle. Of course, you'll see hardly anyone this time of year."

Elizabeth was glad he couldn't see her face in the darkness. His words flowed over her but didn't calm her. "Will it ever be over?"

She hadn't realized she'd spoken the words aloud until she heard him draw a deep breath. "Yes, it will, Lizzie. You said you trusted me. That means that nothing is going to happen to you, to either of us. You got that, kiddo?"

"Yeah, I got that. Since when did you become Superman?"

"Sarcasm, good. I was wondering if you'd lost all your acid."

She sighed. "I never even used to have an ounce."

"I like it, in small doses. You've changed a lot, haven't you?"

"Since you were one of the recipients of that change, you can well imagine what I was like before."

He chuckled. "You weren't a wimp, were you?"

"No, just someone who was very easy, I suppose you could say. And don't laugh, Jonathan! I mean easy as in . . . well, adaptable, malleable."

"Damn," he said.

"Don't be a jerk."

"It's tough, but I'll try. We're lucky, Lizzie. There's a little all-night general store in Damariscotta. We'll stop there and stock up."

"What an interesting name."

"When I was a kid, I called it Scottie."

"Jonathan, why was your ex-wife at your house?"

"She lives there now, and I don't, as of two weeks ago. She got the house in the settlement. After we split, she hoofed it to Europe—to recuperate, that's what she called it. I stayed on until she returned. Thank God you remembered Midge's name."

Jonathan pulled in in front of the small grocery store. It was called Jake's. There were a half-dozen teenagers with motorcycles in front, lolling around. "There's nothing much for them to do, so they cruise Jake's. It drives the old man crazy. Lord, it's cold."

Jake was a picture. Old, grizzled, perfectly bald, with a thick, full white beard. "Mr. Harley, been a while."

"Yes, it has," Jonathan said. "We're here to stock up, Jake."

"First time you brung your missus."

Jonathan smiled down at Elizabeth. "Yes, the first time, but not the last."

It was one o'clock in the morning when they pulled off the dirt road in front of a two-story pine cabin.

"It'll smell musty, but kind of nice too. Cozy. Even in the summer, it's chilly enough here by the ocean to have a fire. Can you smell the salt?"

"Oh, yes," Elizabeth said, inhaling deeply. And the sound of the waves crashing against the rocks just yards from the cabin. She was so tired she wanted to drop, but they had to stow the groceries and air the cabin out. She saw the old screen doors, the wide screened-in porch, the rough-hewn pine paneling, the huge stone fireplace in the living room.

"It's beautiful," she said.

"Let's go to bed now. I'm about ready to pass out."

Elizabeth paused.

"You can sleep in the guestroom, Elizabeth," he said patiently. "I'd volunteer to take it, but the bed's too short for me. Come along, we'll have to make up both the short bed and the long one."

Elizabeth awoke to the smell of the salt air and the sound of the crashing waves. Sunlight filled her bedroom, and she wondered for a moment where she was. Then she remembered, and smiled. In Maine. Christmas Cove. With Jonathan.

It was at least a minute before she remembered, and the familiar fear flowed through her. She sat up in bed and looked around her room. But she didn't really see it. She was seeing the car exploding in flames, knowing that Drake was in it, realizing her helplessness. And she saw Christian Hunter, his eyes filled with concern, standing over her hospital bed. She remembered Christian telling Lieutenant Draper that he'd been cruising in the area. To see his handiwork.

"Good morning."

She raised her head to see Jonathan standing in the doorway. He was wearing old, very faded jeans, a white cotton sweater, and disreputable sneakers.

"How do you feel?"

When she didn't answer him immediately, he walked to her bed and sat down. "Come here," he said, and pulled her against his chest. He wrapped his arms around her back and pressed her face against his shoulder. "It will be all right, Lizzie. You'll see." He kissed her rumpled hair.

"You smell good," she said, rubbing her nose against his shoulder.

"Thanks. Just wait until you fight with the shower to give you something besides rusty water."

"I've always been 'Elizabeth,' even as a child. My father insisted. It has more dignity, I suppose. I like 'Lizzie.' Why do you call me that?"

"Did Timothy Carleton call you Elizabeth too?"

"Oh, yes, probably for the same reason."

"Why did you ever marry him?"

She grew very still. "No one knows why," she said.

He waited, but she said nothing. "When you'd like to tell me, feel free. Now, if you want to get out of this bed, you'd best do it now."

"I'm sorry," she said, drawing back.

"Don't be a fool. I'm the horny man here, and you can't help it that you are the most adorable waif I've ever found on my doorstep."

He patted her cheek and quickly rose from the bed. "I'll start breakfast," he said, smiled, and left her.

"You, Jonathan Harley," she said to the empty room, "are the most unaccountable, wonderful man I've ever met."

The smell of frying bacon made her stomach growl.

"Pancakes too?" she asked, coming into the old-fashioned kitchen.

"You got it. Set the table on the front porch."

They ate breakfast in silence. Elizabeth kept putting her fork down and breathing in the incredible pine-scented salt air. It was heady and clean and pure.

"Any swimming here?" she asked at last.

"Not unless you're a reptile. Well, yes, in the summer. But now you'd freeze your . . . your toes off."

They bundled up and took a walk after washing up the dishes. "No beaches," Elizabeth said.

"Nope, and what there are, are covered with rocks and pebbles. See the boathouse?" He pointed to a structure on stilts that was some fifteen feet out into the water. "The boat is under the boathouse. In the old days, the caretaker lived up top. Later, we can take the motorboat out, if you like, and play tourist in Newcastle. The sun's bright, we should survive."

"I like," said Elizabeth. "I've never been in a motorboat."

"Did I tell you I like your jeans? You look about eighteen and make me feel like a dirty old man." He tugged lightly on her ponytail.

She smiled up at him. "I like your jeans too. Very sexy."

They were standing beneath a pine tree, the only sounds the sea gulls cruising the beach. "You think so?" He bent down and kissed her.

It had been so long, but more than that, she realized that she felt safe, realized that she'd finally come home. She felt something warm flood through her. She'd never felt this way before in her life.

"We've got to stop, Lizzie," he said, raising his head. "The first time we make love, I don't want to do it on a bed of pine needles. It would wreck the mood and your bottom."

The realization made her silent. She just stared up at him, wondering what he was thinking. They'd been enemies for so long. She said suddenly, "Are you all right? Your company, that is? The loan, can you pay it off? You can expand now as you wanted to?"

"Yes. Once you pulled your hooks out of me, things got back on track. In fact, if you want to buy one of those electronics companies I showed you, just tell me which one, and I'll buy the other."

She gave him her most serious business look. "That sounds fair enough."

"Let's take the boat out and you can have your first taste of salt water in your mouth, on your face, and most important, in your eyes."

They motored over to Newcastle and wandered around the town. There were no tourists to speak of, but the inhabitants were about, doing Christmas shopping.

"I don't suppose there's a Mexican restaurant anywhere here?"

He laughed at her wistful tone. "Not that I know of, but we can buy the fixings."

"I wouldn't know where to begin to make a taco."

"Then we'll just have to buy a cookbook."

They did.

The tacos weren't half-bad, but it wasn't until ten o'clock that evening that the wreckage in the kitchen was cleaned up.

"Now for a fire," Jonathan said. "Curl up, Lizzie, and we'll get down-home here and romantic."

She handed him a glass of Chablis and they pulled the sofa closer to the fire. "You want to know something?" he asked, staring into the flames.

"Something earth-shattering?"

"I think so." He took her wineglass and set it beside his on the coffee table.

He turned to face her and grasped her hands in his. "I love you and I want you to marry me. I didn't want to make love with you until I got that out. I'm talking for the rest of our lives, Lizzie."

She looked down at his hands—large, capable hands, warm.

"I was going to ask you," she said, her voice barely above a whisper.

"Were you, now?" He laughed and pulled her onto his lap.

"But I was afraid to. Tell you how I felt about you, that is. In fact I was afraid of how I felt in the first place. Everything's been in such a mess and I just didn't know."

She tucked her head into the spot between his neck and shoulder. "I thought you'd tell me to get lost, with relish."

"Nope. You already told me you loved me. It was up to me to finish it off."

That brought her head up.

"If you find a woman huddled on your doorstep, I think it's safe for a man to assume that she's either a vagrant or a woman who loves him more than anything."

"I was a vagrant."

"Will you marry me, vagrant?"

"Yes."

"There are problems, but we'll work them out."

She shivered.

"No, I wasn't thinking of Hunter. He's been out of my head for at least two hours now. I was thinking about all the damned money, and the power, and the responsibility that goes along with it."

"You wouldn't marry me for all that, would you?"

"No," he said, not at all angry. "I already did that. Well, not really, but that's how it turned out. I was kind of hoping that I'd fall for a nice poor girl who would love me for my jogging abilities rather than my money. Since neither of us is poor, I think it's safe to assume that it's old-fashioned heart-throbbing, don't you?"

"Yes," she said, "yes, I do." She cupped his face between her hands and kissed him. "You're a wonderful man, Jonathan."

"Yes, ma'am, and don't you forget it. And, Elizabeth, there will be problems, don't kid yourself, but we'll handle all of them."

"Yes, I think we really can," she said, a kind of wonder in her voice.

"Can I assume that you're not wearing a bra under that outrageous shirt of yours?"

She gave him a look that made him shake. "Why don't you find out for yourself?"

Jeans were hard to get off and they were both laughing at their contortions. Until they came together. Elizabeth heard the raucous squawk of a sea gull, felt the warmth of the fire on her bare skin. Then she felt his hands and his mouth, touching her, learning her body. When his mouth was at her breast, she arched her back to draw him closer.

"So nice," he said, and his breath was hot against her skin.

She felt his hand stroke over her ribs, lower to her abdomen. He rested his hand on her belly and came up onto his elbow. "You're beautiful, Elizabeth. And a natural blond."

"What did you expect?" Her voice sounded unnatural to her, high and thin, and she squirmed beneath his hand.

"I expect," he said, his voice warm and deep, "that you will be my last lover and that you'll love what I plan to do to you every night for the next forty years or so."

"And what about me?" Her hand found him and began stroking. "What about what I plan to do to you?"

"Just don't do it with such enthusiasm," he managed, "or you're going to wonder what happened to me."

It wasn't too much longer before she felt him deep inside her, covering her, watching her face closely as he moved. She felt his fingers find her between their sweating bodies.

"Jonathan," she whispered, then felt her body explode. And through those seconds she knew that he was watching her face, encouraging her with soft words.

"I'm so lucky," she said before she fell asleep in his bed.

"You're not the only one," Jonathan said, his eyes on her face. "I'll keep you safe, love."

He didn't fall asleep as quickly as Elizabeth. Christian Hunter was back, in full regalia. What to do about the bastard? Jonathan knew the man was smart as hell. He made plans until he fell asleep, wrapped around Elizabeth.

The next morning, they went into Damariscotta.

"I have to call Adrian and Milly." And Catherine, she added silently.

"All right. Then we go to Newcastle, to a jeweler's. We're talking engagement ring here, kiddo."

The kids were lolling about in front of Jake's, as usual. Jonathan recognized one of them, and waved.

One teenager waved back. Then, to show off for the beautiful lady, he revved his cycle and took off in a cloud of dirt. Jonathan waited until Elizabeth disappeared into the phone booth, then went inside to buy some bullets for his .22 automatic.

"Catherine?"

"My God, Elizabeth! I've been frantic! Where are you?"

"Safe. With Jonathan Harley. What's going on?"

Catherine drew a deep breath. "I went down to see

Lieutenant Draper yesterday, furious about their behavior. You want to know what I found out? That woman who called you? The one Christian Hunter was keeping?"

"What about her?" Elizabeth felt the cold creeping through her body. She knew . . . oh, yes, she knew.

"She's dead. Run down in the street."

Elizabeth closed her eyes. Christian had killed her because he was afraid she'd talk. But she'd said so little. She hadn't deserved to die. "He's crazy, isn't he?"

"That's what I said to Draper, and that jackass laughed. He said there was no evidence, says no one saw who did it, just some kind of dark sedan. And supposedly Hunter has an alibi. His nurse says he was in his office doing correspondence at the time she was killed. Draper said he spoke to Christian Hunter, who told him that she had left him for another man. They're now looking for this unknown character."

Elizabeth closed her eyes.

"Her first name was Susan. I remembered. I don't even know her last name."

"It was Linski."

"Poor, poor woman. She didn't do anything."

"You want to know what I did, Elizabeth? I called the governor and the mayor. I told them what was going on. I told them that my grandmother was very disturbed that the police were treating this all as a joke. After all, two people have been killed, Drake and Susan Linski. We'll see what happens now."

"Thank you, Catherine. How is your grandmother?"

"Holding her own. She already yelled at me about calling the bigwigs, and I told her to can it. Elizabeth, where are you in case I need you?"

"Christmas Cove, Maine, of all places. Jonathan has a cabin here."

Catherine smiled into the phone. "I thought there was someone. Someone special. Who is he, Elizabeth?"

"Actually, he's a man I started out trying to destroy. Now he's the man I'm going to marry."

"Marry!"

"Yes, it sounds crazy, doesn't it? Be happy for me, Catherine. I'm very sure, you know. For the first time in my life, I'm sure about another person."

"I guess I'm in shock. You're not the only one who . . . Well, I'll tell you later. Funny, isn't it, how things can happen so quickly and yet be right, and you know they're right. You be careful, Elizabeth. I assume your Jonathan knows everything?"

"Yes. You'll like him, Catherine. He's a very fine man."

"If you trust him, then he must be."

They spoke for a few more minutes, then Elizabeth rang off. She spoke to Adrian and to Milly, but didn't tell them where she was.

"You ready for Newcastle?" Jonathan asked her when she hung up the phone. He saw her pale face, and hugged her. "It'll be all right. Come along now, you can tell me everything on the way to Newcastle."

All he said when she'd finished was, "Can you trust Catherine Carleton?"

"If I can't, I might as well hang it up."

"That's good enough for me. Let's go get that ring. You can consider it your first Christmas present. Then I want to make love to you until the sea gulls stop squawking."

"That's impossible."

"Exactly."

25

He loved to touch her, to feel her smooth flesh beneath his fingers, to feel her muscles contract when his fingers splayed across her abdomen. He raised his hand just above her and said, "I want to fill you out, to about here."

Elizabeth laughed even though his voice was serious. "The fat lady in the circus, sailor?"

"Nope, the pregnant lady in my backyard."

She dropped her head, feeling stupid. "I'm not using birth control."

Jonathan lowered his hand, resting it on her hip. "Then let's get married, here, in Newcastle."

"I like the way you problem-solve," she said. She looked at the diamond-and-sapphire ring on her left hand.

"It's either that or birth control. It's up to you."

"Jonathan, about kids and things . . ."

"Hmmm?"

His teeth nibbled around her stomach, his tongue going toward her navel.

"That's why I married Timothy."

His head jerked up, and his voice was incredulous: "He got you pregnant?"

Elizabeth had buried it deep, so very deep. It all came back now, the pain and the humiliation, the hopelessness balanced by the gratitude. "I know people were divided into two camps. The majority feeling was of course that I'd married Timothy for his money.

The minority opinion was that I married him because I wanted a father, a loving one this time. That was a very minor minority opinion, I might add. Actually, it was neither."

"What happened, Elizabeth?" He drew himself up on his side, balancing on his elbow. He gently pushed the hair behind her ear.

"I was going out with this man who was a visiting pianist at Juilliard. He was Italian, from Milan. He was very intense, very talented. One night he raped me. It's as simple as that. He loved it because I was a virgin, you see. I told him I was going to the police, and he just laughed. He said that everyone knew I was hot for him and I'd be ridiculed and my career ruined. Evidently he'd been bragging that he'd finally gotten icy Elizabeth Xavier to bed and that I loved it. I raged and all that, but I saw he was right, so eventually I tucked my tail between my legs and told him I never wanted to see him again.

"I had met Timothy by that time. In all honesty, I was very fond of him. He was like a benign father, I suppose, but he was also very sophisticated, charming, and knew exactly what he wanted all of the time. I'd never met anyone like that before. He came to my apartment. I was crying my eyes out, wanting to die, because I'd found out I was pregnant and didn't know what to do. I was raised to revere life, so I couldn't get an abortion. I told him what the man had done."

He saw the pain in her eyes and shook her shoulders. "And that's why you married him?"

"Yes, but first Timothy had the man beaten to a pulp. He returned to Italy the moment he was out of the hospital. Then Timothy asked me to marry him. I did. And I lost the baby two months later. Everyone believed it was Timothy's, of course. Before I lost the baby, Timothy would just grin when we talked about it, and say he wanted it. He said he could beat any viciousness out of the child if need be, but just think of the talent the child would have. He was in his music-appreciation and musical-philanthropy phase at that time."

Jonathan drew her into his arms. "I'm so sorry, Elizabeth. So sorry." That damned bastard! He'd have had him castrated. He'd have done it himself. And he'd have married her, just as Timothy Carleton had done. It was hard to hate a man, an old man, who'd behaved honorably, who'd done just what he, Jonathan, would have done.

"It's been over a long time. Such a long time. Timothy literally saved me. Although I didn't love him, I did care a great deal for him. I felt safe and like I finally belonged. I would have done anything he wished."

He held her, saying nothing. He was afraid that his own rage would burst out if he did speak, and she didn't need that.

She said after a moment, "Life goes on, you know. And I went on until Timothy decided I was too confining. He didn't want me to perform anymore, but the reason he'd been drawn to me in the first place was of my talent. There were other women, even younger women who had talent, just as I had, but not musical talent. He'd gone on to another phase. The last woman, one that Rod Samuels managed to keep out of the trial, was an artist, about the same age I had been when Timothy first became interested in me.

"Timothy wasn't a bad man, Jonathan, truly. He was a man who didn't want to admit he was getting old, that he was mortal. It got to the point that I just wanted out. I didn't want any of his money. I didn't need it, after all. I could earn my own way. All I was going to do was leave him, and that's why I didn't have an alibi the night he was murdered. I was out wandering around instead of going to that benefit. Somehow Christian must have known about the party and that I was going to be there, safe with five hundred people who could swear I was nowhere near the house when Timothy was murdered. Then he stuck that exquisite silver ice pick into Timothy's chest."

"For you," Jonathan said slowly. "He murdered Timothy for you."

"Not really for me," Elizabeth said, her brow wrinkling. "For someone he'd created in his mind. But she wasn't me."

"No, how could she be? He didn't know you and you didn't know him. Why, I wonder, didn't he just manage to meet you, get to know you? If you divorced your husband, he could have asked you out. Why murder, for God's sake? Certainly not to marry a wealthy widow. He's got loads of money."

"His mind . . . I don't understand it either. If he cares for me—or cared, I should say now—his feelings weren't normal."

"No, more an obsession, I'd say. And now you're a threat to him."

She wrapped her arms around his back and burrowed against him. "You're the first man who's wanted me for me, and not someone you believe I am—some kind of fantasy woman different from other women."

"You're different, all right," he said, grinning at her. "You think I'd fall in love with some ordinary woman? I love your talent, Lizzie. Perhaps someday I'll let you out of bed and have you play the piano for me."

She tried to smile, but it was a failed attempt. "When will it be over, Jonathan?"

He didn't have an answer to that, so he loved her instead, making her forget, for a time. And himself.

He even forgot about the twenty-two automatic in the desk drawer, and the bullets he'd slipped into it.

Catherine faced Brad from across her grandmother's desk. Odd how comfortable, how right, it felt sitting here. She felt strong. She felt in control. "When are you going to cancel it out with Jenny?"

"It's already been started, by her father. The senator called me. I told him I would come down to Washington this afternoon. He wants Jenny on a plane to England by tonight. He's already got her plane tickets."

"Thank God. Then what, Brad?"

"California. A new start. I'm going to try to talk Trent into coming back here, just like you suggested."

"It sounds like the children are plotting behind the adults' backs."

Michael Carleton stood in the doorway. He looked like an old man with saggy jowls, Catherine thought, staring at him, not the high-powered man who was always at her grandmother's right hand. He even looked like he was wearing another man's clothes, at least one size too big for him. He had shrunk.

"No, Uncle Michael," Catherine said slowly, amazed at her control and calm, "we're not plotting, we're simply taking over our own lives. People should live their own lives, you know, make their own decisions."

"That will last only until your grandmother is on her feet again." He sounded querulous. Another surprise, another shock.

"Maybe your life, Uncle," Catherine said. "Not ours." She rose, noticing for the first time how the light from the huge windows was at her back, and in Brad and Michael's faces. The power position. Wherever had she heard that?

"Brad will marry Jennifer Henkle, just as your grandmother wants," Michael said, his eyes narrowed.

"No way."

"The photos—"

"No more, Uncle Michael," Brad said. "I'll be leaving for Washington, as I guess you overheard, then I'm off to California."

"Your grandmother will bring you back in short order."

"I found the negatives of the photos, Uncle Michael," Catherine said. "Brad and I destroyed the lot of them, as well as the photos Grandmother had locked in this desk."

Michael looked from one to the other. Ungrateful little bastards. He would speak to Laurette. She would know what to do about this mess. "You'll see, both of you," he said, and stomped out of the room.

"What are you going to do, Cathy?"

Her eyes lit up. "I'm going to Boston, then . . . well, we'll see." She came around the desk, looked up at her brother, then hugged him. "Good luck, Brad. And call me when things get sorted out."

"You got it, kid."

"I love you, Brad, and don't forget, we do have control now. Don't let anyone tell you otherwise."

He watched her walk from the room, and found himself shaking his head. He remembered some old photos of Laurette he'd seen years ago in a long-forgotten album. If his mind wasn't playing tricks on him, Cathy had the look of her. The future, he thought, was going to prove interesting.

"Where is Elizabeth Carleton?"

Lieutenant Draper looked up to see Moretti standing in his office doorway. "You got me. Took off, and I can't say I blame her. Why? Who cares?"

"I can't get that damned watch out of my mind, that's why."

"It was all a lie, you know that, she—"

"You haven't broken Hunter's alibi?" Moretti interrupted. He was beginning to think Draper was an ass.

"No, that nurse of his backs him up to the hilt. I mean, we haven't really questioned her all that much, she's credible—"

"Yeah, just like Dr. Christian Hunter was credible."

"Look, it was probably a hit-and-run. A guy hit her, realized he was in deep shit, and got the hell out."

"You know something, Draper?" Moretti said, turning to look out the dirty window. "It's a bummer when you think you might be wrong about someone, particularly when you staked everything on being right. Put out some feelers for Elizabeth Carleton. I want to talk to her."

Draper watched Moretti, the pompous idiot, walk out of his office. He was getting soft.

*   *   *

"Are you sure you want to do this, Jonathan?"

She sounded nervous, and he hugged her to his side.

"Yep. What about you, Lizzie?"

She poked him in the stomach. "That's an awful nickname."

"I don't know about that. We can go from Lizzie to lizard to laziness to lippy broad."

"We don't know each other all that well."

"I know how to make you come in an average of five minutes. That ain't so bad."

"You won't be serious about this, will you? This is for life, Jonathan!"

"You'd better believe it." He struck the palm of his hand against his forehead. "My God, you're right. Where are we going to live, anyway?"

"Judge Columbus is ready for you now."

Elizabeth thought her eyes would cross with apprehension. Married! And everything was such a mess. And she knew, knew all the way to her innards, that Christian Hunter wouldn't just disappear. Oh, no, he was out there. Waiting.

"You ready, sweetheart?"

She looked up at him, saw the understanding and tenderness in his eyes, and slowly nodded.

Mrs. Everett led them into the judge's chambers. He'd put on his robe and looked as dignified as a bishop.

Suddenly Elizabeth grabbed Jonathan's hand and jerked it. "Listen to me," she said as quietly as she could. "If we marry, you'll be a target, just as I am. I can't allow it. It's too dangerous. Christian Hunter won't forget, I know it!"

He let her run herself out.

Her hand was sweaty and her fingernails dug into his palm.

"You done?"

"You're not thinking clearly, Jonathan!"

"You're not done." He sighed and waited.

"Mr. Harley?" Mrs. Everett didn't like the looks of

this. Judge Columbus was a busy man, and here these two were dithering. It wasn't as if they were children, for heaven's sake.

"Just a moment," Jonathan said smoothly. "My fiancée is concerned about the disposition of her assets."

"I'm going to beat your socks off! Stop patronizing me. I'm not being a silly woman and you aren't Superman."

"Let's get married, Elizabeth. Now." He rubbed his hands up and down her arms. "Listen to me. I'm already a target. If Hunter is after you, he'll know about me already. The man's crazy. Don't you see, it doesn't matter. We cannot," Jonathan said, looking her square in the eyes, "I repeat, we cannot let him control our lives."

She felt tears in her eyes and her nose started to run. She sniffed.

He pulled her against him. "I'm scared too, sweetheart. I don't want to be scared alone."

She cursed against his shoulder, very explicitly, and he smiled over her head. Mrs. Everett hadn't changed expressions, so he supposed she hadn't heard.

"Oh, damn you, all right!"

Fifteen minutes later, Jonathan and Elizabeth Harley walked out of the courthouse in Newcastle. Neither Mrs. Everett nor Judge Columbus had recognized Elizabeth. Thank God for small favors. Jonathan dreaded the day the press found out about their marriage, but they'd face it when it happened.

Jonathan felt great. Relieved. During the brief ceremony he'd forgotten entirely about Christian Hunter. He was afraid to ask if Elizabeth had. He tried for a leer.

"Do I have to feed you first or can I take you back to the cabin and revert to my horny self?"

"Why not? I have this feeling that it's going to be a lifetime habit."

An hour later they were lying in front of the fireplace. Jonathan drew on her nipple, making smacking noises that made her laugh even as she arched up closer. He moved up to her mouth and gave her more staccato kisses that were dotted with sex words.

And when he brought her to her orgasm, he thought as he watched her face: She is my wife. He came into her deep, and deeper still, and she watched his face as he spilled himself into her.

"Goodness," she said, feeling him slide off her. "We're both sweaty as pigs."

"Oink," he said, and nibbled on her earlobe.

"I never thought I'd have two husbands," Elizabeth said quietly, testing the reality out loud. He said nothing, so she wondered if he were asleep, his leg over her thighs.

"I never thought I'd have two wives," he said, sliding his hand about her waist. "We both lucked out."

"The real world's out there."

"Yeah, but this is our honeymoon. What is it the French call a special orgasm? Oh, yes, the little death. Well, this is our little honeymoon. We'll think about the real world tomorrow, as Scarlett said."

But he was thinking again about his twenty-two automatic and Christian Hunter, and somewhere deep down, Jonathan wanted him to come. He wanted the bastard to find them. He wanted to destroy him so Elizabeth would never be afraid again.

So he'd never be afraid again either. Unfortunately, he knew very well that he wasn't Superman.

They were asleep on a blanket set between two big boulders near the edge of the ocean. The sun was bright overhead, it was incredibly warm for December, in the high fifties, and the wine had done its job.

Jonathan's hand was on her bottom and she was lying with her head against his shoulder.

It was a moment between dream and reality, the sun blotted out suddenly by shadows. Chilly. He pulled Elizabeth closer. Then his eyes flew open.

He stared into the barrel of a black automatic. He followed it upward to a man's face. The man looked haggard, drawn, as if he hadn't slept for a week.

The man was Christian Hunter.

Jonathan jerked upward.

"Don't even think it, Harley."

Christian had stood watching them for a good ten minutes. It was as close as he'd gotten to them during the past two days. But he had looked—oh, yes, he'd looked through the windows at night and seen them making love, seen them laughing together.

He'd wanted to wait. He'd wanted them to let their guard down.

Elizabeth had given this man what she'd refused to give him. She'd refused him her love and her loyalty. And her body. He'd tried to remember if she'd ever laughed with him.

The automatic jerked in his hand. No, no, calm down, he told himself. You've got the upper hand now. You're in control.

Elizabeth heard his voice, but thought it was the beginning of a nightmare. It was so clear, this nightmare. She felt a tightening on her arm. That was odd; a nightmare wasn't supposed to be physical, not like this.

"Jonathan . . ." she mumbled.

"Wake up, dear Elizabeth."

That wasn't Jonathan. It wasn't . . .

"Oh, no!"

"Hello, Elizabeth. Were you dreaming about me, perhaps? Or were you thinking about this macho cretin you married? Oh, yes, I see the wedding ring."

"How did you find us?"

Harley sounded awfully calm, but Christian wasn't fooled, not the trained part of him that was the detached observer, the psychologist. The man was scared shitless.

"At least I waited until both of you had your clothes on. Sit up, Elizabeth, and join the party."

She'd known he would come, deep down, she'd known. "It's all right, Lizzie," Jonathan said, helping her sit up. She felt him squeeze her shoulder. For reassurance, but of course, nothing could reassure her.

"Lizzie? It suits you, now that you're with him."

"Christian . . ." Her mouth felt so dry.

"How did you find us?" Jonathan repeated. He was gauging the distance between him and Hunter, and that gun. That damned gun. His twenty-two was in the cabin. Safe in a desk drawer. He hadn't wanted Elizabeth to see it. He hadn't wanted her to know. He'd played the macho protector sparing his woman, and look what it had gotten him.

"It wasn't hard, not really," Christian said, and smiled down at them. He took a couple steps back and sat down on a boulder and crossed his legs at the ankles. "That attempt of yours, Elizabeth, to flee on the train to Philadelphia was rather silly. Of course I saw you get on the train. Then I phoned ahead to an investigator I knew in Philadelphia. You were followed, naturally. When I found out the man's name was Jonathan Harley, all I had to do was some checking. Not difficult at all. Deeds of ownership are public record, you know, even those for properties tucked out of the way in Maine."

"Why did you wait so long?" Was that her voice? So calm and detached?

"The NYPD, Elizabeth. They were curious about Susan's death. There were questions, and of course I wanted to make Lieutenant Draper happy. He left with a smile on his vacuous face. He really does hate you, you know. He thinks you're a lying bitch. I would have agreed with him, but I didn't think it too politic to do so. And my nurse is so guileless, you know. She trusts me, admires me even. She believed what I told her."

What did one say to a crazy man? But he seemed so uncrazy. Jonathan looked at him, really looked, and what he saw wasn't at all chilling. He looked like an aristocratic Englishman with his thin, fine-boned face, his long, narrow hands, his tweed jacket and corduroy slacks. He found himself wondering briefly why Elizabeth hadn't fallen for him. He was good-looking, smooth, and rich. But she hadn't.

"This is a primitive place, Harley, but if all you want to do is hide and screw around, I suppose it's perfect. Why did you marry the deceitful bitch? For her money?"

"I married her because she had the good sense to kiss you off." He saw the long, slender fingers tighten about the gun, and tensed. He should have kept his mouth shut.

"Christian, what do you want?"

Christian looked directly at Elizabeth now and his look was tender and cold and deadly. "I want you to suffer, my dear. I want you to die."

The gun swung about to Jonathan. "No, Harley, don't move! Don't even think about it. You see, if you're a good boy, I might let you die more quickly than Elizabeth."

Jonathan's arms went around her and pulled her closer. The sun went behind a cloud. Elizabeth shivered.

"I've been thinking about it quite a bit—how to kill the two of you, that is. It's got to appear an accident—that, or I'll have to live in South America. Draper and Moretti hate you, Elizabeth, but they aren't stupid and they are sworn to mete out justice, whatever that means. Now, I do believe I'm a bit thirsty. Watching you two is tiring and boring. Shall we go to your cabin, Harley?"

He was going to play with them, Jonathan realized, relief flooding him. He was going to brag and show them how great he was. Excellent. Now he had a prayer of doing something. The twenty-two was in the cabin. There was hope. And Hunter would have to make it look like an accident. How?

"Come, Lizzie," he said, and helped her stand.

"Don't call her that again!"

Jonathan froze at the rage in the man's voice. He looked at him, and now he believed he was insane. "All right, I won't call her that. You're thirsty, Hunter?"

Christian ignored him. "Elizabeth, come here, with me."

She froze. She could feel Jonathan coiling beside her. She took a step forward, then another.

She wondered if she could hurl herself at him. Jonathan could perhaps escape. Yes, he was fast, he was strong. The distance seemed endless, one step after the other. With each step, she saw vivid images of herself, fragments really. She was in high school, playing Christmas carols for the choir, wearing red and green, wishing she could be singing and not playing. Then in Paris with Claude, seeing the Louvre for the first time and feeling insignificant.

One more step. She would save him. She felt strong. She felt in control.

26

Elizabeth felt strangely detached from the woman who was walking toward Christian Hunter. One more step. One foot in front of the other. No more fragments, no more meaningless memories. Just now. She forced herself to keep her eyes on Christian's face, and not on that gun.

One more step.

She heard a sea gull squawk loudly, just overhead. Suddenly she smiled, and looked up, for just an instant. Christian's eyes followed hers.

She jumped straight at him, her hands like claws, trained on the gun. She grabbed his wrist, throwing her weight against him, jerking upward with all her strength. He fell backward. She knew Jonathan yelled, but all she really heard was Christian's surprised intake of breath.

The gun went off, loud and obscene.

"Elizabeth!"

She was rolling with Christian on the rocky beach. He was cursing her, slamming at her with his fists. It was over quickly.

"Stop where you are, Harley! Or the bitch is dead!"

Jonathan stopped cold. Hunter had her pinned beneath him, the gun pointed at her temple.

Christian didn't move. He saw that Harley was still now, and he looked down into Elizabeth's face. He gently pressed the muzzle against her temple.

It was cold, so cold.

He felt her beneath him, quivering just slightly, and pressed himself against her. He heard a yell of rage from Harley, and just smiled. "You like that, Elizabeth?"

All she could think about was that she'd failed. She stared up at him, saying nothing.

"That was a stupid move, Elizabeth," he said, and lifted himself off her. "Come along now. No more attempts to save this stupid husband of yours, or I'll put a bullet in the middle of your face."

She believed him.

Jonathan thought of Rambo at that moment, and nearly laughed aloud. What would Rambo do? He'd not have a shirt on, that was for sure, and there'd be a magazine of bullets strapped across his chest, and an M16, or whatever the newest military toy was, in his hands, pointed at his enemy like a huge phallic symbol. Too bad Stallone wasn't here to write a script for him, a script in which the hero won out.

All he said was, "Are you all right, Elizabeth?"

She nodded and came up on her hands and knees. She was aware of pain in her ribs. She shook her head, clearing it, and rose slowly.

"Now, let's go."

Christian kept the gun pointed at her throat now as he walked beside her. Jonathan was just ahead of them. He'd taken karate classes a while back, had gotten pretty good, but suddenly he couldn't remember a thing. It was like his body belonged to someone else. He'd always thought self-defense was a game, nothing more, not really. What wasn't a game to him was jogging. How could he disarm a man with jogging? Or a dynamite breaststroke, for that matter?

"Rustic," Christian said. "Just the spot for newlyweds to scream and yell in bed with no one to hear them. Open the door, Harley."

Jonathan opened the door and walked inside. His eyes went immediately to the small desk on the far side of the living room. Top drawer, under a couple pieces of paper. Loaded and ready to go.

"Get me a Scotch, Harley, neat. Dear Elizabeth and I will wait for you in here."

He was walking away from the desk. Think, you damned fool, think!

"Well, Elizabeth, it was all the watch, wasn't it?"

He sounded so very normal, amused almost.

"Yes," she said, "it was the watch. Timothy had never worn it until the day he was . . . until the day you murdered him."

"That was stupid of me," Christian said easily, stretching out on the sofa, looking relaxed and very pleased with himself. "I knew then that you would think about it, wonder perhaps. Unfortunately I had no idea that the old bastard hadn't ever worn it. Too bad. But I'd already lost you by then, hadn't I, Elizabeth?"

"I was never there for you to lose, Christian."

"Even though I saved you from Rowe Chalmers? You're ungrateful, Elizabeth. I wanted you so much that I didn't even mind that you'd been screwing him."

"No, Christian, it wasn't me you wanted. You killed a man who'd never harmed you and all because of a phantom you created in your mind. She was never real, Christian."

Jonathan heard her speaking and sloshed some Scotch from the glass. God, she was telling him he was insane.

The ice cubes fell onto the counter, sounding like bullet cracks. It was then that Jonathan began wishing frantically for something to put in that Scotch. Rat poison. Anything.

"You want to know something, Elizabeth?"

Jonathan breathed a sigh of temporary relief. Hunter sounded calm, as if her words hadn't penetrated. Perhaps they hadn't. He put two ice cubes into the glass, but waited a moment.

Christian continued, "I used to go to Susan after I'd been with you. I wanted you so badly, but you never wanted me. I didn't realize it then, I believed you so scarred, so wary, vulnerable, but you were just toying with me. You were afraid I'd tell Moretti that I'd lied for you and that you were your husband's murderer."

"No," Elizabeth said. "No."

"Well, no matter now. Ah, my Scotch. Sit down, Harley, and be a good chap. Elizabeth, you will take a drink first, if you please."

Thank God he hadn't found any poison. Jonathan watched her take a small sip, then another. Hunter waited a moment, then nodded to himself, satisfied.

Jonathan watched him sip the Scotch. It was good stuff. He was remembering so many movies where the hero kept the killer talking to gain time. Didn't movie plots come from real life? Hell, it was worth a shot. Maybe the Scotch would slow Hunter's reflexes.

He prayed that Elizabeth wouldn't try to go after Hunter again. He saw her hands fisted in her lap.

"You know, Hunter," Jonathan said finally, "there's not a chance in hell that you'll get away with this."

Christian's eyes slewed toward him. He looked disdainful, contemptuous. He gently rolled the Scotch around in the glass. The ice cubes clicked together. The noise sounded like death itself to Elizabeth.

"Christian, listen to me. I'm the one who hurt you. I'm the one you hate, not Jonathan. He has nothing to do with you. Let him go."

"Shut up, Elizabeth!"

"Let her beg, Harley. I find her devotion touching. Misguided, but touching nonetheless. My dear, I do wonder why you married him, though. Fear of me, perhaps? You knew retribution was coming and you wanted to attach some fool to protect you?"

"He's a man," Elizabeth said quietly, looking Christian straight in the eyes. "He's honest and loyal and the best thing that's ever happened in my life. Let him go, Christian."

"You're boring me now, Elizabeth." Christian set the glass on the table beside the sofa. "You want to know something? I knew you were involved with him, even before I found out who he was. And you lied to me, told me he was just a business acquaintance. But I knew, Elizabeth, I knew you were betraying me."

"No, no, I wasn't."

"Well, it's a little late now. I think it's time to end this farce. We're going for a ride. Get the boat keys, Harley."

Jonathan just stared at him for a moment. The damned boat. Both of them found drowned in the Atlantic off Christmas Cove? Jonathan walked toward the desk, but Hunter's voice drew him up.

"The boat keys are on that hook over there, Harley, by the window."

Jonathan got the keys and tossed them to Hunter. He caught them, grabbing Elizabeth's arm as he did so. "I told you not to try anything, Elizabeth." He bent her arm painfully behind her and she winced, but made no sound.

"Now, Harley, I want you to fetch some nice strong cord for me."

"No."

Christian wrenched her arm back and upward. Elizabeth bit her bottom lip but was still silent. "Now, Harley, or I'll break her arm."

"I don't have any, at least not here in the cabin."

"Where?"

"The boathouse."

"Let's go."

He waved the gun at Jonathan.

Suddenly Elizabeth stopped. "No, Christian, I'm not moving. You want this to be an accident? Well, I won't let you. If you want me dead, then shoot me now, here. Even Moretti will be after you."

Jonathan sucked in his breath. Hunter would shoot, he knew it. The man was crazy, and so twisted that the thought of the New York D.A. after him probably didn't make a ripple in his mind.

Christian looked down at Elizabeth. He smiled. "You want it here and now, my dear? All right."

"Look, Peabody, I *am* the district attorney. And this is a possibly critical situation. Get over to Jonathan Harley's cabin in Christmas Cove. He and Mrs. Carleton are in danger, I'll bet on it."

Homer Peabody looked at the plate of beef stew in front of him, warm and spiced with tangy mustard. His wife thought he was crazy to eat mustard on beef stew, so he usually ate it in his office. It was getting cold even as this idiot crank was bending his ear. He started nodding, then realized that he was on the phone. "All right, Mr. Morelli—"

"Moretti! Anthony Moretti, you damned fool!"

"Yeah, Mr. Moretti. I'll get right over there. Don't you worry, now."

"Take some men with you. Hunter is dangerous. He's already killed three people!"

"Yeah, I'm on my way."

Moretti cursed and slammed down the phone.

Homer Peabody shook his head sorrowfully at the crank's rudeness. Wasn't nothing going to happen. He'd been here for fifteen years. There was a murder once, a long time ago, but it was an out-of-stater who'd stabbed his wife. The district attorney of New York calling him! Fat chance. He scooped up a spoon of stew and took a satisfying bite. He'd go out to Christmas Cove—oh, yeah, he'd go. He took another bite and chewed thoughtfully. That mustard was the best.

Moretti dialed the number of the state police. His hand was shaking. That damned fool Draper had lost Hunter, and now he was long gone. After Elizabeth Carleton. He felt it in his gut. And it was his fault. "Shit," he said softly.

"I beg your pardon?" said a woman's outraged voice on the other end of the line.

"Excuse me," said Moretti. "I need to speak to Mark Cunningham."

"He's at lunch at the moment."

Moretti stared at the phone. "Then get me his next in command! This is a damned emergency!"

"You needn't yell or use profanity," said the woman. Moretti gritted his teeth.

Then the line went dead. The woman had cut him off. He cursed, then dialed the number again.

Elizabeth didn't even see his fist coming. It slammed against her jaw.

Jonathan dived toward him, but Christian grabbed Elizabeth under the arms and pressed the gun against her breast. "Just stop, Harley."

"I'm going to kill you, Hunter."

"Sure you are, buddy. Sure you are. Now, pick up the bitch and let's get to the boathouse. You try anything, Harley, and I'll put a bullet through her." Christian knew Jonathan Harley was at the edge. He added very softly, "I don't care if I die, Harley. It's even possible that after I fire once you'll get to me. But she'll be dead. Very dead."

Christian dropped Elizabeth to the floor. "Pick her up, Harley. Now."

Jonathan lifted her over his shoulder. He hoped her jaw wasn't broken, and almost laughed at his concern. It seemed so trivial, but his blood still boiled with rage. He wanted to kill Hunter, very badly now. He had to think, to come up with something, dammit, not react like a bumbling fool, like a man who would lose everything if he lost her.

He walked out the front door of the cabin, steadying Elizabeth with his arm across the back of her thighs.

He saw Hunter's shadow behind him, off to his left. The terrain was gentle here, no dangerous crags or hidden sharp rocks. Just sweet sweeps of winter grass.

At the boathouse he gently laid Elizabeth on the floor and straightened.

"The cord, Harley," Christian said, waving the gun at him.

You're going to tie me up, then take Elizabeth out and dump her in the ocean.

"You got it," Christian said, and Jonathan started, not realizing that he'd spoken aloud.

Unfortunately, the cord was in plain view. It was

strong nylon cord used on the motorboat. Jonathan reached for it, his mind racing. Oh, yeah, he knew what he'd do now. He felt the rush of air behind him and lurched around, but he wasn't fast enough. The butt of Hunter's gun hit him on the temple. He sank to the wooden floor without a sound.

Elizabeth opened her eyes very slowly. She was first aware of the loud hum of an engine, then movement beneath her. And Christian Hunter. She didn't rub her hand against her aching jaw. No, she just cracked her eyes open a bit. Christian was at the wheel, steering the boat out of the cove, out into the open sea. Where was Jonathan? She nearly cried out when she realized he wasn't there in the boat. What had Christian done to him? Killed him already? She felt bile rise in her throat and she felt the utter horror of helplessness. For an instant, the last year and a half rolled through her mind, and she saw herself weak and vulnerable, then strong, but driven to bury that other Elizabeth.

"No."

Christian turned quickly about to face her. "Hello, Elizabeth. Not much longer now, my dear." Even as he spoke, he turned off the motor.

"What did you do to Jonathan?"

"I killed him," Christian said calmly.

She managed to come up on her hands and knees. The boat was swaying gently in the swell of the waves.

"I killed the damned bastard," he said again.

She raised her face and looked at him. He was smiling. *I killed him.*

The sun was bright overhead. She heard Jonathan telling her, a smile in his voice, "Cover up, love. I don't want to make love to a peeling lobster. Even though it's December, that sun is damned hot."

Christian was smiling at her. He looked boyish, happy, with a lock of hair over his forehead.

She felt the salt breeze on her face, felt her hair lifting and falling about her shoulders. *I killed the damned bastard.*

Everything fell into place.

Elizabeth lurched to her feet and the boat swayed precariously.

"Sit down!"

But she didn't. She didn't see anything, feel anything, but knew that she wanted to die and to kill. Both.

"Sit down!" He brought the gun up, pointing it at her stomach.

The gun meant nothing. It was a little piece of black metal.

Her eyes narrowed on him and her world became only her hatred.

Then she jumped.

Christian drew back, his legs hitting against the motor. She was on him like a wild thing. He pulled the trigger, knew that he'd hit her.

She felt a prickling in her arm. Nothing more, just an irritating little sting. Nothing but a piece of black metal. It couldn't hurt her.

Her fingernails were on his face, tearing downward. She heard him howl, felt his hands striking her, in the stomach, in the chest.

She was yowling like a wild animal, screaming with rage.

He got her arms down, and she brought up her knee and sent it into his groin. He froze, then screamed.

"I want you to die!"

Her voice sounded hoarse, crazed. And she kicked him again, and with all her strength heaved him overboard. But he grabbed at her, pulling her with him. She hooked her leg around the motor and smashed her fist into his stomach.

She felt his grip loosen and drew back her arm. Her elbow went into his throat. He made an odd gurgling sound, then plunged backward into the water.

He thrashed and she watched him. He called out to her. She watched him, not moving.

Then the water closed over his head once, twice.

Elizabeth felt fierce triumph. *I killed him.*

"Elizabeth!"

A woman's voice . . . but no, that made no sense. She turned slowly and saw another motorboat careening toward her. A woman waving frantically toward her. It was Catherine. Rowe Chalmers was at the wheel.

"Elizabeth!"

She looked down at the frothing waves, stirred up by the other boat. She didn't even wonder how and why Catherine was here, Rowe with her. She just stared down at the water. She was aware that she was moving to the edge of the boat.

"Elizabeth, for God's sake, no!"

Rowe's voice, filled with fear.

Then Rowe pulled the boat next to hers and cut the engine.

Catherine scrambled over the side and grabbed Elizabeth. "Oh, God, we saw him, saw you fight with him. It's over, Elizabeth. What's wrong with you?" She shook her.

"He killed Jonathan. He killed my husband."

She tried to pull away from Catherine, but Rowe grabbed her. She fought him, but he jerked her over into the other boat. "Hold on to her, Catherine," he ordered.

He started the motor, and the boat leapt forward, back toward shore.

Elizabeth huddled low, a low keening noise coming from her mouth.

"My God, he shot you!"

Suddenly she felt a searing pain in her arm. Nausea rose in her throat and she leaned over the side and vomited.

Catherine held her, then pulled her back, holding her head on her lap. "We got here as fast as we could," she said, realizing that she was babbling, but it didn't matter. "I even talked to Midge, Jonathan's secretary. She was worried. She wanted to come with us. She wanted—"

"Christian murdered my husband."

"Oh, God, Elizabeth, I'm so sorry." She began rocking Elizabeth, saying meaningless words. So she'd married Jonathan Harley . . . and now she was a widow once again. Catherine closed her eyes.

"We've got to get her to a hospital," Rowe said. He was pale. He pulled the boat next to the dock at the boathouse.

"I don't care," Elizabeth whispered. "I don't care."

"Stop it, of course you care!" Catherine's eyes met Rowe's and he slowly shook his head. He jumped out of the boat and tied it up, then stopped cold.

Jonathan Harley stumbled out of the boathouse, blood streaming down his face, his hands still tied behind his back.

"Elizabeth!"

She didn't raise her head, just kept moaning, "No, no . . ."

27

"The bullet went straight through the fleshy part of her upper arm. She'll be all right, but she needs blood. Mr. Chalmers has her type and he's donating at this moment. Now, Mr. Harley, please calm down, you'll need a couple of stitches in your head."

Dr. Carruthers paused a moment at the close of his very reasoned talk, fully expecting Mr. Harley to fold his tent and cooperate. Instead, Jonathan asked sharply, "What is her type? Why didn't you ask me?"

Dr. Carruthers sighed. "You need all the blood you've got. You were hurt too, you know. Now, please, Mr. Harley."

But Jonathan ignored him for the moment, watching the IV dripping clear liquid into Elizabeth's arm. Her face was pale as death to his frightened eyes.

Dr. Carruthers said patiently, "We'll replace the glucose solution that she's getting now with blood. Then she'll go back to the glucose."

He nodded to the nurse, but Jonathan said, "Just a moment, please." He leaned over his wife and said very softly, "It's over, love. He's dead. Believe me, Elizabeth. It's you and me now, no more shadows, no more monsters hiding in the dark." He kissed her mouth.

"Mr. Harley, your head, sir."

He turned to face Carruthers again, and thought inconsequentially that the doctor's nose was long and thin, just like Christian Hunter's. "All right," he said.

But he didn't move until the gurney was wheeled out of sight.

Catherine Carleton and Rowe Chalmers stood in the sterile corridor, waiting.

"She'll be all right, Cathy," Rowe said as he rolled down his sleeve. "Hell, she's going to get my blood now, she has to do just great."

That drew a small smile. "Yeah, I know."

"And so will Jonathan."

"That poor man. Lord, I'm so tired."

She turned and pressed herself against Rowe's chest, her face on his shoulder. "What if we hadn't found them, what if we hadn't gotten that boat, what if—?"

"It's over, Cathy. Now we need to call the police."

"You folks here with a Jonathan Harley and an Elizabeth Carleton?"

They turned to see a paunchy older man with nothing but a circle of thin gray hair on his head. He wore a gray uniform with the shirt buttons bulging over his stomach.

"I'm Homer Peabody, *the law.* You want to tell me what's going on here?"

Rowe frowned. "Who called you, Mr. Peabody? We were going to in another couple of minutes."

Homer didn't like that question and mumbled under his breath, "Mr. Morelli, a fellow from New York."

"His name is Anthony Moretti and he's the district attorney of New York."

"Ah, shit," said Homer. "Well, yeah, he called me. I got out to the cabin as soon as could be, and saw the rear end of the ambulance. I followed you folks here."

Catherine and Rowe exchanged looks.

"Very well, Mr. Peabody," Rowe said at last. "We'll tell you all we know. Then you'll have to speak to Mr. Harley."

Homer wrote down everything just as he'd been taught to do a long time ago. Big facts with little facts. It could all be important. He looked aghast when he heard about a lady pushing a man overboard.

". . . I suggest that someone try to find Christian Hunter's body," Rowe concluded.

"Let the damned fish have him."

Catherine smiled at Jonathan Harley. He was a handsome man, she noted objectively, even though his jaw was a bit too square for her taste. More objectively, he looked like hell at the moment with the big square of white bandage over the side of his face and the blood on his shirt.

"You Jonathan Harley?"

Jonathan gazed at Homer and nodded.

"I'm Homer Peabody."

"Yes, I know. You're the sheriff, right?"

"Yes, sir. Now, these folk here tell me your wife killed a guy named Christian Hunter."

"I sure hope so," said Jonathan. He smiled at Catherine, and continued the smile, a bit less easily, toward Rowe Chalmers. "Glad you came along when you did." He'd already told them that, of course, babbled it really, so afraid that Elizabeth was dying that he could scarcely make any sense at all. He continued to Homer Peabody, "I want to see Hunter's body. I want to know for certain that the bastard's dead."

"Now, see here, Mr. Harley, the fellow's—"

"—an insane shrink, oddly enough," Catherine said.

"I can't get this all down with all of you butting in," said Homer, licking the end of his pencil irritably.

"Look," Rowe said, "Mr. Harley is exhausted. He needs to get some rest. This Hunter hurt him also, you know, slugged him with a gun. Mrs. Harley isn't in any shape to talk to you now. You've got our statements. Can't we just leave it for a while?"

"But where's this Elizabeth Carleton?" Homer asked. "That fellow Moretti said—"

"We're married," Jonathan said. "She's now Elizabeth Harley."

"All right." Homer carefully wrote that in his book. He'd have to get the coast guard out to find Hunter's body. He carefully folded down his notebook. It was his first big case, and it didn't even sound like murder. A woman kicking a man overboard? Weird, that's how it sounded to him.

The three of them watched Homer Peabody amble away. Rowe shook his head and said, "You know that Moretti called him and the little bastard didn't do anything?"

"If Moretti called me I doubt I'd pay any attention either," said Jonathan. He stuck out his hand. "Thank you, Chalmers, Catherine."

"I just wish we could have gotten there sooner," Catherine said, shaking his hand. "I asked that you have the room next to Elizabeth's. I'll bet that old Peabody will be coming back. Rowe and I will be at the White Duck Inn if you need us."

"Count on Moretti showing up," Rowe added.

"Poor Homer, I wouldn't like to be in his boots when Moretti does show up," said Catherine.

"How is your grandmother, Miss . . . Catherine?"

"She's hanging in, that's about it. Thank you for asking."

"Mr. Harley, it's time for us to get some rest."

Jonathan laughed at the nurse's cajoling voice. "I'll see you guys later," he said.

Moretti arrived at the hospital at ten o'clock that evening. He had no qualms about waking up Jonathan, who himself had no qualms about being rude to the D.A.

"A little late coming to reason, aren't you, Moretti?"

Anthony Moretti was tired, frantic because he, in his own mind, had very nearly been responsible for Elizabeth Carleton Harley's death. And Jonathan Harley's death, he added to himself as he eyed the big man facing him with ill-disguised contempt.

"Yeah," he said. "Look, Harley, I'm damned sorry. They haven't found Hunter's body as yet, but I understand that the tides are peculiar in this area. He could easily have been washed out to sea. Did he admit to murdering Timothy Carleton?"

"Bragged about it, you mean? Yes. And he killed some woman named Susan. He was afraid that this Susan would spill the beans to Elizabeth. As a matter of fact, she had called Elizabeth, but you knew that, didn't you?"

"Yeah, I knew that," Moretti admitted.

"And he blew up Drake, Elizabeth's chauffeur."

Moretti looked down.

Jonathan sighed. "At least you tried to get Peabody off his butt." His head throbbed, but he wanted to see Elizabeth, to hold her, reassure her. To reassure himself.

"The state police even screwed things up for a while," Moretti said, shaking his head in disgust, unwilling to admit that he hadn't been able to tell them exactly where to go. Somewhere in Christmas Cove, a Jonathan Harley's cabin, that's all he had known. Hell, it should have been enough. Even old Peabody had beaten them there.

"You knew about the watch too," Jonathan said, wondering what would happen to him if he were to smash his fist in Moretti's face.

"Look, Harley, I was wrong, okay? You and your wife are alive."

"Find Hunter's body," Jonathan insisted.

Moretti nodded, then walked to the window. It was pitch black outside. They were in the small community hospital in Newcastle. He said, more to himself than to Harley, "You want to know what the real kicker is? Catherine Carleton coming to save your wife. With Rowe Chalmers. Just like the cavalry riding in in the nick of time. Hell, it's like a bloody soap opera."

"People change, thank God," Jonathan said, and knew that any intended irony would go right over Moretti's head.

"I'll let you get some rest now, Harley," he said, turning. "And I'll speak to Mrs. Harley in the morning." Tentatively Moretti held out his hand to Jonathan.

"Oh, shit," Jonathan said, and shook Moretti's hand. Jonathan left his room the moment Moretti took off. He quietly opened Elizabeth's door and stared toward the bed. He tried to hear her breathing, and when he didn't, he panicked. He rushed to the bed, then drew up, feeling like a fool. But she was so pale. He didn't know what to do, but he did know that he didn't want to leave her. She had on a white hospital gown, and he could see the bandage on her left arm. He gently drew the covers up and slipped in beside her, careful of her IV.

Nurse Nancy Cooper looked in several hours later. She blinked, then smiled. No harm, the poor man was distraught, she'd heard all about it. Lord, the Harleys had provided enough gossip to keep all of eastern Maine in conversation for weeks. She quietly closed the door.

She was still smiling when the gun butt came down on the back of her head. Just a very small cry came from her mouth before she collapsed.

"I think I've aged about two decades," Catherine said.

"Me too, and that makes me an old man," said Rowe.

He reached for her, and Catherine came willingly into his arms. She felt suddenly very much alive, shedding her fatigue magically.

"Marry me, Rowe," she said.

He said nothing.

"We make a good team."

"You're too young for me, Cathy."

"And too rich, isn't that what you mean? And too much of a spoiled rich girl?"

"No and no, just too young."

"Bull."

"You've already begun running your grandmother's empire. You're a natural at it. I'm small potatoes, Cathy, small Boston potatoes."

"The same is true of Elizabeth and Jonathan. Will their marriage fall apart?"

"I set out purposely to seduce Elizabeth. I used her.

If you want to be real honest about it, I betrayed her. I needed money and I was willing to do anything."

"And you finally told Grandmother to shove it."

"Only after Elizabeth told me she knew. I was going to marry Amanda for her money. Doesn't that make you wonder about my motives?"

"Look, Rowe, I'm asking you to marry me. Only my motives are in question. All that other crap is in the past. None of it matters now. Remember how I was—not a pretty specimen, that's for sure."

"True."

"Doesn't the fact that we're reformed baddies make any difference? Haven't we paved part of our road to heaven by helping Elizabeth and Jonathan?"

"And *you* set out purposely to seduce me."

"True again, and you didn't answer me."

"You're twenty-four and I'm thirty-six."

"You're very immature for your age and I'm a brick now."

"It all balances out, huh?"

"You got it, big boy. How 'bout I seduce you again?"

"I don't suppose I have anything better to do at the moment."

"Jerk. Sexy jerk."

"It won't be easy—you know that, Catherine. . . . And stop it, I can't think when you do that."

"Then don't think for the next hour or two."

Jonathan was aware of something wet dripping on his face. He raised a hand to dash whatever it was away. It kept dripping.

He forced himself to consciousness and looked up. The room was dim and Christian Hunter's blurred face was over him.

It was a nightmare, he knew it. It was from his head injury. He had a concussion. He wanted to turn away, to scream for the ghost to go back to hell where it belonged.

"Wake up, Harley."

A ghost with a voice, a very soft voice.

Drip, drip.

He was suddenly wide-awake, alert. Elizabeth's IV fluid was dripping on his face. He didn't move, his mind striving to refuse this final ugliness.

The dripping stopped.

"I said to wake up."

"You're not dead." Was that his voice, disembodied and thin as water?

"No, bastard, I'm not."

Christian Hunter's face was clear as light now. Jonathan saw the deep gouges on his left cheek from Elizabeth's fingernails. He saw that Hunter was wearing a white coat, that he looked perfectly natural save for the scratches. He noticed the name on the white coat—Dr. Daniel Carruthers. God, had he killed that poor harried man with the long, thin nose?

"I have some very nice potassium chloride here, Harley. I'm going to inject it in Elizabeth's IV. See, I've already stuck the needle back in her arm. Only about forty cc's, that's all it'll take. Unfortunately, she'll die very quickly, not what I had intended, no, not at all. You know, don't you, that her IV is a glucose solution. I stick this stuff in, and her heart will start beating irregularly, then very fast. Probably she'll wake up with a tightening in her chest, then she'll die in just a matter of seconds. Too bad. Do you want to watch me do it?"

Elizabeth stirred, mumbling something.

"You're not going to do anything, Hunter. In fact, you're going to hang it up. Either that or I'm going to kill you. And I won't have to go to South America."

"Then I think I'll shove this gun into your mouth and pull the trigger, Harley. I guess you recognize it, don't you? It's your twenty-two automatic, you know. Oh, yeah, I knew it was in the desk in your cabin. I had no trouble at all getting it."

"Jonathan."

Both men froze at the sound of Elizabeth's voice. Soft, slurred, helpless.

"You'll die with the stitches still in your damned face."

"Jonathan, where am I? Jonathan?"

"Shush, love. Everything is fine, just fine."

"Like hell it is," Christian said in a loud voice. "Wake up, Elizabeth. I want you to know that you're going to die. Wake up, damn you!"

Elizabeth opened her eyes.

"God, no. You can't be here. You're dead, dead . . ."

"No, but you soon will be."

"I pushed you overboard. I saw you go under."

"I'm an excellent swimmer, but you've already guessed that. No, Harley, don't move. I'm tired of telling you to keep still. Now, why don't you hold your wife while I insert the potassium chloride?"

Jonathan felt her begin to tremble. She was awake, completely lucid, and terrified.

Suddenly Christian jumped at the sound of a buzzing noise.

"Damn you, you bitch!"

He ripped the call button from Elizabeth's hand.

"Too late, Hunter. Too late."

Jonathan jerked his head toward the door. Christian momentarily shifted his attention, and Jonathan jumped at him. He was entangled in the bedcovers.

Elizabeth screamed.

She jerked the IV needle out of her arm and stumbled from the bed. The two men were rolling about on the floor, entangled in the covers.

She saw Christian's gun, and wondered blankly where he'd gotten another one. His had gone into the ocean with him. She saw Jonathan gain a firm grip on his gun hand, jerk it above his head, and smash it against the floor.

Christian jerked his hand free and pressed the gun against Jonathan's throat.

Elizabeth very calmly grabbed his hair and yanked with all her strength. As Christian yelled and his gun hand came up, she raised her foot and smashed his hand against the floor.

He yelled again and the gun skittered across the floor.

Jonathan's hands were around his throat, squeezing.

Gurgling sounds. Obscene gurgling sounds.

Then she saw Christian raise the hand that held the needle. He was bringing it down toward Jonathan's back.

"Jonathan, watch his hand!"

She saw the hand disappear between the men. They rolled over, just once. She heard a sharp intake of breath.

The outside door burst open. Homer Peabody stood silhouetted in the harsh corridor light.

"Do something!"

Homer drew his gun and stared.

Elizabeth heard pounding, running footsteps.

She heard a scream.

"Jonathan," she whispered, and threw herself to her knees, trying to get to Christian's face.

Suddenly Jonathan drew up. He was breathing hard.

Elizabeth looked down to see the needle sticking out of Christian's heart.

His eyelids flickered a moment, and he was staring up at her. He said nothing. Then his eyes rolled and his body jerked.

It was then that Homer Peabody jerked Jonathan away, pointed his gun at Hunter, and yelled, "Halt or I'll shoot!"

But Christian Hunter didn't do anything.

He was dead.

"That was Catherine," Jonathan said, and hung up the phone. "Laurette Carleton died."

Elizabeth gingerly shifted her arm in its sling and rose. She saw Kogi standing in the doorway to the living room, waiting for her to ask for something, anything. She merely waved him away with her good hand.

"The funeral will be on Friday."

"Odd, but I think I want to go," said Elizabeth. "That poor bitter old woman."

"She had her guns aimed at the wrong person. Sit back down, love, and rest."

"You and Kogi," Elizabeth said on a sigh, but she sat back down on the sofa.

"On Saturday you and I, Mrs. Harley, are flying to Montego Bay. I've decided I want to see you with some sexy tan lines."

"Sounds like a wonderful plan to me," Elizabeth said. "But . . ."

"But what?"

"My business, your business, everything . . ."

"Why don't you meet with Adrian, Coy, and Rod and all the rest of the gang, and I'll do the same with my cohorts. We need to get away. The press is having another field day and I'm tired of flashbulbs going off in my face. It's giving me premature wrinkles."

He walked to the sofa and eased down beside her. "When we get bored from making love in Montego Bay, we can discuss what we're going to do about everything. Okay?"

"Sounds like another good plan, and I have no more buts."

"Excellent. Now, pucker up, lady."

She did. Just before she closed her eyes, she saw the newspaper Kogi had slipped onto the coffee table. Her picture was on the front, and the headline read: "ELIZABETH X CLEARED."

"Jonathan, look."

He gave a deep sigh and watched her. She read a moment then turned to face him. "A verdict of not guilty just isn't the same, you know, as 'cleared.' Cleared is like being scrubbed clean and everyone told about it. There's even a statement from Moretti."

"He probably wants you to back him in his next election."

She laughed. For the first time in so long her head was filled with exhilarating glorious music. Her fingers played the song that was in her mind. It took Jonathan a few moments to realize that Elizabeth's tapping fingers were playing music on his shoulder blade.

"Beethoven?"

She grinned at him. "Nope. That's *Life Is Just a Bowl of Cherries*."

About the Author

Catherine Coulter lives in Mill Valley, California, with her husband, a physician. She is the author of eighteen previous bestselling Regency and historical romances.